"Marry me, Eden,

Brodie said, his tone deadly quiet.

Her body went perfectly still, and she stared at him, all the remaining color draining from her face. "What?"

His tone was flat. "Marry me. Now. As soon as possible."

"Are you serious?" she whispered, her eyes still dark with shock.

He gave her a tight half smile. "Very."

"Why?"

"You know why, Eden. After last night and this morning, you shouldn't even have to ask."

Her eyes welled up with tears, and she looked away, despair washing over her face. "Don't do this to me, Brodie," she whispered brokenly. "Don't make me choose."

Dear Reader,

Welcome to another month of wonderful reading here at Silhouette Intimate Moments. We start right off with a bang with our Heartbreakers title, penned by popular Linda Turner. *Who's The Boss?* will immediately catch you up in the battle raging between Riley Whitaker and Becca Prescott. They're both running for sheriff, but there's a lot more than just a job at stake for these two!

Next up is Sharon Sala's *The Miracle Man,* our Romantic Traditions title. This one features the classic "stranded" hero—and the heroine who rescues him, body and soul. *The Return of Eden McCall,* by Judith Duncan, wraps up the tales of the McCall family, featured in her Wide Open Spaces miniseries. But you'll be pleased to know that Judith has more stories in mind about the people of Bolton, Alberta, so expect to be returning there with her in the future. Another trilogy ends this month, too: Beverly Bird's Wounded Warriors. *A Man Without a Wife* is an emotional tale featuring a mother's search for the child she'd given up. You won't want to miss it. Then get Spellbound by Doreen Roberts' *So Little Time,* an enthralling tale about two lovers who never should have met—but who are absolutely right for each other. Finally, in *Tears of the Shaman,* let Rebecca Daniels introduce you to the first of the twin sisters featured in her new duo, It Takes Two. You'll love Mallory's story, and Marissa's will be coming your way before long.

Enjoy them all—six great books, only from Silhouette Intimate Moments.

Yours,

Leslie Wainger
Senior Editor and Editorial Coordinator

Please address questions and book requests to:
Silhouette Reader Service
U.S.: 3010 Walden Ave., P.O. Box 1325, Buffalo, NY 14
Canadian: P.O. Box 609, Fort Erie, Ont. L2A 5X3

THE RETURN OF EDEN McCALL

JUDITH DUNCAN

Published by Silhouette Books

America's Publisher of Contemporary Romance

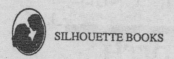

SILHOUETTE BOOKS

ISBN 0-373-07651-7

THE RETURN OF EDEN McCALL

Books by Judith Duncan

Silhouette Intimate Moments

A Risk Worth Taking #400
Better Than Before #421
*Beyond All Reason #536
*That Same Old Feeling #577
*The Return of Eden McCall #651

*Wide Open Spaces

Silhouette Books

To Mother with Love 1993
"A Special Request"

JUDITH DUNCAN

is married and lives, along with two of her five children and her husband, in Calgary, Alberta, Canada. A staunch supporter of anyone wishing to become a published writer, she has lectured at several workshops for Alberta's Department of Culture and participated in conventions in both British Columbia and Oregon. After having served a term as 2nd Vice President for the Canadian Authors' Association, she is currently working with the Alberta Romance Writers' Association, which she helped to found.

Chapter 1

Layers of cigarette smoke hung over the four pool tables, as if trapped there by the wide brass shades suspended low over the green baize surfaces. An indistinct shape moved in the semidarkness beyond the light, creating a current, and the smoke drifted up, disappearing in the shadows above. At the offside table, shards of reflected light glanced off the brightly colored balls as they disappeared, one by one, in the black wells of the side and corner pockets. When only the white cue ball remained, a silver belt buckle came into view, bisected by an upright pool cue. There was something disconnecting about the darkness that hovered thick and heavy beyond the brass fixtures. It was as though it dismembered the players, leaving only the arms and hands playing the game.

The adjacent bar vibrated with the bass beat from the jukebox and the Saturday night crowd, but tonight this room was quiet, intense, the only sounds the sharp report of ball against ball and the terse utterances as the players called their shots. They were all focused on the game, each intent on the next shot, on laying down a winning game. There were no casual bystanders, no spectators tonight—just the players. And the game.

Brodie Malone braced his shoulder against the doorframe and hooked his thumbs in the front pockets of his jeans, his expression unsmiling as he watched the foreman of the Circle S Ranch make a hustler's run against his opponent. Ross Wilson could work a table with the best of them, and he was running hot tonight. But then, nothing put Ross on his game quicker than racking up against one of the narrow-eyed pros from the city. Ross didn't have much use for their attitude, their arrogance or their custom-made pool cues. And he let it show. If the old precept was true, that a good pool player was the sign of a misspent youth, then Ross Wilson had definitely done his share of misspending. There were damned few around who could beat him.

Which, Brodie figured, didn't say a whole lot for himself, seeing as he was one of those few. A flicker of grim amusement lifting one corner of his mouth, he shifted his weight and tested a ridge in the floor with the sole of his boot. Everyone in Bolton knew that Brodie Malone hadn't exactly grown up with a halo hanging over his head. He'd had the kind of reputation that a small town never forgets.

Forcing his thoughts away from that old disturbing track, he lifted his head and watched the action at the table closest to him. It was a quiet night for a Saturday, with mostly local players at the tables and regulars in the bar. Not the usual weekend jam of urban cowboys who drove down from the city for a night of living it up at the Silver Dollar Saloon. But with the weather the way it was, he had pretty much expected a slow night. Cold, miserable, with slicing gusts of wind and rain—it was more like November than the end of May. He wouldn't have been here himself if there wasn't a private party going on in the banquet hall downstairs, or if half his staff wasn't down with the flu. On a night like tonight, he liked nothing better than to roll out the Vette, stick a good blues tape in the cassette player and find a long, straight stretch of empty highway, then take it to the limit. And he knew a lot about taking it to the limit.

One of the players set a glass of beer on the edge of the pool table, and Brodie folded his arms and stared at it. He'd just had all four tables recovered and leveled; in fact, the invoice was still sitting on his desk. And that table was his particular favorite.

Brodie exhaled heavily. Sometimes he felt like a damned den mother. He unhooked his thumbs and straightened. "Better keep the beer off the tables, boys," he said, forcing an easy tone into his voice. "Ruby shot the last person who spilt a drink on a table."

There was a round of guffaws, and someone moved the glass. The grizzled face of Artie Shaw appeared in the light, his battered straw Stetson shoved to the back of his head. He shot Brodie a tobacco-stained grin as he stooped over to line up his next shot, the twinkle in his eyes apparent even in the semi-darkness. "Better watch out for Ruby, boys. She'll cut you off if you do her wrong."

Checking a small twist of humor, Brodie turned and left, another round of guffaws following him. Art having his fun, no doubt. Ruby Taubbs managed the Silver Dollar Saloon, and she was a force to be reckoned with. She had worked in the bar here in the Bolton Hotel for as long as Brodie could remember. In fact, she'd marched him out more than once in his own misspent youth. Every cowhand within a hundred miles had tangled with her at one time or another, but he knew if push came to shove, there wasn't one of them who wouldn't go to the wire for her.

Brodie suspected that the cow-eyed devotion had to do not so much with Ruby's hard-nosed attitude but with her blatant female charms. Most of the time she looked as if she managed a Nevada brothel. With curves in all the right places, and some that weren't, she wore getups that came right off the Las Vegas strip. But it wasn't just her choice of clothes that created the illusion; it was the way she strutted her stuff and flashed her bright-red fingernails and brassy red hair. Ruby was the glitter and glamour of a bygone era, and she sported enough rings and jewelry to sink a decent-size boat.

But with Ruby, what you saw wasn't necessarily what you got. She had a mouth on her that could stop a tank, but she would give a bum the shirt off her back. She was also one of very few who he would trust at his back if the chips were down. Brodie knew from her employment records that she was on the far side of fifty, but she'd made it very clear that that piece of information better go no farther than his desk. And besides all her other attributes, she was worth her voluptuous weight in gold. Not only could she handle a crowd better than anyone he knew, she also had a sixth sense when it came to false ID and trouble, and she could handle a touchy situation better than a union mediator.

When he and his silent business partner had bought the place two years before, they had considered bringing in a business manager. But it had taken him about four minutes to realize that Ruby knew more about the business than any MBA. And they had offered her the job on the spot. It was her advice they'd relied on more than the architect's when they'd renovated the hotel, expanding the then dingy bar into the Silver Dollar Saloon. Yeah, Ruby was worth her weight in gold, and right now, because the regular bartender was working the private party in the banquet room downstairs, she was handling the bar side alone.

Brodie rolled his shoulders and exhaled heavily. A long stretch of empty highway was looking better all the time.

He crossed the narrow hallway that branched off to the rest rooms and entered the saloon area, the heavy thump of the jukebox making his eyeballs throb. Somewhere along the line he was going to have to get a half hour of sleep, or he would be walking into walls by closing time. Between the hotel and his video store, he'd been covering for sick staff for over a week, and he was beginning to feel like Tuesday's toast. Which didn't do a whole hell of a lot for his mood. A week like this was about two days too long.

Skirting the hardwood dance floor, he almost smiled when he saw Ruby propped against the customer side of the bar, her stance drawing the slick fabric of her clinging pants even tighter as she leisurely leafed through the latest tabloid. There wasn't an empty glass or a dirty ashtray in sight. So much for being shorthanded on a Saturday night.

She languidly turned a page, the light above the bar catching in the rhinestone combs holding up her elaborate hairdo. She turned another page, then spoke. "So, stud muffin, has anyone set fire to the new pool tables, yet?"

Resting one arm on the chest-high surface, Brodie leaned back against the bar and laced his hands together. He knew damned well that she was trying to get a rise out of him, both with the dig about the tables and the stud-muffin crack. There was a hint of irritation in his voice when he answered. "Give it a rest, Ruby. I told you, they are *not* new tables."

She cast him a long, castigating look, then flipped another page. "You could have fooled me."

Her testy tone aroused a hint of humor, and Brodie relented with a small smile. "Okay. So the bill was a bit more than we budgeted for."

She shot him a cutting look through the sweep of her false eyelashes. "Malone, kings have been ransomed for less money than that."

"Those are high-quality tables, Ruby Jean."

She shot him another chastising look and flicked her scarlet-nailed thumb in the direction of the poolroom. "Do you really think that bunch in there knows the difference?"

Holding her gaze, he gave her a crooked grin. "But I do."

She stared back at him for a second, then turned back to the tabloid on top of the bar, a smile tugging at her mouth. "God, but you're a pain in the patoot."

Hooking his heel on the brass rail along the bottom of the bar, Brodie swept the room with a swift glance. "So what's going on downstairs?"

"The Valmers are having a twenty-fifth anniversary bash." Ruby turned another page, her tone tart when she added, "The booking form is on your desk, Malone. Do you read *any*thing I put on your desk?"

Another tug of amusement surfaced. "Not if I can help it."

She made a disgusted sound. "I figured as much."

He glanced at her, deciding to needle her a little. He lowered his voice to a lazy drawl. "That's why I've got you and Rita, sugar. To look after me."

Ruby gave him a swift poke in the ribs, then grinned when he let out a sharp huff of air. "Nice try, Malone. But that macho act isn't going to work with me. You wouldn't be caught dead handling a banquet arrangement. That's sissy stuff."

His mouth lifted a little. He couldn't really put up much of a fight with her there. It wasn't that he actually considered it sissy stuff. Dealing with that aspect of the hotel business frustrated the hell out of him. If anyone ever wanted to find out how picky and indecisive someone was, give them a banquet to arrange. It was true that he left that stuff up to Ruby and Rita.

Rita Johnson ran the restaurant and coffee shop, and between the two of them, they could put together a function faster and better than any high-priced hotel. And between the two of them, they spared him a lot of grief.

The phone on the corner of the bar rang, and Ruby reached out, punched a button for an in-house line, then answered it, her tone businesslike. "Ruby Taubbs."

Brodie glanced across the bar and grinned to himself. Ruby had more damned facets than a five-carat diamond.

"So what's your problem, Slugger?"

Slugger, otherwise known as Dave Tucker, was the regular bartender who'd gotten stuck working the private party downstairs. Brodie waited, hoping like hell it wasn't a bad-news call—like a plugged toilet or a crisis in the kitchen. He was too damned tired to deal with another crisis tonight.

Tucking the phone against her shoulder, Ruby drew a notepad toward her and clicked the end of a ballpoint pen. "Give it to me again." She began jotting down a list of items, and Brodie watched her. Finally Ruby spoke. "No. Don't bother. The boss is here holding up one end of the bar. He can run this stuff down to you." There was another pause, and Ruby chuckled. "You've got a smart mouth, Tucker. Too bad I can't say the same for your brain."

Still chuckling, she hung up the phone and straightened. "That must be one hell of party going on down there. Slugger's running out of booze and ice."

Brodie reached for the list, but Ruby slapped his hand away. "Keep your hands to yourself, Malone. I'll fill it. You're so falling-down tired, you couldn't bag popcorn right now." She cast him a scolding look as she went behind the bar. "You can take this order down, then give us all a break and go home. You're beginning to look like something your dog dug up."

Levering himself away from the bar, he tried to ease the bone-deep fatigue out of his shoulders. "You can't manage this place on your own."

She snorted. "Does this crowd look like they're going to bust loose? Of course I can manage it on my own."

Brodie wearily massaged his eyes, then cast another look around the bar. In spite of the noise level, it was a soft crowd. Mostly people out for a couple of beers and a little Saturday night socializing. No big deal. He just didn't like dumping it all in her lap. But he also knew he wasn't much good to her the way he was. He turned and rested both arms on the top of the bar, watching as she fished an empty liquor box out from under the counter. "I'll schedule some extra time off for you later in the month. After this past week, you sure in hell have it coming."

"Don't give me a hard time here, Malone," she responded, a touch of annoyance in her tone. "You've filled in for me often enough, so don't make a big deal out of it when I do it for you." A telltale glint appeared in her eyes. "Besides, you're crowding my space. I'd planned on picking an argument with old Ronald Sanderson tonight."

Restraining a smile, Brodie stared at her. "You just can't leave it alone, can you?"

She chuckled and set the empty liquor box on the low counter behind the bar. "Not a chance. That man's politics need some serious readjustment."

Brodie gave her a small smile. "You just like riling him, Ruby Jean. And you know it."

She nodded in agreement. "Darn right I do."

There was a burst of laughter from one of the tables, and Brodie turned to check it out. They were kids from town— probably celebrating someone's coming of age. He wondered if he'd ever really been that young.

He turned back, watching as Ruby selected stock from the shelves behind the bar, then slipped the bottles into cardboard sleeves in the box. She closed the lid, then lifted a bag of ice out of the freezer unit and set it on top. Ruby slapped the ice. "There you go, bucky. All packed and ready to roll. And for God's sake, don't fall on your face going down the stairs. There's some high-priced juice in these bottles."

He rounded the end of the bar and shot her an amused glance. "Yes, Mother."

She ignored the dig. "And I don't want to see your face back here until Monday night, you got that?"

"I think I'll buy you a dog. Then you'll have something to boss around at home."

"I don't need a dog, Malone. I've got you."

If he hadn't been so bloody tired, he wouldn't have let her get away with that crack, but he knew he had to have his wits about him if he started a sparring match with her. If he didn't, she would take him to the mat in ten seconds flat. He almost smiled. There was nothing slow about Ruby Jean. Not even on a bad day.

The banquet room downstairs was part of the new wing he and his partner had added when they'd taken over the hotel. Structurally part of the basement, it was a large room that could seat a hundred people banquet-style. Rather than create a plain, serviceable room in a windowless hole, they'd decided to go first class and go after small convention business. They had added space for a couple of smaller conference rooms, another kitchen, then changed the grade at the back of the hotel so that the east wall of the banquet room opened up onto a closed-in courtyard.

Everyone in town had thought they were nuts, including the bank that held the mortgage. Bolton was a small town set in the middle of southern Alberta's ranching country, population a little over a thousand, and an hour-and-a-half drive from Calgary. Too far to draw the city crowd, they had said, and not the place that even small-time organizers would consider. But the remodeling and new addition were probably the smartest things they'd done. They were beginning to get regular return clientele for during-the-week corporate retreats and seminars, and there wasn't an open weekend slot for the next six months. Their accountant smiled every time he audited the books. Brodie would have smiled about it now, except he was too damned tired. He was definitely running on empty. He would deliver the booze and the ice, then he was out of there. Eight hours of sack time was looking better by the minute.

As soon as he passed through the fire doors into the lower kitchen, the noise from the Valmer party hit him, and his eyes started to throb again. It was a good thing that Slugger was still up and healthy, or he would have been stuck working down here tonight. Carl Valmer had been elected mayor that fall, and it had definitely gone to his wife's head. Given a choice, Brodie would rather have his eyes poked out than deal with some of the types that would be here tonight. He had a long memory where some people were concerned, and he went out of his way to avoid them if possible. It was easier on his gut if he did.

A twinge of dark humor surfaced. That was twice tonight he'd slipped onto that old track. A week of practically no sleep was definitely messing up his head.

Adjusting his hold on the box, he shouldered his way through the swinging doors used by the kitchen staff, and the noise level immediately increased. Brodie felt as if someone had just dropped a piano on his head.

Slugger was behind the bar, helping one of the waitresses unload a trolley of clean glasses. He looked up and grinned as Brodie set the box on the back counter. "Hey, man. What took you so long? Did you take the long way down, or what?"

Brodie broke open the bag of ice and dumped some in the thermal bucket sunk in the counter. "Ruby had to do her nails first."

Slugger chuckled and reached in front of him, lifting a bottle of rye out of the box. "Well, you got here just in time. We're down to the fumes."

Brodie swept a practiced glance over the bar. "How are you for mixers? Do you need more orange juice?"

"Nope. We've got two jugs in the cooler. Everything else is topped up. We were just running low on the hard stuff."

Brodie slapped the bar and turned to go. "Then I'm outta here."

Slugger rammed a jigger on the top of the bottle. "Right. We'll see you Monday."

The band started up again, blasting a seventies tune from their high-amp sound system, and Brodie shook his head and started to walk away, a small twist of amusement surfacing. He would never have figured either of the Valmers for seventies rock fans. Carl? Most likely down-home country when he was away from his wife. And Sheila was the type who would trot off to the symphony, whether she liked it or not.

He was about to push through one of the swinging doors when the crowd separated and he caught a glimpse of a woman across the room. Her back was to him, but there was something unnervingly familiar about the long sleek body in a slender red dress, something about the dark hair pulled straight back in a simple twist. A funny feeling unfolded in his gut, and he shook his head, disgusted with the way his mind was malfunctioning tonight. The lack of sleep was definitely screwing up his head. Now he was seeing old ghosts.

He went to push the door again, but right then she turned, presenting her full profile to him, and Brodie froze, the moving bodies turning into a weird blur. He stared across the room, feeling as if he'd just been slammed in the solar plexus. His mind wasn't playing tricks on him after all.

Eden McCall was back in town.

The pink neon light from the video store flashed off and on in the darkened street, the flicker creating a sporadic film of pink in the inky puddle collecting along the curb. Rain perforated the surface and rattled against the window, and Brodie stared out, his thoughts detached as he watched a gust of wind send rain skittering along the pavement. His apartment was on the second floor of the video store, and the living room window offered an unobstructed view of the dark, deserted street below. Another gust of wind rattled against the building, buffeting the street lamp across the intersection. Brodie shifted his gaze and watched the light glimmer and twist through the leaves of the huge old poplar tree in front of the store, his thoughts trapped in limbo.

It had been a hell of a jolt, seeing her again. Seventeen years. Seventeen damned years. Half a lifetime ago. It had taken him a long time to get her out of his system, and he didn't want to be reminded of what a fool he'd been. He didn't want to remember her, didn't want to remember how he'd felt after she'd packed it in. And he didn't want to remember the bitterness that had damned near screwed him up for good.

Things had changed. He was no longer the long-haired kid from the wrong side of town. He had built two successful businesses, and he had learned to play the stock market with the best of them. Hell, he wasn't even the same person he'd been back then. But for some reason, seeing her again had kicked off feelings he thought he'd buried years ago. Feelings he hadn't experienced for a long, long time.

Folding his arms across his naked chest, Brodie rested his shoulder against the window frame, watching the reflection of the pink light flashing on and off across the rain-slick street. So why in hell was he standing here at three o'clock in the morning, staring at an empty street, a caged-cat feeling eating a hole in his gut?

A twist of black humor surfaced, and he watched the rain against the windowpane. Maybe he was standing here, feeling like a caged cat, because he'd been reminded that getting tangled up with Eden McCall was the stupidest thing he'd ever done. And he'd done some damned stupid things in his time. But she had topped them all.

He had been so wound up in hormones and fantasies that he'd been dumb-blind as far as she was concerned. He had thought she was different. But when push came to shove, she'd been no different from the rest, no different from her old man or her mother. She had cut him down without a second glance, and it was a lesson he'd never forgotten.

But then, life had a way of teaching some hard lessons. And there were some things he would never forget. Like what it was like growing up without a mother. Like living in the worst rodent-infested dump in town, with a father who was as mean sober as he was drunk. Like seeing what the stigma of being labeled "white trash" had done to his sister. Like watching his old man use booze to dodge reality. Not that it mattered much. Drunk or sober, Mick Malone never accepted responsibility for one damned thing. It was always someone else's fault—the fact that he couldn't hold down a job, that he couldn't stay sober for more than two days in a row, that his family damned near froze to death every winter. Yeah, his old man had an excuse for everything.

Experiencing a hot, searing rush in his belly, Brodie clenched his jaw. He wasn't going to get sucked back into the old rage—he'd spent too many years trying to get out from under it. Shifting his position, he braced his arm against the frame as he stared at the street below. He could have done without this crap from the past tonight. He was just too damned tired to keep it in perspective. And besides, it didn't matter anymore. It had been over and done with for a lot of years. But maybe, in one way, she'd done him a big favor. He'd taken all the bitterness and anger he'd felt at nineteen, and he'd used them to his advantage. He'd vowed that he would show them all, then shove his success down everyone's throat.

And that was pretty much what he'd done. But somewhere along the line, the bitterness had changed into a kind of emotional detachment. He had businesses to run, staff to worry about, bills to pay. His father had died when he was twenty-one, when Brodie was away working the oil rigs in the North Sea. And in some ways, the old Brodie Malone had died with him. He'd done a lot of growing up after that. A hell of lot.

Except a piece of that past had turned up tonight. And as clearly as if she were standing right there before him, he could see her face, smell her, feel her. And he remembered what it was like to have her hot and naked beneath him.

Jarred by the sharpness of the recollection, Brodie swore and slammed his fist against the wall, disgust washing through him. Where in hell was his bloody mind, anyway? The very last thing he needed was to start remembering what it had been like with Eden McCall.

"What's the matter? Someone stiff you at the bar?"

Brodie turned and watched his seventeen-year-old nephew come out of the shadows, his bare chest gleaming in the faint light coming from outside. It always gave him a start when Jason came on him unawares. It was like looking back twenty years and seeing himself—same build, same dark curly hair, same square face. Even the blue eyes were the same, only there was a stillness in Jason's that his had never had, a kind of guarded coolness, a kind of caution. And no damned wonder. The kid had been through half-a-dozen foster homes before Brodie got him. Brodie's sister had died on the streets when Jason was not quite six, and because of the life she'd lived, Social Services had stepped in. If Brodie ever wanted to uncork a full-blown rage, all he had to do was think about the bureaucracy and the three years of battling the system he'd gone through before he got custody of the kid. He wanted to wring someone's neck every time he thought about it. And tonight was not a good night to think about it.

Bracing his hand against the wall, he met his nephew's gaze, managing a tight smile. "Don't give me a hard time, Jase. I'm in a bad mood."

Jason gave him a slow, off-center smile. "Tough." He braced his weight against the corner of the hallway and folded his arms. "Lydia called tonight."

Brodie exhaled heavily and straightened. Lydia was his mainstay at the video store, and she'd been off sick for two weeks. He hoped like hell this wasn't more bad news. She'd worked like a dog setting up the new displays after they'd remodeled, and it wasn't until she developed pneumonia that he found out she'd been coming to work when she should have been at home in bed. He still felt like a louse about it.

Jason shrugged. "She said to tell you she's got an okay from the doctor to come back to work. She'll be back on Monday."

"Not unless I talk to her doctor first."

The teenager shrugged again and hooked his thumbs in the waistband of his jeans. "I told her you'd say that." A lopsided smile appeared. "She said she'd get a damned note, but she was coming back Monday whether you liked it or not. She said if she's stuck at home one more day, she's going to go nuts." He shifted his position, scratching his back on the corner. Then he spoke again. "I set up the hard drive on the new computer tonight, and all the inventory is loaded."

There was the click-clack of nails on the hardwood floor, and his dog ambled out of the shadows and immediately dropped down at Jason's feet, his head on his paws. He gave Brodie a wounded look. Max was a reject from the RCMP canine program and too damned smart for his own good. He was put out at Brodie for not taking him along, and he was still sulking about it. Brodie almost smiled. No doubt Max had gotten even by sleeping on his bed.

He crouched down in front of the dog and scratched his neck along his collar. He spoke to his nephew. "I thought you were going to go over to the Jacksons' tonight to overhaul the dirt bikes."

"I changed my mind."

Brodie heard the flat edge in the teenager's voice, and he suspected something had gone wrong. That tone usually meant that someone had tried to push Jase into doing something he didn't want to do. Jason didn't march to anyone's drum, except his own, but sometimes it was a damned lonely drum.

Brodie gave Max another scratch, then stood up, meeting his nephew's gaze. Jason stared back at him, a touch of cynicism hovering around his mouth. There was a hardness, a maturity there, that went far beyond his seventeen years. The school of hard knocks had left its mark on his nephew, as well. He studied the teenager a moment longer, then spoke, his tone quiet. "Have you got something on your mind, Jase?"

Jason held Brodie's gaze for a moment, then looked away. "I'll work it out."

Brodie made no response. He probably should push it, but he let it go. Maybe it was just as well the kid didn't want to talk. Tonight was not a good night to get into a heavy-duty discussion. There were too many old ghosts sitting in the shadows, and he didn't want anything to trigger them into taking shape. The last thing he wanted was to start remembering.

He'd spent too many years trying to forget.

Chapter 2

A light breeze shivered through the leaves of the climbing honeysuckle that clung to the veranda trellis, and Eden Mc-Call pulled the quilt tighter and huddled deeper into the large white wicker chair. Resting her chin on her upraised knees, she watched the first rays of daybreak seep over the horizon, turning the sky shades of orange and coral and casting the undersides of the clouds in midnight blue. The vivid colors bled through the laurel-leaf willows that bordered the east side of the property, sending shards of brightness shimmering through the leaves as they twisted and turned in the wind. It was an awesome spectacle to watch, with only the soft rustle of the leaves and the early morning twitter of birds marring the perfect stillness of the clear, cool morning.

She tightened her arms around her knees, quietly absorbing the beauty. The McCall house was situated on a slight rise of land on the very outskirts of Bolton, the location offering a panoramic view of the eastern horizon. Eden watched the changing sky, knowing she could never reproduce the purity and blend of color on canvas, no matter how hard she tried. But then, she never had—there was no way she or anyone else could ever truly reproduce an Alberta sunrise. It was simply too intense, too overwhelming.

She shivered and hunched her shoulders against the chill, savoring the peace. The whole town was Sunday-morning quiet, no sounds of traffic, no slamming of doors, no children playing in the street. Hushed. Still. Just the sounds of sparrows and the soft rustle of the leaves.

Across and down the street, a pink neon light flashed in the window of what had once been the first bank in town but was now a video store, the persistent blinking oddly out of context in the still, deserted street. But then, the store itself was out of context, situated the way it was on the edge of town. The old sandstone bank faced what had once been the main road into Bolton, but the street was little used now. Years ago, a new access road had been built that connected with Main Street six blocks away, and that new road had changed the face of the old access road forever. The other businesses had either been torn down or had fallen into crumbling disrepair. Now only the old bank remained, a reminder of another era.

Experiencing a twist of regret, she redirected her gaze and looked across the yard. It had stopped raining during the night, and the dawn was fresh and sparkling, the grass still beaded with dew, the trunks of the trees still dark and shiny.

Another breeze stirred, and she drew the comforter higher around her shoulders, then locked her arms around her knees, watching the colors shift and change, turning the undersides of the clouds even more vibrant. God, but she'd missed this wide open sky. The wide open spaces. How many times, she wondered, had she sat out here as a teenager, watching the sun creep over the horizon?

She inhaled deeply, savoring the blend of fragrances, trying to ignore the sudden unexplained lump in her throat. She had missed this—the wide openness, the sense of space, the stillness. It filled up something deep inside her. But she also knew that this sense of well-being was only temporary.

She did not want to be here. There were too many old regrets. Too much old guilt. But she had felt obligated to come. Her father had suffered a heart attack and had to be hospitalized, and her mother had begged her to come home. And with the mess her own life was in, coming here had offered her an escape. So she had stored what was left of her life in Toronto, packed up Megan and come home. She'd only arrived two days ago, and already she had misgivings. Her mother was not going to make it easy.

Three robins settled on the lush expanse of grass that rolled down to the trees, and Eden watched them hop from spot to spot, harvesting the earthworms that had surfaced. The yard had always been her mother's showcase, and Ellie McCall spent hours in it. It was beautiful but, for Eden, oddly sterile. The shrubs were all precisely pruned, and the flower beds were designed and edged with the same precision. Even the flowers were arranged in a precise color scheme, with a precise symmetry. Controlled. Exact. Rigid. Just like her mother.

Her throat cramped again, and she shifted her gaze, trying to will away the sting of tears, angry with herself. God, she was such a mess. Her life was a mess. But then, maybe she had it coming. She never should have married Richard. She'd known it was a mistake right from the beginning. And she probably would have bolted two days before the big splashy wedding her mother had organized, but Ellie McCall had convinced her that she was being ridiculous, that it was only prewedding jitters, that everyone had them. It had been her own unexplored intuition speaking loud and clear, but she hadn't had the self-confidence or experience to recognize it for what it was. Maybe that was why she'd hung onto one piece of herself, when she'd kept the McCall name. That was something she hadn't handed over.

It had taken her a lot of years to stop being the perfect, well-behaved daughter and the pliant, obedient wife, and to learn how to stick up for herself. It had taken her even longer to learn how not to give in to that feeling of inadequacy every time someone made her feel incompetent. She knew she still had a long way to go, but now that she'd come this far, she would never let it happen again. That weakness had cost her too much in the past, and it would cost her in the future if she let it. And the most likely place it would happen would be right here in Bolton.

It had also taken her a lot of years to admit how emotionally unhealthy her family was—to face the fact that her mother was a master manipulator and her father was a bully. Only they never manipulated or bullied her openly—not like they had her brothers—they had manipulated and bullied her softly, surreptitiously, with her own sense of inadequacy, her need to please, her easily provoked feelings of guilt. And in some ways, that covert manipulation had been far more damaging and twice as hard to fight against. Especially when the first enemy she had to battle was herself.

That was one reason her visits back to Bolton had been very few and very far between. Since she and Richard got married thirteen years ago, she doubted if she had been home more than five times. She couldn't fight them, so the easiest defense had been to stay away. But living with Richard had taught her more than how to be a perfect hostess; it had taught her about power. Even so, she wasn't sure she would have been able to dredge up the courage, or fight off the guilt and sense of failure, to leave him if she hadn't found out about his endless string of affairs.

Then she had been forced to face herself—and admit how damned spineless she was. When she'd made the decision to divorce him six months ago, she'd thought she knew what she was letting herself in for. She'd known things would get nasty, but she hadn't been prepared for how nasty.

He had been so cold and remote by then that she hadn't expected much of a reaction from him, other than sneering personal attacks and chilling disdain. But she had been wrong—dead wrong. His retaliation had been swift and ruthless, and she'd soon learned why he had the reputation he did as a corporate lawyer. He had stripped her of nearly everything she owned, but he hadn't been able to strip her of her daughter or her hard-earned self-respect. And if nothing else, she knew she would never be that kind of victim again. But that didn't make it any easier to be here, watching the sun come up, surrounded by painful memories.

Her history of mistakes was long and hard. And the worst one was rooted here. She often wondered what would happen if she had the power to go back in time and undo that one terrible, terrible wrong.

"Damn, but I'm good. I bet myself a trip around the block you'd be sitting out here, and here you are. What's the matter, Pooky. Is this damned family getting to you?"

Eden quickly wiped her eyes on the corner of the quilt, then stuck a smile on her face and turned toward the familiar voice. Her brother, Chase, was standing below her at the far end of the veranda, nearly hidden in the thick foliage creeping up the trellis. He had his arms hooked over the veranda railing, his cowboy hat pulled low over his eyes, and he was grinning that grin that had gotten him into more trouble than she cared to think about.

Resting her chin on her knees, she studied him, her smile becoming more genuine. "Well, I'll be damned. Chase Mc-Call actually standing on McCall ground. It's a wonder the sky hasn't fallen in."

He stared at her, still grinning that damned grin, a bad-boy glint appearing in his eyes. "Don't push your luck, little sister. Unless things have changed, there's a rain barrel at the corner of the greenhouse that's just begging to be used."

Eden stared right back. "You wouldn't have a hope in hell, bucko. I've learned to fight dirty in my old age."

"You wanna bet?"

She laughed and shook her head, oddly reassured by his presence. He was a little over four years older than she was, and she had idolized him ever since she could remember. It meant a lot that he had come to see her. Chase had walked out of this house when he was eighteen years old, and he'd never been back. But he had come this morning because he knew she was in town, and because he knew that she would be feeling very shaky and alone.

It wasn't easy, but she managed to give him a small smile. "No. I don't want to bet. I like it just fine where I am."

Chase watched, the humor fading from his eyes, his gaze steady and unwavering. After a long moment he spoke, his tone husky. "So how are you doing? You hanging in there okay?"

Her throat closed up on her, and she nodded. Her own voice was uneven when she finally responded. "Yeah. I'm hanging in there."

Chase turned his head and stared out across the yard. There was a long silence; then he turned back, a small smile tugging at the corner of his mouth. "Damn pain in the butt, this sentimental crap."

For some reason his wryness released the cramp in her throat, and she met his gaze, a real grin appearing. "Don't worry about it, Chase. I won't tell anybody."

The laugh lines around his eyes crinkled, and he leaned over and broke a stem off the clump of high ornamental grass, sticking the stalk in his mouth. He stared at her a moment, amusement glinting in his eyes. "You've got a smart mouth on you, you know that?"

"I'm getting there." She motioned toward the road. "So what are you doing skulking around town at five-thirty in the morning? And does your wife know what you're up to?"

He grinned and flicked the stalk of grass away. "Hell, I wouldn't be caught dead skulking. And as for my wife, she's home in bed—by my good graces, I might add. Judd Carver has a two-year-old stud he wants her to look at, so I'm on my way to pick him up."

Her chin still on her raised knees, Eden watched him, wanting to laugh. She decided to give him a hard time, instead. "You mean you're skulking around town dragging a horse trailer behind you? That's pretty pathetic, Chase."

He narrowed his eyes, the glint definitely dangerous. "Do you want to have that talk with the rain barrel?"

She laughed and shook her head. "No. I don't want to talk to the rain barrel."

He gave her another warning look. "You might want to remember that." He indicated her quilt. "So haul your butt out of that blanket, woman. I've come to take you to breakfast."

She rolled her eyes. "Yeah. Right."

"Hell, yes. I'm dead serious. I'm taking you to breakfast."

"And just where are you going to find breakfast at this time in the morning?"

"Barker's Café is open." He jerked his head in the direction of the road. "So come on."

Tempted to dump the blanket and go, Eden hesitated, knowing she shouldn't. Finally she sighed and shook her head. "I can't, Chase," she said, her voice laced with regret. "Megan is still asleep, and I can't just go off and leave her."

He studied her. "What time does she usually wake up?"

"About seven. Seven-thirty."

"If she wakes up and you aren't there, will she get in a panic?"

"No. She'll go watch TV."

"Well, hell, then. I'll have you back here in an hour, max."

Oddly bolstered by his coaxing, she hesitated, reconsidered, then shook her head again. "I can't. I'm not dressed and—"

"What have you got on?"

She straightened and opened the quilt, revealing her ratty old sweat suit and the fuzzy bunny slippers Megan had given her for Christmas.

Chase straightened and gave the railing a decisive slap. "Good enough. Let's go."

Laughing, she shook her head again. "I can't, Chase. I can't go like this and if I go back there, I'll wake Mom up for sure."

He gave her an impatient look. "Hell, Eden. This isn't some high-class establishment in Toronto. Molly Barker isn't going to throw you out if you have slippers on." He turned and started toward the road. "Come on. I need a shot of caffeine before I get downright cranky."

She paused, wrestling with her conscience, then threw off the quilt and scrambled to her feet. "Oh, hell. Why not? I may as well scandalize Mother right off the bat."

Waiting for her to come down the veranda steps, Chase shot her an irritated look. "Ma gets scandalized if you breathe funny." As soon as she came alongside, he draped his arm around her shoulders and altered his stride to match hers. "Besides, who's going to tell her? I sure as hell won't."

The little roadside café had changed very little since Eden had been there last. The same row of chrome-trimmed stools along the front counter, the same plate-glass showcase by the front door, the same high-back booths along the windows. The only thing that had changed was the decor. The old moose head above the door was gone, and the gaudy geometric-patterned curtains had been replaced with vertical blinds. And the stools and the seats in the booths were now upholstered in a subdued tan instead of the bright orange that Eden remembered. She was surprised that she did remember. It had been a long time ago.

There was only one other customer at the counter, and Eden didn't recognize either him or the waitress seated at a back table having a cigarette and coffee. Eden wondered if this was still an after-school hangout for the high school kids.

Chase selected a booth with a view of the highway and the rolling rangeland beyond, then headed for the men's room. After settling into the long, narrow seat, Eden propped her chin on her hand and gazed out, watching the sun clear the horizon.

She loved this place, loved the country around Bolton—the open rangeland to the east, the mountains to the west and the most incredible scenery she'd ever seen in between. Although they had lived in town, they used to spend a lot of time at the McCall ranch, and she could never remember feeling as free as she did on the back of a horse, racing across the open prairie.

She sighed and shortened her gaze, looking at the pasture across the road. It had been a dry spring, but the range grass was finally turning green, and she thought she spotted a patch of crocuses nestled in the shortgrass. She wondered how long it had been since she'd picked crocuses. That thought left her with a hollow feeling, and she shifted her gaze. She would have to bring Megan back later.

"Molly was in the kitchen, so I told her to send us out a tall stack of her pancakes with all the trimmings. That okay by you?"

Swiveling her head, she glanced at her brother, who set two cups of steaming coffee on the table. She shifted and took the mug he pushed toward her. "Sounds great."

Chase slid into the booth and dropped his Stetson on the seat beside him, then ran his hand through his hair. It was exactly the same dark color as Eden's, but hers was straight where his was slightly curly. Only now she could see the odd thread of silver, and she experienced a funny sensation in her middle. Chase with gray hair. It didn't seem possible. He took a sip, then set his cup down and rested his arms on the table, his shoulders hunched. "So, Pooky. How are you really doing?"

She gave him a rueful grin. "I'm doing just fine, Chase. Especially if you stop calling me Pooky."

He chuckled and repositioned his mug. "Now don't get your tail in a twist and a bean up your nose, Miz Eden."

Amusement flicking through her, she studied him. "You've been hanging around those two old reprobates at Tanner's again, haven't you?"

Chase lifted his head and grinned at her. He took a sip of coffee, then set his mug down, his expression turning serious. "They're going to be damned disappointed if you don't get out to see them this time," he said quietly.

Eden held his gaze for a moment, then looked away, a familiar homesickness washing over her. Burt Shaw and Cyrus Brewster were two old cowboys who lived at the Circle S with her half brother. Burt had been like a benevolent old uncle to her, and Cyrus, who had once been the foreman at her father's ranch, had put her on her first pony. Burt had suffered a stroke a few years ago, and they were both getting on in years, and every time she thought about them, she got an achy feeling inside. Richard could never understand why two old men should mean so much to her, and she wasn't sure herself. But whenever she thought about something happening to them, she got so homesick she could hardly stand it.

A strong, callused hand lifted her chin, and she looked back at her brother. His gaze was solemn. "Hey," he said softly. "Don't start beating yourself up, Eden. You should have left that jerk years ago."

She managed an uneven smile, then wrapped both hands around her mug. "So how are things with Tanner and Kate?"

Chase studied her for a moment, then took the hint. "Great. They got some good news a few days ago. Kate's ex got married again, and somewhere along the line, he had a change of heart. He's letting Tanner adopt the boys. So they were pretty happy about that. And Kate's pregnant again."

Eden's head shot up. "You're kidding!"

"Nope. We found out day before yesterday." He shook his head, wry amusement glinting in his eyes. "Two boys, two girls—another on the way. I figure ol' Tanner is headed for an even dozen."

"Oh, Chase. That's such wonderful news. Another baby—and the boys. God, they must be thrilled to bits."

"They're pretty happy, all right." He looked down and toyed with his mug, his expression altering. Finally he spoke, his voice gruff. "If anyone deserves the good things in life, it's Tanner."

Something in Chase's voice set off a chain of half-forgotten recollections for Eden. A violent argument between her parents, and the awful cold shock she'd experienced when she realized they were fighting about a half brother she didn't even know she had. She remembered the first time Chase had taken her to the Circle S to see Cyrus, when she met Burt Shaw and a tall, dark man with the skin of a half-breed and oddly familiar eyes. She had been twelve years old, and she remembered how patient he'd been when he showed her how to braid a horsehair bracelet, and how in awe of him she'd been. And she remembered the night Chase left home after an ugly, violent row with her father, and how panicked she'd been when he slammed out the door, scared to death she would never see him again.

But the memory that was the clearest in her mind was the night she'd found out Chase was back at the Circle S. He had written sporadically when he'd been away on the rodeo circuit, and she had taken to stopping off at the post office every morning on her way to school, hoping for a letter or a postcard. But then she had found out he was back, and she'd sneaked out late that night, without her parents knowing about it, and had gone out to Burt Shaw's ranch.

She had been sixteen years old, and that was the night that Chase had told her the whole story. How her father had lived with an Indian woman before he and her mother were married. That there was a kid involved, and how that kid's mother had committed suicide when Bruce McCall came back from Texas married to Ellie. How her father had abandoned that kid to the worst possible circumstances, and how their mother had denied the boy a decent home. How Cyrus Brewster had finally found out what was going on and had taken him in, eventually taking him to live with Burt Shaw. He told her a story that shattered every illusion she'd had about her family.

Then he told her that the tall, dark man, with the oddly familiar eyes—the man who always treated her with such quiet patience—the man she knew only as Tanner, was the half brother her parents had fought about. Something had been destroyed that night, but she had also found something very special to replace all that had been taken away. Something solid and steady and reliable. And that something was Tanner. She completely understood Chase's feelings about him. Tanner had been an anchor for both of them. And he had been there for her every single time she needed him.

He was the one who had showed up in Toronto six months ago, when things really started getting ugly with Richard. She hadn't said anything to anyone about what was going on, but somehow Tanner had known. And he'd come. He had been there with her when she found out that Richard had cleaned out the joint account, and he had been there when Richard got a restraining order to keep her out of the house. Without saying a word, Tanner had gone to the bank and opened an account for her, arranging for a line of credit that she would never have been able to arrange on her own. But then, that was Tanner. He had that quiet way of taking care of things.

"What are you thinking about?"

Waiting for the tightness in her chest to ease a little, she finally leaned back and gazed at her brother, dredging up an unsteady smile. "I was just thinking about Tanner—how he always seems to be there when we need him."

Chase twisted his mug around, the corner of his mouth lifting in a rueful smile. "Well, he was sure as hell there for me. I don't know where I would have ended up if he hadn't taken me in when I left home." He paused, caught in his own thoughts, then shrugged. "Seems ironic. Dad won't even acknowledge he's alive, but he's the glue that holds the family together." His arms still resting on the table, he raised his head and looked at her. "Did you know that he even made a sizable donation to Milt's campaign fund?"

Eden couldn't help it; she laughed out loud. Her other brother had always had a major issue over Tanner's existence, and getting a big donation from him must have been a hard pill for Milton to swallow. She was still grinning when she responded. "So how is the new McCall Member of Parliament doing?"

Chase cast her an amused look and shrugged again. "Doing fine, by the sounds of things. Loves the action in Ottawa. Seems to be doing a good job for his constituency."

"And no doubt enjoys being out from under Dad's thumb."

"No doubt."

Propping her elbows on the table, she laced her hands together under her chin. "And how are you and Devon doing?"

It was amazing to watch the change in her brother's face when she mentioned his wife. If anyone ever wondered if Chase had made the right decision about coming back after years away, all they had to do was see his face when anyone mentioned Devon. She smiled to herself. Devon Manyfeathers had definitely brought her brother home.

His voice was soft and husky when he answered. "We're doing great." He met her gaze, a glimmer of humor appearing. "Although I'm going to be damned glad when that baby gets here. I'm turning into a bloody wreck."

Eden smiled at him. "Prenatal jitters, huh?"

His expression turned rueful. "Hell, I don't know. I think I'd be fine if she'd just sit in a chair and knit or something, but I caught her cleaning out stalls yesterday. When I gave her hell, she dumped a load of manure on my boots."

Laughter welled up in her, but Eden managed to check it. But her voice still had a tremor in it when she responded. "She's got four months to go, Chase. And if that's how you're behaving, I don't blame her. You're probably driving her nuts."

He gave her a semidisgusted, semiamused look. "Hell. You women are all alike."

"Yes, we are." She took a sip of coffee, then cupped the mug between her hands, assessing her brother. When Chase had come back to Bolton and bought the Silver Springs Training Stables, she had wondered if it was a wise move for him. But it was obvious that he'd learned to deal with their father better than she had. A flicker of humor surfaced. But then, Chase's solution was pretty radical; he simply refused to deal with his father at all. As far as she knew, he hadn't talked to him in years.

"Eden?"

She glanced back at her brother, a funny feeling unfolding in her stomach when she saw how solemnly he was watching her. He stared at her for a moment; then he glanced down, as if he saw something that disturbed him. Folding the paper napkin by his cup, he hesitated for a moment, then finally spoke. "I know you don't want to talk about it," he said, his voice low. "But both Tanner and I have some pretty major concerns about the divorce settlement.''

She stared across the café, her mind registering the sound of a vehicle passing on the highway. She wanted to forget all that, to put it out of her mind—at least for a little while. But obviously it wasn't going to be that easy.

"Don't do that, Eden," he said, an undertone of quiet warning in his voice. "Don't act as if nothing's going on here."

Feeling as though she had something heavy inside her chest, she forced herself to meet his gaze. Chase was watching her, a steely look in his eyes. "Did he ever get rough with you?"

Releasing a heavy sigh, she shook her head. "No." She hesitated a minute, picking at an imperfection on her mug, then looked out the window. "I just wanted out, Chase," she said, her voice low and uneven. "And I didn't care what it cost me. As long as I got Megan, nothing else mattered a damn. I just wanted it finished."

"So he got the house and the bank account and his business, and you got zip."

She glanced at him, then back down at her mug, making a small defensive gesture with her hand. "I was the one to leave, which went against me. And I didn't want to get into a big custody battle with him. All I wanted was Megan—and something to live on for a while. So I accepted a cash settlement, and I got my car and Gran's furniture. And I kept the investments Dad had set up for me."

Chase's response was blunt. "And he was the one who was screwing around."

She straightened and met his gaze, her own tone steady. "I don't care, Chase. I'm out. And maybe he did me a big favor."

Making a disgusted sound, he leaned back in his seat. She saw the look on his face. Before he had a chance to say anything, she cut him off. "If I hadn't found out what was going on," she answered evenly, "I probably would have stuck it out for another thirteen years." She gave him a wry smile. "Don't get your tail in a twist over it, Chase. I'm not quite as spineless as I used to be."

His mouth thinned, and an angry glint appeared in his eyes. "You were never spineless," he responded, his tone flat. "It was just that the old man and Ellie knew what buttons to push."

Shifting the mug in her hands, Eden turned and looked out the window, aware that for the first time in weeks, she could take a deep breath. Maybe, just maybe, she would be able to throw the sleeping pills down the drain, and maybe she would be able to eat without her stomach going into full revolt. And maybe then she finally would be able to conquer the awful feeling of dread that was never far from the surface.

Chase shifted his feet under the table, and she glanced back at her brother. He sat hunched forward, his elbows resting on the edge of the tabletop, his head bent. She experienced a twist of apprehension, suspecting that he was going to challenge her about how she had handled things. And she didn't want to explain. It would only make things worse if she tried.

There was a drawn-out silence; then he glanced up at her, his gaze intent. Then the laugh lines around his eyes creased a little, and a twinkle appeared in his eyes. "So if you've got all this backbone, why haven't you told me to stuff it?"

She managed an off-center smile. "I will. Right after you pay for breakfast."

He grinned and glanced across to the kitchen area. "Just working the angles, huh?"

"Darn right."

Another vehicle pulled up outside, and Eden glanced out the window. She watched as two men got out of a brown, mud-spattered pickup, and she experienced an odd, misplaced feeling when she didn't recognize either of them. There had been a time when, if she didn't know someone, they were strangers in town. Now she was the one who was a stranger.

"Well, I'll be hornswoggled. If it isn't Eden McCall. What are you doing back in town, honey? Or did you come home to straighten out your brother here?"

At the sound of the familiar voice, Eden turned, her expression brightening. Molly Barker, carrying two filled plates and the coffeepot, crossed to the table. She grinned up at the older woman. "Hi, Molly. How's it going?"

After setting the plates down in front of them with swift efficiency, Molly began refilling their cups. "Well, I'm doing just fine, sugar." She gave Chase a reprimanding look. "Your lout of a brother didn't tell me you were here."

Eden's grin deepened. "That's because he's crass and has no manners. You know how he is."

The older woman chuckled and set the coffeepot down, then wedged into the space beside Eden. "You just go on and give him a hard time. I figure for all the hell-raising he did, he has it coming."

Chase gave her a disgruntled look, but there was a twinkle in his eyes. "Hell. It's been years since I spun my wheels in your parking lot, Molly. Can't you cut a guy a little slack?"

Molly let out a snort. "If you had any more slack, you'd hang yourself." She turned to Eden. "So how's life treating you, sugar? Are you home for a while?"

Eden shrugged. "For a while. It depends on how Dad does."

Molly's eyes darkened with sympathy. "I heard he's a bit under the weather. How's your ma holding up?"

"Pretty well. The doctors are encouraging."

She patted Eden's hand. "That's good. That's real good." Leaning back in her seat, she swept a glance around the café, her gaze lighting on the waitress at the far end of the room. She heaved an exasperated sigh. "That girl can drag out a coffee break longer'n anybody I know." Slapping the tabletop, she heaved herself out of the booth. "I guess I'd better get back to it—get some more hotcakes on the griddle." She turned and winked at Eden. "Tell you what. I won't tell your ma you came in here in bunny booties if you come back and have a coffee with me real soon."

Chase thought the bootie thing was pretty funny, and Eden kicked him under the table and shot him a quelling look. Then she smiled up at Molly. "I'll be back, Molly. You can count on it."

The sun was well above the horizon when Eden had Chase drop her off at the post office corner, her slippers now stuffed in her pockets. She knew that if he had a choice, he would just as soon not run into their mother, but that wasn't the reason she wanted to walk home. The town was still quiet and the streets empty, and she wanted to have that quiet, undisturbed time to reconnect with the familiarity of the place she'd grown up in.

This was home, and in spite of everything, she felt grounded here.

She didn't walk down Main Street and out to the old access road, which would have been her shortest route home. Instead, she went home the long way—turning at the library, going past the old stone church where she'd been married and along the street where her best friend had lived.

It was almost as if she'd never been away. Yes, there had been some changes—the Martins had put new siding on their house, some fences had been replaced, and one old house had been pulled down and a new bungalow built in its place. But there was still that unforgotten flavor of familiarity. The sun still dappled through the branches of the huge old poplars the way it always had, and the hedges of caragana and lilac and cotoneaster were just as familiar. The funny little grates in the storm sewers along the curb were the exact same ones that had been there years ago, and the rust-pitted street signs bore the same names they always had. Even the sensory perceptions were the same—the sun warm on her face, the cement cold beneath her bare feet, the feel of a mountain breeze at her back. And the same scent of spring wafted through the air. This was home—and she experienced a sense of rightness that she hadn't felt for a very long time.

She came to the vacant lot that was now carpeted yellow with dandelions and paused, remembering the summer when she and Susan Kovak had built a playhouse in the cluster of trees shading the back corner. It had been so long ago, but the images were still so clear. Mud pies decorated with caragana pods, the broken crockery and rusty spoons they had collected, the wooden boxes wedged between the tree trunks for cupboards. It had been a wonderful, carefree, childhood summer, full of imagination and friends.

But there were other memories farther along the street, where the pavement ended and farmland began, where a sagging barbed-wire gate now closed off an old, overgrown road. Memories of roses and hot summer nights that she didn't want to recall.

She had been seventeen when her parents had sent her away to a private school—and that had been seventeen years ago. But the memories of what had happened that summer were still far too vivid. A wave of painful nostalgia and old guilt surged through her, and Eden stuck her hands in the pockets of her sweat suit and started walking again, the ache in her chest so big she could barely endure it. At least that was one memory that she would not have to confront. He had left town years ago; the last she'd heard, he was working on an oil rig in the North Sea. Gone forever out of her life.

But the sight of that closed-off lane was a wrenching reminder of all she had lost. The ache intensified, and she turned toward home. Coming back was going to be much more difficult than she thought.

Chapter 3

The heavy, overcast sky pressed down, and rain beat against the window, the dreariness of early evening infiltrating the office at the back of the video store. Brodie drew one of the boxes on the side counter toward him, then pulled out his pocket-knife and slit the packing tape across the top. Closing the knife, he slid it back into his pocket and opened the flaps.

It was the first full day he'd put in at the video store since the flu epidemic, and the paperwork had piled up so high, it had taken him most of the day to wade through it all. It was after six, and he still had to go through this shipment of new releases, check the invoices, then enter the new inventory in the computer. Somewhere along the line, he was going to have to get something to eat, or he'd be ready to chew someone's leg off.

Max wandered into the office with his leash in his mouth and dropped it at Brodie's feet, then looked up, a soulful look in his eyes. Brodie shook his head, a wry grin appearing. Max might not have had what it took for the canine unit, but he definitely could have made it as an actor. Brodie reached down and scratched the dog's head, his smile deepening as Max closed his eyes. "You're going to have to hang in there, fella. I've got work to do."

Max gave him another woebegone look, then wandered out again and plopped down in the doorway, his head on his paws, watching him with a morose expression in his eyes. Brodie experienced a twist of amusement. He guessed he was going to have to break down eventually and take the pooch for a run. He could only take that pitiful expression so long.

Turning back to the boxes, he unloaded the shipment of new videos on the counter, then started checking them off against the invoice. He would finish this box, then take Max and jog over to the hotel, see how things were going over there and grab a bite to eat. After being stuck behind a computer all day, he was going to need to burn off a little steam.

He was stacking the videos according to titles when he caught a movement just outside the office door, and he glanced up. A girl of about six or seven, dressed in a bright yellow poncho and red rubber boots, crouched down beside Max, then began to very carefully stroke his head. Her hair was light brown, and some fuzzy tendrils had worked loose from the thick braid that hung down her back, and there were bits of grass caught in her hair. She wasn't a pretty kid, but there was something about the expression on her face that made Brodie pause. She lifted her chin a little, and he restrained a small smile. This one had independence written all over her.

He watched her pet Max for a minute, then spoke, his tone quiet so he wouldn't startle her. "Be careful of his ears, okay? He doesn't like to have them touched."

Her head came up and she stared at him, a startled look in her eyes; then she looked back down at the dog, a hint of color creeping up her face. "Okay." She gave Max's back a long stroke and spoke again. "What's his name?"

"Max."

Very softly, as though she was compelled to disagree but knew she shouldn't, she spoke. "I would have called him Silver Chief or Goliath."

Holding back a smile, Brodie folded his arms and leaned back against the counter. Obviously she thought old Max was worthy of a far more dignified name. He cleared his throat. "Well, his name is really Maximilian. But we call him Max."

He saw her mouth the name; then she gave her head a single nod, as though it met with her approval. Continuing to watch her, he tipped his head to one side. "Do you have a dog?"

She shook her head. "My dad wouldn't let me have one. He said they were too messy."

He made no response, but he noticed the mutinous lift to her chin, and he heard her mutter, "But when I get big, I'm going to have one."

Amused by the hint of belligerence, Brodie studied her, liking the careful, gentle way she had with the dog. She might be small, but there was something about her that seemed older somehow. Crossing his ankles and refolding his arms, he rested his weight against the counter, continuing to watch her. "How old are you?"

"I'm eight." She gave another little grimace. "Well, almost nine." She leaned over and looked in Max's ear. "Why does he have hair in his ears?"

"It helps to keep bugs and dust out."

"Like a fence."

Brodie stared at her, the corner of his mouth lifting. He wondered how many kids would equate the hair in a dog's ears to a fence. This kid's mind was definitely on a different wavelength. "Yeah," he said, "like a fence."

She carefully smoothed the hair down Max's back. "My mom says that maybe now I can have a kitten—after we get a new place to live." The chin lifted again, and the stubborn expression reappeared. "My dad wouldn't let me have a kitten, either."

His mood reflective, Brodie studied her. A divorce, by the sounds of things. And "dad" hadn't scored too many points as far as the kid was concerned. He wondered if she was from around here. He was dead certain he'd never seen her before—and he was sure he would have remembered her. "Do you live around here?"

She shook her head. "We're just visiting my grandma and grandpa." She chuckled when Max, who was reveling in the attention, lifted his head and licked her face. "That tickles, Maxie." She looked up at Brodie, giving him a shy little smile and an awkward shrug. "My mom's looking for a movie for us to watch tonight."

Realizing that she was explaining what she was doing in his store, Brodie gazed at her, amusement making his mouth lift. This one was a little too shrewd for an eight-year-old.

"Megan?"

"I'm here."

Brodie caught a movement at the edge of the free-standing display rack just outside the office door. The woman spoke again. "Honey, you shouldn't be in here," she scolded softly. "This is somebody's office, and—"

His arms still folded in front of him, his weight resting against the counter, Brodie turned his head, prepared to reassure the kid's mother. Only it wasn't just some kid's mother he was facing.

It was Eden McCall. And she was staring at him as if she'd just seen a ghost. Brodie stared back at her, his expression hardening. The last thing he wanted after Saturday night was a face-to-face confrontation with her. And he sure in hell didn't like it that she was here. He didn't like it at all. He spoke, his tone abrupt and unwelcoming. "Eden."

She stared at him, the color gone from her face; then she closed her eyes and drew a deep breath, as if it hurt her to do it. Brodie watched her, unmoved, unmoving. She was thinner than he remembered, and there was an unfamiliar fragility about her—as though she was recovering from a long illness. Realizing that he was noticing things he didn't want to notice, he made himself disconnect. She was bad news. Very bad news.

He glanced at the kid, who was busy with the dog, then back at her mother. Eden was still staring at him, a stunned expression in her eyes, and he gave her a cold, unpleasant smile. "It's nice to see you, too," he said, his tone bitter.

He saw her try to recover, to catch her balance. She abruptly stuck her hands in the pockets of her raincoat, her lips as colorless as her face. "I—" She paused and took another deep, uneven breath, then spoke, her voice unsteady. "Hello, Brodie."

His expression shuttered, Brodie watched her, mulling over her reaction. If he hadn't known better, he would have thought it was more than just shock he saw in her eyes. But he wasn't going to get drawn into any kind of speculation. All he wanted was her out of his store.

When he didn't make any response, she made a stiff, nervous gesture with her hand and forced an unsteady smile. "I didn't know you were still in town."

His tone was cynical when he responded. "I'm sure you didn't." Something flickered in her eyes—a kind of stricken look, and he realized that he was getting sucked into the same old feelings he had experienced when she'd turned her back on him years before. And he didn't want to connect with her at any level. He'd spent all Saturday night trying to put things into perspective. This was simply someone he had known a long time ago. With an indifferent shrug, he erased all expression from his face and forced himself to remain detached. "I've been around for a while."

Eden stared at him as if she'd just had another shock; then she abruptly looked away. Her dark hair was pulled back in a twist, exposing the long line of her throat, but some tendrils had slipped loose and now curled around her face and the back of her neck. With her body obscured by the dark raincoat and her profile cast by the gray light from outside, she looked isolated and oddly vulnerable, like a solitary figure in an old painting. Brodie tightened his jaw and looked away, resenting her presence. Of all the damned luck, her showing up while he was there.

"I'm glad things have worked out for you," she said softly.

He cast her a sharp glance, her comment catching him off balance. She was standing with her hands in her pockets, her gaze downcast, intent on aligning the sole of her jogger along the join in the carpet. There was something in her pose that struck him, and he narrowed his eyes, trying to identify what it was.

A small voice spoke from the floor. "This is Maximilian, Mommy. Isn't he a nice dog?"

Eden looked at her daughter, forcing a strained smile. "Yes, he is," she answered. "He's wonderful." As if bracing herself, she straightened. "Megan, this is Mister Malone." Then she glanced at Brodie but didn't quite meet his gaze. "This is my daughter, Megan."

Megan acknowledged him with a curious look, then opened her mouth to speak. Brodie suspected it was to give him a polite reply. He was in no mood for polite, but he didn't want to drag the kid into this. Forcing his face to relax, he gave her a crooked smile. "Let's drop this Mister Malone stuff, okay? My friends call me Brodie."

She assessed him for a moment, her gaze wide-eyed and intent, then her eyes lightened, and a dimple appeared at the corner of her mouth. "My friends call me Meg."

Something about the directness in her gaze got to him, and he found himself reaching over to extend his hand. "Nice to meet you, Meg."

Rising up on her knees, she held his gaze and took his hand. The dimple appeared again. "Nice to meet you, too."

There was a rustle of rainwear beside him, and Eden spoke. "We'd better get going if you want to watch the movie tonight, Megan."

Megan let go of Brodie's hand and gave Max another stroke, then reluctantly got to her feet. The dog immediately rose beside her, his eyes bright and his tail wagging, his expression decidedly hopeful as he nuzzled the little girl's hand. A wistful look swept over her face, and she knelt and hugged the dog, burying her face in the thick ruff around his neck.

Brodie watched the exchange, experiencing an odd feeling in his gut. She didn't look like her mother. In fact, he couldn't see even a hint of Eden in her. Suddenly aware of what he was doing, he switched off altogether, his expression hardening. He didn't need this. And he sure as hell didn't need it now. His face set in stiff lines, he turned and collected his jacket off the counter. It was time to clear out.

Not wanting to get into any long, drawn-out thing with Eden, he spoke to the kid. "I hope you enjoy your movie. The checkout's at the front of the store." Then without so much as a glance in her mother's direction, he brushed past them. Ten minutes with Eden McCall—or whatever her name was now—was ten minutes too much.

Eden stood in the arch of the bay window in the formal dining room, watching the gray rain fall in the yard, her position partly obscured by the ornate drapery. Heavy dusk had infiltrated from outside, secluding the room in shadows and silence, and she stood in the gloom, trying to will away the awful sensation in her abdomen—a sensation comprised of regret and old shame.

The shock of seeing Brodie Malone again had shaken her right down to her shoes. She had never expected to see him here. Never. The last she had heard, he was working out of the country—and that had been years ago. It hadn't even oc-curred to her that he might have come back here. Granted, there had been countless times when she had wondered where he was, what he was doing. All these years—and he had been right here the whole time. The awful ache in her chest ex-panded, and she folded her arms, trying to retain some warmth. She wondered how she would have reacted if she'd known.

Her vision suddenly blurring, she swallowed hard, huddling in the warmth of her sweater. Of all the mistakes she had made in her life, Brodie Malone had been the worst—and the most unforgivable. She had been seventeen years old—an insecure, uncertain seventeen-year-old—and she had caved in because she didn't have the backbone to stand up to her parents. Her mother had raged at her when she'd found out she was seeing Brodie, telling her that she wasn't old enough to know what she was doing, and that getting tangled up with him would ruin her life. It was nothing more than a silly, girlhood infatuation that she would come to regret.

And she hadn't stood up to her parents when they decided to send her off to an exclusive private school before her first year of art college. Nor had she stood up to the sneering, belittling attitude some of her classmates had had over Brodie and her silly, schoolgirl crush.

But it hadn't been a silly schoolgirl crush. She might have been young and naive and full of impossible dreams, but what she'd felt for him had been real. She just hadn't realized it then. She knew it later, though—after she had lost it all. And it was something she had never been able to forgive herself for—for what she had done to him. If she could go back and undo one thing in her life, that would be it.

"What's the matter, Mom? Aren't you going to watch the movie with us?"

Eden quickly wiped her face on the cuff of her sweater, then squared her shoulders and fixed her expression. She had a smile on her face when she turned to look at her daughter. "Nothing's the matter, honey. I was just watching it rain."

Megan stared at her, an intent, assessing look in her eyes. She finally spoke. "Are you crying because of Daddy?"

Experiencing a surge of emotion, Eden clenched her jaw and swallowed hard. She waited for the awful cramp to ease; then she answered, her voice uneven, "No. I wasn't crying about Daddy. I was just feeling a little bit sad, that's all."

Megan continued to stare at her; then she gave her mother a discomfited grimace. "So do you want to watch the movie?"

Eden somehow managed to hang on to her uneven smile. "Would you mind a whole bunch if I didn't?" she queried softly. "I don't think I'm in the mood for the 'Three Stooges' tonight."

A glint appeared in her daughter's eyes, and Megan flashed her an off-center grin. "That's okay. Martha's going to watch it with me. She says since Grandma's gone to the hospital, she's going to put her feet up and take a bloody break."

Martha Briggs had been the McCall housekeeper for years, and she was the only person Eden knew, besides Chase, who wasn't intimidated by her mother's imperiousness. And sometimes Martha forgot what a parrot Megan was. Her expression stern, Eden stared down at her daughter. "You know you aren't supposed to use that kind of language, Megan. And you'd better never use it in front of Grandma, or she'll wash your mouth out with soap."

The look in Megan's eyes said she would like to see her try, but for once she didn't debate the issue. "Okay, Mom."

"Don't give me that 'okay, Mom' routine, Megan Anne. Or *I'll* wash your mouth out with soap."

Megan gave her a semisheepish smile, then turned to go. "I was just telling you what Martha said, that's all." She stopped at the French doors and turned, meeting her mother's gaze with a steadiness that went far beyond her years. "Don't worry," she whispered softly. "We're going to be okay, Mom. We don't need him."

It was all Eden could do not to let Megan see how her response had affected her. Eight years old and her daughter was giving her comfort. She managed another forced smile. "I know we are, honey." She had to wait a moment to collect herself; then she spoke again, her voice very husky. "You go on and watch the movie with Martha. I think I'll just stay in here for a while."

Megan considered her for a moment, then nodded and turned to leave the room. "If it's really good, I'll come tell you."

"You do that."

Eden watched her daughter disappear; then she turned back to the window, hugging herself against the dampness. Sometimes she wondered what she'd done to deserve her daughter. Meggie had come into her life so unexpectedly—almost like a miracle appearing out of nowhere. She had gone five long years, and every month it was the same—that unquenchable hope that she would be pregnant, then the devastating disappointment when she wasn't.

Early on, she had tried to persuade Richard to enter a fertility program with her, but he'd absolutely refused, saying it wasn't his problem. So she had done it on her own—and found out she wasn't a hundred percent. She'd gone through the whole treatment process on her own, but still nothing. Her life had seemed so damned barren and empty, and it got to the point where she couldn't even paint anymore. There was just nothing inside her to transpose onto canvas. Realizing she was sliding into a severe depression, she had gone against Richard and found a job—a wonderful, fulfilling job in a privately funded art gallery, a job that would give her life some purpose. She'd had the job exactly four weeks when Richard had phoned her from work one day, saying there was a baby available through private adoption. They had brought Meggie home from the hospital two days later.

She had been so thrilled, and so grateful that he'd gone along with the adoption, especially when he'd said he would never consider raising a child that wasn't his own, that she'd never really thought about why he had done what he had. But when Meggie was about five months old, and her boss at the gallery suggested she come back part-time, Richard had gone into one of his reproving withdrawals, telling her that he had given in and gotten her a baby. Hadn't she better stay home and look after it?

It was then that she'd realized that the adoption had been his way of effecting control over her life. Her involvement in charity work was acceptable, and she'd always known that he'd viewed her painting as a harmless hobby, but her getting a real job was different; that smacked of independence. To this day, she could remember the feeling that had risen up in her—a feeling of real rage when she realized what his getting her a baby was all about. It had hit her then that if she gave in and did what he wanted, she would be signing herself over to him for the rest of her life. And it was that tiny, happy, precious baby that had pushed her forward. She wanted to be the kind of mother her daughter would be proud of—and that had nothing to do with a career or a profession, it had to do with self-esteem and inner strength. And going back to work part-time had been her first step toward gaining some control in her life, of working toward self-respect.

Richard's displeasure had been cold and debasing, but for the first time in her life, she had not caved in when faced with that kind of cold disapproval. She had never been able to take a stand for herself, but she had been able to take a stand because of Megan.

Eden sometimes wondered if that was why he had never put up much of a fight for Megan—because getting her was what had effected a change in Eden. But then, he had never really shown much more than a superficial interest in their daughter—it was as though she was a disruptive puppy that he'd brought home to keep Eden amused. He had threatened her once with a custody battle—and Eden had no doubt that he would have gone through with it if he hadn't gotten what he wanted. But it wouldn't have been the child that he wanted—it was Eden's capitulation on the settlement that he was really after. And Eden knew it. So she had given him whatever he wanted, and she had gotten the only thing that really mattered to her, and that was her daughter. Everything else was inconsequential.

"Missy?"

Eden turned. Martha was watching her from the doorway, her ample, apron-swathed figure outlined by the light behind her, her gray hair like a corona around her head. There was a look of motherly concern on her face. "Are you sure you won't come watch the movie with us? It might help you take your mind off things."

Eden shook her head and tried to smile. "No thanks, Martha. I'm not in the mood."

Martha studied her a moment, then pursed her mouth in a worried expression and turned to go. She was about to head down the hallway toward the study when Eden spoke. "Martha?"

The older woman turned, and Eden braced herself and swallowed hard. "Is Brodie Malone married?"

Martha gazed at her a moment, then heaved a heavy sigh. "You've seen him, then?"

"Yes."

As if wanting to avoid any questions about Brodie, the housekeeper went over to the rosewood dining room table, making a tsking sound as she used her apron to wipe a smudge off the high sheen surface.

"Martha?" Eden prompted softly.

The other woman released another heavy sigh and finally met Eden's gaze. "No. He's not married."

Eden's voice wasn't quite steady when she spoke again. "He said he's been around for a while."

Resting her hand on the back of one of the chairs, Martha rubbed her palm back and forth across the polished wood, her hesitancy obvious. "Yes, he has."

Knowing why the housekeeper was reluctant to discuss Brodie, Eden pressed her. "Please, Martha," she whispered.

Martha exhaled heavily and met her gaze. "We used to see him around town now and again after his father died. But he's been back permanent for quite a while. He opened his first business—oh, ten, twelve years ago, maybe more. He had a video place by the old bakery for years. Then he bought that old bank building a while back and renovated it. Then maybe two years ago, he bought the hotel and renovated it, too. Turned it into a bloody showplace, he did." She drew herself to her full height, a look of smug satisfaction on her face. "Some say he's done real well for himself. But then, I never did agree with your folks about that boy. Always said he had some bloody backbone in him, given a chance."

Unable to meet Martha's gaze, Eden turned back to the window, refolding her arms tightly under her breasts. It was so ironic that he'd come back here. Ironic that he'd been here all along and she hadn't even known it.

"Did he say anything about his nephew?"

Eden turned her head and looked at the housekeeper. "I didn't even know he had a nephew."

"He took the boy in a few years back. Nobody really knows much about it, except his sister died. I expect he was around Megan's age when Brodie brought him back here."

Eden turned back to the window, cataloging the information. It was as if they were talking about a complete stranger.

"You're sure you won't come watch the movie?"

She turned and gave the housekeeper a small smile. "No, thank you, Martha," she answered huskily.

Eden wasn't sure how long she stood at the window, watching the rain, feeling so empty inside that she felt almost stripped. Life had a way of rising up to haunt a person sometimes.

Finally realizing darkness had settled in, she sighed and straightened her shoulders, then turned from the window. This was getting her nowhere. Maybe if she made some popcorn for Martha and Megan she would feel better. There was something very comforting about the smell of freshly popped popcorn on a cold rainy night.

She was in the kitchen, trying to find the air popper in the bottom cupboard, when Ellie McCall came in the back entryway. Locating the small appliance, Eden rose and set it on the counter, glancing at her mother as she entered the kitchen. "So how was he tonight?"

Ellie McCall slipped out of her raincoat, carefully folded it and placed it over the back of the chair, refusing to look at her daughter. Eden experienced a start of alarm when she saw the deep tension lines around her mother's mouth. In spite of her age and her silver hair, Ellie McCall possessed that cool, elegant beauty that was almost ageless. But she had never looked as old as she did right then. Her mother's voice was tight when she answered. "Not good."

"What happened?"

Her mother finally met her gaze, a strained look around her eyes, the track lighting above the island leaving her face stark and colorless. "He had another attack—a small one, the doctor said—but they feel it would be best if they moved him to a hospital in Calgary."

Eden stared at her mother, digesting this latest bit of information. It was obvious by her mother's brittle posture and clamped mouth that she had interpreted this move as a serious deterioration in her father's condition—but then, her mother had a tendency to do that, to always see the worst-case scenario. Eden stuck her hands in the pockets of her slacks and leaned back against the counter. Keeping her voice perfectly calm, she spoke. "That's not necessarily a bad thing, Mom. It makes sense that they would want him somewhere close to a good cardiac care unit if something happened. I'm not sure that Dr. Bradley is treating him as aggressively as he could."

Her mother's mouth thinned into a hard line, and she shot Eden a condemning look. "And since when have you become such an authority on medical treatment? Surely this infinite wisdom wasn't the reason it took you so long to come home when your father was hospitalized."

Even two years ago, a cutting, sarcastic response like that would have made Eden feel foolish and inadequate. Now it just made her tired. Folding her arms in front of her, she stared at her mother. "Mom," she said, her voice very, very quiet, "if you're going to start acting like that, I'm going to move out to either Chase's or Tanner's."

Her mother went very still, a stunned expression widening her eyes. It was the first time Eden had taken a stand against her, and she knew Eleanor McCall wasn't going to take it lying down. Her mother opened her mouth to retaliate, but Eden didn't give her a chance to get started. "I mean it, Mother. I came home to help look after Dad. If you're going to start treating me like some half-wit child, I'm going to leave." She gave her a minute for everything to sink in; then she turned back to the cupboard, keeping her voice even. "Where do you keep the popcorn?"

There was a long pause; then her mother finally answered, a funny waver in her voice. "It's on the right-hand side of the top shelf of the pantry."

Eden slid open the heavy oak pocket door and found the jar exactly where her mother said it was. She was pouring the kernels into the popper when her mother spoke from behind her. "Your father wants to see Chase," she said, her voice strained and unsteady, and Eden got an instant knot in the pit of her stomach. She knew why her mother had told her that—she wanted Eden to try to talk her brother into going to see him. She mulled it over for a moment, then responded. "When are they moving Dad?"

"I don't know if they are. He's adamant about staying here."

Eden put the top on the popper, letting her hand rest on the appliance as she stared down at the tiled counter. Finally she released a sigh. "I'll talk to Chase. But I won't promise anything."

There was a strained pause; then her mother spoke, her voice a stiff whisper. "Thank you." Eden heard her mother leave the kitchen as she continued to stare down at the counter, an emotional weariness washing over her. Deciding that popcorn was not a good idea after all, she emptied the popper and put it away, then reached over and shut off the track lights. She wandered over to the breakfast nook that opened onto the east veranda and stood looking out, a sense of loss sweeping over her. There was an old wrought-iron gate at the bottom of the yard, leaving a gap in the high hedge, and through it she could see the flashing pink neon sign of the video store.

The pain in her chest returned with a crippling force. God, but she had loved him. He had been her whole world. He had been wild and cocky and reckless, and he had made her feel things—wonderful, wild, reckless things that she had never experienced before or since. It was as if something bright and shiny had died in her when he was gone from her life.

Her parents had said he was nothing but trash and trouble, but they had been wrong. So very wrong. An old rage of injustice welled up in her, and she clenched her jaw against it. She was so damned glad he had made a success of his life. She really was. It was justice at its best that he had shown them all. But Lord, the shock of seeing him again had unearthed some painful emotions. It was as if she were raw and exposed all over again, only the hurt was far, far worse. With one cold, distasteful look, he had stripped away the past seventeen years, and it was as if she was back on the doorstep of her prep-school dorm, with her classmates looking on as she watched him walk away. And when she had tried to make amends for the past, when she told him she was glad that things had worked out for him, his bitter rejection had caused such a sick feeling inside her that she still hadn't gotten over it.

But then, she had that coming. What she'd done had been unforgivable. But it wasn't until today, until she'd come face-to-face with him, until she was confronted with the look of loathing in his eyes, that she really realized how destructive her betrayal had been. She would never forget the look on his face when he left her at the door of his office, his face hardened into a expression of loathing—how he had slipped between her and the video rack, going out of his way to avoid touching her.

Their breakup had happened so long ago that she would have thought he would have forgotten all about her. But his reaction was just as bitter now as it had been back then.

Renewed guilt rolled through her. It was as though it was happening all over again.

Chapter 4

Eden stood staring out the plant window over the kitchen sink, her arms folded against the early morning chill, a cup of cold coffee clasped in her hand. She had been there since first light, and she was so tired that she felt completely numb inside. Unable to sleep, she had spent the night moving from window to window, trying to outdistance the panic that kept trying to break loose.

And it wasn't just Brodie who kept her awake. It was a renewed fear and uncertainty and a terrifying feeling of inadequacy. She had nothing. She *was* nothing. All her life she had handed over control to someone else, and all her life she had let someone else influence her decisions to the point where she didn't even know who she was anymore. And now she had the responsibility of raising Megan on her own.

It had all come down on her in the middle of the night. With that awful feeling of loss devastating her defenses, the self-doubt had come rolling in like a great crashing wave. She wasn't alone. She knew that. She could always lean on Tanner or Chase, or, if worse came to worst, there were her parents. But she didn't want to be trapped by that kind of debilitating dependency anymore. She wanted to get her self-respect back, to feel that she had the strength and ability and wherewithal to take care of Megan and herself. And the only way she could do that was to let go of all the lifelines.

There were times when she really believed she could handle the future, but last night it had scared her to death. And this thing with Brodie—God, but she hadn't expected the waves and waves of loneliness. It was as though he had died. And maybe in some ways he had. She had hoarded special memories of that summer they spent together, and when things were really bleak, she would remember what it had been like. And now she wouldn't be able to do that anymore. The look she'd seen on his face when he left the store would always get in the way.

Swallowing back the ache in her throat, she turned her wrist and looked at her watch. Seven. Two hours until she had to leave for the hospital. Looking back out the window, she watched the trees against the gray sky, their branches stark and monochromatic in the soft drizzle. She had taken the morning shift at the hospital with her father, and even after a few days, she was beginning to dread it. Both her parents had been very upset with her over her divorce, but once she had actually signed the papers, her mother had clamped her mouth shut in extreme disapproval and had not uttered another word about it. Her father wasn't so accommodating. He continued to rant at her about how ridiculous she was being, insisting that there was no way she was capable of raising Megan on her own. And on at least two occasions he'd phoned Richard and told him exactly that. It was useless trying to reason with him, or even explain. So she didn't even try.

"Hi, Mom. Whatcha doing?"

Fixing a smile on her face, she turned to face her daughter. Genuine amusement surfaced when she got a good look at her. Her hair was sticking out from her braid as if she had just stepped out of a wind tunnel, and her face still had the imprint of the quilt on it. Her baseball pajamas were on inside out, and there was now a large tear in one knee. Eden wasn't even going to ask how that had gotten there. "Hi, muffin. Did you have a good sleep?"

Megan climbed onto the back bench of the kitchen nook, scratched her nose, then propped her chin on her hand. "Yep."

She rubbed one eye and gave an unladylike yawn. "Are you going to the hospital again?"

Eden stifled a sigh. "Yes, I am."

"Can I take the movie back by myself?"

Eden studied her daughter, a funny sensation unfolding in her stomach. Feeling oddly exposed, she turned and set her cup in the sink. Her voice wasn't quite steady when she responded. "Yes. But be sure and tell Martha where you're going." Taking a deep breath to quell the unsettled feeling in her stomach, she spoke again. "And try to be quiet, Meg, please. Grandma is used to sleeping in, and any unusual noises disturb her."

Megan heaved a sigh. "I know. But it's so boring here, Mom."

She turned and met her daughter's gaze. "I know it is, honey. And I know you're upset because you're missing the last two weeks of school. But once Grandpa gets better, I won't be going to the hospital every day, and maybe we can find something to do. And once school is out here, things will be better."

Martha entered the kitchen, tying a huge chef's apron around her middle. She ruffled Meg's hair in passing, her greeting cut short by the sharp ring of the telephone. Swearing under her breath, Eden made a grab for it and caught it before the second ring, praying that her mother had unplugged the phone in her bedroom. Waiting a second to regain her composure, she spoke into the receiver. "McCall residence. Eden speaking."

There was a slight pause, then a soft, disagreeable laugh. "Well, Eden. It's nice to know you still have some sense of propriety left."

Eden's stomach dropped, and she clutched the portable phone and turned her back to the others, her hands suddenly clammy. "What do you want?"

Richard gave another unpleasant laugh, and Eden could almost see him leaning back in his leather executive chair, his feet on his desk, his free hand tucked behind his head. "Well, sweetness," he said in that condescending tone that made her skin crawl, "as I recall, the custody agreement states reasonable visitation rights. And I've decided I'm going to exercise those rights. My lawyer and I have decided that it's only reasonable that Megan should spend the summer here with me."

There was a brief pause, then he spoke again. "I'm giving you until Friday of next week to make arrangements."

For one awful moment Eden thought she was going to be sick, and she clenched her teeth and closed her eyes, trying to will away the awful churning sensation in her belly. "Now," he continued in that same reasonable tone, "I know you aren't going to want to be separated from our little chick, so of course you're welcome to come with her."

Panic radiating through her, Eden went into the formal dining room and leaned weakly against the wall. Her voice seemed to come from a long way off when she whispered, "Why are you doing this, Richard?"

"Why, sweetness," he answered, his tone amazed. "I want to spend some time with my daughter. Surely, after what you did to me, that's not too much to ask. And I did sign the custody papers in good faith."

Eden's legs started to tremble, and she sank down onto the floor, her fingers turning white on the phone. She knew what he was doing; he was trying to force her into some sort of degrading association with him. Nothing would please him more than to humiliate her. Fighting against the panic, she took a painful breath, knowing that if he had one inkling of her reaction, he would push her to the limit. Easing in another stabilizing breath, she spoke, trying to keep her voice calm. "I'll have to talk this over with Megan and see what she wants to do."

There was a brief pause; then he spoke, a smooth, malicious edge to his tone. "Well, my pet, I'd hate to have to charge you with contempt. If my visitation rights aren't addressed, I'll have to reevaluate the whole custody issue, especially since you've taken her out of the province without my consent."

Her whole body trembling, Eden braced her elbow on her knee and covered her face with her hand, trying to think past the fear welling up in her. He was never going to let go. Never. God, she had to stay calm. And she must not let him back her into a corner. Drawing on sheer willpower, she finally answered, her voice so evenly modulated that it didn't even sound like her own. "I'll have to call you back. I'm just on my way to the hospital, and Megan's still asleep."

He started to say something, but she cut him off. "I'm sorry, Richard. I can't talk now. I'm due at the hospital. I'll call you later." Her hands were shaking so badly she was barely able to press the Disconnect button. She clenched her teeth together and pressed another button to get a dial tone, then let the phone drop onto the floor, ensuring a busy signal if he tried to call back. Unable to stop the awful trembling that gripped her, she covered her face with her hand again, feeling as if she were coming apart piece by piece. It was supposed to be over. She had given him everything he wanted. Everything.

A small warm arm slipped around her neck, and her daughter whispered anxiously, "What's the matter, Mommy? What did Dad want?"

Knowing that she somehow had to get it together for her daughter, Eden pulled Megan between her upraised knees and pressed her daughter's head against her own neck. She knew she was going to have to give her an explanation, and she was going to have to do it without frightening her. She had never lied to Megan—not once—but she would do whatever it took to make sure this child was not dragged into whatever sick, twisted game Richard was playing. She would not let that happen.

Steadied by the first stirring of rage, Eden gently smoothed the wild tangle of Megan's hair away from her mouth; then she tightened her hold and spoke, her voice even. "Your father wants you to go back to Toronto and spend some time with him. That's all." She pressed a kiss against Meg's head, then hugged her. "But don't worry about it, sweetheart. If you don't want to go, you won't have to. We'll work something out."

Megan slid both her arms around her mother's neck and hugged her back, her voice quavering and muffled when she answered. "I don't want to go." There was a pause, and she tightened her hold even more. Then she spoke again, her voice stronger and tinged with defiance. "I won't go. And he's *not* my father."

Closing her eyes, Eden tipped her head back against the wall, fighting the unexpected and near-hysterical urge to laugh. God, trust Megan to strip it down to the bare bones. Because it was true. Richard was technically not her father—except on paper. She wondered if that was why Megan had always seemed so removed from anything Richard said or did—because she'd simply discounted his position in her life. It showed a peculiar kind of logic if she had.

Oddly reassured by her daughter's comment, Eden gave her a hug, a small wobble of amusement still in her voice when she responded. "That's true, sweetheart. He's not your father. And we'll work something out. I promise."

Megan gave her another hard squeeze, then lifted her head and looked at her, her face pale and pinched, a mulish glint in her eyes. "I won't go. And he can't make me."

Wanting to reassure her, she gave her daughter a small smile as she tucked a loose strand of hair behind her ear. "Just don't worry about it, okay?" she said softly.

Megan stared at her, then nodded and got to her feet. "Can I have my cereal now?"

Getting the feeling that her daughter was trying to distract her, Eden got to her feet, shuddering when she saw the phone on the floor. If she'd learned one thing over the past few months, it was that Richard got some sort of sick pleasure out of terrifying her. She would give herself time to calm down, to see this more rationally; then she would call her lawyer as soon as she got back from the hospital. She would move to Siberia if she had to, but she was not going to allow Richard to continue playing these vicious little games where Megan was concerned.

After three hours at the hospital, Eden was so tired she could barely function. They had put her father on some new medication that sedated him, but he seemed oddly agitated, as if he were having bad dreams. She finally got him to settle down, but he would get restless the minute she moved away from him, so she had spent the past two hours standing by his bed, rubbing his back and humming old melodies. For all the issues she had with him, it hurt to see him like this, to see the frailness in him. He had always been so indestructible. And now he was simply a weak old man.

They were just clearing away the last of the lunch trays from the rooms when her mother appeared in the doorway, a frantic, distraught expression in her eyes, alarm leaving her face ashen. She motioned for Eden to come into the hallway, and

Eden frowned. Her mother wasn't due here for another hour, and Eden wondered if she had just received bad news from the doctors. Making sure her father's oxygen nose vent was in place, she checked that the safety rail was fixed, then left the room.

Her mother, her hand pressed to her chest, grasped her arm and whispered tightly, "Darling, I think you'd better come home."

Bracing herself for bad news, Eden kept her face calm.

Ellie McCall drew a deep breath, then looked back at her daughter. "Richard called, and I let him talk to Megan. And she's—"

"You *what?*"

Fear glimmered in Ellie's eyes and her mouth started to tremble. "I let her talk to Richard."

Alarm closing around her lungs, Eden felt the color drain from her own face. Her voice low and furious, she fired back, "I told Martha not to let him talk to her if he called. I told her."

Ellie met her daughter's gaze, her own feverish. "I know. I know. She told me. But I thought you were overreacting, so when he asked if he could speak to her, I let him. I didn't think there was any harm. After all, he is her father and—"

"Where is she?"

Her gaze stark, the older woman pressed her hand hard against her breastbone, her face turning even whiter. "I don't know. She's disappeared. We've been looking for her for over an hour—"

Eden stared at her mother, alarm paralyzing her for an instant; then she stepped back into the room and snatched up her jacket and shot a furious look at her mother. "Damn you, Mother! Why couldn't you, just this once, leave well enough alone? But no! You always think you know best!" Casting her mother one last furious look, she sprinted for the exit stairs, panic and adrenaline rushing through her. God, if anything happened to that kid, she didn't know what she would do.

Eden ran all the way home, a frantic prayer playing over and over in her head, her heart hammering so hard she could barely breathe. *Please, baby. Please be okay.*

She burst in the back door of the house, her fear increasing when she saw the look on Martha's face. "I told her, missy. I did. But she wouldn't bloody listen."

Her breathing so labored she could hardly get the words out, Eden pressed her hand against her chest. "I know you did." Taking a stabilizing breath, she tried to think. "Do you know what he said to her?"

Her face etched with worry, the housekeeper shook her head. "No."

Eden paused a moment, trying to process, trying to think, then she headed for the phone. "Maybe she tried to get to Chase's. She went with you Sunday, and that's the only place she'd know to go."

Martha twisted her hands together, the stricken look intensifying. "I thought of that. I drove out. There was no sign of her on the road, and she wasn't there. I didn't want to alarm Devon, so I didn't say anything. I said I was looking for you."

Knowing that panicking was not going to help, Eden pressed her hand to her forehead, trying to force some rationality past the panic. What would Megan do? Where would she go? Where was the first place to look? Where . . . ?

The video. The damned video. She had asked to take it back. It was at least somewhere to start.

Dropping her hand, she looked at the housekeeper. "Where's the video, Martha? Did she take the video back?"

Martha stared at her, then turned and hurried toward the study, Eden on her heels.

Martha stopped just inside the door. "It's gone, missy. It was on the coffee table, and it's gone."

Eden whirled and headed back down the hallway. "Does she have a jacket with her?"

"I don't know. She just disappeared."

"Stay here, Martha," she yelled as she snatched one of Megan's jackets from a hook by the back door. "I need you here if she comes back."

Eden hit the ground at a dead run, a new rush of panic surging through her. God, let her be there. Let her be sitting on the floor in the corner, watching a movie on the big screen. Let her just have forgotten the time. Just let her be there.

Fear and hope burgeoning inside her, Eden pushed through the heavy glass door, her gaze desperate as she checked the corner in front of the big-screen TV. Empty. She checked between the racks, the fear pushing higher.

A kindly voice came from behind the high counter by the exit door. "Can I help you?"

Feeling trapped and frantic, Eden turned toward the voice, her legs shaky beneath her. "My daughter brought back a video sometime today. One of the 'Three Stooges' movies." Forcing herself to take a deep breath, she somehow managed to get out the next sentence. "Did you see her?"

The woman came around the counter, concern showing in her eyes. "Yes. Yes, I did. She brought it back a couple of hours ago. She stopped to play with the dog for a bit, then she left."

Eden closed her eyes and sagged against the wall, a sob twisting loose. "Oh, God. Oh, God."

The woman's expression sharpened with alarm. "What's the matter? Is something wrong?"

Struggling to control the awful shakiness in her legs, Eden clenched her hands and swallowed hard. Richard couldn't have gotten his hands on her. Not yet. There wasn't time. She clenched and unclenched her hands and made herself meet the other woman's gaze. "She's disappeared. We can't find her, and we don't know where she's gone."

There was the scrape of a chair, and another voice spoke. "I'll take it from here, Lydia."

A strong hand gripped her wrist, and Eden opened her eyes, something wrenching loose when she met Brodie Malone's flat, unreadable gaze. Grasping her shoulder, he forced her down into the chair, his tone firm when he said, "Sit down. And tell me what's going on."

Cold to the bone and scared to death, Eden sank into the chair, the solid pressure of his hand on her shoulder strangely reinforcing. She stared at him, her heart hammering in her throat; then she drew a deep, stabilizing breath. "Megan's disappeared. And we can't find her."

Leaning back against the end of one of the racks, he folded his arms and stared at her, his expression unreadable. "What happened?"

Her voice shaking so badly it was almost impossible to get the words out, Eden told him. His expression tightened, and by the time she finished, his jaw was set in a hard line. Unable to hold his gaze, Eden clutched Megan's jacket against her chest, so cold inside she couldn't stop shivering.

There was a long silence; then Brodie spoke, his tone businesslike. "Is that Megan's jacket?"

Clenching her hands to stop the trembling, Eden nodded.

He unfolded his arms and withdrew the garment from her hold. "Max. Come," he commanded. The dog appeared from around a rack, his tail wagging. Grasping his collar, Brodie crouched down in front of him, then took the dog's head between his hands, making eye contact. "Max. Find." He lifted the jacket off his thigh and placed it on the floor in front of the animal, repeating the command. Max pricked his ears and looked at Brodie, his body absolutely motionless. Brodie gave the command again, and Eden couldn't believe the startling change in the dog.

The significance of what was going on finally penetrated, and she locked her arms under her breasts, her mind refusing to function as she watched.

The dog pawed at the jacket, rolling it over on the floor as he sniffed it; then he raised his head and started toward the door. Brodie disappeared briefly, then came back with a jacket, yanking it on. He picked up a cellular phone from the end of the counter and jammed it in his jacket pocket, then started toward the door. "Let's see what he's got."

Not entirely comprehending, Eden stumbled to her feet and followed him. "How...?"

"He flunked out of the RCMP training school, but he knows how to track. We've used him before."

He held the door open for her and followed her out. He gave another command to Max, and the dog started to search.

A kind of shock setting in, Eden numbly watched the dog. "But it's so wet."

"The sidewalk and road are dry. He might get lucky."

The dog continued to circle, sniffing the ground; then his head came up, and he looked at Brodie and barked once. Brodie gave him another command, and the dog took off. Brodie caught her by the wrist, pulling her after him. "Come on. We don't want to lose him."

Eden stumbled after him, the panic and fear she had experienced earlier giving way. Damn Richard. Damn his vindictive maneuvering. Lord, they had to find her. She was so little. And she had to be so scared.

The dog headed down the road leading out of town, his nose to the ground, and Brodie shot her a quick glance. "We're going to have to hustle to keep up," he said, his tone curt.

Letting go of his hand, she nodded and started to run. About a half mile up the road, next to an uncut hay field, Max stopped and began scanning the ground; then he began to circle. Realizing what had happened, Eden braced both hands on her thighs and bent over, fighting for every breath, her face wet with perspiration and tears. God, if only it hadn't rained all night. If only...

A strong hand gripped her upper arm, drawing her up. Maintaining a hold on her arm, Brodie caught her by the chin and forced her gaze away from the searching dog and up at him. "Stop it, Eden," he commanded firmly. "Stop. I want you to look at something." She stared numbly up at him, her chest heaving and hurting, her breathing still raw. He gave her a small, warped smile. "We aren't at a dead end, yet." He took her by the shoulders and pulled her in front of him, then pointed toward the field. "See that old barn in the trees, and if you get the right angle—no, not over there, over here—can you see a faint line through the tall grass?" He tipped her head up, then pointed again. "See it?"

Aware of the heat of his body at her back, she finally saw what he was pointing at, and she nodded.

Resting his hand on her shoulder, he gave her a reassuring squeeze. "I think someone has walked through there in the last couple of hours. And I think they were headed for that old barn."

Swallowing hard, Eden wiped her face with the heel of her hand. "Let's check it out," she whispered.

Taking her hand, Brodie gave a command to the dog, then led her down into the ditch, the tall wet grass soaking her slacks. They reached the barbed-wire fence, and before she could separate the wires to crawl through, Brodie hoisted her over, then used the fence post to vault over. He lifted the bottom wire so Max could crawl under. Grasping the dog's collar, he spoke to Eden. "Wait here a minute." He took the dog a few paces into the hay field, then crouched down in front of him, making Max look at him. After a moment, he rose, sending the dog toward the barn.

Coming back, he reached out his hand toward her. "Come on," he said gruffly. "It's going to be rough walking."

Feeling more hopeful than she had since she found out Megan had disappeared, she slipped her hand into his, grateful for the support, for the steadying effect. Grateful that he was there.

The grass in the field was tall and wet, and the ground beneath was soggy and uneven, and Eden tightened her hold on his hand, partly to steady herself, but more to draw on his strength. They were halfway across the field when three staccato barks rang out, and Brodie squeezed her hand. "She's there."

Suddenly blinded by tears, Eden stumbled on the uneven ground, and he tightened his hold to steady her. By the time they reached the far end of the field, Eden was soaking wet from the waist down, and her legs were trembling so badly she could barely walk. The barn was old and leaning, with the roof caved in and broken in the middle. What was left of the slab siding was weathered and gray, and the beam across the door sagged in the middle. A row of spruce trees formed a windbreak, and Brodie led her through a gap in them.

Just before they reached the barn, he stopped and pulled her to a halt. "I think it's better if we don't let her know we're here," he said, his tone quiet. "I don't want her trying to make a break for it and climbing up through the hole in the roof."

Feeling as if every nerve in her face had gone numb, Eden nodded. Giving her hand another reassuring squeeze, he led her to the sagging doorway, and with Eden's heart jammed up in her throat, they entered the crumbling structure. The gray light from outside did little to dispel the gloom, but even in the heavy shadows, Eden could see that there was nothing left inside except support poles where the stalls used to be. There was a wild flutter in the rafters, and two sparrows skimmed over their heads, frightened by the intrusion.

Max, his attention riveted on the loft above, stood at the bottom of a ladder, his tail wagging slightly. "Good boy," Brodie murmured very softly. "Good boy." Letting go of Brodie's hand, Eden started for the ladder, but he caught her arm and held her back. He shook his head. "Not that way," he whispered so quietly she could barely hear him. "It won't hold your weight." He checked out the stripped interior, finding the remains of a manger in one corner. He looked up, and Eden followed his gaze, spotting the hole to the loft right above it, a faint gray light showing through. Steadying himself against the wall, he stepped up on the manger, then reached up and caught the edge of the hole. Readjusting his hold, he effortlessly and silently pulled himself up. There was the sound of fabric against weathered wood as he hooked his arms in the opening, then levered himself the rest of the way through.

Her heart laboring against the awful tension, Eden stuffed her hands in the pockets of her jacket, her gaze never wavering from the square hole that had swallowed him up. There was an agonizing silence; then Brodie spoke, his voice soft. "Megan. Wake up, honey. Your mom's here."

A sob of relief wedged in Eden's throat, and she swallowed hard against it, refusing to allow herself the luxury of falling apart. They had found her, and she was safe, and that was all that mattered. Not taking her eyes off the hole, she waited, her stomach churning. She heard Brodie shift his weight. "Come on, Meg. Your mom's here."

There was the sound of movement in the far corner, and dust filtered down between the cracks, and Eden clenched her hands. There was another movement; then Megan's tearful retort. "No! No! I'm staying here. I won't go stay with him! I won't! He's *not* my father."

Brodie's voice was soft and reassuring. "Your mom said you don't have to go if you don't want to. She'll work something out." There was a slight pause; then he spoke again, quiet censure in his tone. "You've scared her half to death, Meg. And I don't think that's fair, do you?"

There was another pause, and Brodie spoke again. "Good girl. Now, you're going to have to come to me, honey. This wood's pretty rotten, and we could get in a real wreck here if I try to come to you. Okay?"

More dust sifted down; then, after what seemed like forever, there was the sound of footsteps across the creaking boards. Eden closed her eyes, a sickening relief rushing through her, the surge so strong that it made her vision blur and her heart hurt. He had her. Thank God, he had her.

Realizing he was going to need help getting Meg down, she quickly wiped her face and went to stand below the hole. Brodie's voice came from right above her. "I'm going to hand her down. Okay, Mom?"

Swallowing hard, she forced some strength into her voice. "I'm right here."

There was a slight pause; then he spoke again, a trace of humor in his voice. "She's got a sleeping bag and a big bag of groceries up here—and a jug of water."

Eden closed her eyes, not knowing whether to laugh or cry. No one could ever say her kid was short on determination. She wiped her hands on her slacks and reached up. "Hand them down."

He lowered a large plastic bag that was tied at the top, and as soon as she took it from him, he tossed the sleeping bag down. "You're next, Meggie. Feet first."

He lowered Megan into Eden's outstretched arms, and the minute Eden had her, she started to shake. Locking her daughter in a crushing embrace, she turned her face against Megan's head, clenching her jaw against the awful swell of tears. God, she had been so scared. So damned scared.

Megan wrapped her arms around her neck, her voice shaky with tears, her tone a mix of belligerence and fear. "I won't go. I won't. And if he comes to get me, I'll run away. I will."

Struggling against the awful pressure in her chest, Eden hugged her tight, her voice wavering. "Tell you what. If he shows up, I'll run away with you."

She heard a light thud as Brodie landed beside her, and she lifted her head and looked at him, wanting to thank him. But there was no way she could get the words out; her throat was just too tight. He stared at her a minute, then swept up the plastic bag and sleeping bag. He straightened, avoiding her gaze as he touched the small of her back. "Let's get out of here. It wouldn't surprise me if this place came down around our ears." He turned and snapped his fingers. "Come on, Max. Time to go." The dog relinquished his post, his tail wagging as he came over to Brodie.

With Megan still clinging to her, Eden responded to the pressure of Brodie's hand, and she turned toward the door. Once outside, Brodie dropped the sleeping bag and groceries on a pile of old wood, then pulled out the cellular phone, fixed the mouthpiece and hit a button. Putting the instrument to his ear, he stared out across the rain-sodden landscape. "Lydia, is Jase still there?" He cast a glance at Eden, then made a quarter turn away. "Tell him to get the Jeep and meet me on the north road out of town. By Mitchell's hay field. And tell him to be quick about it." Resting his hand on his hip, he looked toward town. "Yeah. We got her. Thanks, Lydia."

He thumbed a button and looked at Eden. "Do you want me to call Martha?"

Unable to loosen her hold on her daughter, still unable to answer, Eden nodded.

There was a slight softening in his eyes when he spoke, his voice gruff. "I need the number, Eden."

Swallowing, she took a steadying breath and told him. Knowing she should be the one to talk to Martha, but afraid she would burst into tears if she tried, Eden nestled her head against Megan's. "Are you okay, muffin?"

Tightening her hold, Megan gave one sharp nod.

Eden rubbed her daughter's back. "I'm not going to let him take you, honey."

His conversation brief and to the point, Brodie finished and folded up the phone, then stuffed it back in his jacket pocket. Crouching down, he rolled the sleeping bag into a bundle, tying it together with the attached strings. Collecting the plastic bag, he stood up and approached Eden. "Here. You take this stuff, and let me carry her."

Eden gave her daughter a squeeze. "Can Brodie carry you?"

She got another nod, and Brodie reached for her, a small smile appearing when Meg put her arms out toward him. "You're lucky you didn't get lost in the tall grass, short stuff. That's quite a hike."

She gave him a disgruntled look, but her mouth lifted enough to reveal her dimple. "I'm not short stuff."

He lifted her out of Eden's arms, effortlessly swinging her up onto his shoulders. "Yes, you are." He glanced at Eden, his expression narrowing when he saw her face. "Are you going to be able to make it, Mom?" he queried, his tone of voice meant for Megan. Clutching the bulky grocery bag against her chest, Eden clamped her teeth together and nodded, the awful ache in her throat getting worse. Settling Megan on his shoulders, Brodie reached out and tried to take the sleeping bag and groceries from her. "Here. Let me take those."

She shook her head, knowing if she unlocked her jaw she would start to cry. He gave her a steady, unreadable look. "Give them to me, Eden," he commanded firmly. Staring at him, the awful paralysis spreading, she let him pull the items from her grasp. He stared at her a moment longer, then repositioned one of Megan's legs. "Hold on, kid. We're going to have to move it, or we're going to get soaked. There's another rain cloud headed this way."

Eden wasn't sure how she got back across that field. It was as if her legs weren't even there, and she was shivering so badly that she had to clench her teeth to keep them from chattering. But it was a different kind of cold. It was as though she was experiencing a delayed reaction to all the stress that had accumulated over the past six months, and the panic over Megan was the last straw. And she just couldn't hold it all in any longer. She was aware of her daughter talking to Brodie, and she was aware of Max rollicking in front of them, but the periphery was one big blur. She simply fixed her gaze on Brodie's broad shoulders and followed him.

A black Jeep Cherokee stopped on the road, and the driver executed a perfect police turn, then parked on the shoulder. A tall form got out, the stance oddly familiar, and Eden stumbled, then refocused on Brodie's back.

The driver left the Jeep and waded through the tall grass in the ditch, taking Megan and the bags from Brodie, then scrambled up the steep grade to the road. Brodie turned, his face like granite as he lifted Eden over the fence and set her down on the other side. "Stay there." He climbed over and let Max through; then, without meeting her gaze, he caught her by the upper arm and started up the steep grade to the road.

"I can manage," she whispered, her lips stiff.

"Just shut up, Eden," he responded roughly. "You couldn't get out of a wet paper bag right now."

They reached the road, and as the driver turned to face them, Eden experienced a staggering jolt of recognition. It was Brodie. It was as if he'd appeared out of one of her old memories and was now standing there watching, a closed expression on his face. Then reality registered, and she closed her eyes, a sharp pain radiating through her chest. It wasn't Brodie. It had to be the nephew Martha had told her about.

Reaching the vehicle, the real Brodie let go of her. "Give me your jacket, Jase."

The teenager set Meg on the fender of the vehicle, casting Eden an unreadable look before he silently stripped off his jacket and handed it to Brodie. Without saying anything, Brodie dragged Eden's damp jacket off her, then helped her put on the dry one. His voice was expressionless when he spoke. "This is my nephew, Jason." He started doing up the snaps on Jason's jacket, and Eden stared numbly at his face. He avoided her gaze when he spoke to his nephew. "This is Eden McCall and her daughter Megan."

Jason nodded his head and folded his arms, watching her with an oddly intent look. Eden stared at him, then looked back at Brodie, her mind not connecting with anything. Brodie jerked his chin toward Megan. "Get her strapped in the front seat and put Max in the back." Finishing with the snaps, he opened the door and directed Eden into the back seat. He climbed in beside her and closed the door, his expression grim. Jason got in and looked at his uncle in the rearview mirror. "Where to?"

Brodie's tone was clipped when he responded. "Home."

Eden huddled in the warmth and dryness of Jason's jacket, her trembling hands wedged between her knees, aware—so desperately aware—of the man beside her. She knew that this awful reaction of hers was overblown, and she knew it wasn't entirely because of the fright Megan had given her. In her mind she could rationalize it. It was as if everything was hitting her at once, sending her whole body into shock. The six months of stress, the alarm over her father, the emotional jolt of seeing Brodie—the phone call that morning.

And it didn't help that she hadn't slept a wink the night before, or that she was soaking wet and cold—so cold. In her mind, she knew that now they had found Megan safe and sound, she should not be having the reaction she was. But even though she knew it, she couldn't stop it from happening. And the harder she tried to stop the awful trembling, the worse it got. It was as if her whole nervous system was shutting down on her, and there wasn't anything she could do about it.

Swallowing hard, she clamped her thighs tighter together, her vision blurring. God, if she started crying she would never stop. Vaguely aware of the conversation between Brodie and Jason, she locked her jaw and looked blindly out the window, trying to will away the awful constriction in her chest and throat. Maybe that was the problem. She had bottled up so much over the past few months—it was as if there simply wasn't room for anything more, and it was finally spilling out, whether she wanted it to or not.

A warm, strong hand grasped one wrist, trying to separate her hands. "Let go, Eden," Brodie said gruffly. "Let's get you inside."

She looked at him, her vision dulled, not quite comprehending. His dark hair was damp and ruffled by the wind, and there was a grim set to his jaw, but there wasn't a trace of expression in his eyes. He pulled her hands free of her thighs. "Come on. It's time to get out."

She turned her head and looked out the window again, dazedly realizing that they were parked in front of the garage behind the video store. Numbly responding, she followed him out of the vehicle, aware that Jason was carrying Megan in through a side door. "Where is he taking her?" Eden whispered unevenly.

"He's going to make her a cup of hot chocolate in the staff kitchen, and then he's going to keep her busy for a few minutes."

As soon as she stumbled out, he slammed the car door; then, without looking at her, he simply picked her up and carried her toward the door that Jason was holding open for him. She started to protest, but he shook his head, his jaw set. He shouldered his way through, then started up the wide stairs that led to the second floor.

"Is Megan—"

"Don't worry about Megan. Jase and Lydia will take care of her."

Reaching the top, he shifted her weight and pushed open the door. He carried her inside, kicking the door closed behind him, then set her down on a leather sofa. "Just stay there."

He disappeared, and Eden closed her eyes, giving herself over to the cold and shivering. She heard him return, and she locked her hands between her thighs again, every muscle in her body in full revolt. He pulled her hands free, and then she felt his hands at her waist. She looked at him, nothing quite registering. "You're in shock," he said flatly, "and you're wet and cold." With swift efficiency, he stripped off her wet slacks, socks and shoes, then stripped the jacket off her. Without meeting her gaze, he wrapped her up in a comforter, tucking it around her shoulders. "Are you still a tea drinker?"

Her gaze fixed starkly on his tanned, angular face, she whispered unevenly, "I'll be sick."

Finally he looked at her, his gaze flat and unreadable. He stared at her a moment, then sighed and sat down on the coffee table facing her. Leaning forward, he rested his forearms on his thighs and stared at the floor, his hair only inches away from her hand. Finally he raised his head and looked at her, a resigned expression compressing his mouth. "What in hell is going on?" he asked, his tone blunt.

The memory of the anger, of the distaste he had silently expressed toward her the day before rose in Eden's mind, and the pressure in her chest increased. If only, over the past seventeen years, he had been able to forgive what she'd done—just a little. A single sob broke loose, and she covered her face with her hand as the guilt and regret that she had stockpiled for seventeen years welled up with devastating force.

Fighting the emotions inside her, she got out the words, her voice breaking. "Could you give me a few minutes?"

There was a long pause; then Brodie spoke, his tone oddly subdued. "I'll throw your clothes in the dryer, and I'll check on things downstairs."

Eden hung on until she heard the door close behind him; then she finally let it all go. She had to. There was no holding back any longer.

Chapter 5

The cloud cover had dropped and it had started to rain by the time he returned. Eden sat curled up in the corner of the sofa, the quilt pulled tightly around her. Resting her forehead on her upraised knees, she listened to his movements in the kitchen, trying to ignore the dull throb in her head. She would have given anything if she could have left before he got back. But she couldn't; he had her clothes—and her daughter. It wasn't dread that made her want to bolt, it was good old-fashioned pride. She did not want him to see what a mess her face was in. She hadn't cried like that in months, and she knew it was going to show. On the plus side, she felt totally emptied. For the first time in a long time, her insides weren't tied in knots.

Raking her hair back from her face, she released a shaky sigh and lifted her head, regarding his living quarters. It was a huge apartment—the whole upper floor, which she remembered from when the building had still been owned by the bank. The second floor had been leased to a dance school, and she had taken lessons here when she was Meg's age. She wouldn't recognize it now, though. The hardwood floors had been refinished in a dark stain, the walls painted an off-white and the windows had been enlarged. Dark wooden shutters covered them, the louvers were open to let in the meager, gray light.

The room itself was spacious and uncluttered. A wall unit was built along one bearing wall, housing an elaborate sound system, a TV, some cabinets and bookshelves, and a sizable number of hardback books. There were two leather sofas, both black and at right angles to one another, and one chrome-and-black enamel floor lamp in the far corner. The two end tables were chrome and glass and looked very expensive, and the table lamps were lean, angular modifications of the old-style bankers' lamps, the aerodynamic shades a dark red.

It was a beautiful, oddly comforting room, in spite of the sparseness and space—very much like its owner, in many ways. But it was the coffee table that made her heart contract. It was a very old, flat-topped, brass-bound leather trunk that had been beautifully restored. She remembered that trunk. She and Brodie had found it in the attic of an old abandoned house one hot summer day. It made her throat cramp up all over again, knowing that he had kept it.

She heard him leave the kitchen, and she lifted her chin a little, deliberately keeping her gaze averted as she tried to erect a little false bravado. She wasn't sure how she was going to get through this.

There was the sound of wood and leather creaking as he sat down on the trunk; then a glass with two fingers of amber liquid was thrust in front of her. Her gaze flew to his face.

He took her hand and molded it around the glass. "You look like you could do with a stiff drink."

Caught completely off guard by his bringing her a drink, she stared up at him.

A tug of wry humor lifted one corner of his mouth, and a small glint appeared in his eyes. "Bash it back, McCall," he ordered, the glint intensifying. "I know from experience that you can do it."

That little touch of familiarity set off something warm and fuzzy in her chest, and Eden gave a soft unsteady laugh. "I'm older and wiser now."

He gave the glass a nudge. "Drink."

Right then she would have downed straight lye if he had asked her to. Bracing herself to toss back two straight ounces, she stared at him for a second, then downed the contents. It was very, very good Scotch, and it burned a path of heat all the way down to her stomach.

She wordlessly handed him back the empty tumbler, and Brodie set it on the trunk beside him. He braced his arms on his thighs and loosely laced his fingers together, then looked at her. "So what in hell is going on, Eden?"

It surprised her, the sudden feeling of absolute ease she had with him. He had never once given her any reason to doubt him, and that feeling had somehow survived. She held his gaze for an instant, finding something strong and steady in the dark blue depths; then she looked down and began toying with the corner of the quilt. She drew a deep uneven breath and started to talk. She told him a bit about Richard's reaction to the divorce, and she told him the whole story of what had happened that morning and why Megan had bolted. She left nothing out.

When she finished, there was a long silence. Finally Brodie spoke, his tone oddly clipped. "What did Megan mean when she said he wasn't her father?"

Frowning, Eden continued to pleat the fabric of the quilt; then she sighed and met his unwavering gaze. "Megan is adopted. I wasn't able to have kids." She paused, methodically straightening the fabric; then she released another sigh and continued. "I don't think he ever really wanted a baby. The only reason he arranged the adoption was to pacify me. And the only reason he's pushing this visitation thing is because it's a way of getting back at me."

"Have you told your family what's going on?"

She shook her head. "I can't. Tanner's wife went through a really messy divorce. Her ex-husband tried to abduct her kids a couple of times, and I know this would really upset her. She's pregnant, and so is Devon, so I don't really want to drag any of them into this."

"And your parents?"

She forced a tight smile. "My parents' sympathies are with Richard."

"Who's your lawyer?"

She told him.

"What's his number?"

She looked at him, her expression startled; then she looked down and began pleating the quilt again. "I just don't have the energy to talk to him right now," she whispered unevenly. She flattened the material, then met his gaze again. "I'll call him tomorrow."

He stared at her, the rugged angles of his face set, his full mouth clamped in a hard line, but there was something in his eyes that made her heart skip a beat. "What's his number?" he said again, an intractable tone in his voice.

"I'll call him tomorrow."

The muscle in his jaw flexed, and she caught a glimmer of suppressed annoyance in his eyes. "I'm going to call him now."

She held his gaze a moment, then looked down, experiencing a sudden flutter in her chest. It would be so nice to dump all this in someone else's lap—just for a little while—until she could get her feet under her.

"Eden?"

Swallowing hard, she dismissed her guilty conscience and gave in to the déterminée tone in his voice. Her own voice wasn't quite steady when she gave him the Toronto number.

"I'll need to know your married name."

She kept her gaze averted. "I kept McCall. His is Dodd. Megan goes by both—hyphenated."

She could feel him staring at her; then he finally turned and headed toward the kitchen. As soon as he left the room, she leaned her head back against the sofa and closed her eyes. Just this once, she would let someone else deal with the whole damned mess. Just this once.

It was a long time before she heard him reenter the room, and it took a huge effort to open her eyes. She watched him, her stomach tightening when she saw the grim expression etched around his mouth. She silently took the dried slacks and socks he handed her. "Thanks," she said softly.

He looked at her, an intent, assessing expression in his eyes; then he finally spoke. "He's going to call Dodd's lawyer right now, and he'll get back to you either later tonight or tomorrow morning." He paused, his gaze still fixed on her; then he turned, slapping his thigh in a gesture of finality. "I'll let you get dressed. I'll be downstairs."

She watched the door to the stairs close behind him; then she shut off her mind and resolutely pushed back the quilt, suddenly feeling very hollow. It was definitely time to go home.

Megan didn't even notice Eden's arrival downstairs. Eden wasn't sure she would have noticed an earthquake. Her daughter was standing between Jason's knees in front of a computer, mud smeared down one side of her face, her braid unraveling, her attention riveted on the screen. Her face was flushed with excitement as she let Jason guide her hands on two joysticks, her concentration complete. But it wasn't her daughter who made Eden's heart stall; it was the young man who was seated behind her. For some reason it made her chest hurt to see the two of them together like that. Megan was standing between Jason's knees, his hands over hers, his expression animated as he gave her instructions for the game she was playing. There was something almost boyish in his face right then, although Eden couldn't imagine anyone ever referring to Brodie's nephew as a boy. There was too much disillusionment and hard living ingrained in his face for that.

Eden had only a faint recollection of Brodie's sister. She'd left Bolton the year Eden started high school, and she had left amidst all kinds of rumors. The one thing that Eden did remember was that she had been gorgeous—tall with a model's figure, and long, dark hair and eyes that were a deep, bottomless blue. She had been a female version of Brodie, only with a different kind of wildness in her. Eden had heard that she had been found dead in a back alley in Vancouver. She didn't know that there had been a child involved. She wondered what kind of life Jason had led—and how he had survived.

But what made her heart catch now was the carbon-copy likeness between Jason and Brodie. Same thick, curly hair, same sharply chiseled jawline, same straight nose, same full mouth. The only difference was that Brodie had worn his hair long—rebel long—where Jason's was cut in a trendy block cut. Jason laughed and said something to Meg, and the cramp around Eden's heart tightened. So alike. God, they were so alike.

The computer made a sound like a small bomb blast, and Megan made a face, disgust crinkling her nose. "Damn it. He got me, Jase. I didn't see that one coming."

Eden looked up at the ceiling and heaved a sigh of weary resignation. She was going to *have* to do something about that kid's language. But what, she wasn't sure. She had been very careful not to say so much as "damn" in front of her—maybe it was just this tomboy phase she was in, and maybe it was Megan simply exercising her will for independence. She heaved another sigh and looked at her daughter, a touch of wry humor surfacing. Maybe she was going to have to resort to soap after all.

Deciding to let it slide this once, she approached them. "It's time to go, Meg."

Both Megan and Jason looked at her, his expression closing down, hers changing into one of "oh, boy, I'm going to get it" wariness. It was an expression that Eden was intimately familiar with. Megan was not exactly a dull, docile child. Eden sighed. There were times she wished her small daughter wasn't quite so headstrong.

"Get your things together, Megan. It's time to go home."

Meg glanced up at Jason, and he nodded, a glimmer of humor hovering around his mouth. Meg held his gaze and heaved a sigh, then reluctantly let go of the joysticks and stepped out from between his knees. "Thanks, Jase," she said, her voice soft.

He gave her hair a light tug, then rose, meeting Eden's gaze with an unsmiling, unreadable expression. "Brodie's on the phone. I'll get him."

Eden started to protest, but he walked away before she could say anything, and she stared after him, a feeling of dread unfolding in her middle. Dealing with Brodie in a crisis was one thing; confronting him now was a different situation altogether. The memory of that first meeting was still too clear in her mind.

Realizing she was staring at nothing, she turned to her daughter. "Do you know what Jason did with your things?"

They found the sleeping bag and the bag of groceries sitting by the door, with Eden's and Megan's jackets folded on top. Max was lying beside them, and Eden crouched down and scratched his neck. "Thanks, Max," she said softly. "I owe you a very big bone."

Max rose and shook himself, then stood before Megan, his eyes bright, his tail wagging. She chuckled and knelt down and gave him a hug. "You wanna play? Do you want to go outside and play?"

Eden grasped the sleeping bag and jackets, then rose. "Not today, Meg," she said firmly. "We're going home to have a little talk, you and I."

"Aw, Mom."

"No 'aw Mom,' Megan. Pick up your bag of groceries and let's go."

Completely skirting the issue of what she'd done, Megan gave the groceries a baleful look. "Aw, Mom. It's so hard to carry, and it's heavy. And my arms are aching. Can't we just leave it here?"

Eden experienced an unexpected urge to laugh, but she squelched it. The slug of Scotch kicking in, no doubt. "No, we can't leave it here. And it wasn't too heavy or too hard to carry when you went out to the barn." She handed her the sleeping bag. "So now you can carry everything back home."

Megan cast her a disgruntled look, then sighed and picked up the bag. "Maybe Jase or Brodie would carry it for me."

A voice spoke from behind them. "I don't think so, short stuff. Your mother's looking pretty determined about this."

Eden glanced up to find Brodie and Jason standing at the end of a video display, Brodie with his hands in his back pockets, Jason with one arm braced against the frame. Megan whirled, her eyes widening, a sheepish blush creeping up her cheeks. She stared at them for a moment, then hiked up the heavy bag of groceries, an equally sheepish grin appearing. Eden heard her mutter another soft "damn" under her breath.

"Megan," Eden said, a warning tone in her voice. "We had a little talk this morning about soaping out your mouth. Only it won't be Grandma who does it. It will be me, if you don't cut that out."

Trying to get a firm grip on both the sleeping bag and the groceries, Megan looked up at her mother, a tiny hint of defiance in her eyes. "If I was a boy, I'd be allowed to say it."

"No. You would not be allowed to say it." Feeling decidedly harried, Eden gave her daughter another stern look. "Now what do you say to Brodie and Jase?"

Megan juggled her load again, then looked up at Brodie, her expression suddenly tinged with shyness. "Thank you for helping my mom." Then she turned her gaze to Jason, her voice going husky. "And thank you for coming to get us, and for teaching me that neat game." Then she turned, bending over so she was nose to nose with Max. "And thank you for finding me." Her voice dropped to a whisper. "I didn't like it there much." She looked up at her mother. "And thank you—"

Knowing that her daughter would drag this out to the limit if she let her, Eden interjected, "I think that will do, Megan Anne. You don't need to carry it to the extreme." A funny flutter taking off in her midriff, Eden steeled herself and turned to face Brodie. It took everything she had to meet his gaze. "Thank you, Brodie," she said, her voice suddenly uneven. Wanting to say things she couldn't say, she steadied herself with a deep breath, her voice huskier than before. "For everything."

Without a trace of expression on his face, he stared back at her, his gaze dark and unreadable; then he tipped his head in silent acknowledgment. Caught by that dark, unreadable look, Eden stared up at him, wanting so badly to reach out and touch him one more time.

A very old sorrow rolled in on her, and she clenched her jaw and turned away, the sudden ache in her throat nearly unbearable. She wondered if she'd ever really gotten over loving him.

It had stopped raining by early evening, but new storm clouds were again piling against the jagged ridge of the mountains, and the setting sun cast the dark, heavy cloud formations in auras of gold and purple.

Skirting a big puddle on the sidewalk, Eden pulled her jacket around her and took a deep breath, savoring the damp, clean air. God, but it was beautiful out. Still wet and cool, but the solid dismal cloud cover overhead had broken up, and now there were traces of clear sky amidst the dark, tumbling clouds.

She had put Megan to bed and, at Martha's suggestion, had gone for a walk. It was the time of evening she liked best—that time when the sun started to sink and the first filtered grayness of twilight settled in. The time of night when robins twittered their distinctive evening call and the leaves on the trees were almost still. It was one of the advantages of living on the outskirts of town—the stillness, the lack of traffic, the closeness to the countryside.

The coolness was invigorating, and she inhaled deeply again, feeling the stretch in the back of her calves as she climbed the slight incline. Instead of turning at the top of the street and heading toward the center of town, Eden paused, trying to will away the sudden flight of butterflies in her stomach. The barbed-wire gate across the overgrown road was down, lying in the tall grass along the adjacent fence. She stared at the old road, her throat closing up on her.

Experiencing the powerful tug of old memories, she steeled herself and stepped off the pavement, taking the path she had taken many times before. The road was even more overgrown, with the wild bushes crowding in, the twin tire tracks indicating that the old trail was still occasionally used.

Once, long, long ago, it had been a thoroughfare that had cut through to the main county road, but it had been abandoned when the new road had been built decades before. Eden had always loved it. The trees had taken over the ditches, and silver willow and berry bushes had encroached on the grade, closing it in like an old country lane. About two miles down, by the old wooden bridge, there was an old abandoned clapboard church and cemetery. It was a secluded, undisturbed spot that had drawn her ever since she could remember. She had discovered it when she was about seven, when she had been out exploring on her bike, and it had become her secret place, back then.

A slight breeze stirred, and Eden pulled up the collar of her jacket, then stuffed her hands in the pockets, a heavy melancholy pulling at her. She had been fighting with it ever since she'd left Brodie's shop, and for some reason, it was worse tonight. It was as if every old regret, old guilt, old shame had risen up to plague her, their weight leaving her bleak inside. She desperately needed to be by herself, to let the loneliness and painful nostalgia run their course, and to allow herself time to think. She had this wrenching need for solitude—and for comfort. And maybe she would find both at the old church.

The calls of the robins overlaid the stillness of dusk, and the long grass alongside the lane drooped with moisture, dampening the legs of her jeans. Eden shrank deeper into the warmth of her jacket, trying not to let the desolation overwhelm her. She had so many things to be thankful for. She'd had a long talk with her small daughter, and she had been able to explain to Megan what her father was really up to. And her lawyer had called after dinner, assuring her that Richard was simply playing games, and that he would have some serious legal maneuvering to do before he could make a contempt charge stick. And her mother seemed repentant for allowing Richard to talk to Megan, which meant she would be more cautious in the future.

But it was hard to keep reminding herself that things weren't as bleak as they seemed, especially when she felt so damned unhappy inside. And the source of that unhappiness was Brodie. There had been that one instant in his store—when he'd stared at her with that hard, unreadable look—when she would have given her soul to see even a glimmer of forgiveness in his eyes. Seventeen years ago she had been so young and stupid and self-absorbed—so damned confused and unhappy—that she hadn't really thought about what she'd done to him. She had seen his anger, and she had seen his bitterness, but she had never really looked beyond that. He had told her that he loved her, and he had made promises to her about their future, but deep down in her heart, she'd never thought that she could really hold on to someone like Brodie Malone. She had felt so insignificant and ordinary compared to him, and probably her mother had sensed that and used it against her. Her mother was very good at zeroing in on people's weaknesses.

But there was more to it than that. Had she been asked three days ago what his reaction would be if he saw her now, she probably would have said that he wouldn't even remember her. That he had probably forgotten all about that long, hot summer. But his reaction told her differently. She had always felt that she had betrayed him; now she *knew* she had. And that, if she were honest with herself, was why she felt so sick and twisted up inside. She only wished she could explain, could tell him how much she regretted what she had done. But she knew, from the look on his face when she'd left him, that she would never get that chance. He would do whatever it took to make sure their paths never crossed again.

Experiencing a new surge of unhappiness, Eden lifted her head, trying to disconnect from the ache inside her. The lane stretched before her, the slashes of color on the Western horizon slinking lower, the sky fading to a dusky blue. She wondered how many times she had walked this road. Or, she reflected painfully, how many times she had sneaked out and met Brodie at the top of it. He used to wait for her there, looking blatantly male and forbidden astride his black motorcycle, and they would ride down to the old church.

It had been their own private hideaway back then, and he had taught her things, shown her things, that still made her heart race whenever she thought about them. He had been an intense and urgent lover, demanding and unrelenting, but he had also been an unbelievably tender and patient one—never once sacrificing her gratification to heighten his own. He had destroyed every misconception she had about sex, and he had shown her things that had broken down every inhibition she had. He had tutored her and taught her, and he had praised her for her first unsure steps into her unexplored sexuality. He'd never hesitated to let her know how much she pleased him, or how much he delighted in her.

And Brodie had been a very tactile lover. Big snug, enveloping embraces. Small intimate touches. He made her feel protected and cherished, and so very much appreciated. All that had been painfully absent in her marriage, right from the beginning. She couldn't count the nights that she had lain awake as Richard slept, feeling empty and alone, aching for that kind of touch, that kind of physical gentleness. There were times when she couldn't keep the loneliness at bay, when she would remember those times with Brodie. And the emptiness would be so wrenching, it was like losing him all over again.

She swallowed hard and hunched her shoulders, the cool, damp breeze cutting through the fabric of her jacket. Going to the church might be a mistake, but it was a pilgrimage she had to make. It was as if she had left part of herself there, and she had to go back and reconnect, to find something that she had lost a long time ago.

She rounded the bend in the road, and the trees crowded closer, forming a half-canopy overhead as the road dipped to the small narrow bridge with tall weeds growing between the plank decking. But she didn't cross the bridge. She followed an overgrown trail that branched off, the old driveway nearly obliterated by silver willow, wild rosebushes and tall grass. Two crumbling stone cairns marked the entrance to the churchyard, and Eden found a packed trail through the bushes that had proliferated. Ducking under a low-hanging branch, she followed the path through to the other side, wondering if it was a trail that deer used to go down to the creek.

She reached the other side and stopped, a funny feeling unfolding in her midriff. It was the same, yet different. In the soft twilight, the weathered clapboard church appeared unchanged, but one of the big old spruces had toppled, and the small poplar saplings that she remembered were now full-grown trees. The vibrant sky reflected back from the broken shards of glass in the windows—windows someone had boarded up from the inside. Eden paused, an ache of renewed nostalgia clamping around her chest. It was as if all the ghosts of girlhood were rising up and closing around her, pulling at her like whispers on the wind.

Feeling as if her presence was an intrusion, she found the back stoop in the tall grass, checked for soundness, then climbed up on the sagging structure. With her back to the church wall, she sat down and drew up her knees, locking her arms around them. Her mood introspective, she stared across the shallow valley, trying to will away the empty feeling inside her. She had been happy here. So very happy. Deliberately pulling away from that thought, she shifted her gaze toward the stand of spruce growing farther along the creek, wondering if the small footbridge was still there.

Consciously resisting the pull of old memories, Eden watched the changing sky, listening to the rustle of the leaves and the small nighttime stirrings in the bushes. A bat flitted across her line of vision, and she watched it disappear into the silhouettes of the trees. A feeling of being watched pricked at her senses, and she turned, expecting to find deer on the trail from the creek. Only it wasn't deer. It was Brodie Malone.

Her heart stalled, then dropped in a sickening rush, and she stared at him, a wild, tense flutter taking off in her middle. He was standing by the base of a dead cottonwood, one hand braced against the trunk, the other resting on his hip, and it was apparent that he had been out running. His chest rose and fell from exertion, and his hair was matted and wet. He had a white towel draped around his neck, and he was wearing a pair of navy sweatpants and a faded red tank top. Even in the half-light, she could see the dark stain of perspiration on the front of his jersey.

His gaze unwavering, he caught the corner of the towel and wiped his temple, then rested his hand back on his hip, his eyes narrowed. His face was shuttered, but there was a grim set to his jaw, and his anger was as real as the sweat on his brow. He was not at all pleased to find her there; that was obvious.

Feeling as if every ounce of warmth had drained out of her, Eden tightened her grip on her wrists and swallowed hard, fighting against the knot of trepidation inside her. He stared at her a moment longer; then he gave his head a disgusted shake and turned to go.

Her heart racing, Eden watched him, a shock of realization cutting through the paralysis. She had never expected to see him again. But for some reason their paths had crossed one more time. If she let him go without saying what she needed to say, she would lose a God-given chance to try to put things right. Compelled by a kind of desperation, she scrambled off the stoop. "Brodie! Wait." He paused, his back to her; then he shook his head again and started walking. A new wave of desperation filled her, and she spoke again, her voice breaking. "Please."

He paused, then turned to face her, jamming his hands on his hips. He stared at her, fury etched into his face. "What in hell are you doing here?"

Stuffing her hands in her pockets, she hunched her shoulders. "My father had a—"

"No, damn it," he shot back, jabbing his finger toward the ground. "I mean *here.*"

Feeling fearfully unsure, she clenched her hands into fists, her heart pounding even harder. Taking an uneven breath, she put everything on the line. "You know why. Because of everything that happened here." She took another stabilizing breath and plunged on, knowing the next step would take her into very deep water. "Because," she said, her voice very unsteady, "in spite of what you think of me, I was happy here. Maybe the happiest I've ever been."

He stared at her, the muscles in his jaw twitching, his anger making his eyes blaze. "Then if you were so damned happy, why in hell did you pull the stunt you did? You never gave us a chance. You know damned well you didn't. When I came to see you at that damned prep school of yours, you acted like I was something that had crawled out from under a rock."

Shame washed through her, and Eden felt the heat of it all the way to her scalp. She had humiliated him in the worst possible way, and it was a guilt she would carry with her until the day she died.

He gave her a bitter smile, his expression filled with disgust. "What's the matter, Eden? Cat got your tongue? Or are you trying to think of some damned excuse?"

Collecting what courage she had, she held his gaze, knowing she had to face him with this. "There is no excuse," she whispered unevenly. "I don't know if I can even explain. What I did was wrong. And I know you won't believe this, but it wasn't calculated or even planned—I just simply reacted. And I've been sorry about it ever since."

He stared at her, as though caught off guard by her admission of guilt, the anger in his eyes dulling just a little. When he finally responded, his voice was a little less harsh, but the sarcasm was still there. "So why don't you give it your best shot, McCall? You were always good at explanations."

Eden looked away, the ache in her throat so intense that she was afraid she was going to cry. She waited for the knot to ease; then she looked down and began toeing a clump of grass, her hands still buried in her pockets. Finally she started to speak, her voice soft and uneven. "I was young and stupid, and I was so unsure of myself, I don't think I had a thought that was my own. My parents kept telling me how foolish I was, how naive I was, how what I was feeling was nothing but a silly infatuation." She lifted her head and looked out across the valley, her mood bleak. After a long hesitation, she continued. "And I guess I never really believed someone like you could really be serious about someone like me."

There was a strained silence; then Brodie spoke, his voice devoid of any expression. "What do you mean—someone like you?"

She shrugged, a humorless smile lifting one corner of her mouth. "Young and foolish." Her expression turned solemn, and she absently toed the clump of grass again. "Insignificant and ordinary." She released a heavy sigh, unable to meet his gaze. "I had no idea what you saw in me."

She heard him shift position, and she could feel him watching her. "You were the beautiful, elegant Eden McCall," he responded, an edge of bitterness in his voice. "Surely you were aware of that."

She gave another dismissive shrug, a kind of sad detachment settling on her. "Was that all there was, Brodie?" she said, her voice quiet. "Everything on the outside? Nothing on the inside?"

He approached her, but she didn't look at him, an almost dispassionate despair making her feel deadened inside. He caught her face and jerked her head around, his own face etched with anger. "You know damned well there was a hell of a lot more to it than that."

She stared at him, her expression stark. "But I didn't know that then," she whispered unevenly. "And it had nothing to do with you. It was me, Brodie. It was how I saw myself." Feeling the burn of tears, she swallowed against the threat. "By the time they finished with me, I didn't know what was real and what wasn't," she whispered, her voice catching. "And by the time I figured it out, it was too late."

Jamming his hands back on his hips, he looked away, an angry set to his jaw, his profile taut and unrelenting. He stared off across the landscape, his mouth clamped in a hard line, and Eden buried her hands deeper in her pockets, her shoulders braced against the hard knot in her middle. "I'm sorry, Brodie," she said, her voice catching. "What I did was stupid and unforgivable, and it's something I'll always regret."

He turned his head and looked at her, his expression taut and controlled. He stared at her a moment, then spoke, his voice flat. "It's a little late for that, isn't it?"

Eden looked down at the ground, toying with the clump of grass with the side of her runner. She waited until the contraction in her throat eased, then answered, her voice low. "Yes. I guess it is." She lifted her head and stared at the church, her expression stark. "But I was the one at fault, and I needed to tell you that." A light breeze blew some hair across her face, and she tucked it behind her ear with trembling fingers, then stuffed her hand back in her pocket. "You deserved better."

He didn't respond, and Eden's vision blurred. She turned her head so he couldn't see her face. Easing in an unsteady breath, she spoke again, her voice trembling slightly. "And I want to thank you for your help this afternoon. I would have never found her if it hadn't been for you and Max."

"She would have gone home by dark."

Forcing a shaky laugh, Eden responded. "You don't know Megan."

There was another long pause; then Brodie released a heavy sigh and spoke. "It's going to be getting dark soon. I'll walk you back to town."

Tears spilled over, but Eden didn't want to give herself away by wiping them. She knew the last thing he wanted was a two-mile walk back with her. She had to swallow twice before she was sure her voice wasn't going to give out. "You go ahead. It's a full moon tonight, so I thought I'd take a walk along the creek."

She could feel his gaze on her, but she kept her eyes fixed on the distant horizon, more tears slipping down her face. *Go, Brodie,* she pleaded silently. *Please. Just go.*

Eden stood stiff and unmoving, and it wasn't until she heard him leave that she allowed herself to let go.

Now it was finally finished. Nothing had been left unsaid. And there was nothing more to say.

Chapter 6

By the time Brodie arrived back in town, the last light of dusk was fading from the sky and the full moon was sitting high above the Eastern horizon, the broken storm clouds drifting across it like ships at sea. His body was wet with sweat, the muscles in his legs ached and his lungs felt as if they were on fire. He had pushed himself every step of the way, hoping that a grueling pace would keep his mind focused, would keep him from thinking.

Finding her at the church had thrown him for one hell of a loop; his first instinct had been to turn around and get the hell out of there. Any more contact with Eden McCall was something he could do without. But there had been something in her stillness that had made him hesitate. And it was a hesitation that he knew damned well he was going to regret.

Slowing to a walk, he swore and jerked the towel from around his neck and wiped his face, anger surging up in him. He wanted to smash someone's face in. That son of a bitch ex-husband of hers came to mind. Richard Dodd needed someone to take him by the throat and give him a damned good shake. Using a kid for that kind of retaliation was sick, and if he ever got his hands on Eden's ex, it would not be pretty.

But that wasn't the only thing that was eating a hole in his gut. It was Eden. It had been bad enough that afternoon, when she'd gone into emotional shock on him. But tonight it had been worse. He was feeling things he did not want to feel. And she had no damned business being out there alone. Not in the state she was in.

It didn't help that he felt like a bastard for cutting out on her the way he had—but she was just too damned vulnerable, and after that afternoon, he was feeling a little too raw himself. He knew it had cost her big time to confront the past the way she had, and the way she had stood in front of him, unable to meet his gaze, had set off feelings he thought he'd gotten rid of a long time ago. So he had taken the easy way out and left.

Frustration bordering on anger churned in his gut, and he jerked open the side door and took the stairs three at a time, wishing like hell her ex was within swinging distance.

After stripping off his soaked tank top in the hallway, he fired it and the towel in the washing machine on his way past the laundry room. Then he headed for his bathroom, hoping a shower would put things back in perspective. If it didn't, he was in big trouble.

But there were things he couldn't ignore when he stripped down and stepped into the shower enclosure. Like the fact that he was fully aroused, that his pulse rate had nothing to do with the two-mile run, that his lungs kept trying to seize up. He braced his arms on the tile surface and closed his eyes, letting the hot water pour over him. He tried like hell to shut down, but old feelings kept rising up like steam, making his pulse run thick and heavy. Gritting his teeth against another pulsating rush, he clenched his hands into fists, trying to stop the response. He didn't want to feel as if his skin was rubbed raw every time he took a breath.

He'd thought he had everything under control, and he had damned near made it through the afternoon. He simply did what he had to do. He didn't think, didn't let his thoughts stray. He'd even got her clothes off without his anatomy kicking into gear. He had actually thought he'd beaten this thing with her. Then, later, he had tossed the quilt back on his bed and stretched out on top of it, hoping he could get a couple of hours of sleep. But he caught the lingering scent of her on his bedding, and all hell had broken loose. His mind, his body—it was as if someone had pulled a plug, and suddenly the erotic memories came pouring in, and he lay there, his jaw clenched, his whole body primed and throbbing. And he remembered—in absolute living detail—what it had been like when he was nineteen years old, and he was deep inside her.

Realizing he was doing it to himself all over again, Brodie swore and roughly adjusted the temperature setting, the shock of straight cold water doing little to ease the throbbing heaviness between his thighs. He didn't want this. Damn it, he did not want this. Feeling as if the walls were closing in on him, he turned off the water, then dragged his hand down his face. This was getting him nowhere. There wasn't enough cold water in the world to wash away what he was feeling.

He pushed open the door and dragged a towel off the rack, roughly drying himself. He needed a distraction. Any distraction. And he wasn't going to find it here.

His bedroom overlooked the side street, and Brodie went over to close the wooden louver shutters, sharply aware that all he had to do was turn his head and he could see her old bedroom window. Slamming the shutters across the windows, he got a change of clothes out of the pine wardrobe, and tossed them on the bed. His jaw fixed in rigid lines, he pulled on a pair of cotton slacks and a shirt, leaving the buttons undone. He jammed his feet into a pair of loafers, then headed for the door. But another surge of pure, hot sensation washed through him, engorging him even more, and he closed his eyes and rested his forehead against the wall, a thousand emotions warring inside him. He didn't want to want her, damn it. He didn't want to get sucked back into all those old feelings. But the image of her bleak face took shape in his mind, and he knew he could not leave her out there alone.

Swearing angrily, he snatched up a jacket and yanked open the bedroom door. He needed his bloody head examined.

He paused at Jason's room, ramming his arms into the jacket. "Do you have the keys for the bike?"

Jason looked up from his desk, his expression impassive. "Which one? The dirt bike or the Harley?"

Brodie's voice was clipped with annoyance. "Which one do you think? The Harley, damn it."

His nephew stared at him for a moment, then leaned back and straightened one leg, fishing a set of keys out of his front pocket. He tossed them to Brodie, who caught them one-handed and snapped, "If I'm not back by eleven, close up downstairs for me, will you?"

Jason folded his arms and rocked back in his chair. "You going to the hotel?"

"No," Brodie answered, his tone short. "I'm not going to the hotel."

Jason's mouth lifted in a small smile. "Little tense, Unc?"

Brodie shot him a foul look, then tucked the tails of his shirt into his slacks. "Just lock up, okay?"

Anger and frustration had built to dangerous levels by the time Brodie got downstairs, and he was ready to rip the door off the hinges before he managed to unlock the side entrance of the garage. He slapped his palm against the switch for the automatic door opener, then went over to where the two bikes were parked. Tossing the helmet on the workbench, he straddled the Harley, stuck the key in the ignition, then hit the switch. The bike rumbled to life, and Brodie knocked the kickstand away and flicked on the headlight. Grasping the clutch, he rolled open the throttle, then kicked it into gear. He was in no mood for a nice little ride.

By the time he reached the old roadway, the roil of frustration had eased enough that he could at least think rationally. He was ticked off at himself, and he still wanted to throttle the son of a bitch she'd been married to, but it was the hollow feeling in his gut that had his heart pumping. He wasn't sure what he would do if she wasn't there. He wasn't sure what he would do if she was.

Not wanting to scare her to death, he killed the engine and light and coasted the last hundred yards, the full moon casting eerie shadows on the overgrown road in front of him. He rolled to a stop on the verge across from the trail, then rocked the bike back on the kickstand and dismounted, unsnapping the top two snaps on his leather jacket. His expression hardening, he followed the path through the trees to the church clearing.

The churchyard was awash with moonlight, the only sound the rustle of leaves. An owl hooted, and something scurried through the underbrush, but that was the only sign of life. And there was no sign of Eden. His insides tightening into a hard, cold lump, he started down the path to the creek, but a foreign sound stopped him in his tracks. He turned and caught a glimpse of something pale by the back step of the church. His stomach twisting with consternation, he started across the yard.

"Eden?"

There was a soft, muffled sound, and his heart jammed up in his chest, then started to pound with a different rhythm. She was wedged into the corner, her frame nearly obscured by heavy shadows, her arms locked around her upraised knees, her head down. He didn't think she even knew he was there. Something twisted loose in his chest.

Crouching down in front of her, he brushed back her hair. "Don't, Eden," he whispered, his tone uneven. "Don't."

She went still, and he saw her wipe her face against the sleeves of her jacket. Then she drew a deep shuddering breath, and Brodie knew he could not leave her all huddled up like that. He caught her by the upper arms, pulling her up with him as he stood. "Come here, baby," he murmured gruffly. "Come on."

She resisted for a moment, then relented, her arms sliding around him. "I'm so sorry, Brodie," she sobbed against his neck. "So sorry."

"I know you are," he whispered. Pressing her head to his shoulder, he gathered her up in a tight embrace, his hand tangled in her hair. Shifting so she was flat against him, he shut his eyes, the rush of sensation so intense that he had to grit his teeth against it. He tightened his hold on her, his heart hammering, his breathing constricted. She moved, sending a shock wave of heat through him, and he clutched her head, the feel of her almost too much to handle.

His fingers snagging in her hair, he tucked his head against hers, forcing himself to remain immobile. Every muscle in his body demanded that he move, and his nerve ends felt as if they were stripped raw, but he tried to ignore the feelings pounding through him. She had no idea what she was doing to him, but he was all too aware of what was happening.

It took him a while, but he finally got himself under control, and he could finally breathe without it nearly killing him. Releasing a shaky sigh, he adjusted his hold on her, drawing her deeper into his embrace, his lungs constricting. He had never seen her come apart like this, as if there was so much pain inside her that she finally had to get it all out. The thought of her sitting out here all alone, going through something like this all by herself, sobered him like little else had, and he pressed her head against him, a dozen regrets settling in his chest. If only... If only...

Knowing there was no percentage in that kind of thinking, he tightened his arms around her and simply held her, the fullness in his chest expanding. She was so damned thin. And vulnerable. And he wasn't sure how he was going to get them both out of this without getting in a wreck. He was so close to the edge that it wouldn't take a whole hell of a lot to push him over. And she felt so good, and smelled so good, and Lord, he wanted to feel her flush against him.

Unable to control the urge, he widened his stance a little, pressing her against his hard ridge of flesh, turning his face against her neck and clenching his teeth. He hoped she was so far out of it that she wouldn't notice the state he was in.

But she wasn't that far out of it. She went still in his arms; then she made a low, desperate sound and twisted her head, her mouth suddenly hot and urgent against his. The bolt of pure, raw sensation knocked the wind right out of him. Brodie shuddered, and he widened his mouth against hers, feeding on the desperation that poured back and forth between them. She made another wild sound and clutched at him, the movement welding their bodies together like two halves of a whole, and he nearly lost it right then. But the taste of tears cut through his senses, and he dragged his mouth away from hers, his heart pounding like a locomotive in his chest.

Wrong. God, this was wrong. She was an emotional wreck, and she didn't know what she was doing—she was just reacting, reaching for comfort. And it was dangerous. There was too much old familiarity between them, too much need, and it would be too easy—God, so easy to just let it happen. So easy.

Trying to regain some control, he jammed her head against his neck, holding her with every ounce of strength he had, fighting for every breath. Somehow he had to put the brakes on. Somehow.

Inhaling jaggedly, he nestled her head closer, turning his face against her head. "Easy," he whispered against her hair. "Easy, baby. It's okay."

An anguished sob was wrenched from her, and she clutched him tighter, as if she were trying to climb right inside him. There was so much desperation in that one small sound, so much fire, it was like a knife in his chest. Her arms locked around him, she choked out his name; then she moved against him, silently pleading with him, pleading with her body—and any connection he had with reason shattered into a thousand pieces.

The feel of her heat against him was too much, and he clenched his jaw, turning his head against hers. His face contorting from the surge of desire, he caught her around the hips, welding her roughly against him. God, he needed this—the heat of her, the weight of her. Her. He needed her.

Eden made another low sound, then she inhaled raggedly and pulled herself up against his arousal, her voice breaking on a low sob of relief. "Brodie. Oh, God. Don't stop. Please—don't stop." She moved against him again, and Brodie tightened his hold even more, unable to stop as he involuntarily responded. Body to body, heat to heat, and suddenly there was no turning back.

Shifting her head, he covered her mouth in a hot, deep kiss, and she opened to him, her mouth moving against his with an urgent hunger. It was too much—and not nearly enough, and Brodie lifted her higher and caught her behind the knee, dragging her leg around his hip. With one twisting motion, his hard heat was flush against hers. Grasping her buttocks, he thrust against her again and again, a low groan wrenched from him as she moved with him, riding him, riding the hard thick ridge jammed against her. But that wasn't enough, either. Brodie nearly went ballistic, certain he would explode if he didn't get inside her.

Making incoherent sounds against his mouth, Eden twisted free, and a violent shudder coursed through Brodie when he felt her hands fumble with the snap, then the zipper, on his pants. The instant she touched his hard throbbing flesh, he groaned out her name and let go of her, desperate to rid them both of the barrier of clothes.

Somehow he got her slacks off, and somehow he got her shirt open, but the instant he felt her hand close around him, he lost it completely. Jerking her hand away, he hauled her up against him. On the verge of release, he dragged her legs around him again, then backed her against the wall of the church. Wedging his arm between her and the roughened wood, he clenched his eyes shut and thrust into her, unable to hold back one second longer. The feel of her, tight and wet, closing around him drove the air right out of him, the sensation so intense he couldn't move.

Eden sobbed out his name and locked her legs around him, her movements urging him on, and Brodie crushed her against him, white-hot desire rolling over him. Angling his arm across her back, he drove into her again and again, pressure building and building. A low guttural sound was torn from him, and his release came in a blinding rush that went on and on, so powerful he felt as if he were being turned inside out. He wanted to let it roll over him, to take him under, but he forced himself to keep moving in her, knowing she was on the very edge. She cried out and clutched at his back, then went rigid in his arms, and she finally convulsed around him, the gripping spasms wringing him dry.

His heart hammering, his breathing so labored he felt almost dizzy, he weakly rested his head against hers, his whole body quivering. He felt as if he had been wrenched in two.

He didn't know how long he stood there, with her trembling in his arms, not an ounce of strength left in him.

It wasn't until he shifted his hold and tucked his face against hers that he realized her cheek was wet with tears. Hauling in an unstable breath, he turned his head and kissed her on the neck, a feeling of overwhelming protectiveness rising up his chest. There was no way he could let her go. Not yet. God, not yet. He waited a moment for the knot of emotion to ease; then he smoothed his hand up her back. "Can you hang on to me for a minute?" he whispered thickly.

She nodded once and tightened her arms and legs around him. Brodie withdrew his arms from around her back, then managed to struggle out of his jacket with her still clinging to him. He tossed it on the church step, then tucked her head firmly against him. Sharply aware of her uncovered breasts pressed against his bare chest, he tightened his hold as he lay down with her, his jacket forming a meager bed. With her still straddling him, he drew her head into the curve of his neck and released an unsteady sigh. She tightened her hold on him, then settled her weight fully on top of him, shuddering as she took him deeper inside her.

Hit with a rush of emotion, Brodie nestled her tighter against him and closed his eyes, slipping his hand under her blouse and jacket. Needing the feel of her naked skin, he ran the heel of his hand down the lower curve of her spine as he kissed her on the neck. He felt her shiver again and melt around him, and his heart rolled over. She'd always done that—shiver and go boneless whenever he rubbed that pressure point low in her back. One of the thousand things he remembered about her.

Struggling with a thickness deep in his chest, he began stroking her back, feelings he didn't want to acknowledge crowding in on him. Sliding his hand higher, he rubbed the back of her neck, and he felt her swallow, then swallow again, and he realized she was struggling with some very raw emotions as well. His own throat closed up a little. In spite of what had gone before, he didn't want her thinking this was a simple act of retaliation on his part, or, worse, meaningless sex. Sex had never been meaningless with her. Never.

Feeling a little raw himself, he cupped his hand along her jaw, then applied pressure with his thumb to get her to lift her head. Inhaling unevenly, he covered her mouth with a soft, searching kiss, trying to give her some consolation. He knew by how still she went that she was not expecting that, and Brodie experienced a flicker of anger. It was almost as if she expected him to push her away and storm off in disgust, and it made him mad as hell that she thought so little of herself.

Determined to show her that tonight was somehow tied to the past, he tightened his hold on her jaw, his tone commanding as he whispered against her mouth. "Open up for me, babe."

Her breath caught, but she yielded to the pressure of his thumb, and Brodie adjusted the alignment of his mouth against hers, deepening the kiss with slow, lazy thoroughness. Working his mouth softly, slowly against hers, he drank from her, probing the moist recesses, savoring the taste of her. Her breath caught again; then she finally responded, and he grasped the back of her head, her hair tangling like silk around his fingers. His chest tightening, he massaged the small of her back, and he felt her muscles go slack, as if he had released the rigid tension inside her.

Slipping her arm under him, she mimicked his caress, and Brodie let his breath go in a rush, an electrifying weakness radiating through his lower body. She did it again, and he tightened his hold on her hair, feeling himself grow hard inside her.

Dragging his mouth away from hers, he kissed her ear, tracing the shape with the tip of his tongue, then trailed his mouth down her neck. Her breathing grew ragged and uneven, and he shifted his hand under her clothes, lightly, so lightly, rubbing the side of his thumb over the tip of her breast.

A soft sob was wrenched from her, and she caught his hand, pressing it hard against her small breast, until Brodie could feel the frantic beat of her pulse beneath his palm. His own breathing suddenly ragged, he caught her around the hips and rolled, drawing her under him. Shifting his weight so he was anchored deep inside her, he braced his weight on his elbows, then took her face between his hands, holding her head as he kissed her with a thoroughness that made his own heart stammer. This time he was going to make it so good for her that there would be no doubt in her mind what was happening. This time he was going to show her, in spite of everything that had happened in the past, that he wanted this. Wanted her.

He flexed his hips, and she rose up to meet him, tightened her muscles around him, and his mind clouded with desire. He would likely go to his grave still wanting her.

Moonlight cast long, faint shadows through the trees, and off in the distance, a lone coyote yipped. The call was answered, then answered again, until a discordant yodel resonated along the length of the shallow valley, the sounds carrying for miles on the cool, clear air.

Brodie glanced down at the woman asleep beside him, a disquieting feeling settling in his gut. She was lying with her head on his shoulder and her arm around his chest, the rhythm of her breathing indicating a very deep and heavy sleep. As if it was the first decent sleep she'd had in a very long time. Disturbed by that thought, he tightened his arm around her to keep her warm, then stared up at the nighttime sky. He watched the clouds skim in front of the full moon, his mood somber.

Never in his wildest dreams had he expected something like this to happen. Not now. Not after so many years. As far as he'd been concerned, once she was married, she was out of reach, and from then on, he'd set about exorcising her from his life. But now she was back, newly divorced, and here they were, back at the church. Just like old times.

His expression grew more somber. He knew what the knot in his gut was all about. It was a feeling he was well acquainted with. It was recognizing the fact that he'd probably just made the worst mistake of his entire life. No matter how unbeliev-able it had been with her, it was no quick fix. Sex had always been the one thing that was absolutely right between them—it was the other stuff that had screwed up their lives. Like her parents.

A memory of old man McCall took shape in his mind, and Brodie rested his free arm over his eyes and clenched his jaw, an old anger rising up inside him. Anger over that last meeting he'd had with the son of a bitch. Anger over the life Eden had lived. Anger over what she had tossed out the window seven-teen years ago.

Experiencing an acid rush in his belly, he shifted his arm and stared at the sky, determined not to think about that. He wasn't going to get sucked back into that old crap—not tonight. To-night was a reprieve he'd never expected.

Eden stirred beside him, and Brodie glanced at her and rubbed his hand up her arm, wishing they weren't lying on his jacket. The night had turned chilly, and he could tell from her skin that she was cold. He had covered her with every article of clothing he could reach, but he also knew he had only mo-ments before he would have to wake her. He wasn't looking forward to that one little bit.

Tightening his arm around her, he watched her for a mo-ment, then stared back at the star-bright sky, trying not to think at all. He felt as if everything was closing in on him, and he didn't know why.

She stirred again and murmured his name, and Brodie glanced down at her, realizing she was caught in that half-conscious state between sleeping and coming awake. He wondered if she'd ever made that slip with her husband. He experienced a hollow sensation in the pit of his stomach.

"Close the door."

He looked down at her, a small twist of a smile working loose. He would have been happy to oblige, if only they'd had a door to close. His expression softened just a little as he watched her come awake. She had always been slow at it. He remembered how easy it was to arouse her when she was like that, how quickly she responded, how soft and yielding she was. But he shut that thought down almost immediately. He couldn't afford to slide into that trap again. He had made one mistake; he wasn't going to compound it by making another. Besides, it had to be past midnight, and he knew that as soon as she came fully awake she would start shivering.

Wishing there was an easy way to do this, he exhaled heavily and gave her a little shake. "Come on, Eden. It's time to wake up."

"I'm cold. Where's the quilt?"

He probably would have smiled if he hadn't been so tied up in knots inside. He knew damned well she didn't have a clue where she was, but, he thought with a certain amount of grim satisfaction, she knew who she was with. Aware that he was heading back onto dangerous ground, he made himself disconnect.

He somehow had to get them both out of this without doing any more damage. Taking a minute to get a grip, he spoke, his voice gravelly. "There isn't any quilt."

She went still, then her eyes flew open, and there was an instant—just an instant—when he saw incomprehension on her face. Then he saw the flash of uncertainty, of apprehension, and it hit him that she wasn't sure what kind of reception to expect from him.

Despite all the reservations he had, despite knowing this had been one big mistake as far as he was concerned, he could not let her think this was meaningless. If nothing else, she had tried to put the past to rest, and he owed her for that. Experiencing a sharp clenching pain in his chest, he caught her head and nestled her tightly against him, trying not to think, trying to give her some reassurance. She'd had little enough of that in her life. And she sure as hell needed some now.

It took a while, but he finally felt her relax, and he eased his hold on her. When he withdrew, she exhaled unevenly and looked up at him, the moonlight revealing the confusion in her expression. His gut churned with something closely related to regret, but he forced a smile, his voice husky when he spoke. "It's getting pretty late, McCall. It's probably past midnight."

He half expected her to bolt, but she closed her eyes and turned her face against his neck, and he felt her take a deep, uneven breath. He sensed again how vulnerable she was, and he gave her a light squeeze. "Come on," he whispered unevenly. "I'll help you find your clothes."

They dressed in silence, and Brodie watched her, aware of how badly her hands were shaking. He stuffed his shirt into his slacks, then went over to her, silently brushing her hands aside. He finished doing up the buttons on her shirt, then helped her into her jacket and did it up, as well. Tucking her hair behind her ear, he tipped her face up and wiped her cheek with his thumb.

Trying to stay detached from the emotions rolling inside him, he gave in to the urge to hold her one more time and folded her up in an enveloping hug. Resting his chin on the top of her head, he rubbed her back, waiting for the tension in her to ease. No matter what, he didn't want her leaving here thinking that he was angry. He wasn't going to try to figure it out right now, but something had happened here tonight that had left him feeling pretty damned shaky. As if something that had been supporting him was no longer there, as if his whole life was pressing in on him. But that was his problem to deal with, not hers. One thing was for sure, though; if this was goodbye, he wanted it to be a kind one.

After a long moment, Eden finally slid her arms around his waist, and he felt her relax. He closed his eyes, simply absorbing the feel of her against him. It had been a long, long time since he'd felt this kind of regret. He gave her a few minutes, then rubbed his jaw against her hair. "We'd better go," he said, his voice low. "You're going to be frozen by the time I get you home."

She drew a deep breath, as if bracing herself; then she slowly withdrew from his hold. Realizing that she wasn't quite steady, he kept his arm around her as they walked across the clearing, the moonlight casting their shadows before them. They reached the trail through the trees, and he took her hand, leading her through to the lane. She stopped dead in her tracks when she saw the bike.

"You still have the bike."

He forced a small smile. "Not the same one. I've only had this one a couple of years."

Releasing his hold on her, he straddled the Harley and nudged the kickstand clear. His legs braced on either side, he started the engine, the low rumble oddly muted by the silence. He leaned forward and glanced at her. Without being told, she slipped on behind him, and he felt her grip the sides of his jacket. Steadying the bike with his legs, he reached back, pulling her arms around his waist so that she was snug against him. Then, not bothering to turn on the headlight, he kicked the bike into gear and let out the clutch, not sure why his chest was suddenly so tight. Old times, maybe. And maybe something else.

Brodie took it easy on the ride home, partly because he was using the bright moonlight to navigate by, but also because it would get damned cold if he picked up the pace. It wasn't until they reached town that he turned on the headlight, and instead of taking the street that ran past her house, he went around the block and parked the bike on his garage pad. A bike—especially his—parked outside the McCall residence would set off all kinds of speculation if anyone saw it. And speculation was something they could both do without. He waited until she got off; then he rocked the Harley back on the stand and dismounted.

She started to say something when he came alongside her, but he caught her around the neck, pressing her face against his chest. His expression unsmiling, he spoke, his voice gruff. "Don't, okay? I don't want to hash over what happened tonight. And I don't think you do, either. So let's just leave it." Experiencing a suffocating sensation in his chest, he tightened his hold on her head, not sure why in hell his legs suddenly felt so shaky.

Gripping the sides of his jacket, she nodded, letting go a tremulous breath. He held her like that for a little longer, until he got a grip on himself. Then he stroked her cheek with his knuckles and spoke, his voice very husky. "Come on. I'll walk you home."

Not quite able to sever the connection, he held her hand as they crossed the street and started up the sidewalk. But with every step they took, her hold on his hand got tighter, and the tightness in his chest grew. He didn't kid himself. Tonight was just tonight. What was past was past, and maybe that was all tonight had been—a ride down memory lane. If so, it had been one hell of a ride. But at least some things had been laid to rest. She'd had the chance to say she was sorry, and he'd come to terms with at least some of the old bitterness. And that was good. And now maybe they could look back and remember the right things they'd shared, not the wrong things that had driven them apart. He hoped like hell that was how the cards would fall.

He walked her as far as the east veranda. Feeling as if everything was closing in on him, he stopped when he reached the trellis, not wanting to step into the light spilling out through the patio doors. He was feeling too damned exposed for anything as civilized as incandescent light. And besides, he wanted to remember her in moonlight.

Brodie let go of her, stuffing his hands in his jacket pockets. He stared at her for a minute, his heart contracting when he saw the look of dismay in her eyes. Fighting the urge to hold her one last time, he reached out and stroked her cheek with the back of one finger, then drew his thumb along her bottom lip. The look in her eyes was enough to rip the heart right out of him, but he knew this had to be it.

Feeling as if his lungs were closing up on him, he pressed his thumb against her lips, his throat suddenly so tight he could barely speak. "Go," he said softly.

She stared at him an instant longer, her eyes glimmering with unshed tears, then she turned and went up the steps. He stood in the shadows until he heard the patio door close, then turned and started back toward the street.

It was a hell of a way to say goodbye.

Chapter 7

Brodie woke up the next morning, his heart racing, as if something heavy was sitting on his chest. Like the walls were closing in on him. And he knew he had to get the hell out of town. He made arrangements with Ruby for the hotel, and as soon as Jase got up, he told the kid that he was taking off for a few days, gave him a wad of cash and made sure he had the number for the cellular phone he was taking. Then he rolled out the bike, packed up the phone and a change of clothes, and hit the road as soon as Lydia showed up for work.

He briefly toyed with the idea of going to Joshua Stone's fishing lodge; in fact, he headed in that direction when he left town. Stone was his silent partner in the hotel, and Brodie had known him for a long time, ever since they worked on the oil rigs together. And Brodie knew if he wanted to get lost for a few days, the fishing camp would be a good place to do it. Stone wouldn't ask questions. Josh Stone knew a lot about silence.

But when Brodie reached the turnoff for the road that would take him up into the mountains, a renewed feeling of claustrophobia closed in around him, and he knew Josh's camp wasn't going to cut it. So he turned the bike around and headed south.

He needed speed. He needed wide open spaces. He needed to be by himself.

He tore up the miles. The sun beat down, turning the asphalt into a wavering ribbon of silver in front of him, but he couldn't outrun himself or the hollow feeling sitting in his gut.

He crossed the U.S. border into Montana before noon, taking the worst damned pass through the mountains he could find, wanting a road that would challenge both him and the bike, a road that would force him to concentrate. And Logan's Pass was definitely the road to do it. Rarely open before the first of June because of snow, it was high, winding and narrow, with sharp hairpin turns, steep climbs and even steeper descents. It was a biker's dream, and it was open. And Brodie took it to the limit. He ignored the spectacular scenery; he ignored the speed limit; he ignored the no-passing markers; he ignored the frigid mountain air; and he used his brakes only when he had to.

By the time he got to Kalispell, his hands were damned near frozen, but the clothes under his leathers were damp with sweat, and he was shivering right down to the bone. He figured he was next door to hypothermia. He picked up a bottle of Jack Daniel's, found a motel, then hit the shower. He had every intention of drinking himself into a stupor.

But intention and hard, cold reality were two different things. He seldom drank—the odd beer now and then, or sometimes, after a hard day, he would unwind with a shot of Scotch. But he'd learned more than he ever wanted to know about booze from his old man, and a full bottle sitting on the bedside table was just a little too much hard, cold reality for him.

So he faced the night stone-cold sober. Stuffing both lumpy pillows under his head, he stared at the stained ceiling, trying to wrestle with the hollow feeling that had dogged him all day. He'd hoped that once he got away from Bolton he would be able to get a handle on what he was feeling. But it wasn't going to work out that way. He couldn't outrun all the things that were chasing him. And he sure as hell couldn't outrun himself—or images of her. Every time he closed his eyes, he saw Eden as she'd been the night before, standing in the moonlight beside the trellis, that awful stricken look in her eyes when he'd told her to go.

But it wasn't just that; there were other disturbing memories taking shape at the edges of his mind, memories he didn't want to let out. He had learned a long time ago how to erect barriers; even as a kid, he'd known how to do it. He had done it with Eden. And now all those things were shifting around in his head, and it scared the hell out of him. He knew deep down in his gut that there was no future for them. There was too much crap in the past, and nothing had really changed.

Draping his arm over his eyes, Brodie swallowed against the sudden tightness in his throat. God, but he had loved her. He would have moved mountains for her, and in many ways he had. He had turned his life around because of her, but for all the wrong reasons. He had done it out of bitterness and revenge.

If he lived to be a hundred, he would never forget the day he'd found out she was getting married. He'd come home on a month's rotation from the North Sea, and someone had told him that she was getting married the next day. It was as if he'd been slammed face first into a concrete abutment. Needing to see it to believe it, he had gone to the big stone church and parked his Mustang across the street. When she had come out, a vision in white, with that bastard Dodd smirking beside her, he had peeled out of there, laying a strip of rubber fifty feet long. Fury and bitterness had erupted inside him, and that was when he'd vowed to show them all. And he'd hung on to that bitterness and cold fury—because what was buried beneath them was too damned devastating to deal with.

But now the bitterness was gone. Now he was going to have to wade through what was left. And he wasn't sure he could do that. He wasn't sure he wanted to. It had been too damned hard the first time around.

Brodie was on the road again by first light. He hadn't bothered to shave or eat; he just gunned the bike and rode out of town. The aftereffects of the ride the day before, along with numbing exhaustion, left him pretty well brain-dead, and he knew he had no business being on the road. He'd slept a couple of hours at most, and he was feeling shaky and definitely hungover, which was a laugh, seeing as he hadn't even cracked the seal on the Jack Daniel's. Deciding not to tempt the devil, he had left the bottle on the nightstand in the motel—a decision he was probably going to regret later on.

He spent the next night in Billings. He was so damned hungry, tired and wind-whipped by the time he rode into town that he stopped at the first restaurant he came to and took a room in the motel next door. The last thing he remembered was sprawling facedown on the bed.

The readout on the digital clock on the nightstand said 3:27 when he woke up. It was too early to hit the road and too late to go back to sleep, and it was there, in that motel room, with the vacancy sign flashing blue through his window, that some of the things he'd been trying to outrun finally caught up with him.

And those things all had to do with Eden McCall. He had always blamed her for tearing up his life. He had never looked beyond that. But what she had said that night in the churchyard had had a ring of truth to it. She had been young, and even as hot-headed as he'd been back then, he had seen the kind of control her parents exerted over her. And she had been unsure of herself; if he'd been a bit more mature, maybe he would have seen that, as well. But that wasn't all he was running from. Part of it was his own guilty conscience.

He hadn't taken one ounce of precaution with her that night at the church, and he had never done that before, with her or anyone else. And even though she had told him she couldn't get pregnant, she still deserved better than that. And he didn't like the nagging feeling that he had used her in some way—or taken advantage of the situation. She had been such an emotional wreck that she hadn't been capable of making a rational decision—and he had known that. But he'd let it happen anyway. The minute he had touched her, it had been like quicksand— once he was in, there was no damned way he could get out. But what made his gut clench even more was knowing that she had every reason to believe what had happened was nothing more than a hit and run. But it wasn't. It had been more than that. One hell of a lot more. More than he wanted it to be.

She had held nothing back, and what she had given him had been real—her passion, her need. She had been with him every step of the way; there was no doubt in his mind about that. But it was that look on her face when he'd told her to go that was going to haunt him for a long time to come. He didn't know if it was guilt or regret, but his throat closed up every time that image took shape in his mind, and the hollow feeling in his chest spread a little more. It had, without question, been one hell of a way to say goodbye.

Brodie wasn't even sure where he was headed when he pulled into the little run-down trading post and gas station that sat huddled beneath some high, rocky outcroppings on a secondary road. He gassed up the bike and grabbed something cold to drink from the Coke machine outside, then wandered into the trading post to stretch his legs. It had the usual selection of souvenir goods: some Indian blankets, T-shirts, a rack of magazines, a carousel of paperbacks. But in the back, tucked away in a corner, was a glass display case of Indian jewelry.

Sitting dead center, on a piece of worn, faded blue velvet, was a wide silver bracelet set with agates. The workmanship was detailed and intricate, the design and quality that of a master silversmith, but it was the stones themselves that caught his eye. Soft mossy green with flecks of gold and brown, they were the exact same shade of hazel as Eden's eyes. He stared at it for the longest time, a taut feeling spreading through his insides. And it was while he was standing there, looking at that damned bracelet, that his conscience caught up with him. Calling himself every name in the book, he strode out the door, firing his half-finished can of pop into the garbage can by the service island. He needed his damned ass kicked.

Jamming on his aviator sunglasses, he mounted the bike, ignoring the helmet hooked on the back of the seat. He hit the ignition switch as he rocked the machine off the kickstand, a bitter taste in his mouth. He *had* used her, damn it. Not for sex. Not that. But he had used her because he had taken all she had to give that night, then walked away.

With the Harley rumbling between his legs, Brodie pushed his sunglasses up and rubbed his eyes, the familiar hollow feeling settling like a rock in his stomach. He didn't, for one minute, think they could pick up where they'd left off seventeen years ago. He was too much of a skeptic to start believing in miracles. And he knew she was only here for as long as her old man was in the hospital. Then she would likely head back to

Toronto. But he had taken the easy way out when he'd taken off, and he knew it.

Pressing his sunglasses back into place, he folded his arms and stared across the road, facing facts that he'd avoided over the past three days. He was running scared. Yeah, too much had happened between them for all the pieces ever to fit back together. But there was one hard, cold truth that he had to admit. It didn't matter if he never saw her again; he was still going to have to deal with some very heavy-duty feelings when she was gone. So here he was, at a crossroads. He could ride off into the sunset and stay away until he was sure she had left town. Or he could go back and face the music. There could never be a big fix; he knew that. But maybe there could be a small fix, something that would let them reclaim some of the past—the good parts of that long, hot summer. Something that would allow them to reclaim the friendship, that ease of old pals. Something that would allow them to let go, once and for all, and move on.

Reacting on sheer instinct, he cranked the throttle and released the clutch, leaning into a sharp curve as he headed north. Less than a hundred yards down the road, he did a leg-stand pivot and headed back to the trading post. He bought the bracelet, then phoned and left a message for Jase that he was on his way home. Then he climbed back on the bike and cranked open the throttle, heading back north. He figured if he pushed it, he could roll into Bolton around midnight.

It was just after eleven when Brodie pulled into the three-car garage he'd built behind the video store. He parked the Harley beside Jason's dirt bike, then swung his leg over the seat and stripped off his helmet. He felt as if he'd been run over by an eighteen wheeler. He had stopped only for gas and bathroom breaks, and every muscle in his body ached. It got damned cold traveling at night, and the road wind had beaten him to death. The corner of his mouth lifted in a small smile as he draped the saddlebags over his shoulder. Maybe he was just getting too old for this.

He used the stairs that led up to the connecting deck on top of the garage, hoping like hell Jase had left the patio door unlocked. He didn't have the energy to walk around to the side entrance.

A small recessed light over the kitchen counter was on, and he found a scrawled note from Jason on the counter. "Hot coffee in the thermos. Got 100% on the math exam. Stone called. Wants me to give him a hand this weekend. See you in the morning. Jase." Brodie read the note, amusement surfacing. Jason said more in his notes than he did in most day-to-day conversations.

The thermos and his favorite mug were sitting on the counter, and Brodie picked them both up in one hand and headed for his bedroom, the saddlebags still slung over his shoulder. He stopped at Jase's door, another small smile appearing when he heard the sound of soft, moody guitar coming from his nephew's room.

Pushing open the door with one finger, he braced his shoulder against the doorframe and studied the kid. The faint illumination from the streetlight outside lay in a rectangle across Jase's face, softening the maturing angles. Brodie wondered what Jase's friends would say if they knew he went to sleep with a CD on every night—usually flamenco or blues, sometimes classical guitar. But then, he wondered if they knew how well he played. Not likely. Jase didn't give much away.

The night-music routine had gotten started a long time ago. When Brodie had finally gotten custody, Jase had been in pretty bad shape. Silent almost to the point of being mute. Wary, with a stare that was like a wounded hawk. Cold, unwavering, unblinking, not giving an inch. He'd had him home three days before he found out that Jase wouldn't go to sleep until the place was dead quiet, and then he would take his pillow and blanket and crawl into the back corner of the closet to sleep.

The kid had just turned nine years old. And Brodie still got steamed up when he thought about it. The next night, he hadn't put the kid straight to bed. Instead, he'd stuck a blues guitar tape in the tape deck, then stretched out on the sofa with the kid, hoping he would trust him enough to fall asleep. But Jason hadn't fallen asleep. He had been transfixed by the music. And the first voluntary thing he had said, in a tone that was more a vow than anything else, was, "Someday I'm going to learn to play like that."

Brodie had gone out and bought him a guitar the very next day, and he would never forget the look on Jase's face when he'd brought it home. Ever since then, Jase had been taking lessons; they'd even built a soundproof room in the basement for him to practice. And ever since then, without fail, Jase went to sleep to music. Brodie sometimes thought the kid absorbed it through his skin.

"You get my note?" Jase mumbled from the bed.

Brodie nodded. "Got your note." He lifted the thermos and mug. "Got the coffee, too. Thanks." He hooked his thumb in the front strap of the leather chaps he wore. "Congratulations on the exam."

A lopsided grin appeared on his nephew's face. "I kicked butt, man."

Brodie's own mouth curved. "I guess. I'm proud of you, sport."

There was a small silence; then Jason met his gaze across the darkened room, his voice husky when he answered, "I know."

A host of feelings nailed Brodie right in the chest, and he shifted against them. The words didn't come that easy for either him or Jase—but the feelings were there. God, were they there. He tipped his head, letting the kid know he'd heard. He held the boy's gaze for a moment, then straightened, his own voice a little gruff. "See you in the morning."

Jason rolled over, his naked back gleaming in the faint light. "Waffles would be appreciated."

A small smile working loose, Brodie caught the doorknob and started to pull the door closed. "Waffles it is."

"Hey, Brodie."

Brodie opened the door and looked at his nephew, who had propped himself up on one elbow. "What?"

"Dave Jackson's dad said he'd help you get the motocross club started. He's checking into insurance and stuff."

Wondering if he was going to regret getting talked into this damned motocross thing, Brodie let his hand rest on the doorknob. The thought of a dozen kids racing around a killer course on dirt bikes was enough to give even him heart palpitations. "I'll give him a call."

"Okay." Jase rolled over. "Good night."

The corner of Brodie's mouth lifted as he closed the door. End of conversation.

Weariness rolling over him, he turned down the hallway. Entering his room, he hit the switch to turn on the lamp by his bed, then dropped the saddlebags on a chair and set the thermos and mug down on the end of the computer desk. He stripped off his leather jacket and undid the front buckle on the chaps, pulling his shirt out of his jeans. He unscrewed the lid of the thermos and filled the mug, then went over to the windows. Resting his shoulder against the frame, he hooked his thumb in the front of his chaps and took a sip of coffee, his gaze fixed on the McCall house.

He wasn't sure what he was feeling. Three days on the road had left him pretty much numb, but he was left with an undefined stirring in his gut—nothing sexual, more elusive than that. A kind of soul-deep restlessness. What would calm it, he realized somberly, was if she were here asleep in his bed. Then he would pull up a chair, prop his feet on the edge of the mattress and simply watch her sleep. He took another sip of coffee to ease the flip-flop sensation in his chest.

Tonight, having her asleep in his bed would have been his soft soul music. His throat tightened, and he turned away. It was going to be another long, empty night.

Brodie didn't spend the night in his bedroom. There was something a little too disturbing, a little too solitary, about his empty, king-size bed, and he'd finally moved out to the living room. He had fallen asleep on one of the sofas, then awoke at six the next morning, his whole body aching from the long ride the night before, his neck feeling as if he'd suffered whiplash. He figured it probably served him right.

He'd had a shower by the time Jase got up, but he hadn't shaved, and his nephew took one look at him, sly humor pulling at his mouth. But the kid didn't say anything. He just took the plate of waffles Brodie handed him. Brodie experienced a small tug of humor himself. The kid knew when to keep his mouth shut. He poured himself another cup of coffee, then leaned back against the counter and took a sip. "So when are you heading up to Stone's?"

Jason shrugged. "Right after school, if that's okay. It's Friday, so I get out early."

Brodie had no problem with it. The kid worked most nights in the video store, and he spent more time at the computer than Brodie did. And he maintained a straight *A* average at school. "It's fine with me. You'd better take the Jeep. That last twenty miles can be bad this time of year."

"I was going to take Max with me."

Brodie nodded. "But watch him. He gets a little carried away up there."

Jase nodded, then worked his way through another waffle. "Are you doing anything this weekend?"

Brodie stared at Jase's profile, his expression turning solemn. Thinking about the bracelet still packed in the saddlebags, he answered, his tone quiet, "I don't know."

All he did know was that he got a rock in his stomach every time he thought about calling her. How in hell did he go about picking up the threads of their old camaraderie and leave all the rest behind?

He didn't go down to the shop. He spent a couple of hours staring out the window, trying to get rid of that knot in his gut. He knew he was going to have to arrange to see her; he at least owed her an apology for not taking any precautions that night at the church, and that wasn't something he could do over the phone. After that, it was anybody's guess.

It was going on ten o'clock when he finally looked up the number and called the McCall residence. He got the answering machine, but he didn't leave a message. He called again at noon and then again at two. It wasn't until six o'clock that evening, when he called from his office downstairs, that he finally got an unrecorded voice on the phone.

Only it wasn't Eden. It was Martha Briggs, the housekeeper. Not entirely at ease with identifying himself, but suspecting that Martha was probably screening Eden's calls because of Dodd, he said who was calling and asked to speak to Eden. Martha sounded decidedly flustered. "Oh! Oh, it's you Brodie. For a minute, I thought it was someone else." He heard a movement; then she continued, her voice clearer, as if she'd shifted the mouthpiece. "She's not here. Her father took a turn for the worse this morning, so they sent him to Calgary."

Standing in his office, his hand on his hip, Brodie stared out the window. "Have you heard from her?"

"Not ten minutes ago. Her mother is staying at the hospital, and she wants to keep the car. Eden asked me to call Chase and see if he could go get her."

Brodie turned and stared at the video racks just outside his office door, thinking about Eden's ex. After what Eden had told him, he wouldn't put it past him to try and snatch the kid. "Where's Megan?"

"I was just on my way out to take her to Tanner's. Chase took her out there yesterday afternoon, and she had such a good time with her cousins. So they're having her back to stay a few days."

The knot in Brodie's belly eased a little. He looked back out the window, mulling over the situation, then making a decision. "Don't bother calling Chase. I'll go get her."

There was a long pause, then Martha spoke again. "Well, now. I think that would be just fine. And it would certainly save Chase a long drive." There was another little pause; then Martha spoke again, a hint of irritation in her tone. "And heaven knows, she could stand a bit of a boost. It's been bloody awful around here, and I think it's beginning to get to her. She's been really down the past couple of days."

Brodie experienced a shot of guilt, and he massaged his eyes, feeling like a first-class bastard. Inhaling heavily, he raised his head, his expression fixed. "What hospital is her father in?"

It was exactly seven-thirty when Brodie got off the elevator at the coronary care unit. He knew from Martha that there were time restrictions even for family members, but he hesitated about making any inquiries at the nursing station. If Eden's mother found out he was there, there would be hell to pay, and that was something they could both do without. He was debating whether he should try to track Eden down or just wait when he caught a glimpse of her through one of the glass partitions. He checked his watch again, then leaned back against the wall, folded his arms and let his head rest against the high-gloss surface. There had been a time in his life, when he was working on the rigs, that he'd been able to sleep standing up. But he didn't think there was much danger of that tonight. There was too much adrenaline pumping through his system.

She came out into the waiting room a half hour later, the strap of a brightly woven knapsack slung over one shoulder, a large white plastic bag stamped with the hospital logo clutched in her arms. She had on joggers, blue jeans and a cotton knit sweater almost the same color as her eyes. And she looked exhausted.

Eden was only a couple of feet away when she looked up and saw him. She stopped dead in her tracks, her eyes widening with shock, and the look that swept across her face left him feeling pretty much like a bastard all over again. He straightened, his gaze locking on hers; then he spoke, his voice gruff. "I heard you needed a ride home."

She stared at him for an instant, then made a flustered gesture with one hand. "I—I was just going down to the lobby to see if Chase was there."

He reached out and pulled the bag from her arms. "I told Martha not to call him."

She continued to stare at him; then she made a quarter turn and covered her eyes with her hand, and Brodie saw her chest heave. His own expression hardening, he reached out and caught her by the back of the neck. "Come on. Let's get out of here," he said roughly.

There were several people already on the elevator when the door slid open, and he held the panel for her, then followed her inside. The ride down to the main lobby was made in strained silence, but as soon as they got off, he grasped her hand and drew her against him, his jaw tightening when he felt how tense she was.

His Corvette convertible was parked in the far corner of the parking lot, and they crossed the hatched crosswalk against a steady stream of people, neither of them speaking. It wasn't until they reached the car that they were really alone. It was still broad daylight, with the sun sitting above the horizon, but a large van was parked beside them, affording them at least a little privacy.

He reached in his pocket and pressed the remote control on his keys to deactivate the alarm and the door locks, then dropped the plastic bag of clothing on the convertible's roof. Before she had a chance to react, he dragged the knapsack off her shoulder and tossed it up there as well. Then he pulled her against him, pressing her ashen face against his shoulder. She had been his best buddy once, and damn it, she needed a hug. And that was why he'd come here in the first place, to try to recover at least that part of their past. He felt her chest heave, and she pressed her face tighter against him; then, on another uneven breath, she slid her arms around his waist and held on for dear life.

Trying to ease the sudden knot in his throat, he tightened his arms around her and rested his head on top of hers, the hard wad of tension in his belly finally letting go. He gave her a few moments to regain her equilibrium; then he began rubbing her back. It took about thirty seconds, but she finally went slack against him, and he felt her take another deep breath. Running his other hand up her neck under her hair, he shifted his head and rested his cheek against her temple.

His voice was low when he murmured, "We have two options here, McCall. We can find a quiet little restaurant and go for dinner, or we can head home, and I'll fix you something spectacular when we get there."

He was rewarded with a shaky laugh. "I think maybe you'd better define 'spectacular.'"

"You want a menu?"

She shook her head and flattened her hands against his back. Experiencing a flurry of emotions, he tucked his head tighter against hers and caressed the base of her skull with his thumb, her hair like silk against his hand. Waiting for the thickness in his chest to settle, he continued to stroke her neck, wishing like hell they were someplace out of public view. He gave them both a minute; then he eased his hold a little and shifted her head so he could see her face. She looked hesitant and very fragile, her eyes revealing her uncertainty.

Knowing he had to somehow maintain a balancing act, Brodie managed a smile. "So, Mac. What's it going to be?" He deliberately used the nickname he'd used years before, hoping to ease the strain. He wasn't prepared for the obvious effect it had on her. He wanted to haul her back into his arms, but he had to get them out of that damned parking lot, one way or another. Deepening his smile into a grin, he lowered his voice into a Dr. Frankenstein monotone. "Speak."

For the first time since she'd reappeared in his life, he saw a glimmer of dry humor in her eyes. "So," she said. "What were the choices?"

He chuckled and rested his arms on her hips, determined to recover that old, easy familiarity. "Dinner in a quiet little restaurant. Or something spectacular at home."

As though she was afraid of what he would see in her eyes, she dropped her gaze. "No restaurant, okay?" she whispered, her voice uneven.

Brodie gazed down at her bent head, her hair shining like satin in the sun, and his chest got tight all over again. "Home it is," he answered, his voice husky.

Keeping one arm around her, he reached for the door handle. Her head came up, a look of surprise in her eyes. "This is *yours?*"

He opened the door, picking up the jacket and ball cap he had brought for her. "Yep. I figured a trip home with the top down was just what the doctor ordered." He helped her into the jacket, then handed her the hat. "You'd better stuff your hair up under this. It's going to get pretty windy once we hit the highway."

She looked up at him, the strain gone from her face, a sparkle of anticipation in her eyes, and Brodie's heart did a barrel roll in his chest. This was the seventeen-year-old Eden—the one who loved speed and taking chances, the one who was game for anything he suggested because she loved the thrill. The one who'd learned to drive his motorcycle; the one who'd gone white-water rafting with him; the one who'd scaled an old wooden train trestle with him at midnight. The one who had been his buddy, his pal. Something sweet and familiar unfolded in his chest, closely followed by another, more sobering emotion. Feeling a little too exposed, he shifted his gaze and tucked a loose strand of her hair under the peaked hat. He had a feeling that this side of Eden hadn't been allowed out for a very long time.

As soon as he was out of the heavy stop-and-go traffic, he took her hand and pressed it against his thigh, covering it with his own. Her only response was to turn her hand palm up, lacing her fingers through his. When he glanced at her, she was sitting with her head tipped back against the headrest, her eyes closed, as if absorbing the invigorating rush of the wind. She looked serene and relaxed, but he could see the rigid tension along her jawline, as though she had her teeth clenched. Brodie tightened his hold on her hand, refocusing his attention on the road, his own jaw tensing. He felt as if he was standing at the edge of a deep, dark precipice, with very little room to move, and if he made one wrong move... He shifted in his seat. He didn't dare even think about it.

Twilight had settled in by the time they reached Bolton, and he pulled into his garage and got out, collecting her things from the back before going around to her side. She wouldn't look at him, and he figured maybe she was having second thoughts about coming in. Which was probably best.

But he found out how badly he'd misread her when he helped her out of the car, pulling her against him so he could close the door. The instant their bodies connected, she turned her face into his chest and grabbed the back of his jacket, a shudder coursing through her. His lungs suddenly tight, he gave her a quick, reassuring squeeze, then took her hand and led her up the back stairs to the deck.

He dragged open the patio door and led her inside, dropping her things on the kitchen table. He tried to let go of her, but there was something about the way she was gripping his hand that got to him. Really got to him. He couldn't let go, not when she was holding on so tight.

Feeling as if his heart was suddenly too big for his chest, he turned toward the bedroom. He wasn't sure what he was getting into, and right then he really didn't give a royal damn. She needed someone to hang on to for a little while, and she needed to be held. And right then, he was in no shape to do it standing up.

As soon as they entered the twilight-filled bedroom, he stripped off her cap and tossed it in the direction of the computer desk, then let go of her hand and stripped off her jacket. Her chest was rising and falling, and Brodie abruptly looked away, his response thick and heavy. Clenching his jaw, he turned away to remove his jacket, and when he turned back, Eden was pulling her sweater off over her head. The sight of her bra, soft and transparent over her breasts, was damned near more than he could handle.

Clamping down on the ache pulsating through him, he caught her shoulders, his voice tight and uneven when he whispered, "Eden—honey." He turned her to face him, feeling as if every muscle in his body was stretched to the limit. He lifted her face, gazing somberly into her eyes as he ran his thumb along her jaw. "That's not the reason I brought you here," he chastised gruffly. "I wanted us to have a chance to talk. And because I wanted to hold you for a little while. Sex wasn't on the agenda." Trying to ignore the hot, heavy sensation pumping through him, he eased in an uneven breath and rubbed his thumb along her collarbone. "And I sure in hell don't want you doing something you're going to regret later," he said, his voice very unsteady.

She stared up at him, her face devoid of all color, but it was the starkness he saw in her eyes that made his heart lurch. Doubt, uncertainty—and a desperate need. She looked down, pulling the sweater free of her arms. "This is one thing I've never regretted," she said, her voice shaking. "Never."

His heart jumped into overdrive, pounding so hard that it felt as if it would come through his ribs. He shouldn't want this. But he did. God, but he did. Like he wanted his next breath. He stared at her, his pulse laboring, his breath jammed up in his chest, fighting to maintain his common sense, his equilibrium. Her eyes filled up with tears, and he saw her try to swallow as she reached up and unsnapped the front clasp of her bra.

He inhaled sharply and caught her hand, blood rushing in his ears. It took him two tries before he could get the words out. "Ah, Mac. Are you sure about this?"

Holding his gaze, she stared at him with a look of defiance flickering in her eyes, tears spilling over. Her voice breaking, she said, "Yes. Very sure."

His good intentions shot to hell by the need he saw in her eyes, Brodie tightened his hold on her hand and tried to regain some control. He knew exactly how this was going to end. And he also knew that once he touched her, he would not be able to let her go. Struggling with the thick surge of desire, he clenched his jaw and rested his forehead against hers, his body painfully engorged. The pressure eased just a little, and he squeezed her hand, then turned away and yanked his shirt free of his jeans, his whole body primed and throbbing. This time he did not want one shred of clothing between them—nothing. This time he wanted it all.

By the time he turned around, she had shed her clothes, and the instant he reached for her, she choked out his name and came into his arms. His heart laboring against the frenzy in his chest, he caught her against him and carried her down onto the bed. Flesh against flesh. Body to body. And it was too much. Dragging in a ragged breath, he closed his eyes in a grimace of raw pleasure as she shifted beneath him and opened to him. On a ragged groan, he settled himself in the hot cradle of her thighs. And lost himself in her tight, wet heat.

Chapter 8

His whole body trembling, Brodie clenched his jaw, his heart still slamming in his chest, the intensity of his release leaving him totally spent. It was the sense of smell that returned to him first. The musky scent of sex, sweat and hot skin. And the feel of her tight around him, gripping him, anchoring him deep inside her. God, it felt so good. So damned good.

Drained dry by the thick, wringing climax, Brodie inhaled unevenly and turned his face against her sweat-dampened neck, the rush of blood still pounding through his head. He lay unmoving until his pulse rate quieted; then he stirred, his body heavy, his muscles slow to respond. Dredging up what little strength he had left, he braced his weight on his forearms, his chest contracting when he realized how desperately Eden was hanging on to him.

Sensation wrenched loose in his chest, and he closed his eyes and rested his head against hers, his throat suddenly contracting. Every time was like the first time with her. Or the last.

Not wanting to think about that, he drenched his senses with the heated scent of her, trying not to think at all.

Finally getting it together, he inhaled unevenly and lifted his head. Murmuring her name, he reached behind him, loosening her hold around his back, then pressing her down against the bed. She lay with her eyes clenched shut, and he could feel her trembling beneath him. Smoothing her damp hair back from her face, he leaned down and softly kissed her mouth, then lifted his head and gazed down at her. "Look at me, Mac," he whispered huskily.

She drew a deep, tremulous breath, then opened her eyes, and Brodie gazed down at her, his expression softening as he caressed the line of her jaw. "You okay?"

She nodded, then closed her eyes again, her arms tightening around his back as she lifted herself up and buried her face against his neck. Brodie experienced a rush of throat-clogging emotion, and he grasped the back of her head, holding her close. He wished like hell he had a way of stopping time. If he could, he would hang on to this moment for the rest of his life.

Releasing a reluctant sigh, he gave her one final kiss on the neck, then lifted his head. He gazed down at her, his expression sobering as he stroked her temple with his thumb. This hadn't been part of his game plan—to fall into bed with her the minute they got in the door. He hadn't been prepared for that.

But he hadn't expected her to push it to the limit, either. She had never done that before—never demanded something from him, never told him exactly what she wanted or needed. And even though he knew that this was probably another big mistake, and that he was digging himself in deeper and deeper, there was no damned way he could have stopped once he had her naked in his arms. But even if he had been able to put on the brakes, he couldn't have done that to her. Not when she had given him that kind of emotional honesty. But that didn't excuse the fact that he'd had no means of protecting her this time, either, and if nothing else, that was one issue he was going to have to deal with.

He caressed her again, then spoke, his voice quiet. "Eden."

She opened her eyes and looked at him, that same expression of uncertainty in her eyes. Wanting to reassure her, he managed a wry smile. "There's something we have to talk about, honey." He saw a flicker of dread, and he experienced a twist around his heart, but he held her gaze, maintaining the off-center smile. "I owe you a big apology, Mac," he said, his voice a little uneven as he rubbed his finger along her bottom lip. "This is twice now that this has happened, and I haven't used any protection." He gave her a crooked grin, rubbing the back of his finger back and forth across her cheek, hoping to make it less awkward. "You got off the mark pretty quick, McCall. If you'd given me a head start, I could have raided the stash in Jason's room first."

She stared up at him, clearly confused; then comprehension dawned. She gave a startled laugh, a blush creeping up her cheeks. Her tone was slightly scandalized when she said, "I beg your pardon? Exactly what stash are you referring to?"

He tucked a strand of hair behind her ear, then met her gaze, giving her a long, level look. "He's seventeen years old. What do you think he has stashed in his room?"

She narrowed her eyes, a hint of laughter in her expression. "And you *know* about this?"

"Hell, I gave them to him. He got the big lecture about safe sex when he was fourteen."

"I see."

The tone of her voice amused him, and he grinned at her. "I figured you would." Propping his weight on one elbow, he ran his finger along her bottom lip, his expression turning serious. He hesitated a moment; then he shifted his gaze and met hers dead on. "I should have taken care of you," he said quietly. "That was pretty damned irresponsible of me."

She held his gaze for a moment, then looked away, running her hand along his shoulder. "You don't have to apologize about that," she whispered, her voice uneven. "I told you that I can't get—"

He lifted her chin, forcing her to look at him, his voice gruff when he interjected. "I just don't want you to think I was being careless with you. That was never my intention."

Her expression softened, and she almost smiled, her touch feather light as she traced the outline of his ear. "You've never been careless, Brodie," she chastised softly. She looked back at him, a hint of dry humor appearing in her eyes. "And just out of curiosity, since when have you needed a head start?"

Feeling as if he'd just gotten caught in a double play, he lifted back some hair that was stuck to her cheek. He fixed the silky strands in among the rest, then looked down at her, a small smile appearing. "Don't give me a hard time, McCall. You know damned well what I meant."

She laughed and squeezed his lips together in an exaggerated pucker. "God, but you're cute when you put your foot in your mouth."

He leaned down and kissed her, then lifted his head, smiling into her eyes. "Do you know that this is the first time we've made love in a real bed?"

She stared up at him, her eyes suddenly clouding; then she swallowed hard and shifted her gaze. She swallowed again, then spoke, her voice breaking. "Don't," she whispered. "Don't, okay?"

His expression sobering, Brodie caught her along the jaw, turning her head so she had to look at him. "Don't what?" he commanded quietly. She hesitated, her expression stark, unhappiness dilating her eyes. He gave her head a small shake, prodding her to answer. "Don't what?"

She took a deep, unsteady breath, then looked away, her face drawn. "Don't bring up the past." She paused, obviously struggling; then she looked up at him, despair in her eyes. "I want to forget what happened," she whispered. "At least for now." She frowned and looked away, as if her emotions were too raw to hold his gaze. Finally she looked up at him, her face drawn and anxious. "I don't want to spoil this, Brodie."

He stared at her for a moment, then began fingering the wild tumble of her hair, a cold jolt making his gut knot. He understood what she was saying—perhaps too damned well. There had been some bitter realities that they had simply pretended didn't exist back then; they had lived in their own isolated little world. Only that world didn't exist anymore. And he wasn't prepared to start resurrecting the past. He had enough reservations about the present.

Brushing back some stray wisps of hair at her temple, he finally met her gaze, his own somber. "I don't want to spoil it, either," he said quietly.

Trying very hard to smile, she swallowed hard and stroked his collarbone. "I wasn't sure. You cleared out of town pretty fast."

Brodie stared at her, his gaze narrowing. Sensing that if he were to move off her right then, she would bolt, he rubbed his thumb down her throat. Finally he spoke. "How did you know I'd taken off?"

Still avoiding his gaze, she tried to smile again. "I phoned the store."

He knew by the way she was skirting his gaze that she didn't want him to see how his disappearance had affected her, and he experienced a sharp pang of regret. He knew she deserved some kind of an explanation, but he didn't want to get into the real reasons why he'd taken off. Because she was right; there was nothing to be gained by dissecting the past. Realizing she was waiting for him to say something, he released a heavy sigh. "I needed some time to think," he said, his voice gruff. "I wasn't very proud of myself that night at the church. And I figured I'd pretty much taken advantage of a bad situation."

She finally looked up at him, her gaze direct. "You didn't take advantage of anything," she whispered. "I knew what I was doing."

In another time he would have challenged her on that, but not now. He dredged up an off-center smile, injecting a touch of humor in his tone. "You sure as hell did."

She tried to smile back, but he saw how hard she was struggling, how much old pain was still there, and he deliberately softened his expression. Still smiling down at her, he tried to lighten the mood. "In spite of what's off-limits, this is still the first time we made love in a real bed."

A startled look flashed in her eyes; then she gave an uneven laugh and hugged him hard, pressing her face against his neck. "Yes," she said unevenly. "I guess it is."

Sliding his arms under her, he hugged her back, kissing the curve of her shoulder as he shifted his hips between her thighs. Her breath caught, and she clutched him tighter, and Brodie went very still. He gave her a moment to settle; then he moved his hips again, deliberately maximizing body contact, and there was another sharp intake of air.

Shifting his hold, he again braced his weight on his elbows, then grasped her face between his hands. "Look at me, Eden," he commanded huskily.

He heard her swallow; then she eased her death grip on his back, and he pressed her head back against the pillow. Holding her gaze, he slowly flexed his hips again, rocking hard against her, and she arched her neck and closed her eyes, the pulse point in her throat beating erratically.

Watching her face, he moved again, and he could feel the tension mount in her. And he knew. He had felt her climax earlier, but she was in such sensory overload that it would take nothing—nothing—to push her over the edge again.

His fingers tangling in her hair, he gripped her head. "Look at me, Mac," he said softly. "I want you to look at me."

As if it cost her an unbearable effort, she did as he asked, her eyes glazed and dilated. "Stay with me, baby," he whispered; then he moved again, and she tried to arch her neck, but he held her head immobile. "Stay with me."

His gaze locked on hers, he slowly moved against her, in her, maximizing the pressure against her. She clutched his arms, her eyes glazing even more, and she drew up her knees alongside his hips, her body arching with tension. His breathing turning erratic, he continued to move, watching her respond, her tightness driving him on. She gripped his arms, a desperate look turning her eyes black; then, on a fragmented moan, she twisted her head, her whole body arching, and he felt her contract hard around him, her release shuddering through her. Feeling as if something wild and unbearably beautiful had been set loose in his chest, he closed his eyes and gathered her up in a fierce embrace, experiencing feelings that went far beyond the sexual.

It took several moments for her to come back down to earth, and he grasped her by the back of the neck, holding her tight and secure. Finally she shifted under him, letting go a long, shaky breath.

Her arms locked around his shoulders, she buried her face against his neck, her whole body trembling. "Oh, God. Brodie. You didn't..."

"Shh." He slid his hand up the back of her head, holding her tight against him. "Shh. It's okay. It's okay."

"But you didn't..."

Experiencing a rush of tenderness, he smiled and hugged her hard. "No, I didn't," he interjected unevenly. "But you did, and that's what counts." He brushed back her hair and turned his face against her neck, kissing the flushed skin, then smiling again. "Watching you does big things to a guy's ego, Mac. Let me tell you."

She tightened her arms around him, still trembling a little. "Just when did you turn into a voyeur?"

He grinned. "About ten minutes ago."

She hugged him again, then ran her hand down his spine. "Well, let me tell you," she whispered unevenly. "You do some pretty spectacular things yourself."

Bracing his weight on his arms, he lifted his head and gazed down at her, smiling into her eyes. "Then we both had a good time."

He gave her a minute; then he braced himself again and withdrew. Locking one arm around her, he rolled over, taking her with him. Holding her firmly against him, he reached down and picked up his T-shirt off the floor; then, tightening his hold on her, he gently pressed the garment between her wet thighs. She inhaled sharply, pressing her face against his neck, and Brodie drew her leg across his, nestling her firmly against him. A small smile appeared. He might just have to get this quilt bronzed.

"Why are you smiling?" she asked, a hint of accusation in her voice.

He grinned and hugged her. There was no way he was going to tell her about the quilt. He lied instead. "I was just thinking that this beats the hell out of the church doorstep."

She pinched him along his ribs. "You've still got a one-track mind, Malone."

"I know." Running his hand up and down her back, he rested his head against hers, liking the feel of her damp, naked body against his. Eden shifted, and he felt the brush of her long eyelashes as she closed her eyes. He continued to stroke her back. After a few moments he felt her body go slack, and he knew she had dropped off to sleep, which gave him a certain amount of satisfaction. He suspected she had been running on nerves for a very long time.

Releasing a contented sigh, he drew his arm around her and closed his eyes, his throat suddenly tight. He hoped like hell she would still be there in the morning.

* * *

Brodie wasn't sure why he woke up—maybe it was because the room had turned cold, maybe it was the soft tap, tap, tap of an open shutter. Or maybe it was the fact that he was unaccustomed to having someone in his bed. But whatever it was, it was the kind of wakefulness that was sharp and clear, with no blurred edges from a deep sleep or half-forgotten dreams. He opened his eyes, aware of the warmth beside him. The fading sky that preceded dawn was illuminating the room, and Brodie turned his head and looked at Eden, a thick feeling unfolding in his chest.

She was sleeping on her side, facing him, one leg drawn up, her breathing deep and even. The windows had been left open all night, and the room was chilly, cooled by the breeze coming straight off the mountains. Bracing his weight on his elbow, he ran his hand down her bare arm; then he reached over, tugged the sheet loose and drew it over her. He watched her sleep for a long time, until parts of his body started sending him messages that had nothing to do with sleep and everything to do with the woman beside him. For an instant he indulged in a fantasy about easing her onto her back and slipping inside her while she slept, then moving slowly, slowly, so he wouldn't wake her—but then he swore and looked at the ceiling, trying to get his heavy pulse under control. Sometimes he let his fantasies go too damned far.

Eden sighed and shifted beside him, her hand brushing against his arm, and he glanced back down at her, suddenly feeling things he didn't want to feel, wanting things he couldn't have, knowing he would never be able to lie in this bed again without seeing her there. The thickness in his chest climbed higher, and he rolled onto his back, resting one arm across his forehead as he stared into the gloom. This part of their relationship had always been so easy—so damned easy. This was the first entire night they had ever spent together, but it didn't seem like it. It seemed as if they'd slept this way a thousand times before.

Sobered by that thought, he got up and pulled on his jeans, then went over to the windows and closed the shutters to block out the first pink-and-gold streaks of dawn. Casting one last glance at the sleeping form in his bed, he left the room, shutting the door soundlessly behind him.

The chilly breeze coming through the open patio door rattled the blinds, and Brodie closed the door, then went into the kitchen. He filled the reservoir on the coffeemaker and put fresh grounds in the basket, his movements automatic and detached. Flipping the switch to start it brewing, he went and stood in front of the patio door, a hollow feeling unfolding in him. Bracing one arm on the window frame, he stared out, wishing the hole in his gut would go away, wondering what in hell was the matter with him. He should be ecstatic. But he wasn't.

He'd thought he had everything sorted out when he came back from Montana. See her, tell her he was sorry, try to pick up a few threads of their old relationship and leave everything else behind. But what had happened last night had changed all that, and it made him realize he'd been playing big-time games with himself. They could never be just friends. And there was no damned way he wanted them to be just lovers.

Looking away, he swallowed hard, his eyes suddenly burning. It was a hell of a note; he had never found anyone who came close to replacing her. Now she was here, asleep in his bed, and he didn't have a clue why. Maybe she was so damned torn up over her divorce and this thing with her father that she didn't know what she was doing herself. Maybe she was unconsciously looking for a little comfort, a little closeness, someone to hang on to for a little while—and maybe she was simply acting out of a guilty conscience over the stunt she'd pulled seventeen years ago. Maybe her regrets were about how she'd dumped him, rather than why. Who the hell knew?

All he knew for sure was that last night had been real for him. Too damned real. But he was a whole hell of a lot older and wiser than he had been at nineteen. And he didn't ever want to get blindsided like that again.

Exhaling heavily, Brodie dragged his hand down his face, then tipped his head back, trying to release the tension across his shoulders. Hell, he was going to drive himself crazy if he didn't quit thinking about it. Especially when there weren't any damned answers. He turned from the window, rolling his shoulders. What he needed was a long run.

* * *

Early-morning sunlight was casting long shadows through the trees when Brodie turned off the old access road. Wiping his face on the towel around his neck, he walked across the street to his store, trying to cool down. He had done five punishing miles, and the sweat was rolling off him. His lungs felt as if they were about to rip open, but he had dumped his sour mood in the process. In fact, he felt surprisingly cleansed. He wiped his face again, then bent over and caught his ankles, stretching out his hamstrings and the muscles down the backs of his calves, the blood still pounding in his ears. He held the position for a count of thirty, then straightened, shaking loose his arms and shoulders, dragging the towel from around his neck. He hoped like hell he had enough strength to make it up the stairs.

His breathing leveled out, and he mounted the back steps, taking them two at a time. As he turned to pull open the screen door, he caught a glimpse of someone on the McCall veranda, and he took a step back to see who it was.

Martha Briggs was sweeping off the steps, but she kept glancing across the street at his store, and it hit him that she must be wondering where Eden was. Resting one hand on his hip, Brodie considered the McCalls' housekeeper, his expression thoughtful. He'd always liked Martha. He smiled a little, wondering if Ellie McCall had any idea that her housekeeper had kept Jason supplied with chocolate chip cookies for the first couple of years he was with Brodie. He released a sigh. He supposed it wouldn't kill him to call her and tell her where Eden was—and maybe head off an awkward situation.

Tightening his grip on the towel, Brodie slid open the screen door and entered, closing it quietly behind him, the smell of coffee rising up to greet him. Turning toward his bedroom, he chucked the towel and his tank top through the basketball hoop mounted over the hamper in the laundry room, then soundlessly opened his bedroom door.

Eden was stretched out on her stomach, her head turned away from him, her arms shoved under the pillow, and it was pretty obvious that she was still dead to the world. Resting his shoulder against the doorframe, he watched her sleep, a familiar tightness unfolding in his chest. She was here. At least for now. And he was going to make do with that. He'd done some serious thinking when he'd been out for his run, and he'd decided one thing. He was going to quit wrestling with the past and start taking the present one day at a time. It was the only way he could keep from driving himself crazy. She stirred, and the sheet slipped a little. He wondered what she would do if he climbed back into bed and fulfilled his earlier fantasy.

His body instantly responding, Brodie shook his head in disgust and straightened, repressing some very heavy urges. God, but he was turning into a lecher in his old age.

Not quite sure what to expect, Brodie called Martha. He waltzed with the truth a little, telling her that Eden had pretty much had it when they got back from Calgary and had crashed at his place. He figured no one needed to know that Eden McCall had spent the night in his bed. Martha actually sounded pleased about it, saying it was about bloody time someone started taking care of her. Her voice fairly bristling with approval, the housekeeper asked him to pass on a message that she was taking the day off to go visit her sister. Brodie experienced a shot of amusement when he hung up the phone. Who would have guessed? An ally in the McCall camp.

It was going on nine when Eden finally made an appearance. He was in the kitchen, making a second pot of coffee, when she finally stumbled in, looking as if she'd just crawled out of a dog fight. Her hair was wild, he could see the imprint of her hand on the side of her face, and she was wearing an old T-shirt that looked as if it had come out of a rag bag. It wasn't one of his, but he had put her knapsack by the bed, so he assumed it was something she had taken with her. It was a washed-out gray, hung almost to her knees, and it was worn so thin he could have spit through it. For those connoisseurs of nightwear who thought black satin was sexy, they hadn't seen Eden McCall in this paper-thin T-shirt. Parts of his body were already feeling the strain. Deciding he'd better focus his attention somewhat higher, he lifted his gaze to her face.

Looking dazed and not quite awake, she gave a wild-eyed glance around the kitchen. "I never called Martha last night," she muttered, stumbling against the corner of the counter. "She won't know where I am."

Leaning back against the counter, Brodie folded his arms, amusement rising in him. She was not a class act first thing in the morning. He continued to watch her. "I called her."

She squinted up at him, then licked her lips, looking very much as if she'd just fallen off a fast-moving train. "You did?"

Trying to straighten out his face, he nodded. "I did. She said to tell you she's taking the day off to visit her sister."

She gave him a totally confused look. "Oh."

"Would you like coffee?"

She started back toward the bedroom, still pretty much out of it; then she turned, wavering slightly. "Coffee?"

He very nearly laughed. "You know—brown stuff that comes in a mug. Loaded with caffeine and usually served hot."

She closed her eyes and dragged her hair back from her face with both hands, staggering a little; then she opened her eyes again, only she opened them really wide, as if to make them stick. "I'll have a coffee."

He held out his mug to her, and she did the thing with her eyes again, then made her way across the kitchen. She reached for it, took a sip, then released a long, appreciative sigh. "Oh, God. Coffee."

He watched her, barely containing his amusement. She practically inhaled the whole cup. "Feel better?"

She closed her eyes, this time in appreciation, taking another sip. His arms still folded, he continued to watch her face, determined not to let his gaze drift any lower. She had the best set of legs, long—like forever long—and he knew she didn't have a damned thing on under that rag of a T-shirt she was wearing. He wanted to cart her back to bed like some caveman.

It didn't take long for the caffeine to kick in, and he could actually see her come to life. Not a bad thing to do on a Saturday morning.

She finally looked at him, managing a small, sheepish smile. "Hi," she said, her voice still husky from sleep.

He grinned at her. "The mind is finally clicking into gear, is it?"

She slanted a look up at him, then took another sip, holding the mug between both hands, as if absorbing the warmth. "Be wise, Brodie," she said, a warning in her tone. "I need a second transfusion before I'm human."

"Well, you're just going to have to tough it out for a while. This pot won't be done for a couple of minutes."

Putting one foot on top of the other, as though her feet were cold, she rested her hip against the counter. "So," she said, not looking at him, "what got you out of bed so early?"

He decided she needed more than a shot of caffeine to get her blood circulating. "You," he responded, restraining a smile.

She shot him a startled look. "Me?"

Unable to resist giving her a real wake-up call, he reached out and ran his finger down the swell of her breast. "Yeah, you," he answered, his voice deliberately low and provocative. "I woke up, and there you were, all warm and naked, and I started wondering what it would be like to get you on your back, then start making soft, slow love to you while you were still asleep."

She stared at him, transfixed, looking totally winded. As if she'd finally gotten the rush he intended, she turned and set the mug down with enough force to nearly crack it in half. Then she closed her eyes and braced both hands on the countertop, and he saw her chest rise, as if she couldn't catch her breath. It wasn't the response he'd expected—he'd expected her to tell him to stuff his soft, slow sex where the sun didn't shine. But this response was even better—he liked it a lot.

Finally getting some air into her lungs, she turned and looked at him, a dangerous glint in her eyes. "Damn you, Malone," she breathed; then she caught him by the hair, pulled his head down and gave him a kiss that just about blew his jeans to smithereens.

Laughing against her mouth, his whole body going on full alert, he slid his arms around her hips. "Way to go, McCall," he murmured, tasting her mouth.

She gave his hair another yank and deepened the kiss, and Brodie got real serious, real quick, and he dragged her up against him. She made a low sound and slid her arms around his neck, and suddenly Brodie couldn't breathe, either. Grabbing the back of her head, he fought for air, his heart hammering. He changed the angle of her head, then sealed his mouth hungrily against hers. He would never get them to the bedroom in time. Never.

She moved against him, and he nearly groaned, a pulsating heat coursing through him. In desperation, he turned and set her on the counter, wedging his hips between her thighs. She hooked her legs around his waist and moved flush against him, and he nearly lost his mind. This was a fantasy he hadn't even had, yet.

They finally got around to breakfast at about ten o'clock. Brodie made steaks and eggs, and he made sure she ate everything he put on her plate. It bothered him that she was so thin, but he didn't say anything. He knew from the past how stress affected Eden's stomach, and he figured her stomach had had about as much stress as it could take. With that in mind, he confiscated her coffee mug after her second cup. He didn't think she even realized what he was doing.

She insisted that since he'd done all the cooking, it was only fair that she clean up afterward. He let her do it, not because it was fair, but because it gave him a chance to simply watch her.

Filling his coffee mug, he leaned back against the counter, watching her as she scrubbed out the frying pan, up to her elbows in soapsuds. He'd made up his mind on his morning run that he wasn't going to try to second-guess what was going on between them. But he had to admit that he found it damned unnerving how easily they had slipped back into the old familiarity. And it wasn't just the sex. It was the old intimate patterns, like her stumbling out into the kitchen still bombed on sleep, and his giving her a hard time. It was as if they'd spent countless mornings like that, instead of only one. But he also knew it wasn't really real—it was as though they were caught in a time warp, and all it would take would be one small fracture and the illusion would shatter. And reality was something he didn't want to deal with right then.

Shifting his weight against the counter, he lifted the mug to his mouth, watching her work. There was an intentness in her expression, as if she were totally absorbed in what she was doing. She used to get that same expression on her face when she was trying to capture something on paper. He'd spent many an hour lying on his back in some field, watching her with her sketch pad propped on her knees, that same intensity on her face. He wondered if she'd given up that dream, as well.

His gaze fixed on her face, he crossed his ankles. "Do you still paint?"

She shot him a surprised look, then continued with the frying pan, her expression unreadable. It took her a second before she answered. "Not much."

"Why?"

Without looking at him, she gave a dismissive little shrug. "It just didn't seem to work for me anymore."

Brodie experienced a spurt of annoyance. He wondered if that son of a bitch had ruined that for her as well. He locked his jaw to keep from responding.

Rinsing the suds off the frying pan, she tipped her head toward the tea towel lying on the counter. "Would you pass me that, please?"

Still thinking about her ex, he handed her the towel, his expression unsmiling. She glanced up at him; then she looked back down, and he could tell she was thinking about something. Finally she spoke. "Brodie?"

"What?"

"Would you mind telling me about Jase?"

He stared at her profile for a moment, then looked away, cupping his mug in his hand. "There's not much to tell. His mother died when he was five, and he was stuck in foster homes. I got custody of him just after he turned nine."

There was a strained little pause; then she spoke again, a reminiscent softness in her voice. "He's very much like you were."

"He's nothing like I was. He's got his act together."

She set the frying pan on the counter beside him, then folded the tea towel. "He didn't do that by himself," she countered quietly.

He didn't make a response. Her comment had come a little too close to a nerve.

She leaned over and draped the tea towel across his shoulder, deliberately brushing against his fly. Startled out of his reverie by her daring, he looked at her and narrowed his eyes. He knew what she was doing; she was trying to lighten up the mood. He grabbed her wrist, pulling her hand away, barely holding back a laugh. "You're brazen, you know that?"

She gave him a wide-eyed, innocent look. "This from the man who told me what he wanted to do to me while I was still asleep?"

He grinned at her. "You must have me mixed up with some-body else."

He was reaching for her just as the phone rang, and he knew by the double ring it was from downstairs. He gritted his teeth in exasperation. Hell, he'd only been gone three days. It wasn't as if they couldn't manage another day without him. He swore and reached for it just as Eden gave him a slow, provocative wink. He narrowed his eyes again and hit the button for the speakerphone. "What?" he snapped.

Lydia's voice filled the kitchen. "We've got a problem with the computers, Brodie."

Resting his hands on his hips, he stared at the phone. "I don't want to hear about this, Lydia."

There was a thread of amusement in the older woman's voice when she retorted, "Yes you do. We can't get the scanner to work."

"Deal with it, Lydia."

"I *am* dealing with it, Brodie."

Knowing she was probably downstairs laughing at him, he finally gave up. "Try changing the cable."

"You could have told me that right off, you know."

He shook his head; there was no damned way he could win. "Yes, I could have."

"What's with you this morning, Malone? Have you got a woman stashed up there?"

Brodie shot Eden a quick look. She had both hands clamped over her mouth to contain her laughter. He decided to give her a little of her own medicine back. "As a matter of fact, I do."

"Yeah, right. That's why you've been so damned cranky lately."

He reached for the orange button. "Goodbye, Lydia." He punched the button, then started toward Eden, a menacing look in his eyes. "Were you laughing at me, McCall?"

"Yes," she answered, backing away from him, her voice quavering with laughter. "I was."

Before she had a chance to make a move, he had her over his shoulder and was heading for the bedroom. "You're going to pay for that, McCall. Big time."

Laughing and out of breath, she tried to break loose. "You're not going to get one red cent out of me, Malone."

Brodie grinned. That sounded very much like a challenge to him.

Chapter 9

Lying with one hand tucked under his head, Brodie stared across the room, absently watching the thin strips of light flutter as the wind ruffled through the slats of the shutters. In the distance, he could hear the chatter of a water sprinkler, and he wondered what idiot was watering his grass after nearly two weeks of solid rain.

Eden stirred, shifting her head on his shoulder, her breath warm against his neck, and he glanced down at her, slowly running his hand up and down her naked arm. She had fallen asleep after their tumble into bed, and she had been dead to the world for over two hours. He smoothed his hand along her soft skin, his expression sobering. He had spotted a bottle of pills on top of the stuff she had dumped out of her bag, and he knew from the prescription that they were sleeping pills. Those pills bothered the hell out of him. Partly because she needed them at all, and partly because he suspected he had caused her a few sleepless nights over the past few days. He had been a real jerk, taking off like he had. He rubbed her arm again. He didn't care if her old man was sick in the hospital, he was going to let her sleep until she woke up on her own.

He had taken the phone off the hook two hours ago and stuffed the receiver under the pillows. He'd wanted to make sure there wouldn't be another emergency call from downstairs to wake her. Repositioning his hand under his head, he stared back at the ceiling, thinking about what had transpired between them. It was as though she'd never been away. But he was realistic enough to know that they were walking on damned thin ice. He had to keep reminding himself that this wasn't a new beginning; it was simply the past in remission.

She stirred, her body moving against his; then she smoothed her hand across his chest. "What time is it?" she asked, her voice rusty with sleep.

He glanced at the clock radio sitting on his bedside table. "Quarter to three."

"I shouldn't have fallen asleep."

"You're exhausted, Eden," he said, his tone chastising.

He felt her smile. "I wonder why."

He grinned, giving her a little squeeze. "Don't get mouthy, woman. You had a hand in this, too."

"Yes," she said, her tone eloquent. "I certainly did."

He laughed and hugged her hard. "Someone should lock you up and throw away the key." He thought of her ex-husband, and his jaw hardened. By the sounds of things, that was pretty much what the bastard had done. Not wanting to even think about her ex-husband, he changed the subject. "Do you have to pick Megan up?"

She shook her head. "Not until tomorrow." She rubbed her thumb along his collarbone, then released a heavy sigh and spoke, her tone subdued. "But I'm going to have to leave for the hospital pretty soon. Milt flew in yesterday, but he has to go back sometime this afternoon."

Continuing to stroke her shoulder, he remained silent, staring at the flicker of light between the closed slats. There was nothing stopping him from driving her to Calgary, but he knew they would both be better off if he stayed away from her family. He had no use for her old man, and his opinion of her mother wasn't a whole lot better. He didn't even like her talking about them. In fact, he avoided the McCalls whenever possible.

Granted, he and Devon Manyfeathers went back a long way. They'd grown up in the same seedy part of town down by the river, and there was a kind of unspoken acknowledgment between them. But he hadn't run into her that often since she'd married Chase. He knew Chase by reputation, and he'd run into him a few times at the Silver Dollar when he'd stopped by for a beer or to shoot a game of pool.

As for Tanner, he knew him to see him. He'd overheard Rita Johnson telling Ruby about how old man McCall had abandoned Tanner when Bruce had married Ellie. And it was common knowledge that neither Chase nor Tanner had anything to do with their father. Which pretty much said it all, as far as Bruce McCall was concerned.

But then, Brodie knew better than anyone what he was capable of. The old man had come after him with a bullwhip when he found out Eden had been sneaking out to see him. But Brodie hadn't grown up on the wrong side of town for nothing, and he had not been compelled by good manners to stand there and take it. It had gotten damned ugly before it was over, but he'd at least been able to leave under his own steam. When he'd walked away from Bruce McCall, the man was sagging against his shiny new Lincoln, his face and shirt covered with blood, his bullwhip floating down the river. He often wondered if Eden had known about her father's little late night visit.

Realizing that his thoughts were heading onto dangerous ground, he closed his eyes and clenched his jaw, not liking the feeling churning up in his belly. The old anger was seeping back, and he didn't want it. He didn't want to remember how that son of a bitch had tried to whip him like some damned dog. And he didn't want to start wondering if Eden knew about it. There was no damned percentage in it.

Eden shifted her head on his shoulder and spoke, her voice soft. "It's so hard to see him like this," she whispered, as if thinking aloud. "He's so weak he can't even feed himself. And he gets so upset when he can't manage on his own—he keeps trying to pull out the IVs. It's got to be so frustrating for him, when he's always been so active."

Old anger surfaced in Brodie, and the muscles in his face turned hard, his pulse suddenly accelerating. He didn't want to hear about Bruce McCall. And he sure in hell didn't want to hear the anxiety in her voice. Bruce McCall was a bastard as far as he was concerned, and he frankly didn't give a damn whether he lived or died.

Knowing he couldn't lie there and listen to her go on about her father, he eased his arm out from under her and got up, tossing the covers back onto the bed. Deliberately skirting her gaze, he pulled on a pair of jeans and did up the zipper. "I'll go put on the coffee."

He heard her move; then she spoke, her voice soft and unsure. "Brodie?"

He looked at her, his expression shuttered. "What?"

She was sitting up in bed, the sheet clutched across her breasts, watching him with a worried expression. "What's wrong?"

He stared at her for a moment, then looked away. "Nothing."

There was a tiny tremor in her voice when she responded, "Yes, there is."

He swept his shirt off the floor, then turned toward the door. His tone was clipped when he spoke. "There are clean towels in the bathroom cupboard if you want to have a shower." Without looking at her, he left the room, resisting the urge to slam the door after him.

Brodie was standing in front of the living room windows, one arm braced against the wall, his other hand jammed on his hip, the muscles in his jaw still rigid, when Eden finally entered. He turned his head and looked at her, his face taut. Her wet hair was pulled straight back and clipped at the nape of her neck, the severity accentuating the tense pallor of her face.

Lowering her brightly woven knapsack and the plastic bag onto the sofa, she stuck her hands in the pockets of her jeans and lifted her head and looked at him, her eyes unwavering. "You're angry because I was talking about Dad, aren't you?" she asked quietly.

He stared at her for a moment, then looked back out the window. There was so much acid rolling around in his stomach that it felt as if his gut was on fire. And he knew damned well that if they started talking about her father, it was going to get a hell of a lot worse.

He heard her shift her weight; then she spoke again, her voice uneven. "I know how you feel about him, Brodie. I'd have to be deaf and blind not to, but he's old and sick—and in spite of what he's done in the past, he's still my father, and I love him. Can't you understand that?"

Brodie turned his head and looked at her, his expression wooden. "You do what you have to, Eden. But don't try and soft-pedal him to me, all right?"

Her hands still in her pockets, she drew in her shoulders, tension lining her face. "I'm not trying to soft-pedal him," she whispered, her expression pleading. "I'm just trying to explain. That's all."

Turning so his shoulder rested against the window casement, Brodie folded his arms and stared at her. "Don't give me that crap," he said, his tone flat. "You want me to roll over and play dead, but I'm not rolling over for anyone anymore. Especially him."

"I'm not asking you to roll over, Brodie," she said unevenly. "I'm just asking you to try to understand."

"Well, I don't understand. And I never did."

She held his gaze for a moment; then she looked down and began straightening the straps on her knapsack. Finally she looked up at him, a challenging expression in her eyes. "What are you trying to do?" she asked. "Are you trying to make me choose between you and my father?"

Brodie came away from the window, anger flaring in him. "Damn it, Eden. I'm not trying to make you choose anything. I've been down this road before, and I know what you're trying to do."

Her chin came up, and she held his gaze. "I'm not sure you do. I've learned a few lessons since I was seventeen. You would have been quite happy if I'd turned my back on my family back then—but it just doesn't work that way. Everyone has to make compromises once in a while. I've never pretended that my family's perfect—far from it. I'm not asking you to fall in love with them—I'm just asking you to try to understand where I'm at."

Hooking his thumbs in the front pockets of his jeans, he stared at her, his expression unyielding. "So tell me. Just where *are* you at, Eden? Has this all been just a quick roll in the hay—or has it mattered a damn to you?"

She reacted as if he'd slapped her, and she turned away. Brodie half expected her to pick up her bags and leave. The old Eden would have. But she stopped and turned back, hurt glimmering in her eyes. "You really don't know, do you?"

"Know what?"

She looked at him, and he saw a flash of wounded pride in her eyes. "Do you think that I would have come here last night if I didn't love you? Do you think I'm that cheap?"

His pulse hammering in his ears, Brodie curled his hands into fists, his lungs suddenly tight. Trying to keep the edge out of his voice, he spoke, his tone very quiet, very controlled. "Do you mean that, or are you jerking me around again?"

She managed a tight, mirthless smile. "Oh, I'm serious. In fact, I've never been more serious."

Trying to rid himself of the buildup of old anger in his chest, he expelled his breath, forcing his stiff muscles to relax. Holding her gaze for a long moment, he finally spoke, his tone deadly quiet. "Then marry me, Eden."

Her body went perfectly still, and she stared at him, all the remaining color draining from her face. "What?"

His gaze locked on hers, he spoke again, his tone flat. "If you really feel that way, marry me. Now. As soon as possible."

Fumbling for the back of the sofa, she suddenly closed her eyes, and for a minute Brodie thought her legs were going to buckle beneath her. But he stayed where he was, sensing this was the final showdown.

It took a while, but she finally pulled herself together, and she lifted her head and looked at him, her face ashen, her whole body trembling. "Are you serious?" she whispered, her eyes still dark with shock.

He gave her a tight half smile. "Very."

She inhaled unevenly, then folded her arms in front of her. "Why?"

"You know why, Eden. After last night and this morning, you shouldn't even have to ask."

Her eyes filled up with tears, and she looked away, a kind of despair washing over her face. He saw her try to swallow, then try again. As if it hurt her to breathe, she inhaled unevenly. "Don't do this to me, Brodie," she whispered brokenly.

"Do what?"

She looked at him, her expression bleak. "Don't make me choose."

Folding his arms, he stared at her, his expression fixed. "I'm not asking you to choose. I'm asking you to marry me."

She hunched her shoulders and turned away, her body tight, as if she was trying to ward off pain. She tipped her head back, and Brodie watched her, his face feeling like cement. He knew he was backing her into a corner, and he knew he wasn't being particularly nice about it, but he also knew they had to finish this, one way or another. He wasn't going to spend the next seventeen years marking time.

After a long, tense moment she turned, her face deathly white. She looked at him, her gaze stark. "If I married you now," she whispered unsteadily, "it would very likely kill him. And I can't do that. I could never live with myself if that happened." Her eyes pleading with him, she spread out her hand in a beseeching gesture. "Can't we wait until he's better—until he's at least back on his feet?"

His face stiff with renewed anger, Brodie stared at her. "Wait for what, Eden? For your parents to give their approval? For you to decide to live your own life? Exactly what are we supposed to wait for? You know damned well things are never going to change."

Tears caught in her lashes, and she abruptly wiped them away, then folded her arms again. She stared across the room, her profile strained. Finally she spoke, her voice careful, controlled. "You're not being fair, Brodie. My father is sick and deserves a little consideration right now. That's all. This has nothing to do with what happened back then."

His temper flaring, he glared at her, the muscles in his face rigid. "Damn it, Eden. This has *everything* to do with what happened back then. Can't you see that you're doing the same damned thing all over again? You're making a decision based on what they think. And what in hell am I supposed to do— mark time until they change their minds?" Making a conscious effort to check his anger, he paused, forcing his muscles to relax. "They're never going to approve, Eden. You may as well face that fact right now. You can't have it both ways."

Her eyes pleading with him, she made a small gesture with her hand. "I know that. But he's sick, and I can't jeopardize his recovery. I can't do that to him."

His arms folded in front of him, Brodie stared at her, something cold and unpleasant unfolding in his chest. It was almost as if she were dismissing the past. A very old bitterness surfaced. His gaze riveted on her, he spoke, his tone ominously quiet. "So tell me, Eden. Did you know about your father's little visit to see me—the one he made just before they shipped you off?"

Her gaze locked on his face. A startled look appeared in her eyes, but he couldn't tell if it was guilt or shock. He rested his shoulder against the casement, his eyes fixed on her. "So did you?"

She continued to stare at him, her eyes stark; then she wet her lips. "What visit?" she whispered unevenly.

Recognizing the alarmed expression in her eyes, Brodie held her gaze for a moment; then he straightened and turned back to the window, a sick, hollow feeling overriding his fury. Resting his forearm high on the casement, he stood staring out, his jaw locked in self-disgust. When push came to shove, he wasn't a hell of a lot better than her old man. Using that kind of crap as a weapon.

"What visit, Brodie?"

He wouldn't look at her. "Forget it. It doesn't matter."

"It does matter," she answered, a thread of panic in her voice.

He didn't answer her, his expression like granite. What in hell was he trying to prove? He exhaled heavily, and wearily massaged his eyes. There was no percentage in this. None.

"Damn it, talk to me. What visit?"

Exhaling again, Brodie turned and faced her. He didn't say anything.

Her face waxen, she stared at him. "You're not going to tell me, are you?"

Brodie held her gaze for a moment; then he looked away. "No."

There was a long, strained silence; then Eden went over to stand in front of the window closest to her, her arms tightly folded, her profile stark. "I hurt you very badly, didn't I?" she whispered unevenly.

He hesitated, the hollow feeling expanding. Finally he answered, his voice clipped, "Yes."

Her voice was so strained he could barely hear her. "And you don't trust me very much, do you?"

Brodie stared at her profile; then he looked away, reality striking home, and a cold feeling sluiced through his gut. He had never put it together before. Never. Clenching his jaw against the awful sliding sensation in the pit of his stomach, he forced himself to take a deep breath. It was a full minute before he could answer. "No," he responded, his voice rough. "I guess I don't."

She didn't look at him. She just kept staring out the window, her arms locked in front of her. Her voice was very quiet when she answered, "I can't say I really blame you."

The silence was so strained, so brittle, that Brodie could feel it right down to his bones. Suddenly drained, he dragged his hand down his face, then turned and stuffed his hands in his pockets, not sure where to go from here. Because it was true, he didn't trust her—not anymore. He'd lost that trust a long time ago. He just hadn't realized it until she said the words.

The sound of footsteps on the inside stairs broke through his thoughts, and he exhaled heavily. It was probably Lydia. And it sure as hell was bad timing. He could do without this intrusion right now.

A knock sounded, and he shot Eden a quick glance, his mouth compressing into a hard line when he saw how unmoving, how unaware she was. It was as if she wasn't even there.

His expression grim, he opened the door, prepared to give Lydia a quick brush-off. But it wasn't Lydia. It was Tanner McCall. Standing with his feet wide spread, Eden's half brother fixed Brodie with an unreadable stare, his straw Stetson low over his eyes. "Brodie. I understand Eden's here."

Without speaking, Brodie opened the door wider, and Eden's half brother entered. Tanner took off his hat, his face impassive, his gaze fixed on the woman in front of the windows. Eden turned, her arms still folded in front of her, her face white with strain. Tanner looked from Eden back to Brodie, then back to his sister. "I'm sorry to butt in here, Eden," he said, his voice gruff. "But your mother is trying to track you down, and I thought I'd better get word to you."

Alarm registered in her eyes, and she opened her mouth to speak. But Tanner held up his hand to stop her, a small, off-kilter smile appearing. "It's nothing serious. At least, not medically. It sounds like your father's got his tail in a twist, and he wants to talk to you and Chase."

Eden looked from Tanner to Brodie, confusion darkening her eyes, and Brodie saw her waver just a little. Knowing she needed time to get collected, he motioned Tanner to the sofa. "Have a seat, Tanner."

Eden's brother nodded and settled himself on the sofa nearest Eden, stretching out his long legs. Brodie sat down on the sofa adjacent to him, then cocked his leg across his knee, his eyes narrowing as he watched her face. She clasped her hands together and somehow managed an uneven smile. "You could have just phoned, Tanner," she reminded him wryly.

Tanner stared at her, then gave her a small smile. "I tried, but the line's been busy for the past couple of hours. And since I had a bunch of videos to bring back, I thought I'd kill two birds with one stone."

Brodie looked away, clenching his jaw in self-disgust. The damned phone. He'd forgotten that he'd taken it off the hook.

That possibility didn't seem to register with Eden, though. She glanced from Tanner to Brodie, and he could read her discomfort from a mile away. She swallowed and glanced back at Tanner. "How did you know where I was?"

A glint appeared in Tanner's eyes, and one corner of his mouth lifted. "Well, that's a long story. Your mother tried to phone Martha, but Martha wasn't there. So Ellie phoned Chase, and he called me to ask if you were at the Circle S. Apparently your father and Milt had a big falling out, and all hell broke loose." Bracing his elbow on the arm of the sofa, Tanner dragged his thumb across his bottom lip, his gaze fixed on his sister, the glint in his eyes intensifying. "Are you sure you want to hear all this?"

Leaning back against the wide windowsill, Eden folded her hands around the ledge, her weight braced with her legs. Her smile was strained, but there was a faint glimmer of humor in her eyes. "I wouldn't miss it for the world."

The laugh lines around Tanner's eyes deepened. "It gets pretty damned convoluted."

She continued to watch him. "I'm sure it does. But you'd better tell me, anyway."

Tanner gave her a warped grin, then explained. "Well, to make a long story short, I told Chase you weren't there, but for him to head on into the city, and I'd track you down. Kate remembered Martha saying something about going to her sister's when she brought Meggie out. So she called Martha's sister and talked to Martha." A twinkle appeared in his eyes. "I'm not the detective, Eden. I'm just the messenger."

Slouching down in the sofa, Brodie folded his arms and watched the exchange, assessing the situation. Not once had Tanner McCall referred to Bruce as his father—always Eden's father. But what struck him most was the very obvious alliance between brother and sister. For some reason it made his chest hurt like hell.

Eden stood up, and Brodie fixed his attention on her, his expression altering when he saw her nervously wipe her hands down the sides of her jeans. Affecting a stiff, artificial smile, she lifted one shoulder in a dismissive shrug. "Well, then. I guess I'd better get my butt into the city."

His heart suddenly pounding, a nameless heaviness spreading through him, Brodie stood up, deliberately sticking his hands in the pockets of his jeans. Without looking at him, she picked up her things, and Brodie could see her square her shoulders. The same unnatural smile stuck on her face, she looked at her half brother. "Are you coming?"

Tanner set his Stetson down on the sofa, his expression giving nothing away as he looked up at her. "No, I have some business to discuss with Brodie." He glanced at Brodie. "Art Jackson told me you're trying to line up a site for a motocross course. I've got a piece of property that might fit the bill, and I've also got two boys who are pressing pretty hard for dirt bikes. Art suggested I talk it over with you, if you've got a minute."

Keeping his own expression shuttered, Brodie studied Eden's brother, then gave him a shrug, acutely aware of the sudden tension in the room. "Sure. Now's fine."

Locking down his own reactions, he turned and faced Eden, a hole in his belly the size of a basketball. Making damned sure his expression revealed nothing, he looked at her, trying not to feel anything at all.

Hooking the strap of her knapsack over her shoulder, she lifted her head and finally looked at him, her expression fixed, a bruised look in her eyes. She held his gaze for a moment, then glanced at her brother. "I'll see you later, Tanner." Then, without so much as another glance at Brodie, she turned and left, closing the door behind her. And he stood there, staring at the floor, the muscles in his jaw working. Well, he had his answer—history had just repeated itself.

Resisting the urge to drive his fist through the wall, he turned abruptly and went into the kitchen. His voice was brusque when he spoke. "Care for a beer?"

"Beer would be fine."

Going on remote control, Brodie went to the fridge and collected two bottles, hoping like hell Tanner McCall would say what he had to and clear out. He didn't need an audience right now—especially when he felt like ripping the place apart with his bare hands.

He closed the fridge, his expression going still when he found Tanner leaning back against the counter, his arms folded across his chest. Brodie considered him for a minute, then screwed off the cap of one bottle and handed it over. Tanner took it, running his thumb across the label, as if considering the contents. "You know," he said, his tone conversational. "I expect most people think that with all her old man's money, Eden's had it pretty damned easy."

Twisting the cap off his own bottle of beer, Brodie quelled the urge to pitch it through the patio door. His pulse running thick and heavy with barely suppressed anger, he took a long, icy swallow, then turned to face Eden's brother. "So why are you really here?" he asked, his tone blunt.

Tanner turned and considered him with a steady gaze, his expression unreadable. There was a long pause; then he spoke, his tone even. "Maybe to tell you that I know what you're up against." One corner of his mouth lifted a little, and a glimmer of amusement appeared in his eyes. "And to talk to you about this damned motocross club. My boys have been riding me pretty hard about it, and I'd like to know what I'm getting into before I'm in over my head."

Brodie met his gaze for a moment, his own mouth lifting just a little. Then he motioned to the table with his bottle of beer. "Have a seat, then. I guess I'd better fill you in."

But his stomach curled up, and a cold feeling of finality washed through him, when he saw three bobby pins lying on the table. Three bobby pins, and he felt as if the ground had been blasted out from under him. And there was nothing left but a long, hard fall.

He was going to pay for this slip in judgment for a very long time. Because she had done it to him again. Only this time, he'd done it back to her. Anger welled up in him, and he clenched his jaw against it; then he picked up the pins and tossed them in the garbage. She wouldn't stand up to her old man—and he'd hurt her back in return.

The two things should have canceled each other out, but they didn't.

Chapter 10

The elevator door swished shut, and Eden closed her eyes and leaned back against the wall, swallowing against the awful feeling of vertigo that washed over her. She shivered and cupped her hands on her upper arms, trying to provide some self-warmth. She was cold. So cold. And she felt as if one wrong move would send her stomach into open revolt—symptoms the family doctor had diagnosed as nothing more than the onset of adolescence when she was twelve and Chase had left home. Symptoms of a nervous stomach, the school physician had diagnosed when she was seventeen and her parents had sent her away to boarding school. Symptoms of severe stress, her doctor had told her six months ago. She didn't dare think about what was causing the symptoms now.

Opening her eyes, she stared at the flashing floor indicator lights, fighting to contain the nearly unbearable ache in her throat. She couldn't let it run away with her, that awful pressure inside her. She had asked, and he had told her. He didn't trust her—and there was nowhere to go with that. There was no way anyone could go back and pick up the pieces, not when something that precious and fragile had been so irrevocably broken. She knew that. But she hadn't expected it to hurt so much.

Nor did she dare think about what her father must have done to Brodie, something so awful that Brodie wouldn't even tell her about it. She was so damned blind not to have picked up on it sooner. It was like watching something cold and hard settle in Brodie's eyes whenever she mentioned her father. And she had been stupid enough to try to defend her father to him. The ache in her chest worsened, and she gripped her arms, fighting against the feelings rising up in her. He had asked her to marry him—she had never expected that. Never.

Swallowing hard, she tipped her head back and closed her eyes again, trying to will away the awful trapped feeling that suddenly pressed down on her. An hour. All she had to do was get through the next hour; then she could go home.

The elevator slid to a stop, the jolt making her stomach rise, and she swallowed again, moving forward as the door opened. Drawing herself together, she stepped off the elevator, turning toward the cardiac unit, dread like a rock in her abdomen. Another family scene. She wasn't sure she had the resources to get through it. She paused outside her father's room, closing her eyes and taking a deep breath, trying to put on a composed front. Letting her breath go, she schooled her face into an even expression and entered. Her false calm lasted maybe thirty seconds. Chase was leaning against the window ledge with his arms folded, and he looked at her, his eyes hard and assessing, a rigid set to his jaw. And Eden's insides dropped away to nothing. She knew that look. Feeling suddenly very weary, she turned to her father.

Her mother was giving him a drink of water through a straw, and she turned, a compressed, annoyed look around her mouth. "Well, it's about time you got here," she said, her tone sharp with recrimination. "I've been trying to reach you all day." She wiped her husband's mouth with a towel, then set the glass down on the bedside stand and looked back at Eden, clearly miffed by her late arrival. "With the condition your father is in, you could at least have the decency to let us know where you are."

Eden gave her mother an unblinking stare, then went over to the bed. The head had been raised, and her father was lying with his eyes closed, the oxygen vent in place, his hands on the covers. She covered one of his hands with her own, noting the telltale flush in his cheeks and the rapid rise and fall of his chest. Keeping her face expressionless, she rubbed her thumb across the back of his hand. "Hi, Dad," she said softly. "How are you feeling?"

He opened his eyes, his fingers clutching at hers. "I'm going to disinherit that damned brother of yours," he rasped, rage making his mouth tremble.

Trying to keep her voice even, she spoke. "Which one?"

"Milt. That damned Milt. I told him I was going to deed the ranch over to him, and he said he didn't want it." His hand started to tremble, and the flush deepened in his cheeks. "Didn't want it! I told him to get the hell out."

Eden closed her eyes and wearily rubbed her forehead. How many times had they been through this before? She'd lost count. Last time he had been determined to deed it to Chase, and Chase had told him in very specific terms what he could do with the ranch. Exhaling heavily, she opened her eyes. "Dad," she said quietly, trying to use reason. "Milt doesn't want to be tied down here. You wanted him in politics, and he is. He has his own life now."

Bruce McCall jerked his hand away from hers and fumbled with the covers, his fingers shaking with agitation.

Her mother started straightening the bed covers, her movements equally agitated. "After all your father has done for him, you'd think he could assume a little family responsibility." Ellie McCall pulled the bedspread straight, then looked at Chase, a reproachful expression in her eyes. "And you have no sense of responsibility, either, Chase. That ranch has been in the family for a hundred years. You'd think you'd take some pride in that."

With his arms still folded across his chest, Chase shot his mother a warning look. "Don't start with me, Ma."

"Well, the *least* you could do is try to talk some sense into Milton."

Chase never moved a muscle. "I am not saying one word to Milt. It's the first time in his whole damned life that he's stood up for himself. I don't see why everyone can't just leave him alone."

Bruce grasped Eden's wrist, his chest falling and rising with alarming speed. "Then I'm going to deed it to you, Eden. To hell with my no-good sons."

Aware of the wild fluctuations on his monitoring equipment, Eden looked at her father. "Dad, what am I going to do with a ranch?" she asked with strained patience. "Why don't you deed it to your grandkids?"

"His grandchildren?" demanded her mother. "That's the most ridiculous thing I've ever heard. He doesn't have any grandchildren, Eden. Not by blood."

White-hot anger flared in her, and Eden drew a deep, stabilizing breath, forcing herself not to respond to her mother's unfeeling remarks. She spoke, her voice very, very quiet. "Get her out of here, Chase."

Chase unfolded his arms and straightened, his expression etched with barely disguised disgust. "Come on, Ma. We're going for a walk."

Ellie drew back her shoulders, as if insulted. "I'm staying right here."

"No, you're not," Chase interjected, his tone flat. "We're going for a walk."

Eden's stomach was a mass of nerves by the time Chase herded her mother out of the room, and for an instant she felt like walking out herself. She gave herself a minute to calm down; then she dropped the safety rail on her father's bed and slid her arm under her father's shoulders. "Come on, Dad. Let's get you on your side," she said quietly. "And I'll rub your back."

It took her twenty minutes to get him settled, and another ten before he drifted off to sleep, and the whole time she tried to beat down the anger that was building up inside her. She wanted to shake her mother until her teeth rattled.

Assured that her father was asleep, she quietly raised the safety rail, then closed the drapes, her insides shaking. She had to get out of there before she went off like a bomb.

After checking her father one last time, she left the room, pulling the door shut behind her. God, she was so angry. She was shaking, she was so bloody damned angry.

Not looking left or right, she headed for the elevators, passing the nursing station and the waiting room without so much as a glance. She was almost to the fire doors when Ellie McCall's voice rang out behind her. "I want to talk to you."

Eden stopped, took a deep breath, then turned on her heel. She stared at her mother. "No, you don't."

Her mother's lips were white, and there was a resentful glitter in her eyes. "Yes, I do. You have your nerve, coming in here playing high-and-mighty."

Fury slicing through her, Eden narrowed her eyes, her voice shaking. "I want to know what in hell you meant with that crack about grandchildren, Mother. Whether you want to admit it or not, there are several children carrying the McCall name, and there will be two more within months, and every damned one of them has as much right to that name as I do. Simply because *you* choose not to acknowledge that fact doesn't make it any less real. And don't you dare insinuate that Megan isn't a part of this family. I may not have borne her, but she's *mine*. And don't you ever forget that."

"That's not what I was implying, Eden. And you know it."

"No, I don't know it, Mother. But I do know that Tanner has two beautiful daughters who have McCall blood in their veins as sure as I'm standing here."

Ellie McCall gave her a disdainful look. "You're so transparent, Eden, and so very shallow. You haven't got an ounce of family honor in you." She drew up her shoulders. "And I demand to know where you were last night."

"You can demand all you want. It's none of your business."

Her mother compressed her mouth into an embittered expression and turned her head. "I thought I raised you better than that." Then Ellie turned back, riveting her with a cold stare, her face stiff with barely disguised scorn. "I suppose you were out acting like some dog in heat with that Brodie Malone."

White-hot anger blossomed in Eden, and she took a step toward her mother, her voice low and shaking. "Don't you ever, *ever* malign him again. I'm sick to death of your imperial attitude, and I'm sick to death of this whole McCall image. Brodie is a good and decent man, and if I'd had half a brain in my head, I would have run off with him seventeen years ago."

Her mother's face went deadly white, and for an instant Eden expected her to slap her. But instead Ellie McCall drew herself in, her skin mottled with indignation. "Brodie Malone is nothing but white trash, and you'd do well to remember that."

Her anger accelerating, Eden leveled a finger at her mother, her voice shaking. "I've got news for you. If there's any white trash around, it's us." She paused, trying to get control of the angry quiver in her voice. "I don't know what's with you, Mother. As soon as something doesn't go your way, you act like it's a federal offense. You think you're the only one who's qualified to make judgments. Well, you're nothing but a bitter, twisted woman, and I'll be damned if I'm going to end up like you." Eden drew a deep, energizing breath, disgust rising up in her. "But I do know one thing. You're the one who stirs up all the trouble in this family. You're the one who gets Dad all riled up. And," she said, her voice tight, "you're the one who feeds on hate."

Ellie McCall blanched. "Don't you speak to me like that."

"I'll speak to you any way I want," Eden retorted, renewed anger welling up inside her. "And I'll tell you this. You'd better reevaluate how you instigate these scenes. The two of you have manipulated and bullied us to the point where you've alienated Chase. Now you've alienated Milt. And I can tell you, you're an inch away from alienating me." Eden drew another deep breath, then took a step back. "You'd better think about that, Mother." She turned and got as far as the fire doors; then she came back, her jaw set. Ellie was leaning against the wall, her face nearly the same color as her silver hair, her face drawn with shock.

Eden planted herself in front of her mother, her renewed rage giving her a kind of strength she'd never had before. "Before I go, I want to know about the little visit Dad paid to Brodie when you found out I was sleeping with him."

Stunned by Eden's bluntness, Ellie stared at her; then she suddenly looked away, unable to hold her daughter's gaze.

"What did he do?" Eden demanded, her voice seething. Her mother still didn't respond, and Eden moved so she was standing squarely in front of her. "What did he do?" she demanded again.

Her mother glanced at her; then her gaze slid away, her body drawn tight. A sudden sick feeling washed through Eden, and she knew. She knew. "He went after him with that damned bullwhip of his, didn't he?" she said, her tone edged with awful comprehension. "Didn't he?"

Still avoiding her gaze, Ellie McCall made a quarter turn and gave a barely perceptible nod.

Immobilized with disgust and horror, Eden stared at her mother, her hands knotted into fists. "God," she breathed, "you two really do deserve each other."

She turned abruptly and headed for the elevators, so much pressure boiling up in her that she could barely see. God, how could they? How *could* they? And she had defended them to Brodie? Lord, but she'd been such a fool. She slapped the button for the elevator, dashing away angry tears, then hit the button again. With parents like that, no wonder she was such a damned failure as a human being.

By the time she reached the lobby, Eden had managed to get herself under control, but just barely. She stepped off the elevator as if she'd been shot out of a gun, bumping someone as she pushed through the group of people waiting to go up.

"Eden!"

She kept walking, the frenzy in her chest making her tremble, the anger and the tears mixing into explosive proportions.

"Eden, damn it! Wait up."

Chase caught her by the arm and hauled her up short, and she jerked her arm free and turned to face him. "What?"

He looked as if he was ready for a fight, and she was prepared to give him one.

"I want to talk to you."

"Well, *I* don't want to talk to *you*."

He grabbed her arm and steered her to an empty corner, his jaw set in determination. "Too bad, Pooky. We're going to talk anyway."

Jerking her arm free again, she turned to face him. "So just what do you have to say, Chase? Are we going to discuss our charming little family?"

"What in hell's gotten into you, anyway?"

Folding her arms in a defensive stance, she stared across the lobby. She gave herself a minute; then she spoke, her voice taut.

"You'd better say what you have to say, bro, because I'm not sticking around very damned long."

She heard him release his breath in an exasperated sigh; then he spoke again. "Will you just look at me?"

Her arms still stiffly folded, she turned, her defenses armed. She didn't say anything; she just stared at him. He had his Stetson in his hand, and he slapped it against his leg, then looked away. After a tense pause he looked back at her, his gaze unwavering. "Ma told me what's going on, and I think you're messing with trouble," he said flatly. "And after what you've just gone through, I think you'd be wise to use a little caution."

She clenched and unclenched her jaw, then spoke, her voice deadly quiet. "And why do you think that, big brother?"

Chase met her gaze, and she knew he was an inch away from losing his temper. Totally fed up with her family, she deliberately pushed him. "Mother thinks he's white trash, and you think he's nothing but trouble. So tell me, wise one. How did you arrive at that conclusion?"

A muscle in his jaw twitched, and he drew a deep breath. "Damn it, Eden. Use your head. His father was the town drunk, his sister was a tramp and Ma just told me how he almost ruined your life when you were seventeen. Hell, he rides around on that black Harley like some damned road warrior, and everyone knows he's got a chip on his shoulder."

She gave him a cold smile. "As opposed to your riding in your black truck, with a chip on *your* shoulder."

He narrowed his eyes, a warning glint appearing. "Don't mess with me, Eden."

Angrier with him than she'd ever been before, Eden stared at him, giving him another tight smile. "You want to make judgment calls on what Mother tells you, then let's make judgment calls." She started ticking things off on her fingers. "His father was a town drunk—as I recall, Devon's mother was pretty much a drunk herself. Mother calls him white trash. I can remember Mother referring to your wife as cheap Indian trash. You and Dad damned near tore the house apart when he found out you were sleeping with Devon. They just shipped me off to boarding school."

The look that appeared in Chase's eyes was enough to strip steel. "Don't you ever," he said, his voice dangerously quiet, "*ever* drag Devon into this crap, or you'll have me to deal with."

She cut him off, openly challenging him. "How does it feel, Chase?" she demanded, her voice shaking. "Just how does it feel?" Her mouth started to tremble and tears burned, but she would not let him see her cry. "Of all people—after the way they looked down their noses at Devon—I expected better from you," she whispered, her voice breaking. Then she turned and walked rapidly out of the hospital, blinded by a pain so intense that it felt as if her chest was coming apart.

She was in such an emotional mess, with so much anger churning up inside her, that she knew she shouldn't be behind the wheel of a car. Especially when she nearly tail-ended a vehicle leaving the parking lot, and again when she had to slam on the brakes to avoid running a red light three blocks from the hospital.

Realizing she was heading for an accident if she didn't get herself together, she pulled over and stopped the car. Folding her arms on the steering wheel, she rested her forehead against them, shaking with so many pent-up feelings that she couldn't tell one from the other. Fighting for something—anything—to override the rage, the self-directed anger, that awful, sinking, churning sensation from finding out what her father had done. Drawing up an image of Megan in her mind, she closed her eyes and hung on to that like a lifeline.

Finally the trembling abated, and she swallowed hard, then consciously loosened her grip on the wheel and straightened. Taking a couple more deep breaths and focusing her mind on the task at hand, she put the car in gear and watched in the rearview mirror for a break in the traffic, then accelerated. Twenty minutes and she would be out of the city. She would take the back way home rather that travel the four-lane. And she was going to think of Meg the entire way.

By the time she reached the secondary highway, a funny numbness had settled in and nothing really registered. Not the beautiful scenery. Not the wild flowers blooming in the ditches. Not the mountains turning purple as the sun settled low on the horizon. She simply functioned, and when she pulled into the

McCall driveway, she wasn't even sure how she'd gotten there. It was as if she'd driven all the way home in a daze.

Selecting the key for the back door, she unlocked it and entered, an oppressive silence greeting her. The house was stuffy and still from being closed up all day, the lingering scent of furniture polish and cleaner hanging lifeless in the air. Dropping her knapsack on the kitchen counter, she went into the eating area, drew back the vertical blinds and slid open the patio doors, the evening breeze tinkling through the wind chimes hanging from the veranda rafters. The veranda was cast in long shadows, but heat still radiated from the board flooring, and it was the first time she realized how hot it had been outside.

There was something about the artificial beauty of her mother's yard that set off all the feelings she had experienced at the hospital, and suddenly her chest was jammed tight. She wanted to go out in that yard and throw her head back and scream, then tear up the perfectly pruned shrubs, the perfectly arranged perennials, and throw one of the perfectly symmetrical plant pots through the greenhouse.

She had never experienced that kind of blind rage in her life, and she started shaking all over again. Turning abruptly from the door, she headed for the stairs, the feeling expanding as she stormed up them. She slammed open her bedroom door, went into the bathroom and wrenched on the shower, yanking her blouse free of her slacks. Feeling as if she were coming apart seam by seam, she went back into the bedroom, feeling trapped and cornered. There was a picture in a sterling silver frame sitting on her chiffonier, a formal pose of her parents taken at her wedding. The instant her gaze fell on it, something snapped inside her, and all the pent-up anger and pain exploded. She picked up the picture and hurled it the full length of the room, the glass shattering into a thousand pieces when it struck the marble fireplace.

It was as if that one act released all the emotions dammed up inside her, and everything came boiling out. Stumbling against the corner of the canopied bed, she went back into the bathroom, tore off her clothes and got into the shower, fury ripping through her. Damn them! Damn them all!

* * *

Her throat raw, her face still puffy from her emotional out-
burst, Eden stood staring out the kitchen window, watching
dusk settle in, feeling strangely calm inside. It was as if she had
emptied everything out, and now there was nothing left. It was
a nice feeling, that kind of emptiness. Maybe, she thought with
a touch of black humor, she should have started smashing
things years ago. She sighed and rubbed her bare arms. She
could only dodge reality so long.

The stillness of the house closed in on her, and she turned
toward the hallway. She couldn't handle that along with everything else—especially with dusk infiltrating the rooms. There
was just too much emptiness. Crossing the parquet foyer, she
slid back the heavy dead bolt and went outside, pulling the door
shut behind her. It was a beautiful night, with the twilight soft
and purple, and oddly welcoming.

She stared down the long drive, an ache forming inside her.
She wished Megan were home. It wouldn't be quite so bad if
Meggie were here. The breeze picked up, feathering her hair
across her face, and she absently tucked it behind her ear, re-
thinking her day. She got a nervous feeling in her stomach when
she thought about Tanner showing up to talk to Brodie, and the
churning got worse when she thought about Chase. She never
should have dragged Devon's history into it—but God, she still
couldn't believe he'd said the things he had. Releasing a long,
heavy sigh, she lifted her head, her expression bleak. She never
should have come home.

The sudden rumble of a motorcycle sent her stomach dropping to her shoes, and she stopped, her heart suddenly lurch-
ing. She could recognize the sound of a Harley anywhere.
Knowing she should turn around and go back into the house,
she hesitated, wisdom wrestling with the awful need to know.
Feeling as if her heart was loose in her chest, she went around
the hedge that separated the yard from the street, the frenzy
inside her increasing.

Brodie was astride the bike on the garage pad, his legs braced
to balance the weight, and he was bent over, fiddling with
something along the gas tank. He straightened and rolled the
throttle a couple of times, then pushed the kickstand away and
turned to check for traffic. He saw her standing there, and he
froze, his body going very still. He didn't have a helmet on, and

the corner of Eden's mouth lifted just a little. Still the rebel. Still thwarting rules. Still Brodie.

Her throat abruptly closed up, and she stuffed her hands in her pockets, an awful ache forming in her midriff. An old memory came rushing back—one that was special and poignant, one she had treasured for half her life. Maybe it had resurfaced because of the time of night—that soft purple dusk. And maybe it was because of the black Harley across the street. But it was so vivid that she could almost feel the heat, the stillness, the scent of flowers in the air. God, it was so clear. So clear.

It had been a night just like this one. Purple twilight. Hot. Still.

Her parents had left for the evening, and she'd gone to their meeting place at the top of the lane, her heart hammering, afraid that he wasn't going to be there, afraid that he was. They had been at the church the night before, and they had very nearly made love for the first time—so very nearly. But Brodie had pulled back at the last minute, telling her that he could not take that kind of chance with her, that when it happened, he wanted to make sure she was protected.

She had known what would happen if she went to meet him. She had been so scared and so nervous, but she had gone, anyway. There had been no sign of Brodie when she reached the lane, but his old black Harley had been parked there, nearly hidden in a canopy of trees. And on the seat, lying in subtle perfection, were two long-stemmed pink tea roses.

She had been so overwhelmed by those two roses, and so much in love with him, that she had stood there trembling, her hands clutched to her breast. And like some almost mystical being appearing out of the darkness, he had come out of the trees, his expression intense and unsmiling. He hadn't said anything; he'd just come to her, then reached out and slowly, softly touched her face.

That night had been the first time they'd made love. He had been so careful with her and so damned gentle. It had been so beautiful, so special, so astounding, she had been in tears afterward. She would never forget it. And every time she saw pink tea roses, she remembered that night.

Wrenched by the memory, she watched him, feeling as if her heart was breaking into a thousand pieces. She had hurt him again, and if she could go back and replay the scene in his living room, she would. Without a second thought, she would grab on to everything he offered and never let go. But it was too late for that. She had betrayed him again.

The bike still rumbling between his legs, Brodie folded his arms and continued to stare at her. She wasn't close enough to see his expression, but even in the dusk, she could see the rigidness in him—and she sensed the anger.

Her vision suddenly blurring, she stood there, drinking in the sight of him, remembering what it had been like to be held by him—really held by him—and she hunched her shoulders against the sudden chill spreading through her. She watched and waited, expecting him to gun the engine and ride off, but he just sat there watching her, his legs braced, as if he was waiting for some sign from her.

An unquenchable flicker of hope broke free, and she pulled her hands out of her pockets and straightened, her heart hammering so hard she could feel it down to her shoes. Terror rooting her, hope pushing her forward, she swallowed hard and started down the sidewalk toward him. The crunch of tires and the slam of a car door registered, but she locked her gaze on Brodie and kept walking, her heart pounding harder with ever step. *Don't leave,* she pleaded silently. *Please don't leave. Just give me the chance to say you were right and I was wrong. And please, please forgive me.*

She stepped off the sidewalk, and he was still there, and she collected herself to break into a run, but a voice spoke behind her. "Eden, wait. I need to talk to you."

She stopped and whirled around, a fearful feeling washing through her when she saw Chase coming around his truck toward her. A kind of panic rose up in her, and she whirled and looked at Brodie, then back at Chase, the panic rising higher. "Not now, Chase," she answered, her voice shaking. "Please, not now."

He reached out and caught her wrist before she had time to bolt, his voice gruff with apology. "I know I damn well don't deserve it, but I'd like you to hear me out."

She looked at him, her expression strained and unsure. The somber look in Chase's eyes made her hesitate, and that hesitation cost her. The roar of the Harley broke the silence, and she spun around, the blood draining from her face as she watched Brodie take the corner, then disappear. And she knew exactly why he had left. A member of her family had shown up, and she had turned her back on him one more time. She stared after him, feeling as if the bottom had dropped out from under her, and she covered her face with her hand, a single sob wrenching free.

Chase tightened his hold on her wrist, trying to draw her hand down. "What?" he demanded roughly. "What?"

Turning away, she shook her head, unable to answer. There was a slight pause; then Chase swore, his voice rough with self-disgust. "Ah, damn." He caught her by the back of the neck and drew her around, pulling her head against his shoulder. "I'm sorry, Pooky," he said, his voice husky with regret. "Sometimes I'm thicker than a damned post."

Eden wiped her face on his shoulder, then took a deep breath and pulled back. "It doesn't matter," she whispered.

Heaving a sigh, Chase let her go. Jamming his hands on his hips, he turned away and stared at the horizon; then he released another sigh and turned to face her. "I didn't even see him over there."

Fishing a tissue out of her pocket, Eden wiped her nose, avoiding his gaze. "I told you, it doesn't matter."

"Damn it," he snapped, "it *does* matter. You wouldn't be bawling if it didn't matter."

Her chin came up, and she shot him a hostile look. "I am not bawling."

Chase watched her with a kind of exasperated brotherly tolerance, then dredged up a warped smile. "Would it help if you gave me a good swift kick?"

Her mouth lifted a little. "Probably."

He stared at her for a moment, his expression intent; then he looked down at the ground, his hands still on his hips. "I didn't mean to bust up your party," he said, his voice gruff, "but I do need to talk to you."

Eden looked away, trying not to let her throat cramp up. It took a minute; then she answered, her own voice uneven. "I'm not sure you busted up anything." She wadded up the tissue, then looked at her brother. "Do you want to come in for a drink?"

He shot her a scandalized look. "I'm not going in there."

Feeling too drained to stand, Eden sat down on the curb and locked her arms around her upraised knees. She stared across the street, then drew a deep, stabilizing breath. "Where's Devon?"

Chase sat down beside her, stretching his legs out in front of him, then folding his arms. There was a funny tone in his voice when he finally responded. "She threw me out."

Eden shot him a startled look. "She *what?*"

Chase turned and looked at her, a sheepish half grin appearing. "I told her what happened at the hospital, and she told me I'd better get my face outta there, and I'd better not come back until I apologized." His grin deepened. "I think I'm going to need a note before she lets me back in."

Ten seconds ago, Eden wouldn't have thought it possible, but he made her laugh. A weak, shaky laugh, but still a laugh. "A note, huh?"

He held her gaze for a minute, then stared off across the street. "Yep. I think so." There was a slight pause; then he spoke again. "And she's right," he said, his voice gruff. "I was way out of line, and I owe you one hell of an apology. And I owe Malone an even bigger one."

Her expression turning solemn, Eden picked up two pebbles from the pavement, rolling them in her hand. "All we have to do is look at the past to know this whole damned town owes Brodie an apology," she said, her tone flat.

"You're probably right." Chase swatted a mosquito off his shirt, then refolded his arms and stared into the gloom. "You want to tell me about it?" he asked quietly.

Releasing a long, weary sigh, Eden rolled the pebbles together. "There's not much to tell," she said softly, her voice uneven. "I fell in love with him when I was seventeen years old, and I bailed out on him when the going got tough. And I bailed out on him again today."

"I've got the truck. You want to go after him?"

She smiled tightly and tossed the pebbles away. "It's a little late for that."

Chase looked at her, his expression somber. "It's never too late, Eden."

She tried to smile as she shook her head. It was too late. Her last chance had just ridden out of town.

Chapter 11

It looked as if a tornado had struck. Birthday streamers and wrapping paper cluttered the veranda floor, and the white wicker table was strewn with paper plates, plastic glasses and leftover cake. The brightly colored bouquets of balloons, which were anchored by weights on either side of the steps, swayed and bounced as Eden's two nephews jostled past in their rush to get to the yard.

Settling down in the wicker chair, Eden rested her arms on the armrests and stretched out her legs, smiling at the antics being played out in her mother's perfect yard. Ellie McCall would have a royal fit if she ever saw the mess—wadded up napkins, long threads of streamers, paper hats and, God forbid, globs of cake icing everywhere—along with the remains of a wild peanut scramble. But Eden really didn't care. Megan had had a boisterous, fun-filled birthday party with her cousins and the three new friends she'd made since school got out.

Watching the kids roughhousing on the lawn, Eden crossed her ankles and settled deeper into the chair. The only fly in the ointment had been a call from Richard that morning—and a courier-delivered gift. A beautiful, antique porcelain doll, dressed in elaborate velvet and old lace, which Meg had loathed on sight. One of her new little friends—a shy, waiflike child who wore faded, secondhand clothes and whose mother was struggling to raise her two children on minimum wage—had been in such awe of that doll that it had nearly broken Eden's heart. Meg, who had always been perceptive beyond her years, had recognized the wistful look on her little friend's face and promptly traded the doll for a battered old go-cart that Trisha's older brother had discarded. As far as Megan was concerned, it was a deal made in heaven. And Eden was so damned proud of her daughter's kindness and generosity that she'd had to go into the house to get herself together.

Eden smiled again as two-year-old Casey teetered, then planted her butt in the grass. Mark, Kate and Tanner's eldest, picked up his sister, dusted off her bum and set her on her feet, and Casey immediately toddled off after the beach ball the other kids were playing soccer with. It was so damned nice, having family close by. Especially for Megan. She was thrilled to bits with her cousins, she adored her uncles and aunts and she loved the freedom of ranch life.

Her expression altering, Eden reached for the glass of lemonade sitting on the table beside her. Her daughter's new-found enjoyment was going to make a move that much harder. But she had pretty much made up her mind that she couldn't stay in Bolton. In spite of how important the family connection was for Meg, Eden knew it would be unbearable for her.

Two weeks had passed since that scene in Brodie's apartment, and it had been two weeks of agony. Hoping for the phone to ring. Hoping that she would run into him downtown, scared to death that she would. Knowing that he was just across the street and deliberately avoiding her. She couldn't go on living like this—her stomach was a mess, and she doubted if there had been more than two nights when she'd gotten a decent night's sleep. And the strain of coping with the day-to-day grind was beginning to show. She knew, as much as it killed her to admit it, that she was going to have to put some distance between them, to try to pick up the pieces and make a new life for herself and Megan. She had a good job waiting for her in Toronto, one that would comfortably support the two of them—and Megan had all her friends there. Yet it made Eden's stomach go into full revolt every time she thought about leaving here, about going back. It would nearly kill her to get on the plane.

Realizing that she was slipping into a danger zone, Eden dragged her attention back to the kids in the yard. At least the birthday party had been a roaring success. When Eden had asked her daughter who she wanted to invite, and Megan had named her cousins first, it had given her an uneasy feeling. She wasn't sure how Tanner and Kate would feel about letting their kids come to Bruce McCall's palatial home, and she suspected they wouldn't have come if she hadn't assured them that Ellie would not be there.

Since it was the first time Meg had family close by for her birthday, Eden would have liked to have the adults there, as well, but she was realistic enough to know that would never happen—not in her lifetime. But Kate, God bless her, had suggested a family get-together on Sunday at their place to celebrate Meg's birthday. Eden could have hugged her. She had hoped that her sister-in-law might break down and stay when she brought the kids for the party, but Kate had made an excuse that she had a ton of shopping to do and would pick them up later. Although Kate had never once said anything to Eden about the McCalls, Eden knew how she felt about them. And though Eden completely understood why Kate had refused to stay, it bothered her nonetheless.

The sound of excited barking broke through Eden's reverie, and she turned her head just as Max came bounding into the yard, dragging a bright yellow plastic bag, a party bow stuck on his head. The kids swarmed around him, laughing and squealing as Meg dropped to her knees, burying her face in the dog's ruff as she hugged him around the neck. "Maxie! You came to my party! This is the best surprise *ever!*"

Feeling as if she'd just taken a blow to the chest, Eden abruptly looked away, the sharp, sudden pain transfixing her. It shouldn't have come as a shock. Meg had spent hours with that dog, and it had gotten to the point where she and Max were practically inseparable. But there was more to it than just the dog—Megan had come up with every excuse in the book to go over to Brodie's, and her daughter's conversation had been peppered with references to Brodie, Max and especially Jason. But this . . . This was something she had never expected.

Through the wrought-iron gate, Eden saw a figure cross the street to the shop, and the sudden pain turned into a nearly suffocating ache. It was Jason, his hands in his pockets, his head down. He had obviously brought the dog over for Meg's party. Nailed by a rush of emotion, Eden looked away, her eyes suddenly smarting.

Squeals of delight drew her attention, and she watched, her stomach churning, as the kids dumped the contents of the plastic bag onto the ground and started pawing through it. Excitement bubbling from her, Megan jumped up and came tearing over, her hair full of grass, chocolate icing smeared all down the front of her T-shirt, parcels clutched in her arms. She was practically beside herself. "Look, Mom! Maxie brought presents!" she said, dumping everything in her mother's lap. "He carried them over all by himself, and he's got a bow on his head, and there's licorice and passes to the movies for everyone, and gum balls—a whole bunch of gum balls."

Feeling as if she'd been stripped raw inside, Eden forced a smile onto her face. She checked out the treasures with her daughter. "Well, aren't you just about the luckiest birthday girl around?"

"Look!" commanded Megan, excitement bubbling from her. "See. Here's the movie pass with my name on it—everybody got one. See? It's from Maxie."

A small glimmer of amusement tugged at Eden's mouth. "Yes, I see. Max writes very well for a dog."

Meg shot her mother a disgusted look, then sorted through the other items she had deposited in Eden's lap. "And here's my package of licorice and gum balls—boy, this is *so* neat. That Max brought all this by himself."

Not sure if she could play out this little scene, Eden eased in a shaky breath and touched the two parcels. "And who are these from?" she asked, her voice tight and uneven.

Megan gave an excited little shiver and picked up the largest one. "I don't know. I don't know, Mom." She tore off the wrapping paper and ripped open the lid, then pushed back the tissue paper. "Oh," she breathed. "Oh, wow." Inside was another box—a yellow one with a distinctive trademark—which held a small compact camera. Megan pried off the second lid and lifted out the camera. "Oh, Mom," she said, her voice hushed with awe. "A camera. My very own camera." She looked up, obviously overwhelmed by the gift. "I told Brodie once I wanted to be a photographer when I grew up—and look, he got me a camera."

Meg hugged the camera to her chest, her eyes ablaze with delight, and Eden looked away, her throat too tight, her chest too tight, her heart too tight. She gave herself a minute to forcibly collect herself, then she swallowed hard and looked back at her daughter.

Megan was turning the camera over and over in her hands, inspecting its features, her touch almost reverent. Eden cleared her throat. "What's in the other package?" she said, her voice very unsteady. Her excitement muted by the enormity of the gift, Megan carefully replaced the camera in the box, then picked up the other present. She opened it with far more care, as if conscious of its specialness. It was a long, slender box, and inside was a silver identification bracelet. Her daughter lifted it out of the box, her eyes wide. "Oh, wow. This is from Jason," she whispered. "He has one just like it, only bigger. I told him how neat I thought it was." She stroked the flat metal surface, her voice wobbling a little. "And it's got my name engraved on it just like his does."

Needing very badly to touch her daughter, Eden picked a small twig out of Megan's hair, then tucked some loose strands behind her ear, her fingers not quite steady. She recalled her daughter's reaction when she'd opened the gift from Richard—and how different that gift was from these. That gift was for a corporate lawyer's daughter to display in her room—these gifts were for Meg.

Experiencing a hollow sense of loss, Eden started gathering the scraps of paper and shredded ribbon, stuffing them into a discarded plastic cup.

"Mom?"

Keeping her expression neutral, Eden glanced at her daughter. "Hmm?"

Megan gave a discomfited grimace, a hopeful look glimmering in her eyes. "Would it be okay if I took them over some birthday cake? You know, to say thank you for letting Max come, and for the presents?''

A constricted feeling gripping her chest, Eden forced an uneven smile. "I think that would be very nice. I'll help you fix up a basket as soon as your guests leave, okay?"

Pleasure shining in her eyes, Megan gave herself an ecstatic little hug. "That'll be so neat."

Kate came to pick up her crew at four, and the other three left right after. Megan helped her mother pick up the trash in the yard, with Max sniffing through the grass for any crumbs he might have missed earlier; then the three of them went into the house. Eden smiled as Max sat down in front of the sink, watching the action with bright interest. Her mother would fall over in a dead faint if she knew a dog had been in her house.

With Megan giving orders, Eden fixed a basket of goodies to take over to Brodie and Jase—large wedges of cake with decorations and candles intact, a thermos of lemonade, freshly steamed hot dogs with all the trimmings, chips, napkins, party favors and what was left of a cold roast in the fridge for Max. She insisted that Meg change her T-shirt, and her daughter came bouncing back into the kitchen, wearing a bright red sweater that made Eden smile. She handed Megan the basket at the patio door, smoothed down wisps of hair, then slipped her hands into her pockets. "Well, Little Red Riding Hood, don't talk to any wolves on the way over, okay?"

Megan grinned at her, anticipation sparkling in her eyes. "I won't." She glanced at the dog, who was watching her with anticipation. "Come on, Maxie. Let's go."

Eden slid open the screen for her, trying to ignore the sudden ache in her chest. "Phone me if you're going to be awhile, all right?"

Megan nodded as she brushed by, Max trotting behind her. Meg stopped on the second step and turned, her expression suddenly altering. She looked up at her mother, her gaze direct and very solemn. "Just so you know, I'm really glad I got you for a mom," she said.

Hit by a rush of unbearably strong feelings, Eden took a deep breath, somehow finding the strength to hold her small daughter's gaze and to erect an unsteady smile. "And I'm glad I got you," she responded, her throat aching. Megan stared up at her, as if confirming her mother's answer, then she grinned and hoisted the handle of the basket on to her other arm. "I think I need Uncle Chase's truck."

Telling Max to come, she started down the stairs, eager to be on her way, the silver bracelet glinting on her small wrist, the camera tucked into one corner of the basket, her father's gift long gone. "See you later, Mom."

"See you later."

Folding her arms against the hollow feeling around her heart, Eden watched her daughter and the dog disappear around the corner of the house, grief rolling in on her. She wondered if she would ever recover.

On Saturday Megan and Eden went shopping. The water pistols were Megan's idea. Eden had some reservations about buying them for all the kids, but she really couldn't see the harm, providing some firm rules were established. No squirting in the house. No squirting anyone in the eyes, ears or nose. No squirting grown-ups. No squirting Allison and Casey. And if a fight started, Eden was going to confiscate them all. Megan fervently agreed, almost licking her lips in anticipation.

As soon as the purchases were in the bag, Megan immediately began plotting about getting her hands on her two youngest cousins' weapons. After all, Allison and Casey were too small for water fights. Eden was firm; she'd bought five so everyone would have one—and that meant *everyone*.

When they arrived at the Circle S on Sunday afternoon, Megan practically fell out of the car in her haste to tell her cousins what she'd conned her mother into. The boys were beside themselves. Eden lined the whole bunch of them up, firmly laying down the rules. Everyone nodded, willing to promise her anything while she was still holding the bag of toys. All except four-year-old Allison. She watched her aunt, expectation glinting in her eyes. Eden suspected Miss Allison was going to hold her own just fine.

Kate, who was standing on the back step, rolled her eyes, then shook her head. "Do you have *any* idea what you're unleashing here?"

Eden grinned and came up the back steps, a large cardboard box holding a birthday cake and marinated salad in her arms, feeling lighter than she had for a long time. "Come on, Auntie Kate. What's a little water?"

Holding open the screen door, Kate cast her sister-in-law a long-suffering look. "Did I ever tell you what it was like around here the first time Tanner gave the boys lariats? With Burt egging them on?"

Trying not to laugh, Eden entered the utility room. "No, but I can imagine."

"I don't think so," Kate responded darkly. "Every time I came out of the bathroom or a bedroom, I got ambushed. When I caught them trying to rope Burt's feet, with him giving instructions, I banned the ropes from the house. So Mark roped all the blossoms off my geraniums."

"Poor Kate."

Kate cast her a sharp glance, a glint of humor appearing in her eyes. "You just wait, Eden McCall. At some point all hell is going to break loose with those water pistols, and it's going to be all your fault."

Eden grinned. "Lord, but you're suspicious."

"It's a learned condition. Believe me."

They entered the kitchen, and Eden set the box on the kitchen counter, then dragged the strap of her knapsack off her shoulder. The house was silent—unusually so. "Where is everybody?"

Kate straightened a chair, then leaned over and tested the water level in a huge bouquet of mixed flowers sitting in the middle of the big harvest table. "Chase and Devon took Burt down to the barn to check out the new team of Belgians he and Cyrus just bought. Casey's having a nap, and Tanner's off to some meeting." Kate straightened the bouquet, then turned and gave Eden a grin. "So what do you want to do? Make the potato salad or fry chicken?"

Taking the butcher's apron Kate handed her, Eden gave her sister-in-law a disgruntled look. "How come Devon gets to go look at horses and I get stuck in the kitchen?"

"Because," Kate answered, "you're here and Dev is out looking at horses. And because kitchens give her hives. Now, potato salad or chicken?"

"Potato salad."

Kate gestured toward the fridge. "Then go to it. Everything's in there." She grinned again, a mischievous glint in her eyes. "We should only need a couple of gallons."

Eden cast her sister-in-law a rueful look. "Gee. Thanks a lot."

The kitchen was sweltering by the time Kate finished frying a platter full of chicken, so they decided to have supper on the big old veranda. The veranda had been screened-in the year before, and it was blessedly cool. Devon, back from inspecting the horses, dryly commented that it was probably a wise choice, seeing as it was the only place in the whole house that could be hosed down after.

Cyrus, Burt and Chase returned to the house just before six, with Burt wondering where in hell supper was. Kate told him they would eat as soon as Tanner got home, and that he'd better behave himself or he wouldn't get any birthday cake. His old eyes twinkling with mischief, the eighty-four-year-old told her she was a bossy bit of goods and he had half a mind to fire her. Kate told him she would quit first, and if he didn't clear out of the kitchen, he wouldn't get anything at all. It was all Eden could do to keep from laughing. Burt loved to stir things up, and Kate let him.

Auntie Devon herded the kids into the utility room to supervise the washing of hands, and before very long there was some sort of debate going on. Then Devon's voice overrode the chatter. "The idea, boys," she said in a droll tone, "is to get your hands wet *before* you wipe them on the towel." Kate shot Eden a quick glance, a sparkle of barely contained laughter in her eyes, and she turned, her shoulders starting to shake. Knowing that they didn't dare get caught laughing or the kids would be all over them like ants, Eden headed for the living room. "I think I hear Casey," she said, her voice choked. "I'll go get her."

Eden had Casey up and was putting on her sunsuit when the other kids came tearing up the stairs, arguing over something as they went into the boys' room. Casey clapped her hands, then tried to crawl off Eden's lap. "Oh, no, you don't, little one. Clothes first." She was just doing up the straps when she heard Tanner's voice downstairs. She lifted the toddler up, then kissed her niece and blew a raspberry on her chubby little neck.

She was awarded with a chuckle, and she gave her niece a hug. "Daddy's home. Do you want to go see Daddy?"

Casey jabbered something that Eden couldn't decipher and pointed to the door, giving her a huge smile. Her heart giving a little jump, Eden shut her eyes and hugged her niece again, reveling in the feel of a little one in her arms. God, she was so precious.

The toddler jabbered again and squirmed to get down, and Eden gave her another tight squeeze. "You are a persistent little thing, aren't you?" Picking up a sun hat, she turned toward the door. "Let's go, squirt. You can mash birthday cake in your hair again."

The kitchen was empty and the food was gone, so Eden headed for the veranda. She stepped out, letting the screen door slam behind her. Chase was leaning against the veranda railing, a beer in his hand, a funny expression on his face. Eden shot him an intent look, then set Casey down, steadying her until she got her balance. Then Eden straightened, a light-headed feeling washing through her when she saw Brodie Malone sitting in an old rocking chair at the far end of the veranda, a beer in his hand, deep in conversation with Tanner and the other men. Jason, his arms folded, was propped against the rail beside him, with Max sprawled at his feet.

Shock immobilizing her, she swiveled her gaze to Chase, caught completely off balance. He gave her a warped little smile and lifted one shoulder in a small so-now-you-know shrug, and the bottom immediately dropped out of her stomach. Feeling as if she was standing on thin air, she looked at Kate, who met her gaze briefly, then quickly busied herself with arranging the food on the big trestle table. "Tanner had them out to look at that piece of property," her sister-in-law commented, her voice just a little too innocent. "So I told him to bring them home for supper."

Before she had time to assimilate the fact that she'd been set up, Brodie looked up and saw her, his expression going very still. Eden realized that he'd had no idea she was there. She held his gaze for a frozen moment; then she abruptly looked away, an awful, shaky feeling sliding through her. Oh, God. Oh, God. This had all been engineered.

Her heart fluttering wildly in her throat, she stared blindly across the yard, her stomach rolling over. Lord, how was she going to get through this? How was he?

The screen door slammed behind her, and Megan came tearing out, her braid full of straw and a huge grass stain down the front of her shirt. Max scrambled up, his ears perked, and Megan stopped, throwing her arms wide in enthusiastic welcome. "Maxie!" The dog bounded over to greet her, his tail wagging, his eyes bright. As if she hadn't seen him for days, Megan went down on her knees to give the dog a huge hug.

It was the weirdest sensation—as if she was standing back, looking through a long, narrow tunnel, somehow disconnected from everything that was happening around her. She heard Megan speak to Brodie and Jase, rattling on about them coming to her second party. And she heard Jase laugh. Then Chase caught her hand, giving it a hard squeeze as he ambled past her, crossing to the other men. He gave the top of Megan's head an affectionate knuckle rub as he passed, then spoke, his voice an easy drawl. "Are you ready for another beer, Malone?"

Realizing that Tanner was watching her with a steady, reflective look, Eden flexed her hands and turned toward the table. "Is there anything else I can do, Kate?" she asked, her voice sounding unnatural in her own ears.

Kate gave her a worried look, then forced a smile. "No, that's it." She turned and spoke to the men. "Help yourselves, everyone. Plates and cutlery at the end of the table." She glanced down at Meg. "Meggie, honey, would you please go tell the boys and Allison that supper's ready?"

Needing to distance herself, Eden sat in the porch swing at the far end of the veranda. Drawing up one leg, she locked her arms around it, feeling very shaky. Aware of the thickening sensation in her chest, she stared across the yard. It was ironic—Brodie had just been taken into the bosom of her family, whether he realized it or not, and she was the one who was feeling strangely misplaced.

Aware that that kind of thinking was only going to make her feel worse, she swallowed hard and turned back, knowing she was going to have to play this out somehow. Her gaze fell on Devon, who was sitting on the veranda railing, moving a leaf around with the side of her boot, her expression thoughtful. She lifted her head, her somber gaze connecting with Eden's, a wealth of compassion in her eyes. And Eden knew, from somewhere deep inside her, that Devon Manyfeathers knew exactly how she was feeling. Eden held her sister-in-law's gaze for a moment, then managed a small half smile. Devon stared back at her; then she, too, managed a half smile in return. Oddly braced by that one small exchange, Eden released a shaky sigh and got up. She would get through this somehow.

The leftover food had been taken into the house, the birthday cake and ice cream devoured, and the adults were sitting around enjoying coffee when Eden heard Chase laughing in the house. Then she heard the excited babble of all the kids trying to talk at once. She didn't think much about it until Chase came out, a water pistol in each hand, looking very much like a gunslinger. Devon, her rounded belly pressing against an oversized tank top, was leaning against the veranda pillar talking to Brodie, her arms folded, her ankles crossed. With a bad-boy grin, he leveled the pistols at his wife. "Stick 'em up, Manyfeathers. I gotcha covered."

Not moving a muscle, Devon leveled a look at her husband. "You might want to rethink that, McCall," she said, her tone very dry.

Devilry glinting in his eyes, Chase widened his stance and tipped his straw Stetson back with the barrel of one gun; then he squirted her square in the belly in a one-two action.

It happened so fast that Eden had no idea how she did it, but Devon moved. Grabbing Chase's arm, she swept his feet out from under him, and suddenly Chase was flat on his back on the floor, a stunned look on his face. Devon gave him a sweet, sweet smile as she dumped a pitcher of cold water on his chest. "I told you," she said, still smiling that smile, "that you ought to think about it, slick."

Eden bent over and burst out laughing, loving, *loving,* the look on her brother's face. Before she had time to get her guard up, Chase was on his feet, grabbing her in a headlock. He still had possession of one pistol, and he unloaded it in her face, wrestling to control her arms. "You," he said, his voice breaking with exertion, "are not supposed to laugh." Eden was fighting to reach the other pistol at Chase's feet, but he kicked it away just as she broke free. She backed up, shaking out her arms, affecting a wrestler's stance. Jason was standing behind Chase, laughing at her, and she narrowed her eyes at him, then made a dive for the loose water pistol, grabbed it and let Jase have it square in the chest.

He stared at her as if he couldn't believe what she'd done; then he set his glass down and came toward her, a wicked gleam in his eyes. And then all hell broke loose.

By the time a truce was declared, the veranda was awash and there wasn't a drop of water left in the big wading pool Kate had put out for the kids. The adults were soaked, the kids were soaked, the dog was soaked. The only one who was completely dry was Tanner. Burt had gotten wet helping the boys reload, and Cyrus got blasted by the hose by accident. But Tanner sat there, smiling like a benevolent uncle—at least until Casey toddled over to him with a plastic glass of water, her pants sagging. She jabbered something at him, gave him a big grin, then let him have it. And the startled look on Tanner's face was worth the price of admission.

Praising her niece, Eden propped herself against one of the support posts, so out of breath from wrestling and laughing and inhaling water that she felt as if her lungs were seizing up. Kate went by, shaking water off her hands, her shirt plastered to her, her face flushed. "And I thought the *kids* were going to be the problem?"

Tanner was watching Kate, a look of amused tolerance in his eyes. "Nice shirt," he said gruffly, referring to the drenched T-shirt plastered to her chest.

Chase, who was standing off to the side, his forehead resting against Devon's, his chest heaving, grinned like a fool and tried to get his hands under his wife's oversized tank top. "Yeah," he responded, his tone provocative. "Nice shirt."

Laughter bubbling up in her chest again, Eden leaned over and wrung water out of her hair, then braced her hands on her thighs, still trying to haul air into her lungs. There wasn't a dry square inch on her. But Lord, it had felt good to laugh like that.

A towel appeared in front of her face, and she dragged her hair back and straightened, meeting Brodie's amused gaze. His shirt was soaked, and his hair was all wet and slicked back, and she knew he was an inch away from laughing. "And I thought this was going to be a nice little Sunday dinner."

Her heart rolling over in her chest, she took the towel, laughter still bubbling up inside her. "You mean it *wasn't?*"

Holding her gaze, he shook his head, his eyes still glinting with humor. "I think I can safely say that there was a serious breach of etiquette here."

She managed a shaky laugh, her chest suddenly aching. She didn't think she had ever loved him more than she did at that very minute, and Lord, but it hurt. More than anything, more than her next breath, she wanted to step into his arms and rest her head on his shoulder. She wanted to hold on to him and never let him go.

She shivered, not from being cold and wet, but from all the feelings welling up inside her, and she opened her mouth to speak, to tell him how wrong she'd been. But suddenly his expression shut down and his eyes turned cold. "You'd better get changed," he said flatly, then turned, sweeping up a plastic sand pail that had been tossed onto the floor. Eden watched him go, the familiar pain returning with a vengeance. Feeling as if her blood had turned to ice, she turned and went into the house. She would have to go back to Toronto. There would be too much heartache if she stayed around here.

Casey was in bed and Allison was on her way by the time Eden came back downstairs. She'd borrowed some dry clothes from Kate, then had a long, hot shower. Not because she really wanted one. It had simply provided her with a good excuse to go off by herself, to try to deal privately with the ache around her heart, to try to come to terms with the rest of her life. To try to get rid of the persistent lump in her throat.

Devon was alone in the kitchen, wiping down the stove. She turned as Eden came in and gave her a long, considering look; then she tossed the dishcloth in the sink and wiped her hands on her jeans. "Come on. We're going for a walk."

Eden opened her mouth to protest, but Devon cut her off. "Brodie's gone, Eden. And Kate's putting the girls to bed. Cyrus and Burt are watching a baseball game on TV, and Tanner and Chase have taken the boys and Meg out to check the cattle."

Twisting her straight black hair up under a Toronto Blue Jays ball cap, Devon put her hand on Eden's shoulder and pushed her toward the door. "One of Tanner's brood mares came up lame, and I told him I'd check her out."

Not having the energy to argue, Eden complied. The sun hadn't set, yet, but the shadows were long and the robins were chirping. A cool breeze was coming off the mountains, and Eden closed her eyes and turned her face into it, the wind clearing her damp hair off her face.

Releasing a sigh, she shoved her hands in the pockets of Kate's jeans, appreciating Devon's silence. They were halfway to the barn when Devon finally spoke. "How's your dad doing?"

Eden let her breath go, a weary tone in her voice. "Devon, you don't have to do this."

Devon turned in front of her, resting her hands on her hips. "Listen, Eden. You need to talk to someone."

Her expression hesitant, Eden met her sister-in-law's gaze. "No one wants to talk about him."

"No," Devon agreed. "They don't. Chase doesn't. Tanner doesn't. Kate doesn't. And I'd just as soon not discuss him, either, but you're carrying it all, and the least I can do is listen."

Eden stared at her, then managed a wry smile. "What are you going to do—toss me on my back if I don't?"

Amusement glinted in Devon's eyes. "I might." She stared at Eden for a moment; then she turned and started walking. "So, how's your father?"

Fortifying herself with a deep breath, Eden started talking. "He's better. His cardiologist has recommended a bypass, but Dad is so damned bullheaded about any medical treatment. I think I had him talked into it yesterday, but all that could change tomorrow. You just never know. And I had the doctor talk to Mom about not getting him all riled up, and things have been much better."

"How's your mother been?"

Eden gave a humorless smile and kicked a rock off the path in front of her. "I suppose Chase told you about the blowup at the hospital."

Devon cast her a quick glance and nodded. Eden heaved another sigh. "She's been very distant and very civil." Eden shrugged, another wry smile appearing. "Sometimes I think she enjoys being a martyr."

"And Richard?" Devon prompted.

"I don't talk to Richard. I have my lawyer talk to his lawyer. If Richard has anything to say to me, he has to go through them." She snapped a branch off the clump of willow growing by the trail, absently crushing the silver leaves between her fingers. "He made arrangements to talk to Megan on her birthday, but that's the last I've heard from him." A cramp formed in her throat, and it took a minute before she could get it to relax. "But I wake up at night wondering when he's going to strike next."

"Remember, you've got family here," Devon counseled quietly. "Don't be afraid to ask for help."

Eden shrugged, feeling suddenly very raw. "I don't want to do that," she said, her voice uneven. "Especially with the hell that Kate went through with her ex-husband."

"You don't need to worry about Kate. She's tougher than she looks."

The path narrowed, and Devon followed Eden in silence until it widened; then she stepped back beside her. Her gaze fixed on the trail, Eden thought about how much Devon had changed since she and Chase had been married. Before, she would have stood back and been an observer, offering little and asking nothing. Always removed. But that had changed. Devon had pushed past her natural reserve and cautiousness, and she'd let all her old guards down. Maybe, Eden thought, it was all a matter of trust. Jarred by that random realization, she shoved her hands deeper into her pockets and focused on the landscape, not wanting to think about trust. It hurt too damned much.

They were at the corrals before Devon spoke again. "So," she said, her voice deceptively casual, "I guess that leaves Brodie."

Eden stopped, her chest suddenly tight; then she abruptly turned and started walking back up the path, feeling stripped down to the bone. Devon caught her by the arm, her grip restraining. "Whoa, there. Whoa," she said, using the same, husky, soothing tone she used when she was working with a high-strung horse. "Just talk, Eden. Let's just talk, okay?"

Fighting the growing pressure in her chest, Eden closed her eyes and folded her arms across her middle, her stomach jumping and her lungs unable to function. God, but everything hurt.

Devon slid her arm around her shoulders, gently urging her to move. "Come on. There's a flat rock over here. Let's sit and watch the sun go down."

Too drained to fight, Eden let her sister-in-law draw her off the path and onto the rock. Wrapping her arms around her upraised knees, she rested her forehead against them, her stomach still rebelling against the awful flutter of nerves. Devon rubbed her shoulders for a moment, then started to speak. "I've been where you are," she said, her voice husky with remembering. "I was eleven years old when I met your brother, and I fell in love with him on sight."

Caught off guard by Devon's admission, Eden turned her head, watching her sister-in-law, the tightness in her chest easing a little when she saw the soft, reminiscent smile hovering around Devon's mouth. The other woman plucked a piece of broadleaf grass, then began absently shredding it, her expression intent. "He was my best friend. He was my buddy. He was my soul mate," she continued, her soft smile wavering a little. She dropped the shredded leaf and looked away, her arms draped across her upraised knees.

Sensing the wealth of emotion in Devon, Eden watched her, waiting. Finally Devon took a deep breath and plucked another piece of grass. "He wanted us to get married when I was eighteen, but I couldn't let go of all my fears and self-doubts— and I'm not sure things would ever have changed, except I hurt him one too many times, and I knew if I didn't make a move, I'd lose him for good."

Caught in her own thoughts, Devon began to peel the leaf in strips, her expression heavily reflective. "It was really hard for me to let go of all my protective barriers," she said very quietly. "I'd feel threatened and I'd tried to pull back—to close up—but Chase kept coming at me, kept pushing me." A wry smile appeared, and she shook her head. "Now I can fight with the best of them, and I've learned how to push back." She looked at Eden, her gaze direct and solemn. "But it wasn't easy. I don't think the good things ever are."

Her head still resting on her knees, Eden considered her sister-in-law for a moment, then spoke, her tone guarded. "Why are you telling me this, Devon?"

Devon held her gaze for a minute, then went back to shredding the grass. There was a long pause as she considered her response; then she finally answered. "Maybe because I know what Brodie's life was like. I lived it. My mother was an alcoholic, and so was his father. I was just neglected, but Brodie's father was a mean, ugly drunk. I can't imagine what Brodie's life must have been like. It's bad enough growing up with that stigma hanging over your head—a parent who's the town drunk, living on welfare in a run-down shack, everyone in town looking down on you as if you're nothing but dirt. You feel that stigma every day of your life. But for Brodie, it was worse—his father should have been horsewhipped for the way he treated those two kids."

The reference to a whip made Eden's insides go cold, and she turned her forehead against her knees, feeling for a moment that she might be sick. She waited for the nausea to pass, then she lifted her head and looked at her sister-in-law, her expression drawn. "And just what did he do to them?" she whispered unevenly.

Devon shot her a sharp look, then glanced away. "He didn't tell you?"

"No. He's never talked about it. Never talked about his father or his sister."

Devon sighed and folded her arms across her knees, staring off across the pasture. "Then it's not for me to say," she finally answered. "But I can tell you that Brodie had every reason to be hostile. Except he did something with it. A lot of kids who grow up in those kinds of conditions get buried by them— Brodie didn't. He dug himself out, put it behind him and made something of himself—against all odds, he did that," she said, her voice laced with a hint of anger. "It's too bad some people can't see that."

"Meaning my parents."

Devon looked at her from under the bill of her baseball cap, her dark, solemn eyes suddenly unreadable. She stared at Eden for a moment, then looked back across the pasture. "How old were you when you first got tangled up with him?" she asked.

Eden exhaled heavily. "Seventeen."

"What happened?"

Feeling absolutely lifeless inside, Eden told her. She also made it very clear that the blame was hers.

"You were very young," Devon countered quietly. "You were bound to make mistakes."

A mirthless smile lifted one corner of Eden's mouth. "But I'm not very young now. And I made the same mistake again."

And she had. Only this time it was worse. She had made it for all the wrong reasons.

Chapter 12

With the heavy velvet drapes pulled against the bright sunshine in the formal sitting room, Eden lay on the white brocade French provincial sofa, her arms draped across her eyes. It was so heavy in the house, and she had such a blinding headache that she had spots behind her eyelids. She and Chase had both suffered with migraine headaches as kids. Chase didn't get them anymore, but she did, and she was thankful this wasn't one.

This room had always been off-limits for casual use—white carpets, white furniture, flawless cherrywood tables adorned with antique porcelain figurines, heavy crystal glassware and a silver candelabra, precisely positioned, with tasteful pastel artwork hung appropriately on the Wedgwood blue walls. And that was the reason she was in here—because it was off-limits, and because it was the last place her mother would think to look for her.

Ellie McCall had returned home the previous afternoon to take care of some business for Eden's father and to collect a change of clothes. Her mother had been tight-lipped and coldly civil, occasionally dropping snide little comments, and the strain was beginning to get to Eden—a Miss Ellie headache,

Martha used to call them. Eden had made up her mind that she was not going to get drawn into another battle with her mother. Her father's condition had finally stabilized, and bypass surgery was scheduled in ten days. She was going to stay until he was back on his feet because she felt duty bound, and because she was the only one who could get him to comply with his doctor's orders. Then she was leaving, and she was never coming back. At least, not to this house.

"You know you're not supposed to by lying on that sofa, Eden. It wasn't meant for that."

Keeping her arms over her eyes, Eden spoke, her tone deceptively mild. "Just what was it meant for, Mother?"

"Well, certainly not that kind of abuse."

Moving her arms onto her forehead, she stared at her mother, who was standing in the archway clasping a wide gold bracelet on her wrist. The throbbing in Eden's head increased, and she clamped her jaw together so hard that she could feel the pressure all the way up to the top of her head. Trying to ignore the sudden churning of acid in her stomach, she assessed the woman standing rigidly in the doorway. "There just isn't an ounce of give in you, is there?" she asked quietly.

"And what would you know about *giving?*" her mother responded bitterly.

Eden stared at her, not rising to the bait. "You know what I can't figure out? I can't figure out how come us kids turned out as well as we did, with you the way you are and Dad the way he is," she said, maintaining that same mild tone. "You really aren't very nice people, you know."

Ellie McCall went perfectly still, her gaze riveted on Eden, a strange expression paralyzing her face. Her mother stared at her for a moment, then roughly adjusted her bracelet, her mouth tight. She shot Eden a condemning glance. "To think, after all that your father and I have done for you, that you could actually say something like that. You're a very selfish person, Eden, and you've really disappointed me."

The acid stopped churning in her stomach and Eden experienced a sudden sense of release. "That's fine, Mother. Because you've really disappointed me, too. And I've discovered I don't like you very much."

Her face white and her mouth trembling, Ellie McCall opened her mouth to respond, but Eden cut her off. "I'm not going to get into another yelling match with you, Mother," she said, her tone very quiet. "And I don't want to hear anything you have to say. If you want me to stick around to see Dad through his surgery, then I suggest you keep your narrow-minded opinions to yourself. I'm not playing your little games anymore." She closed her eyes and drew one arm back across them. "You'd better get going," she said in that same even tone. "Or you're going to be late for your appointment with the surgeon."

There was a long, tense silence, then Eden heard the front door close. Letting out a shaky breath, she swallowed against the frantic flutter in her throat, her insides feeling like jelly. For the first time in her whole life, she felt as if she'd been set free.

"Has Grandma gone?"

Eden rested her arm on her forehead and met her daughter's somber gaze. "Yes, she's gone."

Megan crossed the room and knelt down beside her, an anxious look on her face. "I brought you an ice pack," she said softly. "Martha said it would help your headache."

Lightly stroking her daughter's cheek, Eden managed a small smile. "I think," she said, trying for lightness, "that my headache just went out the door."

A sudden glint appeared in her small daughter's eyes, and a dimple appeared at the corner of Megan's mouth. "You mean Grandma?"

Eden took Megan's not-quite-clean hand and rubbed her thumb across her daughter's knuckles, amusement tugging at her mouth. "Yes. I mean Grandma."

Grinning at her, Megan pulled her hand free and scrubbed at her nose, then put the thin white ice pack on Eden's forehead. "Martha said to use this, Mom," she said, her tone warning.

The headache had faded into a low-grade throb, but the coldness felt wonderful. Eden repositioned the pack and smiled at her daughter. "Well, I guess we'd better not argue with Martha, had we?"

Propping her chin in her hand, Megan shook her head. "Nope." She watched her mother for a moment, then began fiddling with a lock of Eden's hair. "Mom?"

"What?"

"Can I go over to Brodie's? He asked me if I wanted to help put new videos on the shelves—and Martha's saved some bones for me to take to Max."

Feeling suddenly very exposed, Eden shifted her arm back over her eyes, her throat closing up on her. Brodie. She had seen him once since Sunday. She had stopped in at the post office to pick up the mail, and he'd been coming out of the hotel. As soon as he'd seen her, he'd turned and gone the other way. Lord, but it had hurt. Swallowing to ease the clog of emotion, she answered her daughter. "Yes, you can go, Meg. But you be home by five, okay?"

"Aren't you going to go see Grandpa?"

Shifting her arm, Eden looked at her daughter, then reached out and wiped a smudge from her cheek. "No," she said, avoiding her daughter's gaze. "They're going to be doing tests on him all day, and Grandma will be there with him."

Rubbing her nose again, Megan got to her feet. "Martha just made some lemonade from real lemons. Do you want some?"

Adjusting the ice pack, Eden shifted her head into a more comfortable position. "No thanks, honey. I'm going to get up in a minute anyway."

"Okay. See you later, Mom."

"See you later."

Eden watched her daughter disappear, then closed her eyes. Lord, but she was tired. So tired.

"Mom," a soft voice whispered from somewhere far off. "Are you asleep?"

Completely disoriented, Eden opened her eyes, not sure where she was. A familiar painting took shape on the wall, and she wet her lips, pulling her hair back from her face with both hands. She blinked a couple of times, then focused on the shape standing in the doorway. "Yes. I'm awake."

"Martha told me not to wake you if you were asleep." Megan made a guilty little grimace, then gestured toward the kitchen. "Dinner's ready."

Still feeling half drugged, Eden lifted her arm and squinted at her wristwatch. Six-thirty. She'd been out cold for four solid hours. Wetting her lips again, she opened her eyes wide and then sat up, her head still swimming a little. She hadn't slept that soundly for days. Maybe she was going to survive after all.

Martha had the table laid out on the veranda. The housekeeper had prepared a simple meal, which suited Eden just fine, and they sat outside after they finished eating, watching the shadows lengthen, watching dusk settle in. Martha was working on yet another crochet afghan, and Eden idly wondered how many the housekeeper had made over the years.

Slouched in her chair, her feet propped up, Eden laced her hands across her stomach as she drowsily watched the housekeeper finish another row. "Did you ever keep track of how many of those you've made?"

Martha glanced up at her, a twinkle in her eyes. "Bloody hundreds."

Eden gave the older woman a sleepy smile. "You aren't supposed to say bloody, Martha. My mother will wash your mouth out with soap."

Martha lifted her arm, yanking a long loop of wool out of the skein. "Not bloody likely," she said tartly. "Miss Ellie knows a good thing when she sees one." She looked at Megan, who was standing with her arms looped over the veranda rail, blowing bubbles through a small wire hoop. "I saw Brodie today," the housekeeper mentioned a little too casually.

Eden tipped her head back and closed her eyes, experiencing the familiar jolt of regret in her middle.

"He's looking very grim—except with the little one," Martha continued, oblivious to Eden's silence. "He would have made an excellent father, he would."

Knowing she was going to end up in tears if the housekeeper didn't stop, Eden made herself take a breath. "Please don't, Martha," she whispered unevenly.

"Well," the housekeeper continued, as if Eden hadn't spoken, "it's cooled down enough. I think I'll go rustle up a cake to take over to old Mr. Ferris. His wife is in the nursing home, and I think he's finding it pretty lonely." Stuffing the crocheting into a huge canvas bag, she heaved herself to her feet. "How would you like to give me a hand, Meggie? You can run the Mixmaster."

Eden had mastered a little trick over the past couple of weeks. If it was really quiet, and if she closed her eyes and stayed focused, she could manage not to think at all.

It was starting to get dark when she finally went in. And the only reason she went in then was because it was well past Megan's bedtime. She entered the kitchen, closing the patio screen door behind her, the brightness of the track lighting making her squint. Megan was at the kitchen table coloring, her baseball pajamas on, her hair freshly shampooed and braided, her face shiny and clean. Eden gave her daughter an amazed look. "Don't tell me you've had your bath already? And without a fight?"

Her head bent, Megan kept on coloring. "Martha said I could take the bubble stuff in with me." She leaned back and appraised her artwork, then selected another crayon. "She said I could fill the whole bloody room with bubbles for all she cared, 'cause she's going to clean it tomorrow."

Knowing the game her daughter was playing, Eden grabbed her around the neck and gave her head a little shake. "What am I going to do with you, Miss Megan?"

Megan giggled and hunched her shoulders up around her ears. "Gotcha, Mom."

Eden gave her daughter's neck another little squeeze, then leaned over to see what she was working on. It was clearly a picture of Max. "Hey. That's pretty good, kiddo."

"Except his body is too long."

"Where's Martha?"

Still intent on her coloring, Megan responded, "She went to take the cake we baked to Mister... that guy."

Eden picked up a crayon off the floor, then turned toward the kitchen cupboards. "Would you like some hot chocolate before you go to bed?"

"Yes, please."

The doorbell rang, and Megan scrambled out from behind the table, obviously wanting to beat her mother to it. "I'll get it! I'll get it!"

Locating the can of chocolate in the cupboard, Eden closed the door and was about to set the can on the counter when Megan screamed, "No! No, I'm not going!"

Alarm shooting through her, Eden dropped the can and started for the hallway. She collided with Megan at the kitchen door and shoved her daughter behind her, the blood draining from her face when she saw a coldly furious Richard coming toward her.

"You bitch," he sneered, shoving her out of the way and making a grab for Megan. "You've stuck it to me for the last time. She's coming back with me, and there's not a damned thing you can do about it."

Fear radiating through her, Eden threw her whole weight against him, prying his fingers off Megan's arm. The minute she was free of her father, Megan whirled and darted toward the front foyer and the stairs. "I'm not going with you. I'm not!"

Richard turned to go after her, but Eden grabbed the doorframe, shoving him back. "Have you gone insane?" she demanded, struggling to stop him. "You can't barge in here and—"

His teeth clenched in fury, Richard grabbed her and shoved her hard against the wall. "I can do anything I damned well please," he snarled, his face shoved into hers. "Your damned brother had a little talk with Sam Carlton at some damned political fund-raiser." He slammed her against the wall again, his smile vicious. "You remember Sam Carlton, Eden. The senior partner of the firm. And your brother told him I'll screw anything that moves, including one of the partner's wives. Unfortunately, Sam is convinced it was his."

Her shock wearing off, Eden jerked up her arms to break his hold and push him away; then she backed up across the kitchen. "What's the problem, Richard?" she snapped back, her tone biting. "You do screw anything that moves, *including* his wife."

He raised his hand to backhand her, but Eden crossed her arms, silently daring him. "Hit me, Richard," she said in a cold, threatening tone. "And I promise you'll be up on assault charges so fast, you won't know what hit *you*."

His face contorted in an ugly sneer, he came toward her. "He terminated me yesterday. I'm out of a job because of you."

"Oh, no, Richard," she responded, her tone defiant. "You're out of a job because of *you,* because you couldn't keep your zipper up."

He smiled another cold, malicious smile. "Well, Ms. McCall, you're going to pay the price, anyhow. I'm taking Megan home with me, and there's not a damned thing you can do to stop me." He pulled a folded paper out of the inside breast pocket of his suit and held it up for her to see. "This is a court order stating that I've been granted temporary custody." He tossed the document on the counter behind her. "And," he said, withdrawing another folded paper from the same pocket, "I have an affidavit from Sharon Tattersol. You remember Sharon Tattersol, don't you, sweetness? She's Megan's *real* mother." His eyes riveted on her, he stepped closer and touched the paper under Eden's chin. "In this affidavit, she states who the father is." His smile turned colder, more vicious. "And the father, my darling—is me."

Alarm for her daughter shot through her, giving her the kind of courage she never had, and Eden snatched the paper out of his hand, turned to the sink and stuffed it down the garbage disposal. Richard tried to wrestle her away from the counter, but she managed to hit the switch, the loud whirring noise demolishing his claim. Practically screaming with rage, he grabbed Eden by the hair and jerked her head back. He was raising his hand to strike her when Brodie came barreling into the kitchen, closely followed by Martha, an empty cake container in her hand. Before Richard had time to react, Brodie grabbed him, twisted his wrist until he let go of Eden's hair, then threw him across the kitchen, his face white with fury. "You touch her again, you son of a bitch," he seethed through gritted teeth, "and I promise you—you won't leave here in one piece."

Grasping the counter to steady herself, Eden sobbed once, then clamped her hand over her mouth, her legs suddenly shaking violently beneath her.

Putting himself between Eden and her ex, Brodie hauled fresh air into his lungs, his rage so intense that he was seeing red. He wanted to kill the bastard. Piece by piece. Little by little. It was as if a lifetime of rage had broken loose in him, all of it focused on the slimy bastard in front of him.

Richard got to his feet, giving his head a little jerk to the side as he straightened his suit jacket. "Well, well. Who's this, sweetness?" he asked, a nasty little smirk appearing. "Is this the man who was in our bed with us the whole time we were married?"

His rage accelerating, Brodie moved, and before Richard shut his mouth, Brodie hooked his arm around his throat, whirled him around and sent him crashing out through the screen door. His strength fueled by rage, he hauled the smaller man to his feet, jerked one arm behind his back and slammed his face into one of the veranda support poles. His jaw clenched in murderous fury, he gave Dodd another sharp shove. "You aren't dealing with a woman now, Dodd," he said, his voice like cold steel. "You give her any more grief and I'll come after you so damned fast, you won't know what hit you." He twisted the arm higher, exerting more pressure. "This is the only warning you're going to get, buddy. You lay off her and the kid, or you can expect a nice little visit from me. Got that?" Richard moved his head in acknowledgment.

Brodie gave him another sharp shove into the post, then let him go, forcibly getting his fury under control. "You get in that Caddy you rented, you get the hell out of town and you get your slimy ass on the next plane to Toronto." Without looking at the man, Brodie picked up the screen door, which had been wrenched out of the frame, propping it against the railing. He gave Eden's ex a cold, furious look. "And don't think you can mess with me, Dodd. Get out of town—now." Giving the other man one last warning glance, he turned his back and entered the house.

A phone was sitting on the end of the kitchen counter, and Brodie dialed a number, then reached for the pen and pad lying beside it. He was jotting down numbers when Jase answered. "I'm sending Martha over to get Megan," he said curtly. "There's a white Caddy parked outside with rental plates. Number..." He straightened the pad and read back the numbers he'd just written down. "Follow him, and make damned sure he's headed to Calgary. And I want to know if he books a flight out of there. Take a cellular with you, and let me know if he makes a detour." Brodie glanced at the open door, making sure Dodd had decided not to come back in. "I expect it's going to be a quick trip, so take the Vette. And, Jase?"

"Yeah?"

"If he gives you any trouble, take him down."

There was a slight pause; then Jason answered, his tone edged. "Happy to, Unc."

Setting the phone back in the cradle, Brodie dragged his hand down his face, then sighed heavily, trying to expel the last of the adrenaline trapped in his chest. Raking his hand through his hair, he went around the island and crouched down by Eden. She was sitting on the floor, her knees drawn up, her elbows braced on them, the heels of her hands pressed against her eyes. Brodie had never seen anyone tremble the way she was trembling. His expression turning grim, he glanced at Martha, who was coming into the kitchen with a shawl in her hand. "I want you to go get Megan from my place and bring her over here. Then I want you to go upstairs and start packing." Needing to keep his thinking untainted by another shot of fury, he glanced away, trying to think of a solution, knowing he had to deal with the logistics first. But that didn't make it any easier to ignore Eden. He glanced back at Martha. "Has Richard spent much time at Tanner's?"

Martha, her face ashen, shook her head. "No. Never. Mostly when Eden came to visit she came alone—and that wasn't all that often. I doubt if Richard even knows where he lives."

He stared at her, formulating a plan. "Okay. This is what I want you to do. Go get Meg and bring her back here, then pack up their things. I'll wait until I hear from Jase to make sure Dodd booked a flight, then I'm taking them out to Tanner's. I don't want to take a chance that he'll double back and catch them here alone."

The housekeeper draped the shawl around Eden's shoulders and gave her an awkward hug, then straightened.

She was at the kitchen door when Brodie spoke again. "Make sure the white car is gone before you move her, Martha. We don't want him getting a second crack at her."

"Don't worry," she said, bristling with indignation. "He will not lay a hand on the little one while I'm around." The housekeeper started to turn away, but Brodie stopped her. "Is there any hard liquor in the house?" Without saying anything the housekeeper headed to the living room, then returned with a bottle of rye and set it on the island. She gave Brodie one sharp nod of assurance, then disappeared.

Brodie waited until he heard the front door shut; then he turned his attention back to Eden, his mouth compressing. She hadn't moved, and she was still shaking like a leaf. He saw a red mark on her arm where Dodd had grabbed her, and his fury soared all over again. Exhaling heavily, he drew her hair back from her face, then slid his hand to the back of her neck, giving her a little shake. "Come on, honey," he said gruffly. "We have to talk. I need to know what's going on here."

She didn't respond for a minute; then she drew a deep, ragged breath and dropped her hands. Knowing he didn't dare look at her face, Brodie caught her by the wrist and helped her to her feet, then led her over to the kitchen table. Placing his hand on her shoulder, he forced her to sit down; then he went back to the counter and cracked the seal on the rye. The glasses were in the second cupboard he checked. He poured a stiff drink, then went back to the table, setting it in front of her. She had her elbows braced on the table, with her hands shading her eyes, and she was shaking so badly the table was quivering.

He caught her arm, exerting controlled pressure as he pulled her hand away from her face. "Drink it, Eden," he said firmly. "Now." He folded her hand around the tumbler and waited. Finally she complied, downing it in a single swallow. Then, without looking at him, she set the glass down, folded her arms on the table and weakly rested her head on them.

Unable to watch her shiver any longer, he drew the shawl up and tucked it around her shoulders. His expression rigid, he pulled her hair free, a fierce, tight feeling unfolding in his chest.

Stuffing his hands into his pockets, he went over and stared out the kitchen window, his reflection coming back at him.

He heard the front door open, and he turned just as Meg came flying into the kitchen, fear in her eyes, her face blotchy from crying. Before she had time to get to her mother, he swept her up, pressing her face tightly against his neck. "Easy, Meg," he whispered softly. "Easy. Everything's okay. It's okay. It's okay." He shot a glance at Martha, and she made a motion for him to follow her. Tightening his arms around Meg, Brodie followed the housekeeper down a hallway and into a study. Altering his grip on Eden's daughter, he sat down in a large leather easy chair and put his feet on the footstool, still holding her face against his neck. Pressing his mouth against her hair, he started to speak. "I need you to listen to me, short stuff," he said softly. "Your mom is pretty upset right now, and she needs a few minutes to get it together, okay?" He gave her a little shake. "Okay?"

She took a deep shuddering breath, then nodded. "Okay," she whispered brokenly.

"I know you're pretty scared yourself, but I really need your help right now."

Megan turned, her arms going around his neck in a tight grip. He felt her nod, and he gave her a firm squeeze, then rubbed her back. Her bones were so small, so fragile, and Brodie had to swallow to keep his throat from closing up. He waited a moment until he was sure his voice was going to hold out; then he rubbed her back again. "Your dad—"

"He's not my dad," she interjected, her voice muffled.

Amusement lifted one corner of Brodie's mouth, and he gave her another squeeze. "Okay. *Richard* is on his way back to Toronto, and Jase is following him to Calgary to make sure he gets on the plane. I've asked Martha to pack up all your things and your mom's, and then I'm taking you out to your Uncle Tanner's."

He felt Megan wipe her face on his shirt; then she sat up, a relieved expression in her eyes. "So he can't get us, right?"

Wanting to smile, Brodie wiped a salty trail off her cheek. "Right."

She looked down and began toying with a button on his shirt; then she looked back at him, a mulish set to her chin. "He can't make me go with him. I'll scream and kick all the way if he tries."

Resting his head against the back of the chair, Brodie studied her, humor tugging at his mouth. He didn't doubt her for a minute. Finally she looked away, making a discomfited little grimace. "I will."

"I know you will," he said, continuing to watch her, liking her grit. "I hope you do." He touched her on the end of her nose, then spoke, his tone serious. "Would you mind a whole lot if you didn't talk to your mom right now?"

Fiddling with the button, she shook her head.

Brodie glanced up at Martha, who was wiping her eyes, then back at Megan. "Do you think you could go give Martha a hand—make sure she packs everything your mom will need?"

Megan nodded, then slid off his lap, and Martha took the little girl's hand. At the door, Megan turned and looked up at him, a fearful anxiety pinching her face, her eyes glimmering with fresh tears. "What if he comes again and you aren't there?"

A fierce tightness clamping around his lungs, Brodie stood up and fished his wallet out of his back pocket, a lump in his throat the size of a baseball. He extracted a card, replaced his wallet, then crouched down in front of the little girl. He handed her his business card. "It tells you all the numbers where you can reach me. This is the store, this is the hotel and these are for the two cellular phones. And this one is the apartment number." He pointed to the last number. "This is a voice mail number. If you can't get me anywhere else, you call that number and leave a message. But be sure to tell me where you are and how I can reach you, okay?"

Megan nodded, and Brodie lifted her face. "Do you know how to make a long-distance call?"

She took a tremulous breath and nodded again. "My mom used to let me dial when we phoned Uncle Tanner or Uncle Chase. And she showed me how to make a collect call, too."

He stroked her cheek with his thumb. "Good girl. All you have to remember is to press one and the area code." He showed her on his business card. "The area code for Alberta is right here with the numbers, okay?"

"Okay."

He gave her head a little shake. "You did the right thing, Meggie," he said quietly. "Going for help like you did. You aren't big enough to help your mom, so that was a really smart thing to do."

Megan studied the card, then looked at Brodie, resolutely blinking back her tears. Staring into the little girl's eyes, he spoke, his voice firm. "If you ever need me again, all you have to do is call. It doesn't matter what time it is, or where you are. You call, and I'll be there as fast as I can."

She stared back at him, assuring herself that he meant what he said. Finally she managed a wobbly smile. "Cross your heart and hope to die?"

He smiled back. "Cross my heart and hope to die."

She put her arms around his neck and hugged him with surprising strength. "Thank you, Brodie," she whispered. "It makes me not feel so scared."

Closing his eyes, he hugged her back, swallowing, then swallowing again against the sudden fullness in his throat. "Good," he managed to get out. "Because you're one tough little cookie."

She surprised him with a shaky little giggle. He gave her another tight squeeze, then stood up, meeting Martha's gaze. "You'd better phone Tanner and tell him what's going on. It might be late before we get out there."

Martha gave his wrist a little squeeze, then caught Megan by the hand. "Come on, pumpkin. Let's go to work."

His hands on his hips, Brodie tipped his head back and stared at the ceiling for a very long time, so many feelings running through him that he felt as if he'd been gutted. Maybe he'd let too much damned pride control his life. Releasing a heavy sigh, he straightened, his face drawn. Now he had to face Eden.

She was still at the table with the shawl draped around her shoulders, but she was upright, her arms resting on the surface, moving the glass back and forth through a wet spot. She was so deep in thought, he doubted if she was even aware he was there.

He got another glass from the cupboard, then picked up the bottle and went to the table. He slid into the space opposite hers, brushing aside paper and crayons. After uncorking the bottle, he sloshed another finger of rye into her glass, then poured a stiff drink for himself. He downed half of it, then hunched forward and rested his arms on the table. He aligned the base of the square-bottomed tumbler with a line in the butcher-block surface, then lifted his head and looked at her. There wasn't a trace of expression on her bloodless face, and the deadened look in her eyes scared the hell out of him. With a mechanical stiffness, she lifted the glass and took a sip, then set it down on the table. "Where's Megan?" she asked, her voice as expressionless as her eyes.

He watched her, a gnawing, uneasy feeling twisting through his gut. "She's upstairs with Martha."

Eden lifted the glass again, only this time she drained it. He knew she hated rye, but it was as if the taste didn't even register.

Glancing down, he twisted his glass around; then he looked back at her. "What went on here tonight, Eden?" he asked, his tone unwavering.

She glanced at him, then looked down, a tight smile appearing. "He brought a court order so he could take Megan back with him."

Brodie shot her an intent look. "Where is it?"

"On the counter."

Anger rising in him, Brodie got up, retrieved the paper and unfolded it. He read the document, then clenched his teeth in an expression of anger and disgust. He wished he'd smashed the son of a bitch's face in. Restraining the urge to hit something, he placed the paper in front of Eden. "Read it," he commanded curtly.

He paced back and forth behind her chair until he got his temper under control; then he dragged out a chair and sat at the end of the table, watching her face. She finished reading the document, then looked at him, numb incomprehension in her eyes. Drawing a deep breath to keep the anger out of his voice, he indicated the bottom of the paper. "It's a court order," he said, his tone flat. "But it isn't a *signed* court order." He made the muscles of his face relax, then inhaled again. "He was trying to snow you, Eden. This piece of paper isn't worth spit."

She stared at him; then she clutched her arms around herself and closed her eyes, a shudder coursing through her. Brodie looked away, unable to handle the agony of the emotions he saw sweep across her face. Moths were swarming around the veranda light, and Brodie watched them, his expression tightly controlled. The house would be full of them in another few minutes. Shifting his gaze, he knocked back the remaining liquor in his glass, then poured himself another drink.

Finally getting a grip on his own emotions, he looked back at Eden. "What's going on, Mac? You've been here a month and a half—why has he decided to get down and dirty now?"

Pulling the shawl tighter around her shoulders, Eden fixed her gaze on the glass as she ran her thumb around the rim. "Apparently Milt ran into Sam Carlton at a political fundraiser. Sam's the senior partner of the firm Richard's with. And apparently Milt gave him the dirt on Richard, right down to the fact that he'd been having an affair with one of the partner's wives. Unfortunately it was Sam's wife—I knew about it." Another tight smile appeared. "He was good enough to tell me all about it when I told him I wanted a divorce." She released a sigh, lifting one shoulder in a semblance of a shrug. "According to Richard, Sam fired him on the spot."

"That's Dodd's problem. It has nothing to do with your having custody. A judge is going to take a pretty dim view of him using those kinds of tactics. I can guarantee it."

Suddenly her eyes filled with tears, and she looked away again, pressing her knuckles against her mouth.

Unable to stand seeing her like that, he leaned over and caught her other hand, giving it a reprimanding little squeeze. "Hey," he said softly. "Don't sweat it. He hasn't got a leg to stand on, and he knows it. Tomorrow morning, you phone your lawyer and get a restraining order. And as soon as I get you and Meg tucked in at Tanner's, I'll come back and talk to the RCMP and see if we can lodge an assault charge."

She turned her hand in his, holding on to him with a desperate strength. "But that's not all," she whispered, her voice breaking.

A cold sensation sliding through his gut, Brodie watched her, tightening his hold on her hand. Finally she took a deep, tremulous breath, as if bracing herself; then she met his gaze, raw fear in her eyes. "He brought an affidavit. He said it was a statement from Megan's natural mother swearing that he is Megan's biological father."

Brodie stared at her, trying to digest the bombshell she'd just dropped on him. Not liking the hard, cold feeling in his belly, he glanced at the counter where the court order had been, then back at Eden, his voice sharp. "Where is it?"

"I garburated it."

He stared at her. "You *what?*"

She wiped her eyes with the side of her hand, then looked at him, a glimmer of defiance in her eyes. "He was waving it under my nose, so I grabbed it and stuffed it down the garbage disposal."

Brodie stared at her, feeling as if he'd just been poleaxed; then he started to laugh. And it was the first time he'd laughed for quite a while. His unexpected reaction dragged a small smile out of her, easing the haunted, hollow look in her eyes just a little. "It isn't funny, Malone," she said, but the hint of a smile remained.

Expelling the last of his amusement on a long sigh, he shook his head, giving her an approving look. "Good for you, Mac. Destroying the evidence. That must have rattled his chains."

The smile still hovered around her mouth as she pushed her glass back and forth through the wetness on the table. Then she suddenly folded her arms and looked away, distress putting that haunted look back in her eyes.

His own face sobering, Brodie looked down and toyed with his drink. Trying to ignore all the feelings turning over in his chest, he studied the contents of his glass for a moment; then he raised his head and looked at her. "If it's true, is it going to make any difference to you?"

She looked up and swallowed hard, then spoke, her voice tight with emotion. "No. It's not going to make any difference. She's mine, and I love her." She huddled in her arms, a terrible anguish lining her face. "I don't know what I'll do," she whispered, her voice breaking, "if he takes her away from me."

Brodie had a nearly uncontrollable urge to go after Dodd right then and there. Locking his jaw against the roiling sensation in his belly, he clenched and unclenched his teeth, trying to bring the new burst of anger under control. The hot, violent surge of adrenaline finally abated, and he looked at her, affecting a calm he didn't feel. "He's not going to get away with this," he said, his tone flat. "He can drag out all the evidence he wants, but all it's going to take is one good lawyer to shoot him down in court. And it isn't going to matter a damn whether he's the natural father or not. There isn't a judge in the country who won't see this for what it really is. This has nothing to do with Megan. This is retaliation against you—pure and simple."

Recognizing the sharp edge in his voice, Brodie paused, making his muscles relax. Resting his elbows on the table, he hunched forward, forcing a calm, reasonable tone. "And this could be another damned stunt, just like the court order." He paused, staring at her profile, then spoke again. "Don't let him terrorize you, Eden," he counseled quietly.

She tipped her head back and closed her eyes, and he could sense her trying to regroup. Releasing a tired sigh, she finally turned her head and looked at him, her gaze stark. "What do I tell Meg? I can't risk him getting to her somehow."

His elbows still on the table, Brodie considered her question. "Tell her the truth. Tell her what he said, but that you don't know if it's true or not. She tough and she's smart, and she knows what he's like. I think the big thing right now is to get her somewhere that's relatively safe—someplace where he doesn't have easy access to her."

The phone rang, and Brodie got up to answer it. He glanced at his watch—nearly an hour since he'd sent Jase on his mission. Too soon for good news. He hoped like hell it wasn't bad. Picking up the phone, he answered, his tone brusque, "McCall residence."

There was a slight pause; then Tanner McCall spoke. "I just got off the phone with Chase," he said, his tone flat. "He's on his way. We should both be there in twenty minutes."

Brodie's gaze connected with Eden, and he saw the flicker of acute anxiety in her eyes. He shifted the phone away from his mouth, his expression fixed. "It's Tanner." Unable to handle the look of relief that swept across her face, he turned away, resting his hand on his hip. "You're taking her back with you?"

There was a hard, dangerous edge in Tanner McCall's voice. "Yeah, I'm taking her back with us." There was a pause; then Tanner spoke again, his tone more controlled. "We'll see you in twenty minutes." Then there was the sound of a disconnect. Brodie smiled a wry smile as he hung up the phone. He didn't envy Dodd if Tanner McCall ever got his hands on him.

"Brodie?"

Sliding his hands into the back pockets of his jeans, he turned.

She was watching him with big dark eyes, as if she didn't quite comprehend what was going on, and he realized the booze was kicking in. "What was that about?" she asked unevenly.

Folding his arms, he leaned back against the counter. "Martha's packing up your things, and Tanner's coming in. We're moving you out there."

Confusion darkening her eyes even more, she made a helpless gesture with her hand. "I can't move out there. They already have such a houseful, and—"

"You're going, Eden," he countered firmly. "After what happened today, you can't stay here by yourself."

Locking her arms around her middle as if her stomach hurt, she turned her head, her eyes welling with tears. "He's never been like this before," she whispered, bewilderment in her voice. "I've never seen him act like this."

Brodie refrained from pointing out that Dodd's safe, smug little ivory tower had just been blown to bits. His reputation was shot to hell; he'd cuckolded the wrong man and lost his cushy job because of it. He stared at Eden, thinking the guy had been some kind of fool. Yeah, he'd lost it, all right. He'd lost it in spades. Keeping the disgust he felt out of his voice, he responded, "And that's why you're going to Tanner's."

He didn't know why, but he was suddenly angry with her. Maybe it was because anger was safe and it shut down everything else he was feeling. And when he was around Eden McCall, he needed to be shut down.

Maybe, he thought grimly, that was how he'd survived all along.

Chapter 13

Rolling his shoulders in weariness, Brodie entered the bar, a dull headache pulling at the backs of his eyes. After three hours of staring at a computer screen and another two hours of wading through paperwork that had piled up on his desk, he was so damned tired he could barely see straight. Probably because he hadn't slept at all the night before. His gut had kept pumping out anger-induced adrenaline; the image of Dodd yanking Eden around just wouldn't go away.

Going behind the bar, he pulled himself a pint of draft, his expression fixed. No wonder he had a damned headache. He'd spent most of the day slamming around with his teeth clenched, wishing he'd pushed the son of a bitch's face in. He'd seen enough of that kind of brute force when he was a kid—it had disgusted him then, and it disgusted him now. Making the muscles in his jaw relax, he went around the bar and sat down on one of the high stools, then took a long drink. Setting the glass down, he hunched his shoulders and rested his arms on the bar, wiping a trail of foam off the side of the glass. The phone was sitting right beside him, and for one brief, insane moment he considered phoning out to the Circle S. Then he gave his head a disgusted shake and took another long drink.

Last night was a night he wasn't going to forget for a long while. It had scared the hell out of him when Megan had come flying in the door and into his arms, damned near hysterical, crying that her dad was at the house hurting her mother. He had literally tossed the kid to Jase, telling him to get upstairs with her, lock the door and not let anyone near her, then he'd practically ripped the door off its hinges when he slammed out. No, it would be a damned long time before he forgot the jolt of pure, hot fury when he'd seen Dodd about to belt Eden. He should have broken the bastard's arm right then and there.

Experiencing another jolt of fury, Brodie forced his muscles to relax again, his pulse running heavy. He hadn't been able to let go of any of that fury until Jase had called, saying that Richard had driven around Bolton for a while, then eventually headed for the city. He'd gone straight to the airport, returned the rental car and checked into the airport hotel. Assured that Dodd was indeed on his way back to Toronto, he had told Jase to cut him loose and come home; then he'd stuck around until Chase and Tanner showed up. He'd told them what had happened; then he'd disappeared. He'd gone home, put on his running gear, then hit the lighted track at the high school and ran lap after lap, until his lungs shut down and his legs gave out. And he'd run again that morning—but he couldn't burn off the feeling in his gut. All he had to do was think about Dodd and he was wound up like a damned top all over again.

"Well, if this isn't Mr. Happy Face hanging over his beer," commented Ruby as she came around the far side of the bar to unload a tray of empty glasses. "What's the matter, Malone? Did someone smash all your toys?"

Ignoring his manager, Brodie took another drink, clenching his jaw again. Damn it, couldn't she leave him alone for ten minutes?

Ruby placed the dirty glasses in the built-in dishwasher, then began wiping the bar. She lifted his glass, wiped up the puddle of foam, then pointedly placed a paper coaster on the damp surface, setting his glass back down with a thud.

"Cut it out, Ruby," he snapped. "And quit treating me like some snot-nosed kid."

"Well," she responded, her tone tart, "if you're going to act like a snot-nosed kid, you're going to get treated like one. You've had your knickers in a twist ever since Eden McCall showed up in town."

She probably would have gotten a smile out of him with the knickers-in-a-twist crack, but the Eden McCall thing really got his temper up. "This has nothing to do with Eden McCall, Ruby Jean. This has to do with people minding their own damned business."

She took his glass and refilled it, setting it down on the bar with more force than necessary. "Don't kid a kidder, sweet thing. I remember how thick the two of you used to be—riding around on that old Harley of yours, sneaking off down back lanes. I always figured you were the reason old Bruce shipped her off to school."

Brodie glared at her. Ruby gave him a phony smile as she reached across the bar and tapped him on the nose with a long, red fingernail. "So what happened, Malone? Did you bail out on her again?"

Brodie jerked his head back, giving her a look that would have made most men quail. "No, Mother, I did not bail out on her," he said, his tone abrupt. "I'm hardly McCall material."

Folding her arms on top of the microwave oven, Ruby studied him, a thoughtful, assessing expression appearing in her eyes. "Don't kid yourself, Brodie," she said, her voice suddenly quiet. "You had such a damned big chip on your shoulder back then, you couldn't see the swamp for the alligators."

He stared at her for a minute, then pushed the full glass of beer away. "You don't know what you're talking about," he said flatly.

"It was your way or no way back then." Her tone was maternally scolding. "You didn't do one damned thing to make it easier for her—you didn't cut your hair or park your bike—everything had to be on your terms." Straightening, she began pulling the daily inserts out of a stack of menus. "You're the best damned boss I've ever had," she said evenly. "And I'd like to think we've got a pretty good friendship going—a little give and take on both sides." She tossed the inserts in the garbage, then started putting in the new ones. "It doesn't take a light bulb salesman to see that you're crying in your beer," she continued, her tone even. "My old grandpappy used to say that blame goes both ways—and it takes a big man to shoulder his share. Maybe," she said, stacking the menus in a pile, "it's time to check the swamp, Malone. Maybe those alligators are really crocodiles."

Someone entered the bar from the side door, and Ruby glanced over, a curious expression settling on her face. "Malone?"

Having had just about enough of alligators and crocodiles, Brodie snapped, "What?"

"Is your life insurance paid up?"

He closed his eyes in exasperation, counting to ten. "What in hell are you talking about, Ruby Jean?"

"I was just wondering," she said mildly. "Tanner and Chase McCall just walked in. And by the looks on their faces, I don't think they've stopped by for tea and crumpets."

In spite of how put out he was feeling, Brodie could not restrain a small smile. "Hell, Ruby. Are they packing guns?"

She raised one eyebrow, giving him a dry look. "No. Does that make this a friendly visit?"

Heaving an exasperated sigh, Brodie gave her a long, level look. "Why don't you go find some dirty ashtrays? Or some old rancher to flirt with?" he asked, his tone blunt.

She grinned and thumbed her nose at him, then turned and sashayed across to a full table in the corner. Turning halfway around on his stool, he rested one elbow on the counter and laced his hands together, watching the two McCalls approach. He wished to hell he had a couple more beers under his belt.

Keeping his face expressionless, he tipped his head in acknowledgment. "Chase. Tanner. Can I get you a beer?"

His Stetson in his hand, Tanner indicated a table off to the side. "There are a couple of things we'd like to talk to you about, if you don't mind."

Ruby was returning to the bar, and Brodie held up three fingers, then followed Eden's brothers over to the table in the corner, his headache back full force. He sat by the wall and rocked his chair back against it, waiting until Ruby deposited three glasses of beer on the table. He caught her eye, giving his head a small shake to indicate no tab; then he folded his arms, his expression giving nothing away. "What's up?" he asked, his tone noncommittal.

Tanner took a drink, then shoved his glass out of the way and rested his arms on the table. He looked up and met Brodie's gaze. "We were wondering if Dodd said anything—made any threats, gave any indication about what he's going to do next."

Brodie gave him a wry half smile. "I didn't give him much of a chance. But no, he didn't say much." But Brodie *did* remember what he had said about Brodie being the man Eden had in bed with them the whole time they were married. The recollection set off a heavy sensation in his chest, and he tightened his jaw, keeping his expression blank. "Why?"

Chase gave him an off-center grin. "Mostly because I want to get my hands on the son of a bitch and hammer him feet first into the ground."

Experiencing a genuine flicker of amusement, Brodie studied Eden's brother, thinking he would like to be there if Chase ever got the opportunity.

Tanner spoke, his expression set. "Unfortunately, Eden's lawyer is away on holiday, and so is Richard's, and Richard isn't answering his phone." He lifted his head and met Brodie's gaze, a cold, stony look in his eyes. "Eden spent all night on the veranda, watching the road. I don't think she can take much more of this, and I want it stopped." He held Brodie's gaze for a moment, then looked down at the table, releasing a heavy sigh. "But there's not a damned thing she can do until her lawyer gets back." He turned his glass around, then looked up at Brodie again. "My concern right now is that Richard might turn up again. If he does, there's a good chance he'd book a room here."

Still leaning back in the chair with his arms folded, Brodie held Tanner's gaze. "If he does, he'll leave here on a stretcher."

Chase gave him a warped grin. "Hell, you disappoint me, Malone. I was thinking more of a body bag."

Tanner downed half of his beer, then stood up. "You'll let us know?"

"I'll let you know."

Tanner clapped his hand on Chase's shoulder, then picked up his hat. "We'd better hit the road, Chase. We've got a herd of cattle to move tomorrow."

Chase finished his beer, then got up, settling his hat low on his head before looking at Brodie. He didn't say anything for a long moment; then he spoke. "You can stand at my back anytime, Malone," he said, his tone gruff. Then he turned and followed his brother. "And thanks for the beer."

Brodie watched them leave, then tipped his head back and closed his eyes, experiencing a familiar hollow feeling deep down inside him. He wondered if she was going to sit on the veranda again tonight, watching the road.

It was well after two by the time Brodie closed up the bar and cashed out. He checked in with Ivan, the night clerk in the hotel; then he pulled up the collar of his jacket as he left through the lobby doors. The town was still, the sky bright with stars, the night air brisk with a tang of autumn. He dropped the canvas cash bag in the bank depository and turned toward home. Normally he jogged the six blocks to the store, but tonight he just didn't have the energy.

The streets were deserted, the streetlights casting halos on the empty road, the moths fluttering in clusters around the mercury vapor elements. Stuffing his hands in his jacket pockets, Brodie walked from one halo to the next, a sudden recollection sending a hollow ache through his belly. He remembered being six years old—when his mother died—and lying in bed at night curled up in a tight little ball, so lonely and scared, so full of dread and panic, that he had been damned near paralyzed by it.

Trying to will away the sudden constriction in his throat, Brodie lifted his head, focusing on the next halo of light. He hadn't thought about that in years, maybe because he had never allowed those memories to surface—maybe because he'd never quite forgiven her for deserting him, for leaving him alone. For an instant he felt as if he was back in an old childhood nightmare, with something dark and shapeless right behind him. And if he looked back, he would see something that would terrify him.

Experiencing a twist of something that felt a little too much like that old panic, he locked his jaw and forced his mind to disconnect. He didn't need that now. Not with everything else going wrong in his life. He did not need to connect with that.

The apartment was dark and silent, but the light was on over the kitchen counter, illuminating a single sheet of paper and a large brown envelope. Stripping off his jacket and draping it over the back of a chair, he wearily scrubbed his face, then went over to read the note, aware that the message light was flashing on the answering machine.

Drawing the paper toward him, Brodie read.

Tanner and Chase McCall came by to see you. Told them you were at the hotel. The Jeep had a flat. Took it to the garage to get fixed. Yearbook photos came. Eden called. Told her you'd be home about two. Jase.

Feeling as if he'd just been sucker-punched, Brodie swore, casting a sharp glance at the clock on the stove. It read 2:19 a.m. Bracing his hand on the counter, he massaged his eyes, not liking the sharp knot of disappointment in his belly, or the sudden shot of realization that had nailed him square in the chest. All this time. He'd been waiting all this time. But he hadn't realized it until right then, until he'd read that damned note, that he'd been waiting—no, hoping—for exactly that, for her to make the next move. And he'd been waiting ever since that last morning together. He had wanted her to come to him.

Exhaling wearily, he straightened, his expression haggard as he reached over and hit the Replay button on the answering machine. The message recorded a hang-up, and Brodie waited for the electronic voice to give the date and time. "Friday, July seventeenth," the voice echoed mechanically, "2:05 a.m." The machine clicked off, and Brodie exhaled abruptly and hit the Rewind button. He had missed her call by fourteen minutes. Slapping his hand against the counter in a burst of frustration, he glanced at the clock again. It was too damned late to call back. He knew that. But damn it, he wanted to pick up that phone.

Needing a distraction, he picked up the envelope and withdrew Jase's yearbook photos. It gave him a jolt, seeing his own eyes looking back at him. A snapshot was clipped on the corner of the largest photo, the picture obscured with a stick-on note. "What do you think? Alike or what?" Jase had scrawled. He pulled off the note, getting another jolt. It was a snapshot of him, looking at the camera. It was almost identical to the pose in Jase's picture, and the resemblance was uncanny. The picture was one Eden had taken during that long, hot summer, and it had been buried in a box of old pictures in the storage room. He remembered that day as clearly as if it had happened yesterday. It was the day they had found the old trunk.

Not wanting to deal with the sudden empty feeling clawing through him, he shut off the light and headed toward his bedroom. Weariness washing over him, he undid the buttons of his shirt with one hand, then pulled it free of his jeans, stripping it off as he entered his bedroom. He was going to have a quick shower, then plant himself in that bed, and with any luck he would be out cold before he hit the pillow.

He had just turned off the water and was stepping out of the shower when he thought he heard the faint ring of the phone. Snatching up a towel, he slammed open the bathroom door. The phone rang again, and he made a dive for it, grabbing the receiver from across the bed. His heart hammering in his chest, he gripped the receiver, hoping like hell it was her. "Malone."

There was a slight pause, then he heard the caller take a breath. "It's Eden," she said, her voice so soft, so unsteady, he could barely hear her. "I know it's late, but I..." He heard her take another shaky breath, as if bracing herself; then she continued, her voice only slightly stronger. "I wanted to thank you," she said, an audible catch in her voice. "I was pretty much out of it last night... and you left before... before..." She paused, and Brodie could almost see her, and he knew she'd been crying. "And I wanted to tell you how sorry I am that you got dragged into my mess."

Rolling onto his back, Brodie dragged his free arm over his eyes, the sound of her voice doing painful damage to his heart. Clenching and unclenching his jaw, he reached down deep for an easiness he did not feel. "Hey, McCall," he said gruffly. "Don't sweat the small stuff, okay? It was no big deal."

"It *was* a big deal," she said, the same heart-wrenching catch in her voice. "You always seem to be there when I need you."

A funny, uncomfortable sensation coursed through Brodie, and he jerked his arm off his eyes and stared at the ceiling, his insides going dead still. It wasn't true. He had never been there when she really needed him. He hadn't been able to swallow his damned pride, so he'd walked out on her. Like seventeen years ago. Yeah, she had acted flustered and ashamed when he'd showed up at her dorm, dressed like a thug. But he had been the one who had walked away. And he had been the one who never went back.

"Brodie?" she said unevenly. "Are you still there?"

Experiencing a sharp rush of self-contempt, he closed his eyes. "Yeah," he said, keeping his voice even. "I'm here."

"I just wanted to thank you, that's all. And I know you're probably in bed and—"

His heart suddenly slamming in his chest, he dragged himself into a sitting position, experiencing a kind of dread he'd only experienced once before. For some reason he couldn't let her hang up on him. Not yet. Not yet. Swallowing against the dryness in his mouth, he spoke, his voice uneven. "How's Meg doing?" he interjected, needing to keep her on the line, needing to hear the sound of her voice.

He heard Eden sigh; then she answered. "She's doing okay. She's pretty upset over her dad, but other than that, she's fine."

Leaning back against the headboard, Brodie drew up one leg, draping his arm across his knee as he stared into the darkness. "And how are you doing?"

"Okay, I guess." There was a pause; then she spoke again, her voice soft, strained, dispirited. "I'd feel better if I could talk to my lawyer. But he won't be back for another two weeks. And Richard's lawyer is out of town, as well. I'll just have to tough it out until then, I guess."

"You should be in bed, Mac," he said, his own voice still not quite steady.

"I know," she answered in the same soft tone. "But I needed to talk to you first."

His eyes suddenly burning, Brodie gouged at them. It was as if his blinders had just been stripped off and he could see. And he realized just how damned badly he *had* let her down. "Have a good night's sleep," he said gruffly. "And I'll talk to you later."

Feeling as if he had a fist jammed in his chest, he hung up the phone, then tipped his head back against the headboard. Why hadn't he seen it before? Maybe it was Ruby's comment about blame going both ways, or maybe he'd gotten rid of a lot of old garbage when he'd thrown Dodd through the screen door. Or maybe he was just a self-absorbed bastard who had to lose her twice before he got the message. He was as much to blame as she was—maybe even more. And he'd sure as hell paid the price.

He opened his eyes and stared into the darkness, the rectangle of light from the bathroom door illuminating his dresser. The bracelet he'd bought in Montana was buried at the back of his sock drawer—the bracelet he had bought because it was the exact same color of her eyes.

His throat closed up on him again, and he closed his eyes, a surge of hard emotion cutting through him. Someday he was going to give her that bracelet, but first he had to right some wrongs. He couldn't go back and fix the past, but maybe he could do something about the present. And the biggest thing facing her right now was Dodd. There had to be a way to get the jerk off her back and out of her life. Then maybe he would have the right to tell her that he loved her. He swallowed hard and closed his eyes tighter. Hell, who was he kidding? It was about time he faced up to the fact that he'd never really stopped loving her.

Brodie was in the video store office, going through some papers, when Lydia showed up for work. She stuck her head in the door, noticing the small leather duffel bag and garment bag stacked by his desk. "Did you decide to clean out your closet, or are you running away from home?"

He turned, dredging up a smile. "I never clean closets, Lydia."

She grinned, folded her arms and leaned against the door-frame. "So what's up?"

He turned back to the counter along the wall, shuffling through the papers he held. "I'm going to Toronto for a few days. Jase will be baching it upstairs, and he knows what has to be done here." He glanced at her, his expression giving nothing away; then he turned back to the counter, extracting a piece of paper covered in his own handwriting and handing it to her. "I'll be staying at the Bradford Arms if you need to get a hold of me—the number's there. I've talked to Ruby at the hotel. If there's a problem, I'm sure the two of you will be able to work it out."

Her expression suddenly serious, Lydia considered him. "This came up pretty sudden, didn't it?"

"Yeah, it did." He snapped the lid shut on his briefcase, then picked up his jacket off the chair. "Jase is taking me to Calgary, so he can pick up the shipment of new releases while he's there." A horn sounded outside, and he grasped the handles of both pieces of luggage in one hand, then reached for the brief-case. "That's him now." Skirting his employee's gaze, he glanced around the office. "I guess that's it."

Lydia stepped out of the doorway, and he went past her. "Have fun," she called after him.

He picked up a cellular phone off the front counter. "Just don't drain the bank account while I'm gone, okay?"

"You're no fun, Malone."

"Yeah. Right." He paused, slipping the phone into the pocket of his jacket. He avoided her gaze. "I'd appreciate it if you didn't tell anyone where I've gone."

"Fine." He had the luggage straps over his shoulder and his hand on the door handle when she spoke again. "Brodie?"

He turned and looked at her.

She was watching him, concern in her eyes. "You take care of yourself," she said quietly. "And get some sleep. You look like hell."

Brodie had never cared much for big cities. And after four-teen days in Toronto, he liked them even less. It was hot. It was humid. And the constant, unrelenting noise got to him. He remembered what it had been like on the drilling platforms in the North Sea. The constant thunder of the ocean against the substructure, the constant clank and drone of the rig. Hell, he'd been able to sleep through a gale-force wind back then. But here, the steady noise kept him awake.

The night lights of the city mocked him, and he turned from the window of his hotel room, peeling off his shirt and dropping it on the end of the bed. Rolling his shoulders, he tipped his head back, trying to release the knot of muscles across his shoulders and up his neck.

Fourteen days. It felt like a hundred. But at least in those fourteen days he'd found out more about Richard William Dodd than he'd ever wanted to know. He'd tracked down a hotshot P.I. outfit through an acquaintance of his, and they had been fast, efficient and thorough. But he'd run smack into a brick wall today.

On the advice of Ken Smith, his private investigator, he'd made an appointment with Eden's lawyer. He knew that Jackson R. Marcus would not discuss Eden's case with him—he hadn't expected him to. In fact, he'd gone under the guise of getting a divorce himself just to check him out. Plain and simple.

The reason he'd gone to check him out was because of some information Smith had ferreted out—that Richard William Dodd and Jackson R. Marcus had gone through law school together. And that they'd been as thick as thieves.

That angle would never have entered Brodie's head, but when he'd told Ken the kind of settlement Eden had received, Ken's instant response was that the whole deal smelled pretty damned rotten. And after his meeting with Marcus today, Brodie had a damned good idea just how rotten. Smooth, pleasant, amiable—Marcus was the kind of man who knew how to play people. Brodie had disliked him on sight.

Undoing the zipper of his slacks, Brodie stripped them off and tossed them on a chair, then sprawled out on the bed. God, but he was so damned tired his eyes felt like they were going to disintegrate in his head. The little sleep he got was punctuated by disturbing dreams. Dreams from his childhood, dreams about his mother. Dreams of Eden. He'd lost count of the number of times he'd reached for her and she hadn't been there.

Turning onto his back, he stacked his hands under his head and stared at the ceiling, trying to figure out what in hell to do. If he told her about the connection between Dodd and Marcus, it would send her into a panic. Yet if push came to shove over Megan, Marcus was not going to give her a fair shake.

Ken had gotten a line on Megan's natural mother, but Brodie had told him to sit on that, more for Megan's sake than Eden's. He didn't want to unearth a can of worms unless it was absolutely necessary. But this thing with Dodd and Marcus had his gut in a knot. And he didn't know what to do about it.

Unable to stay down, he got up and went back to the window. Bracing his arm on the wall, he stood staring out, his expression haggard. It wasn't just the mess Eden was in with her lawyer that had him feeling like a caged cat. He'd done some pretty heavy soul searching since he'd left Bolton, and he didn't much like what he saw.

It had taken him a while to put all the pieces together, and the picture wasn't a pretty one. What Ruby had said about his always having to have everything on his terms had really stuck in his craw. So had her pointed little comment about blame going both ways, about it taking a big man to shoulder his share. He had chewed on that all the way to Toronto and for a good many days after he got there. But it had finally begun to gel in his thick head that the reason he'd been so ticked off when Ruby first laid it on him was because it was true. He'd stuck his attitude in everyone's face, and because he'd had such a damned big chip on his shoulder, it had been his way or no way. And he hadn't put it together until she had hit him with it. But it was true. He had never tried to make things easier for Eden— not seventeen years ago nor in the past few weeks. If he'd handled things differently that morning in his apartment, if he hadn't pushed her, if he'd let her set the terms, he wouldn't be here alone, feeling as if he had a hole in his chest where his heart ought to be.

Trying to rub the exhaustion from his eyes, Brodie took a deep breath against the ache in his chest. Too bad Ruby hadn't sat him down a few years ago and let him have it. Maybe he wouldn't have screwed up the way he had. Exhaling wearily, he rested his hand on his hip and stared back out the window. Wry amusement tugged at one corner of his mouth. Most of what she'd said had been right on the money, but he was still working on the comment about it being time to check the swamp, that maybe the alligators were really crocodiles. But even that was beginning to make sense. Maybe he had been fighting the wrong things all along.

The phone rang, and he glanced at the travel alarm by his bed. It read 12:21 a.m. Which meant it was probably Jase returning his call.

He picked it up before the second ring. "Malone."

"I've been thinking," said Ken Smith without any preamble.

Brodie gave a halfhearted grin. "I'm paying you eighty bucks an hour. You'd better be thinking."

Ken chuckled, and Brodie heard him take a deep drag on a cigarette. "Don't be a wiseass, Malone. I think I've got a plan to shake that creep loose."

Suddenly alert, Brodie tightened his grip on the phone. "What kind of a plan?"

"Well," Ken responded, taking another drag, "you mentioned that Sam Carlton was the senior partner who fired Dodd. He has a hell of a reputation as a litigator. So, since I had nothing to do, I did some checking on him. Do you know," he said, an impressed tone in his voice, "that he hasn't lost a case in twenty-seven trips to the bench? That's a hell of track record, Malone. And I was thinking. He's probably the kind of guy who likes to settle old scores. So I got to wondering if there was any way we could sic him onto Dodd over this custody thing."

His weariness gone, Brodie looked at the jumble of papers spread out on the desk. He was finally able to take his first decent breath in days. "Yeah," he said softly, "I think there is."

"How about we meet for breakfast and map out a strategy? I can meet you there."

Feeling as if there might really be a light at the end of the tunnel, Brodie turned and looked out the window. "Sounds good to me."

"Malone?"

"Yeah?"

"I'm buying."

Three days later Brodie walked into Sam Carlton's richly paneled office, his briefcase holding an itemized record of all the information Ken had dug up. One look at the senior partner and a wad of tension in his belly let go. This man had power—and Brodie would bet everything he owned that he knew how to use it. Graying at the temples, distinguished, eyes like a hawk. This man knew a whole lot about going for the throat.

"Have a seat, Mr. Malone," Sam said, waving at the leather chair facing his desk. "What can I do for you?"

Setting his briefcase on the floor, Brodie sat down and stretched out his legs, then steepled his hands across his chest. He met the older man's gaze dead on. "I want you," he said, his voice even, "to take down Richard William Dodd."

Sam Carlton's eyes instantly narrowed, and he stared at Brodie for several seconds. Then he leaned back and folded his arms across his chest, a slow, predatory smile appearing. "I'm listening."

An hour later Brodie got up and paced to the corner window, feeling as if he'd just been put through a wringer. Sam Carlton was still at his desk, reading through the last of the documentation Brodie had given him. Taking off his glasses, he leaned back in his chair, staring off into space. Then he spoke. "You've done an excellent job, Mr. Malone."

Brodie turned and looked at him. Sam Carlton stared at him a moment, then went on. "To use street vernacular," he said, satisfaction glinting in his eyes, "we've got him by the balls."

Waving to the chair Brodie had just vacated, he reached for the phone. "Have a seat, my friend. The show is about to begin." He hit a button on the phone, putting his glasses back on. "Erica, get Jackson Marcus on the phone for me, please. Tell him it's urgent." He replaced the receiver and lifted a carafe of coffee, silently offering Brodie a refill. Brodie shook his head, wanting to get up and pace again.

Two minutes later the phone rang and Sam picked it up. Brodie watched him, his heart suddenly jammed up in his chest.

"Sam Carlton."

The attorney met Brodie's gaze, a cold smile appearing. "Jackson. Have you got a minute?" He gave Brodie a thumbs-up sign, then leaned back in his chair. "I've just been retained to represent Eden Eleanor McCall. I understand you handled her divorce a few months ago."

There was a long silence, and Carlton rocked back in his chair. "No, Ms. McCall isn't my client, Jackson. I've been retained by someone else." There was another pause, and Carlton smiled, like a tiger going for the kill. "Well, Jackson, I'm suggesting you'd better rethink that. I suggest that you've been in conflict of interest. I can prove in a court of law that you and her ex-husband have had a long and fruitful association." His eyes narrowed, and his face hardened. "I suggest you don't interrupt me, Jackson. And I suggest you listen to what I have to say. I've accessed the records for Ms. McCall's divorce settlement." Another pause, his face hardening even more. "Don't challenge me on how, Jackson. Now," he continued, his tone like steel, "it doesn't appear to me that you represented your client with due diligence. In fact, I would say that between you and her ex-husband, you've taken her to the cleaners."

Staring at Brodie, Sam Carlton tucked his free hand under his arm, listening to what Marcus was saying. If his gut hadn't been in such a knot, Brodie probably would have smiled. He knew a street fighter when he saw one.

Giving an irritated sigh, Carlton spoke again. "Jackson, you're taking off on a tangent here. I have no intention of challenging the settlement. Not," he said, his tone pointed, "unless your associate is uncooperative. I've been retained concerning the custody issue of one Megan Anne McCall-Dodd. Apparently your friend has been making threats, harassing Ms. McCall, and," he added, his tone sharper, "being a general pain in the ass. Now," he added, his tone firm, "I'm prepared to take this all the way. So—" An annoyed expression crossed his face. "I don't like it when you interrupt me, Jackson, so I suggest you listen for a moment. This is what I want. I want you and Richard Dodd in my office at nine o'clock tomorrow morning, I want him prepared to relinquish all rights and privileges to the child, I want him to drop this nonsense about his being the natural father—whether it's true or not. I also want a nice donation made out to the girl's college fund. And I think a nice sum of money for Ms. McCall's pain and suffering would also be appropriate.'' He looked at Brodie and winked, then returned to the conversation. ''No, Jackson. 'I'll see what I can do,' is not what I want to hear. What I want to hear is that you and Mr. Dodd will be in my office tomorrow morning at nine. If you aren't, be forewarned that I am going to report you both to the law society. Then I'm going to marshal my considerable resources, and, as my client so succinctly put it, I'm going to take Mr. Dodd down.'' He smiled again, his tone suddenly cordial. ''Fine, Jackson. We'll see you tomorrow morning at nine.''

After carefully setting the phone back in the cradle, Sam Carlton folded his arms, tucking his hands under his armpits. A sparkle of pure satisfaction appeared in his eyes. ''I think we can safely say we've got them on the run, Mr. Malone. They both have a great deal to lose. If this goes to court, I'll ruin them both, and Marcus knows it.'' He reached forward and opened an elaborately carved box on his desk. ''Have a cigar, my friend.'' He selected one, removed the cellophane wrapper and clipped the end, then picked up a gold lighter. Leaning back in his chair, he lit the cigar and exhaled a puff of blue smoke, then stared at Brodie. ''I'd like to know why you're doing this,'' he said. ''If you don't mind.''

Avoiding his penetrating gaze, Brodie selected a cigar and removed the wrapping. ''I owe it to the lady,'' he answered, his voice husky.

The cigar clamped between his teeth, Carlton leaned back farther in his chair, his arms folded, his hands again tucked under his armpits. He watched Brodie through a haze of smoke. He didn't say anything; he just studied him.

Brodie lit his cigar, then leaned back, meeting Carlton's gaze, a glimmer of amusement surfacing. He wasn't sure why he was at ease with this man, but he was. Birds of a feather, maybe.

''Does she know you're here?''

Skirting the other man's gaze, Brodie leaned forward and flicked a small ash into the crystal ashtray on the desk. "No." Fixing his expression, he leaned back in his chair and met Carlton's gaze. "I'd like to discuss your legal fees."

Still watching him with that same impenetrable stare, Sam Carlton released another puff of blue smoke. "You've pretty much put the cart before the horse, haven't you, Mr. Malone?"

Brodie gave him a level stare.

Sam took the cigar out his mouth and flicked the ash into a potted plant behind him. He rotated his chair back, folding his arms as before, continuing to stare at Brodie. "Most clients come in here and want to discuss fees first." Another glint of amusement appeared. "You came in here with a very different agenda."

Brodie gave him the same impenetrable stare back.

Carlton removed the cigar from his mouth, studied the glowing ember, then looked back at Brodie. "So you want to discuss fees."

"Yes," Brodie answered flatly, not sure if he liked this man after all.

Sam Carlton leaned forward and rolled the remaining ash off on the edge of the ashtray, then leaned back again. He studied Brodie for another moment, then suddenly grinned. "This one is on the house, Mr. Malone." He took another puff on the cigar and blew the smoke toward the ceiling in a long stream, a look of pure gratification on his face. "The truth is, you've made my day."

Chapter 14

It was three weeks to the day from his leaving Bolton that the deal finally went down. Brodie hadn't slept at all for over twenty-four hours. He hadn't eaten. He hadn't shaved. All he had done was stand by a window, waiting for that damned phone to ring. It had gotten messy when Eden's ex had balked at the money. He hadn't balked over the kid, but he had dug his heels in over the cash.

Brodie didn't give a damn about the money. But he figured he owed Sam Carlton that much. Hitting Dodd in the pocketbook was sweet revenge for the senior partner of Carlton, Wilson, Mackey and Fennal, so Brodie had let him have his way. He had no doubt that Carlton would win in the end. It was just that it was taking so damned long, and the waiting was almost more than Brodie could handle.

He looked at the travel alarm on his bedside table. At this very minute Carlton and two of his associates, along with Marcus and Dodd, were probably squaring off. The meeting had been set for ten; it was now after eleven, and Brodie was ready to climb the walls.

The sound of the phone jarred the silence, and Brodie had the receiver in his hand before it finished ringing. His voice was tense and not quite steady. "Malone."

"Mr. Malone, I think you'd better come by for another cigar." There was the sound of an audible puff.

His legs suddenly weak, Brodie sat down on the edge of the bed, bracing his arm on his thigh. "Give it to me," he demanded, his voice thick.

"It was interesting," Sam Carlton said, buoyancy in his tone. "Mr. Dodd was very resistant, threatening action and bodily injury, among other things. So I had my assistant place a call to the law society, explaining to all those present that I was, first of all, going to lodge a complaint against them both. Then I explained exactly what I was going to do to Mr. Dodd. It got very interesting after that, but the outcome was more than satisfactory. I have the signed papers here before me. Ms. McCall has full custody of her daughter, and I have it in writing that he will cease and desist. I also have two certified checks—one made out to Megan Anne McCall-Dodd in the amount of fifteen thousand dollars, which, according to the agreement, we will put in trust for her. I have another check for an equal amount made out to Eden Eleanor McCall." There was another pause, another puff; then he spoke again, his tone rife with satisfaction. "It's in the bag, Mr. Malone. We have indeed taken the son of a bitch down."

Feeling as if everything had let go inside him at once, Brodie rubbed his eyes, knowing there was no way in hell he could answer.

It was as if Sam Carlton hadn't expected him to. "We'll file the original documents here, but I'm having certified copies made up for you to take to Ms. McCall. I have to be in court in an hour, so I'll be out for most of the day. I'll leave the package with my secretary."

Brodie had to swallow twice before he could get his voice to work. "Thank you for—"

"No thanks necessary, Mr. Malone," Carlton interjected. "It's been a pleasure doing business with you."

A debilitating weakness rushing through him, Brodie replaced the phone in the cradle, then braced his elbows on his thighs and hunched over, pressing the heels of his hands against his eyes. Sweet heaven, it was finally over.

It was after two in the morning when he got off the plane in Calgary. The first seat he'd been able to get was on the red-eye, and then only because it was business class. Jase met him, took one look at him and shook his head, then gave him the keys to the Corvette, told him where it was parked and said he would get the luggage. The only verbal exchange was when Jase slid into the driver's seat, turned on the ignition and looked at him.

"She got the kid?"

"She got the kid."

It was just after four when they rolled into Bolton. Jase carried Brodie's luggage into his bedroom, then came back into the living room and stared at his uncle, who was going through the stack of mail. "You okay?"

His throat feeling tight and raw, Brodie answered, his voice gruff, "Yeah, I'm okay."

Jason stared at him for a moment longer, then slapped the wall. "I'm going to crash. I told Lydia I'd open tomorrow."

Without looking at his nephew, Brodie nodded. Tossing the mail back onto the trunk, he went over to the windows, resting his hand high up on the frame. He was so numb with exhaustion that he couldn't regiment his mind, and bits and pieces of thoughts kept surfacing, like flotsam churned up by the tide. He had been so wrong. And so damned blind. What Ruby had said had been true; it had either been his way or no way. But it had taken him more sleepless nights than he wanted to count to figure out why he'd been like that. Yet he'd finally realized that it had been his way of making Eden prove herself to him. And he had never given her an inch—compromise hadn't even been in his vocabulary. He had wanted her on his terms. And if he'd been any kind of a man, there shouldn't have been any terms at all. He hoped like hell that the brown envelope in his briefcase would help make amends for him being such a self-centered bastard. And if he was lucky—damned lucky—maybe she wouldn't turn and walk away.

It was six o'clock when he went into his bedroom and washed his face and put on a clean shirt, then picked up his set of keys off his dresser. Getting the envelope out of his briefcase, he shut off the light and closed the door. He knew he wasn't going to get any sleep until he placed the photocopies of those documents in her hands.

It was just a little after six-thirty when he pulled into the Circle S yard. He parked on the gravel pad by the fence, killed the lights and engine, then picked up the envelope and got out. The air was crystal clear and still, and he heard a door slam down by the cook house, then the voices of the ranch hands as they headed toward the barn. Feeling as if his eyes had been rubbed raw, Brodie opened the gate, his insides twisting into a hard ball. He didn't know what he was going to say to her. But then, how many ways were there to say you were sorry?

He had just latched the gate behind him when the back door opened and a grinning Tanner McCall appeared. He stopped, his hand on the open screen door, his expression suddenly going very still. He stared at Brodie for a moment, then tipped his head. "Brodie."

Bracing his weight on one hip, Brodie tapped the envelope against his legs, his gaze riveted on Eden's brother. "I'd like to talk to Eden, if you don't mind," he said, his tone fixed.

Tanner considered Brodie for an instant, then opened the door wider. "Come on inside. You look like you could use a hot cup of coffee."

Brodie entered the utility room, and Tanner followed him, letting the screen door close quietly behind him. They entered the kitchen, and Kate McCall, who was loading dishes into the dishwasher, glanced up. A startled look crossed her face; then she glanced at her husband, a questioning look in her eyes. His expression giving nothing away, Tanner drew out a chair for Brodie at the table, then one for himself, dropping his Stetson on the counter behind him. Shifting his chair so it was at right angles to the table, he sat down.

Laying the envelope on the table, Brodie leaned forward and rested his arms on the surface, staring at his hands. He felt detached, disconnected, as if he were someone else watching this little drama unfold. A cup of steaming coffee appeared before him, and he looked up, trying to smile his thanks but failing totally. He fixed his gaze on his hands again, knowing he was going to have to give Tanner McCall some kind of an explanation before Eden's brother would let him get within ten feet of her.

Trying to will away the dryness in his eyes, he started talking. "I've spent the last three weeks in Toronto," he began, his tone as detached as he felt. And without looking up, without any change in inflection, he told them everything. His dealings with Ken Smith and Sam Carlton, about the crap he'd laid on Eden, about how he'd screwed up seventeen years ago. He didn't leave anything out. He told them the whole story.

When he was finished, he pushed the envelope across the table. "These are certified copies of the documents Sam had Richard sign. I want to give them to Eden." His expression gaunt, he looked up. Kate was watching him, her expression distressed, her eyes brimming with tears, but Tanner wasn't as easy to read. He was sitting with his arm across the back of Kate's chair, his expression immobile as he ran his thumb back and forth across his wife's shoulder. Finally he looked up and met Brodie's gaze, a solemn look in his eyes. "She's not here."

His mind thick from days with no sleep, Brodie stared at him, a disturbing feeling rolling over in his gut. "Where is she?"

Kate reached up and squeezed Tanner's hand, then answered, her voice unsteady, "We don't know."

"What do you mean, you don't know?"

Tanner's wife wiped her face, then took a deep breath. "Her father's surgery was moved up, and she stayed here until he was through that. Then Tanner and I came home from town one day, and there was a note on the table. She said that she and Megan were going away, and that she'd be in touch." Kate wiped her eyes again, gripping her husband's hand. "We haven't heard from her, and it's been over a week. We think maybe she's gone back to Toronto."

Feeling as if he'd just taken a blow to the midsection, Brodie bolted to his feet, a cold, numbing sensation engulfing him. Too late. He was a week too late. His back to the table, he dragged his hand down his unshaven face, his throat cramped up, his eyes smarting. Too late. She was gone, and he had no one to blame but himself. Unable to see, he gouged at his eyes, guilt slicing through him. He deserved this. God, but he deserved this. He'd been such a self-centered bastard.

A heavy hand settled on his shoulder, giving him a light shake. "Come on. Sit down. You need something to eat and about ten hours of sleep," Tanner McCall said, his tone gruff. "Kate's going to rustle you up some breakfast."

Brodie exhaled unevenly and shook his head. "No. Thanks. I think I'll just head back to town." Making a supreme effort, he turned and tried to smile at Kate. "Thanks for the coffee," he said, his voice thick.

He turned and headed for the door, not sure how much longer he could hang on to the rising pressure in his chest.

Brodie had his hand on the gate when Tanner came out of the house, the brown envelope in his hand. He handed it to Brodie. "You'd better take this with you," Tanner said. "It's only right that she gets this from you."

Brodie looked away, struggling with the tightness in his throat, the burning in his eyes. Finally he answered. "No. You give it to her when you see her." Without looking at Eden's brother, he opened the gate, blindly heading toward the Jeep. He had to get out of there. And he had to get out fast.

He got into the Jeep and slammed the door. He had his hand on the ignition when Tanner appeared at the open passenger window. He tossed the package on the dash. "We'll give you a call if we hear anything," he said, then slapped his hand against the vehicle in a gesture of finality.

Without looking at Eden's brother, and ignoring the package, Brodie turned on the ignition. "I'd appreciate it," he said, his voice uneven. Then he put the vehicle in reverse and backed up, the wheels flinging loose gravel. He just wanted to get the hell gone while he could still see.

His body finally shut down on him that afternoon, and Brodie slept like the dead for the next eighteen hours. He didn't feel a hell of a lot better when he woke up, but his head was clearer, and at least he could think halfway rationally.

He'd learned a lot from Ken Smith in the three weeks he'd spent with the P.I. By Wednesday afternoon he had found out two things for certain: Eden had leased a car in Calgary, and she had withdrawn a fair amount of cash out of her bank account, which left him absolutely nothing to go on. After hitting one dead end after another, he finally had to face the fact that there was not one damned thing he could do. As much as he hated it, the next move was hers. And that scared the hell out of him.

By Friday afternoon he'd had about all he could take of his apartment, the video store, the hotel and the irritating problems that had sprouted up like a damned garden. And he finally said to hell with it all and went for a long run.

When he got back to the video store an hour later he was soaked with sweat, his lungs felt like they were about to rip apart, and his legs felt like jelly, but he felt better than he had for days.

Wiping his face on the towel, he entered the store, needing a long, cold drink of water. He was in the staff kitchen, downing his second glass, when Jason entered, a funny look on his face.

Brodie set the empty glass in the sink and wiped his face, his breathing finally leveling out. "What's up?"

Hooking his thumbs in the front pockets of his jeans, Jase rested his shoulder against the door, watching Brodie with an unreadable look. "We just got a collect call from Megan."

Brodie stared at his nephew; then he turned and slammed his hand against the cupboard door. Damn it, the only time in the whole bloody week that he hadn't been by a phone and the kid had called. Damn it!

Jamming his hands on his hips, Brodie tipped his head back, waiting for the burst of frustration and disappointment to settle; then he turned and faced his nephew again, his expression controlled. "What did she say?"

Watching his uncle, Jase gave a small dismissive shrug. "Not much. She said she really needed to talk to you. Then she said she had to go because her mother was coming. She's going to call back later, after Eden goes to sleep. I told her you'd likely be at the hotel tonight, and I made sure she had the right number for the bar."

"What time is it?"

"Just a little after six." Jase straightened, his thumbs still hooked in his pockets. "I checked the caller ID readout, but it was an out-of-area call."

Brodie hit the cupboard again and swore, then made himself let go of the jam of frustration in his chest. He looked at Jase. "I'm going upstairs for a shower. If she calls again, come get me. And if she can't wait, find out where the hell they are and how I can find them."

Brodie was at the hotel by six-forty. He'd had a shower, packed some clothes and the brown envelope, and had a road map of Canada stuffed in the side pocket of his leather duffel. He had been halfway down the stairs when he remembered the bracelet, and he'd gone back to get it, butterflies the size of bats in his belly.

Now all he had to do was wait. And hope like hell Meg called back.

The call came at just after nine. Brodie snatched up the phone at the end of the bar, tension in his voice. "Brodie Malone."

"I have a collect call for Brodie from Megan McCall. Will you accept the—"

"Yes," he interjected before she had a chance to finish. "Yes, I'll accept the charges."

"Go ahead, please."

"Brodie. It's me. Megan."

Taking a big breath to ease the frenzy in his chest, he spoke. "Hi, Meggie. Jase told me you called."

"Can you come, Brodie?" she asked, her voice breaking. "I think something is wrong with my mom."

He turned his back on the noise from the bar and covered his other ear, barely able to hear her. "I'm packed and ready to roll, honey. You just have to tell me where you are."

"She made me promise not to call Uncle Chase or Uncle Tanner and especially Grandma, but she never made me promise not to call you."

He could hear the panic in the little girl's voice, and his stomach rolled over. "Where's your mom now, Meg?" he said, trying to keep his voice calm, hoping like hell they hadn't left the province. Or that they weren't in Toronto.

"She's in bed. She's always sleeping, and sometimes I hear her being sick in the bathroom. And she just acts funny, Brodie," she said, her voice breaking.

"Hey, now," he said softly. "Don't get upset, short stuff. Just take a big breath, then tell me where you are and what the phone number is, and I'll be on my way in ten minutes."

He heard her take a deep breath, and her voice was stronger when she answered. "We're at Pigeon Lake. Mom rented a cabin. Do you know where it is?"

Brodie let out a shaky sigh of relief. It was a couple of hours north of Calgary, and he could be there in three hours if he really pushed it. Maybe less. "Yeah, I know where it is."

Megan had obviously been paying attention, because she gave him very detailed instructions, right down to the color of the cabin. Brodie wanted to hug the kid. He wrote down the directions, then read them back to her. "Is that everything, Meg?"

"I wrote down the license plate on our car. Just a minute. It's in my pocket."

Brodie already had the license plate number, but he almost smiled at the kid's presence of mind. "That's okay, honey. Don't worry about that. Now give me your phone number."

"We don't have a phone. I'm calling from the phone booth by the store."

For some reason that bit of information just about did Brodie in, and he had to wait a minute before he could clear his throat. "Okay, Meg. I'm on my way. I should be there around midnight—maybe a bit before. Leave the light on outside, okay?"

"Okay."

"Don't worry, okay?"

He could hear tears in her voice. "Okay."

Hanging the phone up was one of the hardest things Brodie had ever had to do. The thought of her standing there in that phone booth all alone made his stomach knot up into a cold little ball, but he had to put it out of his mind. He had a lot of miles to cover.

He waited until he was on the highway before he called Tanner and told him about Meg's call; then he pushed the Disconnect button and dropped the cellular in the passenger seat and cranked open the Vette. This baby was going to fly.

It was half past eleven when he turned down the rutted road leading to the cabin. It was narrow, with trees crowding in, and the driveway was so obscured that he probably would have missed it if he hadn't caught the glimmer of a yard light through the trees. The car rocked in the ruts, and he eased down the rough, narrow lane, the undercarriage scraping. The headlights picked up a blue sedan with rental plates, and Brodie experienced such a jolt of relief that his insides started shaking. Parking behind the sedan, he killed the lights and ignition and got out, closing the door soundlessly behind him. He was just rounding the front of the car when a small, pajama-clad shape came hurtling out of the shadows and into his arms. He swept her up in a fierce hug, and she wrapped her arms and legs around him, hanging on to him for all she was worth.

Tucking her head against his neck, he tightened his arms around her. "Hey," he said softly. "It's okay, short stuff. It's okay." He just held her for a while; then he gave her a little squeeze. "Is there somewhere we can talk without waking up your mom?"

She tightened her arms around his neck. "The sun deck" came her teary, muffled reply.

Giving her another reassuring hug, he carried her up two steps, the light above the side door illuminating the deck through a high shrub. Settling into a wooden lounger, he cuddled her closer and pressed a kiss against her hair, then began rubbing her back. He waited until her grip eased a little; then he tucked his head down against hers. "It's going to be okay, Meg," he said, his voice low. "But I really need you to tell me what happened, okay?"

She sniffled once, then nodded.

Brodie experienced a small tug of amusement. "So what happened, slugger?"

She heaved a tremulous sigh, then eased back in his hold and met his gaze. "I don't know what happened. She got a letter from *him,* but she didn't even open it. She tore it up and threw it in the garbage. And I know she and Grandma had a big fight after Grandpa had his operation." She shrugged and played with the snap of his jacket. "It was over you." She looked up at him, her expression pinched and worried. "Then she said we were coming here. I wanted to come, but she's acting so funny, and I got scared. And I couldn't find your card, but then I found it again. So I called."

He wiped a trail of tears away with his thumb, then spoke, his tone not quite even. "There are some things I want to talk to you about, Meg, before I talk to your mother, okay?"

Watching him with a solemn gaze, she nodded.

He smiled and ran his finger down her nose, then released a heavy sigh. "I love your mom a lot," he started, his voice unsteady. "We used to know each other a long time ago, only something went wrong. And I've made a lot of pretty dumb mistakes, but I really want things to work out between us this time. If that's okay with you."

She stared at Brodie for a moment; then the sweetest smile he'd ever seen lit up her face. "You mean you might be my *dad?*"

He gave her a wry grin. "I don't know. You're kinda hard on dads, short stuff."

She grinned back and gave his chest a poke. "Not *you*, Brodie. I wouldn't be hard on you."

He tucked some of her wild hair back from her face, then met her gaze again. "I'm not sure your mom's even going to talk to me, Meggie. I wouldn't blame her if she didn't. But if she does, we're going to have some things to work out. And we're going to need a chance to talk."

"Like by yourselves."

"Yeah, honey, like that." He wiped a smudge from her cheek. "I just don't want you to think you're being left out, okay?"

She slid her arms around his neck and gave him a hard hug. "That's okay," she whispered. "I'm just so glad you're here."

He closed his eyes and hugged her back, feeling things he hadn't felt since he brought Jase home to live with him. He held her tight for a minute; then he gave her another squeeze. "Do you think you're ready for bed?"

Resting her head on his shoulder, she nodded.

The interior of the cabin was softly lit from a night-light in the kitchen area. Following Megan's soft instructions, Brodie carried her down the short hall to a small bedroom behind the kitchen. He tucked her into bed and sat with her until he was sure she was asleep; then he left the room, closing the door softly behind him.

He stood outside the door to the other bedroom for a long, long time. Now that he was here, now that he'd found her, he didn't have a clue what he was going to say. All he did know was that he wanted back in her life, and he didn't give a damn what he had to do to make that happen.

His insides a tangle of uncertainty, he pushed opened the door and stood there, the faint light from the kitchen falling across the bed. She was sleeping on her side, wearing the thin gray T-shirt, her face turned toward him. Brodie stood there watching her sleep, a thousand feelings piling up in his chest. Guilt, uncertainty, self-doubt, fear, but—most of all—love.

Feeling suddenly very shaky inside, he entered the darkened room and crouched down beside her, his chest filling up with the kinds of emotions he couldn't even define. And suddenly his vision blurred. God, but he loved her.

His hand not quite steady, he gathered her hair back off her face and smoothed it down, the ache in his throat so intense it made his jaws ache. He didn't know what he would do if she walked out of his life and never came back.

Her eyes opened, and she stared at him, then a confused frown appeared. "Brodie?"

He tried to smile as he stroked her cheek with his thumb. "You scared the hell out of me, McCall," he said, his voice gruff.

She stared at him for an instant longer; then she closed her eyes and came up into his arms, holding on to him with a desperate strength. Closing his own eyes, Brodie roughly turned his face against her neck, locking his arms around her. Inhaling raggedly, he tightened his hold on her, an agony of relief rushing through him. She gave a soft sob and tried to pull him into bed beside her, but he held back. Dragging one arm free, he undid the buckle of his belt, pulled the leather free and tossed it on the floor. Then he kicked off his loafers and gathered her up again, clenching his teeth against the powerful surge of sensation as he stretched out beside her. He turned, his face contorting with raw emotion as she came fully into his arms, fusing herself flush against him. His face pressed against her neck, he hung on to her, grateful—God, so grateful—for her. "Ah, McCall," he whispered, his voice shaking. "You will never know how much I love you. And how sorry I am for hurting you."

Making a choked sound, she tightened her arms around him and turned her face into the curve of his neck, then started to cry. He didn't say anything, and he didn't try to stop her. He just hung on to her with all the love and the strength he could muster. And he let her tears heal him from the inside out.

He held her like that for a long, long time, locked in a tight embrace, trying to reassure her, trying to reassure himself. Finally she drew a deep, tremulous breath, grasping the back of his head and holding him close. "I thought I was dreaming," she whispered brokenly.

"Ah, God, Mac," his said, his voice gruff. "I think I still am."

She gave a soft, shaky laugh, tightening her hold on him. "How come you're here?"

Shifting so she was on her back, he braced his arms on either side of her head, holding her face between his hands. He stroked her cheek with his thumb, his gaze somber. "Meg called me. She was pretty scared that night Dodd showed up, so I gave her my business card with all my phone numbers." He brushed back some loose hair from her temple, then managed a small smile. "I told her that if she was ever scared, or if she ever needed me, all she had to do was call, so she did. She told me where you were and how to get here."

Eden swallowed hard and smoothed her hands up his back, her eyes filling up with tears again. "I'm so sorry, Brodie. I keep making the same mistake."

Shaking his head, he pressed his thumb against her mouth. "No, babe. *I* keep making the same mistake." He heaved a heavy sigh, his expression darkening with regret. "It took a kick in the ass before I realized how I've been abusing you."

"But you haven't—"

"Yes, I have, Eden," he countered firmly. "It always had to be my way—I could have done a whole lot of things seventeen years ago to make things easier on you, and I didn't. And I could have done a whole lot of things differently this time around, but I was so damned determined to have you come to me on my terms. And I was wrong. Dead wrong." He stroked her face again, his throat growing tight. "I love you, Mac. And I want you in my life no matter what. It's about time I started showing it."

Tears gathering in her lashes, she tightened her hold, pressing her face against his neck. "Oh, God. I never thought I'd hear you say that again."

Grasping the back of her head and hugging her against him, he turned his face against her, the cramp in his throat getting worse. "You're going to be hearing it a lot from now on," he whispered, his voice uneven.

She clung to him for a long time; then she drew another tremulous breath and kissed him on the cheek, her hand pressed firmly against the back of his neck. She moved her mouth to his ear, and Brodie closed his eyes, a shiver of sensation coursing through him. God, she was soft. So soft.

Exhaling unevenly, he caught her face in his hands, then reluctantly lifted his head. "We need to talk first, babe," he whispered huskily. Tipping her face up, he gave her a soft, gentling kiss; then he looked down at her, his gaze very serious. "I want it all this time, Eden," he said, his tone steady. "A home for Jase and Megan, family vacations. And to do that, we're going to have to talk about my attitude toward your parents."

He saw a glimmer of fear in her eyes, and he touched her face, trying to reassure her. "I don't like your old man very much," he said quietly, pressing his thumb against her mouth when she was about to interrupt. "But that's my problem; not yours."

"But he went after you with a whip, Brodie," she interjected, her voice tight with despair.

He sighed, stroking wisps of hair back from her face. "Yeah, he did. But you never should have found out about that."

"But that was so—"

"Listen to me, Mac," he said, his tone quiet. "I think we need to make a pact. The nasty stuff from the past stays in the past. We can't change it. All we can do is put it behind us, okay?"

She looked up at him, her eyes again filling with tears, and she finally nodded. He leaned down and kissed her. "That's my girl," he whispered against her mouth.

A soft sob escaped her, and she abruptly tightened her hold on him, pressing her face against his neck. "God, but I love you. I was so scared I'd lost you all over again."

Rolling onto his back, he drew her snugly against him as he cradled her head on his shoulder. "We're going to make it this time, McCall," he said, his voice gruff with emotion. "We really are."

He waited until she quieted; then he lifted her face, covering her mouth with a slow, searching kiss. Her breath caught, and she turned in his arms, and Brodie tightened his hold around her, drawing her flush against him. He had finally come home.

Brodie awoke early the next morning to the sounds of Eden being sick in the bathroom. After pulling on his jeans, he crossed the hall and pushed open the door just as the toilet flushed. She was sitting on the floor, her elbow braced on the edge of the tub, supporting her head, and she was deathly pale. He ran a facecloth under the hot water tap and wrung it out; then he crouched down beside her and gently wiped her white face. "Hey, honey," he scolded softly when she tried to take over the task herself. "Just let me, okay?"

He tenderly brushed back her tousled hair, then wiped her face again, smiling just a little when she closed her eyes. "I can do it," she whispered.

"I know you can, but I want to, all right?"

She abruptly pulled out of his hold and heaved again, and he held her head, his expression disquieted. Even years ago, her stomach had been the first thing to react when she was under a lot of stress, and obviously that hadn't changed. But he had never seen her this bad before. He waited until she straightened; then he got up and rinsed out the facecloth and filled the glass sitting by the sink. When he turned back, she had her arms folded on the edge of the tub, her head resting weakly on them, her eyes closed, and she was even paler than before. Brushing her hair back from her forehead, he wiped her face again. Finally she released a shaky sigh and straightened.

He wiped the perspiration off her neck. "Better?" he asked, his tone soft.

She nodded, and he handed her the glass. "Here. Rinse."

She complied, then started to get to her feet. "I need to brush my teeth," she whispered unevenly. He helped her up, flushed the toilet again and put the lid down. Her eyes dark and dilated, Eden started to brush her teeth, but halfway through she gagged again.

Brodie whipped the toothbrush out of her hand and tossed it on the vanity, giving her the glass again. "That's it, McCall. You're going back to bed." He waited for her to rinse out her mouth; then he took the glass out of her hand, slammed it down and picked her up. She started to protest, but he cut her off. "Don't argue with me, Mac."

Crossing the small hallway, he shouldered his way through the bedroom door. "Hang on to me for a minute," he commanded softly. Still holding her, he pulled back the bedding and stacked the pillows against the headboard, then put her down. Pulling the quilt over her, he tucked it around her shoulders, then sat down beside her, stroking her forehead. Eden closed her eyes and swallowed hard, and he could tell she was trying to quell the nausea. She was so white and so damned thin, and the dark smudges under her eyes made him wince. The past few weeks had just about done her in.

She finally opened her eyes and looked at him, and he leaned forward and kissed her on the cheek, his hands braced on either side of her. Lifting his head, he gazed down at her. "Feeling better?"

Eden released a shaky sigh and nodded, her gaze somber. "Brodie..."

Remembering the envelope in his duffel bag, he pressed his finger against her mouth, holding her gaze. "I've got something for you in the car. You going to be okay while I go get it?"

She hesitated for a moment, then slowly nodded, not sure what was going on. He dropped a light kiss on her forehead, then got up. He smiled to himself. Knowing Eden, she would likely throw up again when she realized that Dodd was truly off her back.

It was very early, the faint light before dawn casting the landscape in a soft blue hue, and the birds were just beginning to twitter. The grass was wet with dew, and a mist lay over the lake. The cold, damp air making him shiver, Brodie sprinted to the car. He grabbed the duffel out of the back seat, then sprinted back over the wet grass, taking the stairs in a single bound. Going into the cabin, he closed the door quietly, not wanting to wake Megan. He entered the bedroom, feeling better than he had for a very long time.

Setting the bag on the dresser, he unzipped it and pulled out the package of documents, exposing the box with the bracelet in it. He removed it, as well, then went over to the bed. A gift in either hand, he leaned over and kissed the corner of her mouth, then sat down beside her, hip to hip. Feeling like a little kid at Christmas, he handed her the box first. "This is something I got for you when I was in Montana."

Eden took the box, a confused look in her eyes. She knew when he'd gone to Montana and why, and it was clear from her expression that she couldn't believe he'd gotten something for her then. She stared at him for a moment; then she looked down and opened the box, her hands not quite steady. She folded back the cotton batting, going very still. "Oh, Brodie," she whispered, her voice soft with awe. "It's beautiful."

"I got it because the agates were the same color as your eyes," he explained huskily.

Her fingers trembling, she put the bracelet on, then looked at him, her eyes filling with tears.

Before she had time to say anything, he laid the envelope in her lap, his voice even gruffer. "And I got this for you when I was in Toronto."

She stared at him, as if not quite comprehending. "Toronto?" she said unevenly.

He met her gaze, his expression somber. "I've been in Toronto the past three weeks, Mac," he said quietly.

She stared at him for a moment longer; then she whispered, "Oh, God," and frantically ripped open the envelope. The photocopies spilled out, and she grabbed them up. He watched expressions flit across her face—fear, followed by dawning hope, then wrenching relief as she read the last one. Still clutching the papers in her hand, she went into his arms, holding on to him with all her strength. "Oh, God. It's over. It's finally over," she choked out, shuddering in his arms.

Turning his head against hers, Brodie closed his eyes, a host of emotions piling up in his chest. This was one thing he had done right. This was their new beginning.

His throat so tight he couldn't even swallow, he hugged her hard, loving her so damned much that he felt as if he couldn't hold it all in. Hell, he would even go golfing with her old man if it made her happy.

She finally eased her hold a little, turning her face against his neck. "Thank you. God, thank you."

"You're more than welcome," he answered, his voice thick. Sensing that she needed a little lightness right then, he gave her a squeeze. "You aren't going to throw up all over me, are you?"

She hugged him back, managing a shaky laugh. "No, I'm not going to throw up all over you."

"That makes me real happy, McCall."

Brodie felt her dry her face with her hand; then she relaxed her hold. Taking a deep, steadying breath, she eased away from him, meeting his gaze. "How did you ever manage it?" she said, her voice breaking a little. "How did you ever get him to sign those papers?"

He gave her a kiss, then nudged her hip. "Hike over."

She complied, and he stretched out beside her, then drew her into his arms, nestling her head on his shoulder. Shifting a little to get more comfortable, he gave her a little hug, then started talking.

The sun was up by the time he finished telling her the whole story. Eden was still lying with her head resting on his shoulder, absently stroking his bare chest. "I don't want the money, Brodie. I couldn't care less about that."

"I didn't want that, either," he said, his voice quiet, "but it was kinda Sam's payment. He wanted to stick it to Richard, and that was one way he could make him bleed. I figured he deserved a little revenge.''

Shifting her head on his shoulder, she released a contented sigh. "This is nice, Brodie," she whispered softly.

He caught her under the chin and tipped her head back, kissing her lightly on the mouth. "It's better than nice." He also released a sigh, stroking her bottom lip. "But I'm worried about you, Mac. You're so damned thin, and this stomach thing is out of control."

She pulled away, a funny expression crossing her face. Fumbling with the quilt, she shifted her legs and sat up. She drew a deep breath and met his gaze, looking oddly discomfited. "Uh, Brodie? I don't think this stomach thing is going to go away for a while."

He frowned. "Why the hell not?"

She held his gaze for a minute, then smiled, her eyes bright as she leaned over and gave him a deliberately provocative kiss. "Because I think I'm pregnant."

Epilogue

Large snowflakes started to fall, sliding soundlessly through the halos created by the streetlights, and Brodie turned up the collar of his fleece-lined jacket and hunched his shoulders. By morning the streets would be covered. It was the middle of November and this was the first snowfall of the year, so he couldn't really complain. Although he wasn't nuts about walking home in it at two o'clock in the morning.

He passed a heavily treed vacant lot, and a wry grin appeared. He and Eden had been fighting over that damned lot for two months. He wanted to buy it and build a house on it; she wanted to stay in the apartment over the bank. They had just finished developing the unused space in the old bank: a studio for her, a guest room, a huge room for Jase, with a private bathroom, along with a nursery. He had figured it was going to be a temporary arrangement. She said it was permanent. He figured she should have a proper home. She said she had one. He grinned again. He would give her a few months, then give it another crack. He figured if he kept chipping away at her, he would win sooner or later. Besides—although she didn't know it, yet—he'd made an offer on the lot.

Stuffing his hands in the pockets of his bomber jacket, he angled his head against the falling snow, his expression sobering as a familiar full feeling settled in his chest. He was so damned lucky. It was as if all their hard times were being rewarded with a stretch of good ones.

They had gotten married a week after he brought her home from the lake. It had been what they both wanted, just a small ceremony in the old abandoned church, with just family and a few close friends attending. He'd pretty much left the reception up to Ruby and Rita, which had been a mistake. He'd figured on a small intimate gathering; they'd figured on the whole damned town. He would be an old man before he forgot the shock of walking into that banquet room and seeing all those people. A live band. Magnums of champagne. And enough flowers to fill an entire greenhouse. Of course, he should have known better than to give them free rein. But it had been a hell of a bash, and Eden had been thrilled to bits. Another grin appeared. She hadn't thrown up once.

The only sour note was that Bruce and Ellie had refused to come. He had personally delivered the invitation, and he personally couldn't have cared less if they showed up or not, but he'd made the effort for Eden. Her only response was a hug and a kiss, and a comment that they'd had their chance. She had been so ecstatic over being pregnant that he didn't think anything could have dampened her spirits. But then, he'd been pretty damned ecstatic himself. He would lie in bed at night and feel that baby stir beneath his hand, and he would be damned near overwhelmed with pure, simple gratitude. Yeah, he was a lucky son of a bitch, all right. And sometimes he wondered what he'd done to deserve her.

He approached the store and looked up, as he always did when he came home late from the bar. A light was on in Jase's room, but the rest of the apartment was dark, except for the light in the kitchen. Eden always left it on for him when he was going to be late. Brodie experienced a twinge of disappointment. He'd kinda hoped his lady would be up.

He opened the side door and climbed the stairs, amusement pulling at his mouth. Her falling asleep anytime, anyplace, was something he could handle; it was the morning sickness that had nearly done him in. It had gotten so bad for a while that he'd hated to leave her alone. But that had finally passed, thank God, and now she was finally gaining some weight. He grinned to himself. If Eden sat still for more than five minutes, she was out like a light. It upset her to no end, but he thought it was kinda cute. And Jase and Meggie had started referring to her as Mrs. Van Winkle.

Entering the apartment, he closed the door soundlessly behind him, then stuffed his gloves in his pockets and took off his jacket. He was hanging it up on the antique brass coatrack Eden had found when a voice spoke behind him.

"Hi."

He turned, amusement glinting in his eyes. His lady *was* up. Except she was four-foot nothing, had freckles and wore baseball pajamas.

"You're going to get us in a pile of trouble, slugger, if your mother catches us."

She grinned at him, scratching her head with the pencil she had in her hand. "She's *asleep,* Brodie. Jase says pretty soon we're going to have to set off the fire alarm to keep her awake."

"Don't make fun of your mother, short stuff. She had a hard day."

She rolled her eyes. "She fell asleep when she was making your bed. She fell asleep reading the newspaper. And *then* she fell asleep watching TV tonight." An impish glint appeared in her eyes. "She drooled all over the sofa."

The only thing that kept Brodie from laughing out loud was that he knew it would likely wake up the drooler. Grinning down at Megan, he flipped her under the nose, then went past her into the kitchen. "She did, huh?"

"Yep."

"And you and Jase are never going to let her forget it, are you?"

She chuckled and hitched up her pajama pants. "Nope." She used the bottom drawer to climb onto the counter. "Mom left a turkey sandwich for you in the fridge, and we made homemade soup for supper." Brodie opened the fridge. "The soup's in that yellow thing."

Brodie lifted out the container and the plastic-wrapped sandwich and set them both on the counter, then opened the cupboard door for a bowl.

"Brodie?"

He turned and looked at her, his expression turning serious as he assessed her. He knew that tone of voice. This little lady was worried and needed to talk. He'd heard that tone a lot the first couple of weeks after they'd been married. Eden had been worried sick that Richard would say something to Megan about being her natural father. Brodie hadn't wanted to leave something that serious to chance, so he convinced Eden that they should tell her the truth. So Brodie had. He'd told her that they didn't know if it was true or not—they just wanted her to know, so she could deal with it if Richard ever said something. Megan had handled it amazingly well for a nine-year-old, saying that she didn't care if he was her father or not, he still wasn't her father. The thing that worried her most was that he could still take her away from her mother. Brodie had finally put a call through to Sam Carlton and let her talk to the lawyer. And the attorney had been able to assure her where he and her mother could not.

Lifting her chin so she had to look at him, Brodie studied her face. "What's the matter, Meggie?" he queried softly.

She met his gaze with that level, grown-up look of hers. She didn't say anything for a minute; then she spoke. "Will I be able to marry Jase when I grow up?"

Brodie felt as if he'd just gotten nailed by a ten-ton truck. He had to bite the inside of his cheek to keep from laughing. He wondered if Jase had any idea what he was up against. "That's your plan?" he said, somehow managing to keep his voice steady.

She looked up at him, anxiety in her eyes. "Yes. But will we be able to? Like, will it be against the law or anything?"

Brodie had to give himself a minute before he dared to answer. Clearing his throat, he spoke, using the same level tone. "Does Jase know anything about this?"

She narrowed her eyes, giving him a slightly belligerent look. "No."

Fighting like hell to keep his amusement in check, he answered solemnly, "Well, I wouldn't tell him yet if I were you."

"Well, can we?"

Clearing his throat again, he nodded. "You aren't related, so yes, you'll be able to marry Jase." Sensing that she needed a hug, he picked her up, and she wrapped her arms and legs around him, hanging on to him for dear life. "You won't tell Jase, will you?" she asked, a funny wobble in her voice.

A tight, protective feeling climbing up his chest, he hugged her hard. "No," he answered gruffly. "I won't tell him."

"Promise?"

"I promise."

She gave him a tight squeeze. "Will you tuck me into bed?"

"I'd love to." With her clinging to him like a monkey, he put the soup and sandwich back in the fridge, then carted her down the hall to Jase's old room. He tucked her in, gave her a kiss good-night and closed the door. His chest still congested with a mix of emotions, he turned on the night-light, then turned toward the master bedroom.

He turned the knob and opened the door, the faint illumination from the hallway spilling into the room and lightly touching Eden's face. Undoing the buttons on his shirt, he watched her sleep, remembering the night he'd come back from Montana, when he'd wished for exactly this. Picking up the chair, he set it down by the bed, then stretched out in it, propping his feet on the edge of the mattress. She had kicked the covers off and was lying on her back, one arm thrown wide, her face turned toward him. She had taken to wearing his T-shirts to bed, and the fabric was stretched tight across her rounded abdomen. It was oddly humbling, watching his child move and grow in her, knowing that that child had very likely been conceived that night at the old church. That night when the past collided with the present.

She opened her eyes and shifted onto her side, giving him a sleepy smile. "Hi," she murmured, her voice still rusty with sleep.

Experiencing a nearly suffocating surge of love, he somehow managed to smile back. "Hi yourself."

Eden blinked a couple of times, tucking her hands under her face. "What are you doing over there, Malone?"

Real amusement surfaced. "Just checking out the view."

"All hippopotamuses should be so lucky."

Slouching down in the chair, Brodie grinned at her. "Feeling a bit big and awkward, are we?"

She gave him another sleepy smile. "Next time I'm going to get you pregnant."

Still grinning, he continued to watch her. "Does that mean I get to barf on your shoes?"

"Whatever."

Watching her fight the pull of sleep, Brodie decided to give her a real wake-up call. "Tell me, Mac. How do you feel about being the mother of the bride?"

His pregnant wife frowned at him, clearly confused. "Pardon?"

He waited for a moment, then dropped it on her. "Megan informed me tonight that she's going to marry Jase when she grows up. I figured you ought to know."

She rolled onto her back, slapping her hand against her face. "Oh, God," she muttered, clearly overwhelmed by the news.

"We promised not to tell Jase," he said, enjoying her reaction. "I think it'll be a hell of a deal."

Turning her head, Eden looked at him. "She's going to drive us crazy, Brodie," she commented.

He grinned. "I know."

Narrowing her eyes, she crooked her finger at him.

Curious to know what she had up her sleeve, he complied. Shifting onto the bed beside her, he braced his arms on either side of her shoulders, careful not to put any weight on her round belly. He dipped his head, giving her a long, wet kiss. "Hi, baby. Wanna go for a ride?"

She laughed against his mouth, giving his hair a sharp tug. "I'm on to your little tricks, Malone."

He trailed his tongue across her bottom lip. "You like 'em."

"Yes, I do."

Drawing a deep breath around the renewed fullness in his chest, he whispered against her mouth, "I love you, Mac." Knowing how easily she was moved to tears lately, he didn't give her a chance to respond. He just kissed her again, sliding his hand under her T-shirt, stroking her inner thigh. "So what do you say, Mrs. Malone?"

She gave him a hard hug, then tipped her head back and looked at him, laughter and love shining in her eyes. "Do I get to drive?"

Brodie laughed and rested his forehead against hers. "Somebody better the hell drive. You're redlining my engine."

Eden ran her hands up his back, then shifted so she was straddling his legs. Taking his face between her hands, she lowered her head and gave him a kiss that sent his blood pressure through the roof. "Then hang on, darlin'," she said, her voice husky. "We're going to find out how fast you can get from zero to sixty."

He laughed against her mouth. Hell, his fantasies had never been so good.

* * * * *

Within a few lost souls,
the *Heart of the Wolf* beats fierce
and wild. Feel them, fear them, tame them....

HEART
OF THE
WOLF

Don't miss **SECRET OF THE WOLF (SS #54)**, the
spine-tingling first book in Rebecca Flanders's terrific
new *Heart of the Wolf* trilogy.

After being struck down by a car, he remembered
absolutely nothing of who he was. But as pieces of
his shattered past returned, "Michael" was learning
what real fear was. He knew his family's secret could
threaten the very woman who had so graciously
taken him into her home. And he realized the
terrifying question they were about to face was
not who he was, but *what....*

Find out Michael's secret this July—only from

SILHOUETTE® *Shadows*™

Men and women hungering for passion to soothe
their lonely souls.

The intriguing Intimate Moments miniseries by

Beverly Bird

concludes in July 1995 with

A MAN WITHOUT A WIFE (Intimate Moments #652)
Seven years ago, Ellen Lonetree had made a decision
that haunted her days and nights. Now she had the
chance to be reunited with the child she'd lost—if
she could resist the attraction she felt for the little
boy's adoptive father...and keep both of them
from discovering her secret.

And if you missed the beginning of this compelling
series, pick up the first and second books:

A MAN WITHOUT LOVE (Intimate Moments #630)
Catherine Landano was running scared—and straight
into the arms of enigmatic Navajo Jericho Bedonie.
Would he be her savior...or her destruction?

A MAN WITHOUT A HAVEN (Intimate Moments #641)
The word *forever* was not in Mac Tshongely's
vocabulary. Nevertheless, he found himself drawn
to headstrong Shadow Bedonie and the promise of
tomorrow that this sultry woman offered. Could home
really be where the heart is?

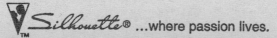

...where passion lives.

He's Too Hot To Handle...but she can take a little heat.

SILHOUETTE

Summer Sizzlers

This summer don't be left in the cold, join Silhouette for the hottest Summer Sizzlers collection. The perfect summer read, on the beach or while vacationing, Summer Sizzlers features sexy heroes who are "Too Hot To Handle." This collection of three new stories is written by bestselling authors Mary Lynn Baxter, Ann Major and Laura Parker.

Available this July wherever Silhouette books are sold.

Romantic Traditions sizzles in July 1995 as Sharon Sala's THE MIRACLE MAN, IM #650, explores the suspenseful—and sensual—"Stranger on the Shore" plot line.

Washed ashore after a plane crash, U.S. Marshal Lane Monday found himself on the receiving end of a most indecent proposal. Antonette Hatfield had saved his life and was now requesting his presence in her *bed*. But what Lane didn't know was that Toni had babies on her mind....

Lauded as "immensely talented" by *Romantic Times* magazine, Sharon Sala is one author you won't want to miss. So return to the classic plot lines you love with THE MIRACLE MAN, and be sure to look for more Romantic Traditions in future months from some of the genre's best, only in—

SIMRT8

THE MEN OF MIDNIGHT

Join RITA-award-winning author Emilie Richards as her miniseries "The Men of Midnight" concludes in August 1995 with MacDOUGALL'S DARLING, IM #655.

Andrew MacDougall believed in his two best friends, a misty loch creature...and little else. Love and marriage were certainly not meant for him. But Fiona Sinclair's homecoming stirred up memories of their long-ago bond, one he knew still existed by its hold on his heart.

Don't miss MacDOUGALL'S DARLING, Emilie Richards's magical finale to "The Men of Midnight" miniseries. Only in— INTIMATE MOMENTS®
Silhouette

FLYAWAY VACATION SWEEPSTAKES!

This month's destination:

Glamorous LAS VEGAS!

Are you the lucky person who will win a free trip to Las Vegas? Think how much fun it would be to visit world-famous casinos... to see star-studded shows...to enjoy round-the-clock action in the city that never sleeps!

The facing page contains two Official Entry Coupons, as does each of the other books you received this shipment. Complete and return all the entry coupons—**the more times you enter, the better your chances of winning!**

Then keep your fingers crossed, because you'll find out by August 15, 1995 if you're the winner! If you are, here's what you'll get:

- Round-trip airfare for two to exciting Las Vegas!
- 4 days/3 nights at a fabulous first-class hotel!
- $500.00 pocket money for meals and entertainment!

Remember: The more times you enter, the better your chances of winning!*

*NO PURCHASE OR OBLIGATION TO CONTINUE BEING A SUBSCRIBER NECESSARY TO ENTER. SEE REVERSE SIDE OF ANY ENTRY COUPON FOR ALTERNATIVE MEANS OF ENTRY.

VLV KAL

FLYAWAY VACATION
SWEEPSTAKES
OFFICIAL ENTRY COUPON

This entry must be received by: JULY 30, 1995
This month's winner will be notified by: AUGUST 15, 1995
Trip must be taken between: SEPTEMBER 30, 1995-SEPTEMBER 30, 1996

YES, I want to win a vacation for two in Las Vegas. I understand the prize includes round-trip airfare, first-class hotel and $500.00 spending money. Please let me know if I'm the winner!

Name_____

Address _____ Apt. _____

City   State/Prov.   Zip/Postal Code

Account #_____

Return entry with invoice in reply envelope.

© 1995 HARLEQUIN ENTERPRISES LTD.   CLV KAL

FLYAWAY VACATION
SWEEPSTAKES
OFFICIAL ENTRY COUPON

This entry must be received by: JULY 30, 1995
This month's winner will be notified by: AUGUST 15, 1995
Trip must be taken between: SEPTEMBER 30, 1995-SEPTEMBER 30, 1996

YES, I want to win a vacation for two in Las Vegas. I understand the prize includes round-trip airfare, first-class hotel and $500.00 spending money. Please let me know if I'm the winner!

Name_____

Address _____ Apt. _____

City   State/Prov.   Zip/Postal Code

Account #_____

Return entry with invoice in reply envelope.

© 1995 HARLEQUIN ENTERPRISES LTD.   CLV KAL

OFFICIAL RULES
FLYAWAY VACATION SWEEPSTAKES 3449
NO PURCHASE OR OBLIGATION NECESSARY

Three Harlequin Reader Service 1995 shipments will contain respectively, coupons for entry into three different prize drawings, one for a trip for two to San Francisco, another for a trip for two to Las Vegas and the third for a trip for two to Orlando, Florida. To enter any drawing using an Entry Coupon, simply complete and mail according to directions.

There is no obligation to continue using the Reader Service to enter and be eligible for any prize drawing. You may also enter any drawing by hand printing the words "Flyaway Vacation," your name and address on a 3"x5" card and the destination of the prize you wish that entry to be considered for (i.e., San Francisco trip, Las Vegas trip or Orlando trip). Send your 3"x5" entries via first-class mail (limit: one entry per envelope) to: Flyaway Vacation Sweepstakes 3449, c/o Prize Destination you wish that entry to be considered for, P.O. Box 1315, Buffalo, NY 14269-1315, USA or P.O. Box 610, Fort Erie, Ontario L2A 5X3, Canada.

To be eligible for the San Francisco trip, entries must be received by 5/30/95; for the Las Vegas trip, 7/30/95; and for the Orlando trip, 9/30/95.

Winners will be determined in random drawings conducted under the supervision of D.L. Blair, Inc., an independent judging organization whose decisions are final, from among all eligible entries received for that drawing. San Francisco trip prize includes round-trip airfare for two, 4-day/3-night weekend accommodations at a first-class hotel, and $500 in cash (trip must be taken between 7/30/95—7/30/96, approximate prize value—$3,500); Las Vegas trip includes round-trip airfare for two, 4-day/3-night weekend accommodations at a first-class hotel, and $500 in cash (trip must be taken between 9/30/95—9/30/96, approximate prize value—$3,500); Orlando trip includes round-trip airfare for two, 4-day/3-night weekend accommodations at a first-class hotel, and $500 in cash (trip must be taken between 11/30/95—11/30/96, approximate prize value—$3,500). All travelers must sign and return a Release of Liability prior to travel. Hotel accommodations and flights are subject to accommodation and schedule availability. Sweepstakes open to residents of the U.S. (except Puerto Rico) and Canada, 18 years of age or older. Employees and immediate family members of Harlequin Enterprises, Ltd., D.L. Blair, Inc., their affiliates, subsidiaries and all other agencies, entities and persons connected with the use, marketing or conduct of this sweepstakes are not eligible. Odds of winning a prize are dependent upon the number of eligible entries received for that drawing. Prize drawing and winner notification for each drawing will occur no later than 15 days after deadline for entry eligibility for that drawing. Limit: one prize to an individual, family or organization. All applicable laws and regulations apply. Sweepstakes offer void wherever prohibited by law. Any litigation within the province of Quebec respecting the conduct and awarding of the prizes in this sweepstakes must be submitted to the Regies des loteries et Courses du Quebec. In order to win a prize, residents of Canada will be required to correctly answer a time-limited arithmetical skill-testing question. Value of prizes are in U.S. currency.

Winners will be obligated to sign and return an Affidavit of Eligibility within 30 days of notification. In the event of noncompliance within this time period, prize may not be awarded. If any prize or prize notification is returned as undeliverable, that prize will not be awarded. By acceptance of a prize, winner consents to use of his/her name, photograph or other likeness for purposes of advertising, trade and promotion on behalf of Harlequin Enterprises, Ltd., without further compensation, unless prohibited by law.

For the names of prizewinners (available after 12/31/95), send a self-addressed, stamped envelope to: Flyaway Vacation Sweepstakes 3449 Winners, P.O. Box 4200, Blair, NE 68009.

RVC KAL